SHATTERED HOPES, MAGNIFICENT FAILURE

The Road to the Nuclear Middle East

by
Mark Hertz

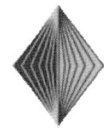

Ytterbium Press
(An imprint of DecaBooks, LLC)

Copyright © 2014 by DecaBooks, LLC
All rights reserved, including the right to reproduce this book
or portions thereof in any form whatsoever.

Cover Designer: Jean Waschow

Shattered Hopes, Magnificent Failure
The Road to the Nuclear Middle East

ISBN: 978-1-938587-18-4

*"The fault, dear Brutus, is not in our stars,
but in ourselves . . ."*

Julius Caesar, William Shakespeare

Table of Contents

Shattered Hopes, Magnificent Failure

Preface ix

Introduction xi

Part I
The Doomsday Arsenal 1
    An Eyewitness Account 1
    Joining the Program: How It All Started 2
    The Weapon in the Desert 3
    The Six-Day War: Who Is In Control? 16
    The 1973 (Yom Kippur) War: One Minute to Midnight 29
    The Doomsday Plan 42

Part II
The Approaching Calamity 55
    Shattered Hopes 55
    The Demographic Storm: The Making of the Jewish
        Theocratic State 60
    Theocratization and the Arab-Israeli Conflict 64
    The Changing World and the Middle East 68
    Is Globalization Working? 70
    Israel and The New Middle East 74
    The Approaching Calamity in the Levant 75

Part III
Reinventing a Homeland: The State of Israel 79
    Too Little, Too Late 79
    The Holocaust and the State of Israel 80
    Reinventing A Homeland: Inside The Bengurionite State 86
    David Ben-Gurion: The Man and His Legacy 89
    The Illegitimacy of Bengurionism 93
    Life In Bengurionite Israel 99

Part IV
How It All Began: The Origins 131
In The Beginning 131
The Israelites and the Exodus 132
Creating a Religion 134
The Divine Promise to the People and the Promising
  Beginning of the Israelites 140

Part V
The People and Its Land: What Went Wrong and Why 145
Creating A Nation 145
The Promise 148
The Hypotheses of Failure 151
Hypothesis of Failure During the Second Temple 163

Part VI
The Diaspora: Recreating A Religion
But Losing A People 185
Weaving a Tapestry of Twenty Centuries of the Lost 185
Reinventing a Religion: The Disastrous Failure of the
  Religious Leaders...192
Losing a People: The Jewish Being and Being Jewish in
  the Diaspora 202
Enlightenment and Emancipation 211
Antisemitism: The Annals of an Implacable and Unending
  Global Phenomenon...228
The Jewish Question 232
The Who, The Why, and The Blending and Bending of
  Truth and Hopes...237

Part VII
Behind the Empty Mirror: The Epilogue 241
The Fallacies of History's Determinism 241
The Thread of Jewish Destiny: From Origins To Calamity 245
Behind the Empty Mirror: The Epilogue 250

Bibliography 255
Notes. 271
Index. 301

Preface

The events narrated in this book are true. They are told to the best of my memory, several decades after their occurrence. This book has benefited from the inputs and impressions I have accumulated and learned from innumerable people over a lifetime. This book is not my story. It's a story that needs to be told about a people and a country in the midst of a crucial region in the world.

Introduction

By all accounts I was born into one of the more illustrious families in Judaism. My maternal grandfather was a direct descendent of Rabbi Levi Itzhak from the Russian city of Berdichev. This rabbi gained worldwide fame as the "advocate of the Jewish people." It is said that he would directly appeal on their behalf to the Supreme Being himself. My maternal grandmother was a cousin of Rabbi Yehuda Leib Hacohen Maimon, a signer of the declaration of independence of the State of Israel, a founder of the Mizrahi movement in modern Judaism, and my godfather. My mother's family inhabited the land between the Mediterranean Sea and the Jordan River for many generations. They lived in Jerusalem, Safed, Rosh-Pina, and Hebron. Their roots in the Promised Land were very deep, extending all the way to the period before the Napoleonic wars in the mid-eighteenth century.

Members of my family had participated with valor and distinction in every armed conflict of the Jewish people in the twentieth century. My father was instrumental in the birth of the Israeli air force. One of my paternal uncles served in the British Army during the Second World War and was a highly decorated officer who participated in missions behind enemy lines in occupied Europe. A maternal uncle was wounded during the 1948 Israeli war for independence. Other family members took part in the Sinai War of 1956, the Six Days War of 1967, the Yom Kippur War of 1973, and all the conflicts since then.

There was political diversity in the family. My mother's cousins were senior members of Menachem Begin's IRGUN organization in the years leading to the birth of the State of Israel. One cousin was captured by the British authorities and exiled to Eritrea, in the horn of Africa. Other family members supported the socialist regime of the new Jewish state.

For almost three centuries the life of my direct ancestors has been intimately woven into the Jewish experience and its struggle in the Holy Land and the Diaspora. At the dawn of the twentieth century my maternal grandfather launched and edited a Hebrew newspaper in the city of Jerusalem. He was also among the few who established the daily newspaper Ha'aretz (The Land)–a major publication in today's Israel.

There is a family tale surrounding the birth of my mother. After my grandmother had suffered two miscarriages, my grandfather decided (as was the custom in his community) to procure the advice of sages.

In 1914 he left Jerusalem on a perilous journey to war-torn Russia, in search of a famous rabbi. Upon hearing my grandfather's story, the rabbi declared: "Return to you wife. In one year from today, a baby daughter shall be born, and she will live and prosper." And, so it came to pass that my mother was born followed by five siblings.

Very few families who dwell today in Judaism or who inhabit the State of Israel had a more illustrious past upon the pages of Jewish history. The family had produced scribes, merchants, scholars, professionals of various types, and warriors.

It was a twist of fate that upon my birth, my parents lived in a house in the street in Jerusalem named after Joseph Ben Matityahu, also known as Josephus Flavius. Born in 37 A.D., he was the son of the Priest Matityahu (Matthias) and a direct descendent of the royal family of the Hasmoneans. Author of several historical books, he narrated the Jewish War against the Romans, the fall of Judea, and the burning of Jerusalem in 70 A.D. Although much maligned by historians, Josephus nevertheless was a witness to the crucial events that led to the destruction of the Second Temple of the Jews in Jerusalem, and to the beginning of the Jewish Diaspora. His analysis of these events continues to be controversial, and his narrative is considered by many to be a biased account of a horrific chapter in Jewish history. Some parallels will certainly be drawn between Josephus writings and this book.

In my lifetime I bore witness to two of the major episodes in the life of the Jewish people in the twentieth century: the post-Holocaust era, and the birth of the State of Israel–with all the implications and the challenging aftermath these events have generated. Ever since boyhood I had pondered upon these radical occurrences and their repercussions to the present age. As a student of history and philosophy, I often wondered at the destiny of the Jewish people and its tortuous past. My personal experiences have led me to believe that the disastrous path of Jewish history is not necessarily the fault of others. As William Shakespeare so aptly said: "The fault may not be with the stars, but with ourselves."

The thesis of this book is predicated on my belief that the often-painful voyage of the Jewish people through history was a magnificent failure. It was an unmitigated disappointment–politically, economically, technologically, and demographically. As I will show in these pages, the Jewish people had failed even during its tenure as a political entity in the land of the judges, and later, in the kingdoms of Judea and Israel.

This book is not a scholarly historical account of the life of the Jewish people in over three thousand years. Although I studied history in college, I am not a professional historian and this book is not a traditional study of historical events. This book is a story, animated by a thesis, and fed by descriptions of key events in the life of the Jewish people. The story also benefits from my personal experiences and those of family and friends. This story is a subjective account of the promising future of an ancient people, and how it managed to turn such extraordinary promise into a resounding failure.

I wrote this book with understandable bias, pain, passion, and prejudice. As a product of the latter half of the twentieth and the early twenty-first centuries, I examined the promise and the failure with the eyes of a social scientist who specializes in the study of organizations. I could also now examine the story of the Jewish people with the eyes of a participant in the past five decades of this story. As I recount in this narrative, in one instance in May 1967 I was a participant in an episode in Jewish and Israeli life that could have influenced world history. Unwilling participant nonetheless, I served as a small pin in a very complex machinery of events of which the history of peoples and nations is made.

How does one evaluate the performance of a people, from its origins over three thousand years ago, to the present time? In this story I address the evaluation from the political, economic, technological, and demographic perspectives. I utterly reject the notion of the "victim" as an overarching explanation for the painful events in the life of the Jewish people. Nor do I commit this narrative to the religious belief that the misery in Jewish history is a precursor to its redemption in a Messianic event to come. This book is simply an account of events in the life of a people, which when taken together, paints a picture of a string of disasters, mistakes, incompetence, and ineptness. By comparison, where other peoples succeeded, the Jewish people generally failed.

The account in this book is an exception rather than the rule of stories of the Jewish people. Most accounts herald the positive aspects of Jewish contributions to world's history and culture. Most accounts also offer a plethora of excuses why, amongst such marvelous accomplishment, the Jewish people had encountered so many obstacles and hatred, which were the reason for persecution and ultimately its failure on the stage of history.

This book considers the outcomes and the performance of the Jews—as a people. The many contributions of individual Jews to history, science, and culture are well documented. But, the performance of the *people* has not been addressed quite generously. In a twist of events, many individual Jews who most contributed to the social and cultural welfare of humanity had suffered criticism, repudiation and even excommunication from their community.

Although excommunication was seldom applied, persons such as the philosopher Baruch Spinoza were excommunicated. Recently, a rabbinical court in Brooklyn, New York, issued an edict of excommunication against U.S. Senator Joseph Lieberman. The Talmud (the authoritative record of rabbinic views on Jewish law, ethics, customs, and case histories) has twenty-four offenses that may be punishable by excommunication. They include such minor offenses as violating the second day of holiday, although it is observed as a matter of custom, not law.

Why has there been such a magnificent failure? This book will attempt to provide some meaningful answers. It is difficult to offer a unique perspective that extends over three millennia and that can explain such a diversity of events, circumstances, and the different components of historical epochs. Nevertheless, one variable that runs through the ages seems to be the gross incompetence, ineptness and corruption of Jewish leadership—political, economic, and religious. This book will argue that, throughout its history, the Jewish people has been misled, misinformed, and incompetently managed, so it continually found itself at the gates of unmitigated disaster.

Consider the current state of the Jewish people, as we enter the twenty-first century. Numerically, there are fewer Jews in the world than the populations of Sao Paulo (Brazil), Calcutta (India) or Tokyo (Japan). Anti-Semitism and hatred of the Jews is a world-wide phenomenon and seems to be on the rise. With its own country after twenty centuries of Diaspora, the Jewish state is in a constant state of war with its neighbors. Internal strife between religious and secular Jews is one of Israel's menacing threats. Europe is today, for all practical purposes, "clean" of Jews. The Nazi dream of cleansing the continent has been a success. By contrast, the Jewish people is still dispersed throughout the world, divided and weakened, and even more hated.

From its humble beginning in the land on the shores of the Euphrates and Tigris (Mesopotamia), the Jewish people found its way to modern times. Some who chronicle Jewish history argue that by simply surviving the horrors of its historical roller coaster, the Jews have shown great accomplishment. I utterly reject this claim. This book will show that by using metrics of a variety of outcomes, the performance of the Jewish people throughout history has been a series of failures, many of which were unrelated to persecutions and other such catastrophic events.

This book will also address five myths of the historical performance and destiny of the Jewish people. The first myth is *victimization*. The key argument is that the continuous adversity in the people's history can and should be attributed to persecution by others, and that Jews were always the powerless victims of oppressive regimes and hateful populations.

The second myth is the compelling *force majeure* of the Diaspora. It supports the belief that by existing for so many centuries in a state of Diaspora, away from and without a homeland, the Jewish people were entrapped in a force beyond their control. This led to the creation of a culture of submission to one's destiny, without any visible or foreseeable means of "breaking the pattern" of misery.

The third myth is the *role of religion*. Its key argument was that the Jewish religion–as developed in the Diaspora–was a force of stability and strength for the suffering people. Religious practices, beliefs, and rituals were strictly observed and united the people in the power of their faith so they could endure the torments of the secular world.

The fourth myth is that of the *inspired leadership*. Its contention was that religious as well as secular leaders of the Jewish people were inspired and inspiring fellows, representing the best that Jewish intellectual and moral existence could offer—in the marvelous tradition of the venerated kings David and Solomon.

Finally, the fifth myth was the *superior* attribution of the Jewish people and the special and magnificent role it is destined to play in the world and its history.

This book will systematically demolish these myths. Compared against benchmarks and metrics of the performance of other peoples in world history, these five myths will be shown to be simply "wishful thinking." The reality as it will be shown in this book was, and is, quite a different story, debunking such hopeful yet outlandish beliefs.

Our narrative now turns to the events in my own life experience in the 1960s. I became the linchpin in a series of occurrences that constituted one of the most fearful incidents in the history of the Middle East. I was instrumental in controlling the traffic on the road to the Atomic Age of the Jewish State.

Part I
The Doomsday Arsenal

An Eyewitness Account

In May 1967 I was 24 years old. I had recently completed my military service and was enrolled as a full time student in both the Hebrew University in Jerusalem and Tel-Aviv University. As tensions in the region had escalated during that month, I was called up as a reservist. I could not imagine that within a week I would be holding in my hands the plutonium core of a nuclear weapon. I also could not fathom that I would be in command of a company of border-patrol soldiers with minimum armaments, in charge of this core, and that I would be the focus of a power struggle between the military and the civilian branches of governments of Israel for the control of the nuclear weapon.

This eyewitness account is being told for the first time, after almost five decades. This story is as relevant today, perhaps more relevant than it was at that time. The more I recollect the events of May 1967, reading through my contemporaneous notes and diary, the more I am convinced of the necessity for this book and my obligation to tell this story. This is an eyewitness account of a series of dramatic events, a few days before the outbreak of the Six-Day war.

It was a lovely day in late May—as is usually the case in the Eastern Mediterranean. I was standing at the gate of the compound where I was in charge of the core of the Jewish nuclear device. On the other side of the fence stood a Colonel, on a mission as a senior army officer. Behind him were four command cars armed with heavy machine guns and bazookas, and two trucks carrying a large contingent of cadets of the officer's school (Training Base Number One). The senior officer wanted to gain access to the facility and take control of the nuclear core. This had put me right in the middle of a nuclear political and military coup. This event was the culmination of a month long power struggle between the prime minister and the generals. The Colonel insisted on gaining access and assuming control of the nuclear device.

I could not let this happen.

Joining the Program: How It All Started

My first encounter with the Israeli program to develop nuclear weapons was shortly after the completion of my military basic training. The year was 1964. At the time I had no idea that I would be so intimately associated with this program in various capacities and responsibilities for the better part of a decade.

My orders were to travel to the Southern Command of the Armed Forces, located in the city of Beer-Sheva. Known as the "Capital of the Negev Desert," the city at that time was a relatively small town. Several developments had begun to emerge in the periphery of the center of the city, composed of buildings that were originally the Arab municipality at the gate of the Negev. The military headquarters were also housed in the original building that served as the police headquarters during the British Mandate, before May of 1948.

After a session of introduction to my new assignment, I was told to join a few other people on the bus, with destination to the town of Dimona, in a southerly direction. Up to that day I had heard rumors about a military installation in the desert but I was not aware of the nature of the installation, its purpose, or its structure.

It was a beautiful spring day with a blue sky and dry warm temperatures. On such a day, one can see forever. The bus ride of about 30 minutes took us to the arid and desolate stretch of road between Beer-Sheva and the small town of Dimona. The black asphalt of the road stood sharply against the light brown and yellow hue of the desert. Suddenly it occurred to me that I would be traveling on this desolate road for some years to come. This sentiment generated in me an uneasy feeling.

The bus turned to the right, going in an easterly direction on a recently paved and lightly traveled road. The short ride of a few kilometers brought us to an elaborate entrance to the installation ahead. The road bifurcated so that the right segment led into the facility and the left out of it. We stopped at the gate, heavily guarded and constructed with fortified concrete, an electric portal, and a very high fence surrounding the perimeter. Two armed guards boarded the bus, conducted a head count, and alighted. We were allowed to proceed.

From the gate we could see the majestic cupola of the nuclear reactor, as it proudly emerged in the eastern horizon of the facility. The installation was built as the Greek letter pi, the northern leg of the three-prong sprawl was the Administration building; a long three-story edifice. The southern leg, to our left, contained several structures that I later learned were the technical buildings.[1]

I was then introduced to the headquarters of the military unit that was housed inside the facility. This was a two-story building of grey cement and long corridors running alongside the exterior of the building. I was now officially a member of unit 1050 of the Army. The unit was composed of regular army personnel to be trained in various technical functions across the facility. These recruits would then spend their compulsory military service as technicians at the site. There were several options for training. One was a short course for "operators" of the technical installations, including the reactor. Another which I joined, was a short course for radiation inspectors. Within a few weeks I graduated from the course and began my service as nuclear radiation inspector.

The course included instruction in nuclear physics, metallurgy, and the ways in which radioactive materials are propagated in land, water, and air. A second component of the course focused on instrumentation and the practical use of such devices for measuring levels and exposure of radiation. We learned to monitor alpha and gamma radiation and to assess levels of accumulation and benchmarks for dangerous exposure.

I had therefore joined the program and would soon be assigned to Institute Number Two as a radiation-monitoring inspector. The program of unit 1050 was conceived out of necessity. When the Ben-Gurion regime completed the Dimona facility, it became painfully clear that there would be a shortage of highly skilled technical personnel. Due to the constraints of security and the location of the facility near the under-developed town of Dimona, the pool of potential applicants from the existing civilians seemed quite small. Thus, the recruitment of talented military personnel seemed to be an optimal solution. These were young men and women in the initial leg of their military service and with the intellectual abilities to be adequately and rapidly trained in whatever skill was needed for the operation of a nuclear installation. This solution also guaranteed at least two years of service for each recruit, because the length of military service at the time was 30 months.

The Weapon in the Desert

For the next five years I was an integral part of building the weapon in the desert—two years in military service and the remainder as a civilian in order to finance my studies at the Hebrew and Tel-Aviv Universities. I served with three different directors of the facility and witnessed key events in its existence.

The Layout of the Facility

Known as *KAMAG* (Kiryah LeMechkar Garyini), the "Town for Nuclear Research" at Dimona was the second such installation in Israel. The first was a small reactor (5 megawatts) erected near the city of Yavne, along the coast of the Mediterranean Sea, some fifteen miles from Tel-Aviv, at Nahal Soreq. This facility was commonly known as *MAMAG* (Merkaz LeMechkar Garyin) or the "Center for Nuclear Research." The Yavne reactor, purchased from the United States, was primarily used for the study and manufacture of radioactive isotopes, with applications in medicine, industry, and non-invasive testing of materials.

KAMAG was a much larger installation. Its reactor was at least five times more powerful. The official figure had been capped at 24 megawatts. The Yavne installation was relatively accessible to researchers and to foreign organizations, particularly from Europe and the United States. By contrast, *KAMAG* was hermetically isolated and inaccessible to all but its carefully selected employees and government officials.[2]

Each building at the facility was named "institute." The nuclear reactor was Institute Number One. To the south stood Institute Number Three, where uranium ore was transformed for further processing. Institute Number Five was responsible for metallurgical transformations of uranium, and Institute Number Four was the official entity in charge of disposing the nuclear waste from the other institutes. Institute Number Six included all the installations that served the infrastructure and which supplied the facility with water, electricity, and other utilities.[3]

Institute Number Two

Nestled in the southeast corner of the facility, directly south of the reactor, stood Institute Number Two. It was an unassuming one story building. It had the appearance of a large warehouse or a Wal-Mart store in the United States. The entrance was a simple door leading to a small lobby, with a pair of double doors on the other side. The official designation of this building was "administrative and maintenance offices."

In reality, the modest appearance of the structure was only the upper and visible portion of an enormous site. Like the "tip of an iceberg", the building was an entrance to a subterranean installation of over 210 feet in depth. Built into the sandy crust of the desert, Institute Number Two was a hidden web of production and research laboratories.

There were two main elevators going down to the various underground floors. Each floor was designated by its depth—in meters—below the surface. Every day dozens of engineers, technicians, and other personnel would enter the Institute via the unassuming doors, then vanish underground to conduct their business. The hidden installation offered two important advantages. It was camouflaged from prying eyes of curious aircraft of foreign countries and it provided a semblance of safety in case of accidents and/or the critical discharge of unwanted nuclear material.

Institute Number Two was the "raison d'etre" of KAMAG. It housed what one might call the "plutonium factor" or the installation in which the Jewish state was preparing the core material for its nuclear arsenal.

The Plutonium Factory

Plutonium is a heavy element produced within atomic reactors by the bombardment of uranium 238 with neutrons. Known as Pu 239, this radioactive isotope serves as the weapon core of the atomic bomb.[4] It is radioactive and highly toxic.

All radioactive elements decay overtime, losing their radioactive potency. The amount of time it takes for an isotope to lose half of its radioactivity is called its "half-life." Plutonium 239 has a half-life of about 24 thousand years. For the human experience, therefore, any plutonium produced in the past half-century is as powerful, toxic, and dangerous as ever for the foreseeable future.[5]

Plutonium emits alpha and gamma radiation. *Alpha* radiation is in the form of particles, consisting of two protons and two neutrons (like the nucleus of the element Helium). Due to their large mass, alpha particles are slow and can travel only to the surface of the plutonium where they can be detected and measured. *Gamma* radiation is a form of electromagnetic emission, such as X-rays. Plutonium emits some gamma radiation, which can also be detected and monitored.

Due to plutonium's ability to reach a "critical mass" with relatively small quantities, its storage and disposal are complicated. The configuration of storage of this element had to be carefully calculated, as also did the care given to the storage of large quantities in a confined space. The warehousing of plutonium was a key concern of Institute Number Two and required dedicated facilities for the task.

Radiation Safety and Monitoring

Upon completion of the course on radiation safety and monitoring, my next assignment was to join the team responsible for this function in Institute Number Two. In time I was promoted to leader of the team with responsibility over at least one floor of the installation.

Radiation at the institute was monitored in three key modes. The first consisted of "radiation tags" or badges worn on the lapel of every employee admitted into the facility. These tags were designed to detect gamma radiation and were periodically inspected by a specialized laboratory. The second mode monitored employees upon leaving the installation. At the exit corridor employees would check their feet and hands in a contraption that resembled a scale. If the reading of alpha or gamma radiation was above permissible levels, an alarm would sound and the employee would be rushed for decontamination.

The third mode consisted of periodic sweeps of the installation and its employees by the team of radiation inspectors. All employees wore protective gear over their shoes; other special clothing was required when entering certain areas of the institute. In time I developed some creative ways to monitor the installation as well as adequate forms to report all readings.

Living with radiation turned out to be a permanent fixture of life inside Institute Number Two. Peril and the challenges of potential accidents loomed everywhere in this monstrous underground facility. Sometimes I would patrol the floors and corridors during the night shift. A few engineers and technicians would be at work around the clock. In most sections of the institute there was a strange calm created by the walls and artificial lighting, reproducing the subterranean life of groundhogs in their web of caves.

We monitored alpha and gamma radiation by using instruments manufactured by a Chicago company. The alpha monitor had a probe that resembled a duck's foot. It was covered with a thin layer of a metallic substance that allowed the alpha particles to penetrate the chamber of the probe. The gamma monitor was a tube-like probe, also known as a "Geiger Counter." We had radiation inspection stations on each floor, equipped with emergency equipment such as breathing apparatus and first-aid kits. At the entrance of each room was an emergency shower in the corridor.

But all these precautionary measures did not prevent a few accidents in the installation. One incident involved an explosion in the lower level of the institute. It caused at least one death. Luckily, I was not on duty the night when the explosive event occurred.

Life in KAMAG

A short walking distance from Institute Number Two, in a westerly direction, there was a public plaza with surrounding buildings. These structures included the main dining rooms of the facility, recreational space, and a variety of small shops that sold snacks, soft drinks, and other items for the consumption needs of the employees.

The dining facility was a step above the normal military or government installations, although the quality of the food itself was comparable to that served in military bases of that era.

Military conscripts were a small part of the total workforce but we served in crucial posts such as the operations, safety, and security of all the institutes. All employees, including military personnel, wore civilian clothes. The living quarters for the military people of the KAMAG unit consisted of hastily constructed three-story elongated apartment buildings in the neighboring town of Dimona. Shuttle vans and buses transported the soldiers/workers to and from the facility.

Recreation for the civilian workers and the military personnel consisted of a few coffee shops and a small number of movie theaters in Dimona and Beer-Sheva. There was also a small library at the facility with a very limited number of books. Very few other leisure activities existed at that time.

The overall climate of KAMAG resembled a modern manufacturing plant. Although a variety of scientists and engineers were employed at the facility, intellectual excitement was sorely lacking. Even the challenges and enlightenment of a research environment were thoroughly absent. The prevailing sentiment was that the task at hand needed to be completed and that the facility was a critical contributor to ensuring the defense and ultimate survival of the country. There was a certain joyless cloud of seriousness hanging over everyone's existence. The feeling—re-enforced by periodic appearances and speeches by government officials of the Department of Defense—was one of duty to produce the weapon, with the recognition that a poor and tiny country had poured its precious and limited resources into building this facility in the desert.[6]

A similar atmosphere existed within Institute Number Two. The long days and nights of living underground with artificial "neon" lighting took a toll on the employees. It was not uncommon for a worker following a 18-24 hour shift to emerge from the Institute into daylight and to seriously inquire: "What time of day is it: morning or evening?"

The inability of any individual employee at KAMAG to be a party of, or to visualize, the entire product of the facility was a vexatious deterrent to a true feeling of accomplishment. Unlike the manufacture of airplanes, automobiles, or home appliances, the final product of KAMAG was shrouded in secrecy and inaccessible to all but the very few.

The French Are Here!

The nuclear facility KAMAG was constructed with the help of the French Government and with French nuclear technology and engineering. In the late 1950s French engineers and technicians arrived in Israel. In 1957 the Dimona project began. Several accounts have been advanced about this chain of events. Michael Karpin (2006) wrote that the KAMAG reactor was similar to the French model at the Marcoule Center, which had a capacity of 42 megawatts.[7] The difference was the nature of the cooling system: graphite for Marcoule and heavy water for the KAMAG reactor.

The similarity in construction and the capacity of the pipes for the cooling system of the plutonium-separation in Institute Number Two have led to the speculation that the true capacity of the reactor was originally over 40 megawatts. Such capacity (upgraded in the 1970s) allowed for the production of over 80 pounds of plutonium.[8]

Karpin's speculation is correct. The capacities of the reactor and the plutonium-separation plant far exceeded the official numbers. The reactor had reached its full capacity within a few months after my arrival. Institute Number Two was in high gear within the year so that by 1967, when the Six Day War began, at least one workable nuclear device was fully operational and ready to be added to the military arsenal.

The French cooperation with Israel in the period 1957-1966 was a strange affair between unlikely bedfellows. On the Israeli side, the Francophiles of the Bengurionite regime moved to the vanguard of the list of important aides to the Prime Minister.[9] The French political rationale for the nuclear alliance with Israel was nourished by President Charles De Gaulle's unique strategic view of the distribution of power in the world and in the Middle East. De Gaulle held a deep-rooted dislike of Great Britain and the United States. He deeply resented the "perfidy of Albion" during the dark hours of the Second World War and the fact that in the post-war period, France's global prestige had deteriorated to the point of becoming a second-rate nation.[10]

French president De Gaulle viewed the nuclear alliance purely in *political* terms. He did not particularly like the Jews or their homeland. Later in his life he would refer to the Jewish people in disparaging terms.[11] But in the period 1958-1966, De Gaulle fully supported the making of the Jewish national nuclear power. His cheer leader was Jacques Soustelle (1912-1990), a gifted scholar in anthropology and an ardent anti-fascist during the Second World War. Under De Gaulle, Soustelle had been governor of the French Colony of Algiers and in charge of France's atomic energy program. He strongly opposed De Gaulle's plan for Algerian independence and in the mid-1960s his views drew a wedge between Soustelle and his president. Soustelle held the Arab world and civilization in very low esteem. Thus, his anti-fascist views and his dislike of the Arabs made him a perfect supporter of Israel and the Jewish cause.

The combination of President de Gaulle's aversion to the English-speaking influence in the region and Soustelle's deeply held convictions generated the perfect set of drivers for the Franco-Israeli alliance in atomic energy.

The French Invasion of 1959-1965

The French arrived in the Negev Desert in cohorts of highly skilled scientists, engineers, and technicians. The Bengurionite government selected the city of Beer-Sheva as the main urban environment to accommodate the important visitors and their families. A large complex of apartment buildings was hastily constructed in the immediate neighborhoods, a short distance from the center of the city. The structure resembled military barracks. They were four-story complexes of grey cement along a major street aptly named "The Peace Road."

Ever sensitive to beauty and their habitat, some French engineers complained to me about the stark, colorless, and depressing environs of their buildings. One engineer who had served in Tunisia was particularly incensed about the lack of trees and anything green in the area. I had studied the French language and French culture and quickly struck friendships with a few of the young engineers. They were favorably impressed with my recitations of poetry by Lamartine and Verlaine, and my affinity for the records of Edith Piaf.

However, the French invaders mainly kept to themselves. Although the city of Beer-Sheva had a substantial influx of Jewish immigration from the former French colonies in North Africa, there was little interaction between the visitors and the French-speaking inhabitants. The visitors from the mainland of France shunned any overture to mingle with their former colonists, and the North-African Jews not only rejected attempts to fraternize with the visitors, but often accused them of discrimination and snobbery.[12]

The French visitors whom I befriended consistently complained about their tour-of-duty in Israel—the drab living conditions, the desert, and the lack of cultural and recreational outlets in Beer-Sheva. One solution was a night club that catered only to them, as well as specialized cultural events and activities internally managed.

But the key mission of the French visitors was to provide a turnkey operation of the nuclear reactor and the plutonium-separation facility and to offer some training and initial maintenance for their Israeli hosts. Upon departure, one of the French engineers confided to me that Israel was—in his view—a strange country, devoid of culture, fine cuisine, and sophistication. He said that the population he had come to know was the refuse from North Africa, rather than the best the Jewish communities there had to offer. He was deeply concerned with the fact that he and his colleagues had just transferred the keys to the most destructive weapon ever devised to this strange country and its leaders.[13]

The Americans Are Coming!

In the mid-1960s there occurred a special event that changed the routine at KAMAG. After the departure of the French contingent, the reactor was fully operational and Institute Number Two had sprung to life. The Institute was now "dirty" or "contaminated," as the production of plutonium had entered into high gear. Some authors, such as Karpin (2006), Richelson (2006), and Cohen (1999), have speculated that Israel attained nuclear weapons capability around 1966.[14] This speculation is quite correct. The possible differences between such speculations and the actual dates are anchored in the definition of "attaining" capabilities. There was a distinction between reaching the point where sufficient plutonium was produced for one or several nuclear weapons and the joint effort between the Israeli Atomic Energy Agency and the agency responsible for developing the actual weapon, known as RAFAEL (The Authority for the Development of Instruments of War).[15]

Another speculation often advanced by historians is that beginning in the early to mid 1960s the United States had knowledge of the activities at KAMAG and knew that Israel was achieving nuclear capability. What is not clarified in these speculations is the level of detail of such intelligence. As more confidential documents enter the public domain with the passage of time (particularly on the American end), they tend to shed some additional, albeit limited, light on what the United States knew and when it knew it.[16]

What The Americans Knew

Five decades after the actual events there is still a gap between the account offered by historians and the reality of the times. The paucity of documentary evidence on the Israeli side has kept the historical reporting within the realm of speculation. What were the accuracy and the detail of American intelligence on the progress of activities at KAMAG? When did such intelligence materialize and how much did it affect American decision-makers in the 1960s?

The importance of these questions is magnified in these early years of the twenty-first century. The successes and failures of Western intelligence agencies in foreseeing and preventing terror attacks and the construction of weapons of mass destruction in unfriendly countries have demonstrated the crucial role of what these agencies knew and when they knew it.

The American interest in the activities at Dimona in the mid-1960s is usually depicted by historians as an episode in the overall U.S.-Israel relations and the events that preceded the Six Day War of 1967. There is a tendency to link the actions of then Egypt's President Nasser to his suspicions about Israel's development of atomic weapons. In early 1967, President Nasser initiated an aggressive policy vis-à-vis Israel by concentrating military forces on the border, thus raising tensions between the two countries (Ferris, 2013).

But, based on reports by American intelligence to their own administration and reliable historical sources in the Arab world, President Nasser was not concerned with the approaching timeline of the completion of an atomic weapon fabricated in KAMAG.[17] In his book on the Israeli nuclear bomb, Karpin (2006) had relied on a May 24, 1967 meeting between Richard Helms and President Lyndon Johnson. Helms was, at the time, the Director of the American Central Intelligence Agency (CIA). At that meeting Helms reportedly had assured the president that Israel did not possess nuclear weapons and that it would not have them in the immediate future.

Most importantly, if this account is correct, the chain of events leading to it began in 1963. At the insistence of President Kennedy, Israel was asked to allow American inspectors to visit the Dimona facility. Prime Minister Levi Eshkol had agreed to the visit and, indeed, the American inspectors first arrived in mid-January 1964. They reported that there was no activity to produce or separate plutonium.

In fact, in March 1965, the United States and Israel had signed a cooperation agreement. The second article of the agreement included the Israeli policy statement about nuclear weapons. This statement continued to be Israel's official policy for the almost five decades. The statement was: "The government of Israel has reaffirmed that Israel will not be the first to introduce nuclear weapons" into the Middle East and the Arab-Israeli conflict. [18]

The day-long American visit of January 1964 could not and did not uncover evidence of uranium enrichment because at that time Institute Number Two was not fully operational. But, this is not the full story. The Americans *did return* to Dimona for a visit some twenty months after their first visit, and several months before Richard Helms delivered his clean report to President Johnson. This time there was ample activity at Institute Number Two and, in less than a year, nuclear weapons capability would be achieved by the Jewish state.

One can argue that the second visit must have produced evidence that KAMAG was heavily involved with plutonium enrichment for weapons-grade production. Therefore, the CIA failed to interpret the report from the inspectors or withheld this intelligence from its own boss. Alternatively, perhaps the Israelis had been highly proficient in disguising their activities to the point of deceiving the skilled inspectors.

The "Great Deception"

Several weeks before the "phantom" visit of the American team of inspectors, a strange event was rapidly unfolding at the Dimona facility. At the time I was team leader of radiation safety and monitoring in Institute Number Two. We were instructed to conduct a special survey of radiation levels in all the underground floors and laboratories and in the ground-level building and its surroundings. Daily readings were especially ordered for the above-ground perimeter of the institute.

A contingent of carpenters, electricians, painters, and builders suddenly descended upon the institute. I became somewhat aware of such activities in the other institutes, particularly in the structure of the reactor and at Institute Number Four, whose function was the disposal of nuclear waste. But the major "face lift" was conducted at Institute Number Two.

The contingent of construction professionals began to tear down walls, seal entrances, and completely revamp the interior of the institute. All underground activity had already ceased and we had granted the institute a clean bill of radiation safety both within the structure and in the immediate surroundings. Within a few days the lobby of the one story building was totally transformed. The passage to the elevators was concealed by a freshly erected and painted wall, aptly decorated with some paintings of desert images. Metal filing cabinets and a pile of used wooden storage crates had appeared and the lobby now resembled the entrance to a storage facility. The "great deception" was in full swing.[19]

The entire underground facility usually bustling with hundreds of workers, scientists, and laboratory technicians had magically disappeared. Above ground there now existed an expansive one-story structure, fully committed to the administrative functions of inventory, storage, and maintenance. The faint radiation to be detected in the immediate vicinity around the building with the finest instruments of the time was not above "background radiation" routinely used as standard for the calibration of radiation-monitoring devices.

Following the "makeover" of the institute, there was a brief visit of the "brass" of the facility. The inspection was a measure of ensuring that the institute was simply a structure built for innocuous administrative purposes. Upon approval by the management, we remained at the institute to continue daily measures of radioactivity with the caveat that all instruments were hand-held and could be carried away from the building at any time. The larger, fixed-to-the-floor radiation detection apparatus had been taken down to the underground floors, out of sight of the casual visitor to the building. All was ready for the visit.

The Visit

The American team of inspectors arrived by mid-morning. Much of their time was allocated to a tour of Institute Number One: the atomic reactor. The visit to Institute Number Two was a sideshow. Those of us on duty that day seemed busy at our administrative chores of paperwork and other clerical functions throughout the building.

The team of two American visitors briefly walked through the lobby and then slowly exited the building. They did not carry any hand-held instruments to measure radiation. Each had a radiation detection tag attached to their lapel, as was the custom for *all* visitors to KAMAG. The tags were standard issue for all. The visitors were always accompanied by management, and they seemed to be affable, unfettered, and cordial.

The visit itself was a brief affair, at least for Institute Number Two. All the effort to give the structure a makeover and a perfect camouflage had been a success. The visitors showed very little interest in the building. As the peculiar party of visitors and KAMAG managers were leaving the premises, a mendacious thought occurred to me. How could they even imagine that beneath the unassuming building, in the "big dig," there was a world of beehive activity where the first Jewish nuclear weapon was being created?

At the time, the comforting thought was that the team of visitors presumably had not detected the deception and had given the facility a "clean bill of health." Or, did they?

The day after the visitors left KAMAG, the builders, carpenters, and painters returned to Institute Number Two. The walls were removed, the entrances to the underground facility were reopened, and the place returned to business as usual. The "great deception" had been a magnificent success. But, the troubling doubt persisted in my young mind: for how long? And, was the team of visitors *really* fooled?

What Did the Americans Know, and When Did They Know It

As I reflect today upon my notes, the affairs of the Middle East, and the world since the mid-1960s, the picture that emerges is simultaneously more complex but also more clarified. In light of the later inspections, requests for inspections, and reports of teams of nuclear experts from the IAEA (International Atomic Energy Agency) in such countries as Iran, Iraq, Libya, North Korea, and even the restructured Soviet Union, it is inconceivable that the United States did not realize, at the time, that Israel was on the verge of joining the exclusive nuclear club of nations.

The American state of knowledge is generally deduced by historians from Director Richard Helms' report to President Lyndon Johnson at the May 14 meeting of the National Security Council in which he unequivocally dismissed the notion that Israel was about to become a nuclear nation.

It is also highly improbable that Director Helms had failed to report the true outcome of his agency's analysis of data from the visit to Dimona and related intelligence. If the minutes from this meeting are correct, then there are two possibilities that might explain the gap between the reality on the ground at KAMAG and the report by Director Helms.

The first alternative scenario may be the reluctance of the field inspectors to file a positive report based solely on speculation and subjective assessment. The deception—in my view at the time—had been successful. The inspectors could not gather credible evidence to the existence of a plutonium extraction facility. Although, as, for example, many argued in reference to the events that led to the invasion of Iraq in 2003, intelligence is a complex compilation of disparate evidence and subjective evaluation, the experts in the field often refrain from making judgment calls and from issuing a potentially explosive report without hard evidence.

The second possibility is based on the assumption that the field inspectors indeed filed a report—based on their subjective assessment—that the facility at Dimona was at a stage which would strongly suggest that the country would very shortly acquire nuclear capabilities in the form of a nuclear weapon system. However, it is also possible that this report was met with a high degree of skepticism at CIA headquarters in Langley, Virginia. The CIA analysts probably rejected conclusions based on speculative assessments. Director Helms would have been told that lacking concrete evidence from the field, the intelligence community believed that, at that time, Israel was not about to enter the nuclear club of nations.

In my view it is also highly improbable that the experienced American inspectors failed to realize that the KAMAG facility was not what it purported to be. The sheer size of the facility far exceeded that of the reactor and laboratories at Nahal Soreq, south of Tel-Aviv. If not for the development of nuclear weapons, what was the purpose of this very expensive facility of such magnitude? Power generation was hardly an acceptable reason for such an enterprise, due to the limited size of the country and its economy.

Similarly, the various structures of the KAMAG facility could not be adequately described or explained away as laboratories for civilian or commercial uses of nuclear fission. Different scenarios with military objectives would have provided a comfortable framework within which the facility and its multiple buildings could be easily positioned.

Lastly, the tight security around the KAMAG facility could have been considered an indication of a well-guarded enterprise.[20] As the field inspectors considered all these variables, they would have at least drawn an inference that there would be a possibility of an *underground* facility. There was adequate space to build such a hidden plant, invisible from the sky and, to an extent, protected from aerial attacks.

President Lyndon Johnson and Israeli Prime Minister Levy Eshkol had previously agreed to the initial American military support of Israel. This agreement was a major departure from the lukewarm relations between the Bengurionite regime and three previous American presidents. With regard to the nuclear issue, Israel promised not to be the first nation to introduce nuclear weapons to the volatile region of the Middle East. This was a "double entendre" of a meaningless promise. If the Americans knew or suspected prior to June 1967 that Israel was ready to become nuclear, the policy of conventional military support was a shrewd move. It made Israel dependent on American supply of conventional weaponry while also reducing Israeli *angst* and fear of its enemies, thus making the nuclear option a much less attractive solution. The United States had become Israel's protector.

The Six-Day War: Who Is In Control?

A Personal Hiatus

The period between my discharge from the service and the Six-Day War of June 1967 was for me a personal time of growth and learning. I immersed myself into studies and work.

I continued my work at KAMAG, as a civilian employee of the facility.[21] This was a period of a continuous effort at self-improvement and personal growth. Six nights a week I was in charge of the late night shift at Institute Number Two. During the days I traveled by bus, alternating between the facility and university to attend classes. The daily bus trips of over four hours allowed me to keep a hectic schedule intermittently laced with catnaps. Expenses for tuition and transportation consumed the lion's share of my salary. I was fortunate to have a home at my mother's modest apartment, where I usually enjoyed a most agreeable and calming Saturday in the delightful company of my mother and sister.

This period of personal hiatus was marred by two "incidents" at Institute Number Two. The first occurred one night when I was not on duty. Engineers and technicians had disregarded standard operating procedures for safely handling radioactive materials. The result was a major explosion in which, I later learned, two employees had died. There was no perilous leak of radiation but the cleanup lasted for several days.

The second incident occurred one night when one of the research engineers decided to move a "glove box" from one room to another room down the hall.[22] I strongly objected. The researcher asked two lab assistants to help with the move, ignoring my arguments for safety abeyance. I remained in the room, nonetheless, to monitor the move. The glove box fell on the ground and its Plexiglas walls shattered. I ordered everyone outside and locked the door. All present in the room may have been exposed to plutonium. Further testing during the reporting and inquiry phase could not confirm or dismiss this possibility. Working without protective masks and an attempt to move a 250-pound large box contaminated with plutonium had been an infantile move by a very intelligent scientist, perhaps driven by glory or the pressures of unrealistic deadlines.

War is Imminent

The month of May is usually a mild and comfortable time in Israel. Western winds caress the eastern shores of the Mediterranean Sea and the vegetation springs to life in a multitude of colors. It is a month of calm and renewal.

But May 1967 was hardly calm. After the middle of the month, the days grew unusually hotter, not only in the atmospheric climate, but in the political and military as well. It was a time of tension, apprehension, and the imminence of war.

The fresh Israeli Prime Minister, Levi Eshkol, was facing the veteran warlord, General Gamal Abdel Nasser, president of Egypt. This rise in tension followed a year of difficult economic conditions in Israel. The Eshkol government continued the discredited economic policies of the Bengurionite tradition. The country descended into a recession.[23]

By the middle of May, 1967, the Israeli public began to realize that there was a tension building at the southern border with Egypt and the northern border with Syria. Eshkol authorized the call-up of the reserves. Over 50 thousand were called and many more received an alert that they would soon be mobilized. This was a bold move, since these were the backbone of the economic activity in the country. Extracting them from the economy deepened the recession and cast a shadow over the government's ability to deal with such a compounded economic-military crisis. Although Levi Eshkol had been a true Bengurionite in creed and deed, he lacked the manufactured charisma of the older statesman. Fueled by the "old guard" of the Bengurionite regime, Eshkol became the target of popular doubt and mistrust, resulting in a lack of confidence in his leadership.

Prime Minister Eshkol decided to wait before committing Israel to an all-out war with its neighbors. He was faced with the specter of the failure in 1956 to obtain support and consensus from the international community. In 1967 he also had to consider his newly established ties of friendship with the United States. The Soviet Union and France insisted that Israel exhaust all diplomatic effort in the face of Nasser's bellicose maneuvers on land and in the Straits of Tiran. The French President, Charles de Gaulle, adamantly admonished the Israelis: "Do not start a war!"[24]

Days of Discontent

While the Israeli diplomats were shuttling between capitals in Europe and the United States, the situation at home continued to deteriorate. The public and the IDF (Israel Defense Force) had lost confidence in their government. The generals were unhappy and ordinary Israelis (in and out of uniform) were clamoring for action.

Sunday, May 28, 1967, was a day of significance. Although already mobilized, I was between assignments. After spending several days at the Department of Defense headquarters in Tel-Aviv[25], the preceding Friday I traveled to Beer-Sheva to say good-bye to my family before leaving for my new destination. The radio was turned on and we could hear the Prime Minister addressing the nation. His speech was hesitant and at times unclear, confused, and bewildered. He tried to explain the reasons for the lack of action and proceeded to reiterate his faith in the support Israel could expect from the United States. This was a disastrous speech. I left my mother's apartment with a heavy heart and much apprehension. So did the majority of the population.

A sentiment of disillusionment permeated the country in the last week of May 1967. Many Israelis, particularly those with strong political and economic connections to the Bengurionite regime and many members of the orthodox religious segment of the population, headed to the international airport near Tel-Aviv in search of flights away from the danger zone.[26]

On the way to my next assignment, back to the Defense Ministry in Tel-Aviv, I had time to reflect and assess in my young mind the events of the past several weeks. The bus[27] had left the brown and yellow surroundings of the desert as it navigated toward the greener plains of the seaside terrain. A sentiment of disillusionment and stressful expectation were on the minds of all and I could see the seriousness and tension in the faces of the passengers. The bus station in Beer-Sheva resembled a beehive of activity, with hundreds of men and women in uniform hurrying to their units. The age difference was evident: young recruits and older reservists mingling in their rush to board the buses to their destinations, or disembarking from buses to their units in the southern command.

With the mass media (radio and print) under the control of the government, the hourly news merely reported the movements of Israeli diplomats abroad. Intermittently, the radio announced the calling signals or password for specific units. It was an eerie experience, reminiscent perhaps of how the members of the French resistance felt during the Second World War as they listened to the BBC.[28]

Mobilizing the Reserves

Although Prime Minister Eshkol was still trying to avert a military confrontation, the generals could not and would not wait. The events of the last two weeks in May continued their uninterrupted pattern of tension and threat. Egypt and Jordan agreed to a military alliance, thus creating a strategic imbalance for Israel, with three enemy forces surrounding it from the south, east, and north. To the west lay the Mediterranean Sea, into which Israelis felt—their sentiment of apocalyptic fate—the Arabs under Nasser and King Hussein of Jordan were going to throw them in a war of total annihilation.

The generals continued the accelerated pace of mobilization. Diplomatic attempts to engender an effort to open the Straits of Tiran had failed. Nasser massed his tanks in the Sinai Peninsula, facing the

Israeli southern command in the Negev desert. By the end of May the Israeli mobilization effort was complete.

But, to appease its friends and foes in the international community, the Eshkol government continued to claim that its intentions were not to go to war unilaterally, and that there was only a "partial mobilization." Within Israel everyone knew that the mobilization was total, the economy was virtually paralyzed, and the army and the air force were posed for immediate action once the order was given.

There was a "blackout" on information sent abroad by foreign correspondents. The Israeli censors insisted upon the terms "partial mobilization" or "precautionary mobilization." This led to a peculiar oddity of the time. An American journalist prepared a cable to his newspaper that the "partial mobilization" was proceeding as efficiently as Ivory soap. The censors allowed the cable to pass. They were unaware of the popular advertisement for Ivory soap on American television, claiming that it was 99.9% pure. The editors understood the meaning and headlines emerged in the American press that Israel was fully mobilized.[29]

The De Facto Coup D'Etat

Several historians have claimed that the IDF general staff and the ardent Bengurionites did not attempt the formal overthrow of the elected government. Other historians have strongly maintained that Eshkol was different from his mentor and predecessor, David Ben-Gurion.

In my estimation, Eshkol was a true and hardened Bengurionite. His personality and his style of management may have been different, but in creed and indeed in his policies, Eshkol remained a disciple of Ben-Gurion and continued the failed economic and geo-political strategies of his predecessor. Moreover, Eshkol's success in winning over President Lyndon Johnson was due to the happenstance of two second-stringers rising to power simultaneously in the fast steps of a predecessor who was a hero in the eyes of the populace. Johnson and Eshkol were kindred spirits. Both had received little support from the followers and close advisors of the previous leaders.

In the case of Eshkol, Ben-Gurion himself was heartily engaged in the weaving of a derogatory campaign against the current occupant of the prime ministership and the ministry of defense. From his retreat at Sde-Boker, the former leader mightily and unashamedly declared that Levi Eshkol was leading the country into an abyss. Ben-Gurion reveled in the joy of key political figures making the pilgrimage to his desert residence to grovel before him and to implore him to return to power to save the endangered homeland.[30]

Unable to return Ben-Gurion to power, the generals and Bengurionite politicians and their collaborators instituted a de facto coup d'etat. Although a knowledgeable historian, Michael Oren, wrote, "Yet, however angry, those generals made no serious attempt to oust Eshkol, never threatened the rule of law" (p. 134). The combination of the military and political cooperative achieved its anti-Eshkol objective in a de facto manner. With underhanded maneuvers they stripped Levi Eshkol of his most important basis of power: the Ministry of Defense. On Thursday, June 1, 1967, retired General Moshe Dayan formally became Minister of Defense.

The appointment met with a strong degree of skepticism by the chief of the army general staff, General Yitzhak Rabin. An astute man of superior intelligence, he clearly understood that his new boss now held all the power and that the prime minister had been reduced to a puppet administrator. General Rabin was also concerned that the new defense chief would tamper (under the guise of key improvements) with the IDF master plan for the air and ground attacks. It was abundantly clear to both Eshkol and Rabin that bringing back Dayan, the one-eyed hero of the war of independence and the war in the Sinai of 1956 as defense minister, was infinitely more than simply to boost the morale of the populace. This appointment meant a total shift in power from Eshkol to Dayan and the generals and, by logical extension, to Ben-Gurion.[31]

For all practical reasons, this was a major de-facto coup d'état. It meant a fundamental shift in power. The finger on the trigger of the conventional forces now belonged to Moshe Dayan. Even more troublesome, the power to deploy unconventional weapons had been taken away from the prime minister. In a strange and unpredictable set of circumstances, I found myself in the middle of this controversial power shift, never before made public.[32] My new assignment and the events associated with my experience in late May and early June 1967 helped to clarify my view of the change in power.[33]

The Assignment and the Weapon

After spending two days on alert on the campus of the Ministry of Defense, I was ordered to report to a wooden structure that housed an office of security command. A middle-aged man in civilian attire received me. He identified himself by his first name and provided his code name "merkaz" (center). He handed me written orders and asked me to sit down. Following a short inquiry about my skills and experience at KAMAG, "Merkaz" had this to say: "Whatever happens in your new command, you don't allow anyone, repeat, anyone into the compound and you don't contact me. I'll contact you if necessary. The number you have is for absolute emergencies." I would later obey these orders to the utmost of my ability, even in the face of superior forces.

The orders consisted of traveling with "Merkaz" to a facility in the center of the country to assume command of the facility and to conduct daily duties of radiation control and monitoring. The facility was an abandoned police station some 20 miles southeast of Tel-Aviv. This was a "Tigert"-type compound, designed and built by the British colonial regime. The facility had a surrounding stonewall and a majestic entrance with heavy gates. There were four mini guard towers facing the only access road leading to the compound. The towers had been designed to accommodate heavy machine guns.

We arrived in mid-afternoon in the company of the "package." This was a wooden crate of about 40 cubic feet in volume. We deposited the crate in one of the rooms inside the main building. The room was empty of any furniture and without windows. I proceeded to open the crate and to uncover a metal container with a removable top. Using both alpha and gamma detection instruments, I measured the levels of radiation in the room and on the surface of the "package." I noted the readings in a daily log. Just before dark, "Merkaz" departed upon the arrival of a contingent of border guard soldiers with their armaments and equipment, including a mobile kitchen and a most-welcome load of military-type issue of chairs, desks, and sleeping cots.

Unlike the Army, the border guard in Israel reported to the Ministry of Police, which in turn reported to the prime minister's office. This was a civilian rather than a military contingent. This arrangement was much more than a symbolic selection of which force should guard the weapon. The border guard allowed the prime minister—hence the civilian authority—control over the core of the nuclear weapon. Such control enabled the prime minister to be the sole entity to authorize the deployment of the country's nuclear might.

The shortcoming of the border guard was their lack of substantial military armament and training. The contingent comprised 36 border guards and their commander. They were armed with personal weapons and four heavy machine guns, which we immediately deployed on the towers of the building. Working in 3 shifts, the border guards supplied me with a constant surveillance of the perimeter.

We posted guards at the massive main gate, some 50 yards from the building. I also ordered barbed wire to be set upon the top of the brick wall surrounding the facility.

The commander of the border guard contingent sat down with me on the large veranda at the entrance to the main building facing the large front yard and the main gate. We discussed the placing of guards, the perimeter to be guarded, and the daily routine for his men. The commander asked very few questions regarding the mission, or the "package" ensconced in the inner room. I ordered a permanent guard at the entrance to the corridor leading to the said room. I also ordered the positioning of the two large trucks that brought the contingent to the gate, thus barricading it from the inside.

I then explained to the commander that the package contained radar-avionic parts for the newly acquired fighter planes. He seemed pleased and satisfied with my clarification. We then established a telephone line hook-up and tested the electrical connections so that the compound would be lit upon the approaching darkness of night.

We hooked up the public announcement system throughout the compound and we then set up a command post in the rooms facing the courtyard in the main building, directly behind the veranda. The commander was a veteran officer in his fifties who did not mind taking orders from a much younger person. He understood the unique aspects of my technical responsibility and channeled his energy into assuring the safety and security of the installation from a military standpoint.

Once we secured the perimeter of the compound, we effectively isolated ourselves from the outside world. We had provisions for about two weeks. The commander initiated a grueling routine for his men, including daily physical activity and training for the unlikely event of air attacks. We were not sufficiently equipped to repel a serious military ground attack but we had a strong cordon of an armed guard surrounding the compound. I was satisfied with the arrangements.

A Time for Reflection

The next day, when all the arrangements had been put in place, I could relax and execute charge of monitoring our precious package. I entered the room and uncovered the heavy lid. Inside the container there was a metallic half sphere, with muted shine, and a peaceful, almost serene appearance to it.

The core of the weapon was in my charge. The trigger mechanism for the weapon was stored elsewhere. A specially equipped aircraft was at readiness at an airfield nearby my facility. Once the order was given, the core would be transported to the trigger facility and the weapon would be assembled. The locations of the assembly and the aircraft were unknown to me.

I was not fooled by the apparent calm surroundings of the room and the container. The sphere was the core of a nuclear weapon: made of plutonium and containing the destructive force of millions of tons of TNT. After taking the necessary measurements of the alpha and gamma radiation, I stood bewildered and amazed at this moment. The first Jewish-made nuclear weapon—the outcome of what the Germans called in the 1930s "the Jewish science" of physics. I stood in silence, reflecting upon the words of Professor Robert Oppenheimer, quoting the verse from the Bhagavad Gita: "Now I am become death, the destroyer of worlds."

Another verse came to my mind, preceding the verse that Professor Oppenheimer had contemplated upon realizing the power of his creation: "If the splendor of a thousand suns were to blaze forth at once in the sky, that would still not be the splendor of the exalted being." I shuddered at the powerful potential of this seemingly harmless sphere to destroy all within the size of an entire city. I could feel the ghosts of Albert Einstein, Enrico Fermi, Niels Bohr, Leo Szilard, and Ernest Lawrence hovering over me as I stood in awe, staring at the incredible artifact in my charge. This was the product of a fantastic investment in treasure and human endeavor. This was also the harbinger of a destructive force of a "thousand suns," the epitome of human folly.

As I stood in contemplation about this moment in time, when a young man of twenty-four communed with the primeval force of nature, I was also thinking of the future. A poem by one of my favorite poets, Robert Frost, came to mind:

> "The woods are lovely, dark, and deep,
> But I have promises to keep,
> And miles to go before I sleep,
> And miles to go before I sleep."

I was also thinking of myself as a boy of eight years of age, penning his poems in the nearby city of Tel-Aviv. One of my early poems came to mind.[34]

> *"I stand alone...*
> *And those I love*
> *And those I care about*
> *Are there, with me...*
> *But I am still alone."*

I was indeed alone. This was much more than the solitude of command. I was gazing at the man-made harbinger of the destructive splendor of a thousand suns. My notes jotted down that same evening reflected the contriteness of being a part of this endeavor, and holding—alone—the primordial power of the universe.

I was also thinking of my father, whose strength and gentleness of character had mingled so exceptionally in his short life. I had known him only during my childhood and adolescence, and he would probably wonder what I was doing with this incredible device, and would probably advise, as he always did: "Do the right thing."

Who Is In Charge?

The first three days were uneventful. We had become accustomed to the routine in the compound. Twice daily I communed with the device. The border guards and their commander performed their duties with professional efficiency and all did their best to make me comfortable. I was grateful and acknowledged their benevolence.

The month of June exploded upon us with hot days and nights warmer than usual. We had begun to settle into the surreal atmosphere of the waiting game. We kept the radio on for much of the day. I had agreed to broadcast the hourly news reports to the troops via the public announcement system throughout the compound. The news was consequently grim and discouraging. The diplomatic "offensive" continued and there were changes in the chain of political command, when the broadcaster announced that retired general Moshe Dayan had been made the Minister of Defense.

That same evening I reflected upon these changes in the power structure and the implications for my assignment and the device under my charge. I hoped to hear from my contact in Tel-Aviv, but the call had not materialized. The silence became a deafening experience of "wait and see."

The next morning I was invited by the troops to partake in a friendly game of ball. I agreed, since this would be good exercise for me and for them. I took off my shirt and we played for a while in the courtyard in front of the main building. After a while, one of the guards from the gate came running and announced that we had a visitor. I walked over to the gate. Outside there was a military command car. An officer alighted. He was perhaps in his late thirties or early forties. He held the rank of "Aluf-Mishne (Colonel)."[35] The officer then identified himself by the name Yaakov. The following conversation ensued:

"Who is in charge?" he asked.

"I am."

"Who are you and what's your name"

"Please state your business here."

"Where is your shirt? Your insignia?"

I identified myself by my first name—no rank, no unit.

"I came to take over command," said the officer, Colonel Yaakov.[36]

"I was not aware of your visit," I answered politely. "Please turn around and leave."

"Don't be insolent," he said. "I need to inspect the facility."

"This is a restricted area. You are not authorized to gain entry," I said forcefully. "Please leave."

Colonel Yaakov then uttered some indignities and ordered his driver to turn around. The commander, who had joined me at the gate, asked for an explanation: why was this officer demanding an inspection? I said that I did not know that it was a mistake, and dismissed the incident.

The next morning Colonel Yaakov returned to the gate. This time he was accompanied by a couple of transport trucks carrying troops. These were cadets, from the army's officer's training school. Again, the symbolism was clear. Instead of regular troops, Colonel Yaakov brought a contingent of cadets. They were, of course, soldiers, under the command of a regular officer, but they were also cadets, not yet assigned to their specific units. They were highly trained and motivated. One more time I went to the gate and confronted his demands to enter and to take charge of the facility. Colonel Yaakov was losing his patience. He yelled: "If we don't gain access I'll be back with tanks and drive right in!" He looked serious and determined. Again I flatly rejected his authority. He was a worthy opponent, expressing both intransigence and will power. Finally, I turned to the commander and said: "If they try to enter by force, use all the force we have available to keep them out."

The commander looked puzzled. I repeated the order and started to walk away. The commander stopped me. "What do you mean by using force?" he asked. "Use live ammunition," I said and returned to the main building. Colonel Yaakov turned around and departed. The commander rushed in. "This is a bad order," he said. "This means civil war."

We sat down to sip a cold drink. He was very apprehensive. I attempted to explain that I was under strict orders to defend the compound, regardless of the nature of the intruder. I then agreed to contact my superiors and to gain some form of explanation. This I did later that evening.

My telephone conversation with "Merkaz" was brief and instructive. He knew about Colonel Yaakov and his visit. He promised to look into the matter and to contact me again in the morning. I instructed the commander to keep his men on full alert.

Next morning the news came after my daily communion with the weapon. I was ordered to *share* control of the compound with Colonel Yaakov and his men. At about noon he arrived with two companies of his cadets. Arrangements were made to house the cadets, and a joint duty roster to guard the facility had been worked out between the commander and the captain in charge of the cadets. As before, the inner rooms of the main building remained out of bounds for *all* personnel.[37]

After the Six Day War I met my contact, "Merkaz," at a Tel-Aviv coffee shop—at his invitation. He looked despondent, old, and depressed. He attempted, unsuccessfully, to explain in broad terms what had happened. He had worked for the civilian authority and deeply resented the intervention of the military. His main concern was the weapon—its safety and the control over its whereabouts and ultimate use. We parted with a handshake. I never saw him again, and I never learned his name.

The Military Takeover and the Nuclear Trigger

The various accounts and events had begun to congeal in my mind. A clear picture began to emerge as I was putting together the disparate pieces of information. The core of the nuclear weapon in my charge was no longer under the control of the civilian government within the authority of the prime minister. The military establishment had taken over the charge of the fearsome weapon.

The generals had acted on the instigation of their mentor, David Ben-Gurion. Three key assumptions or motivators seemed to have guided their drastic action.[38] The first was their strong belief that a national crisis was upon the country. The second assumption was their aggregate conclusion that Prime Minister Eshkol's feeble leadership, hesitancy, and failed policies had brought the country to the brink of extinction. Finally, they believed that when and if the time came, Eshkol would not bring himself to pull the nuclear trigger and to exercise the atomic option.

As late as Monday, May 29th, Eshkol spoke to the Knesset (Israel's parliament) in what appeared at the time—conciliatory terms. After describing the reasons and severity of the crisis, Eshkol said: "It is our duty, first of all, to put international undertakings to the test . . . we are now engaged in extensive political activity for the restoration of freedom of passage."[39] Thus, Prime Minister Eshkol had reiterated Israel's position that the blocking by Egypt of the Straits of Tiran indeed represented a "casus belli," but that he was determined to exhaust all diplomatic avenues before unleashing the might of the IDF upon President Nasser and his allies.

The military establishment in Israel thought otherwise. When retired general Moshe Dayan became minister of defense, we effectively assumed with this act that General Dayan had also gained control of the nuclear trigger. Dayan was not elected by the people nor was he a choice of the prime minister. The legitimate authority vested in the elected government had been usurped.

From my humble vantage point I was thus privy to the forced transfer of control of the plutonium core of the nuclear bomb. The border police represented the enforcement arm of the *civilian* government, whereas the cadets were the *military* arm, reporting to the minister of defense. In so many ways this situation was similar to the 1962 book by Fletcher Knebel, "Seven Days in May," in which the author describes a planned coup d'etat perpetrated by the United States military against a president with pacifist views.[40]

In his book on the Six Day War, Michael Oren described the takeover of the reign of power from Prime Minister Eshkol on the basis of disagreement with the military on the timing of the first strike against Egypt. But, as I describe in this book, the illegal takeover was much more acute, with far-reaching future implications. I am referring to the takeover of the nuclear assets of the country. The finger on the nuclear trigger was no longer that of the elected *civilian* official. When and how to launch a nuclear strike became the sole prerogative of the senior generals. Eshkol had now merely become a puppet of the Bengurionite general staff.

It is perhaps utterly ironic that Eshkol himself was an ardent Bengurionite and the ultimate subservient assistant of the leader. He supported with unbridled enthusiasm the deviant version of socialism that Ben-Gurion so aptly enforced on the country. Eshkol's career as Minister of Finance and Prime Minister will be remembered with trepidation, not so much for his meager achievements but rather for his slogan of what Israel represented: "We want Jews without money and money without Jews." The pupil had been betrayed by his master and by the cabal of the carefully chosen devotees who served as a caste of military officers. Eshkol's only indiscretion was that he dared to fill—albeit legally—the vacant prime ministership when his master, David Ben-Gurion, left the office in one of his typical outbursts of juvenile rage.

As I further explain in Part VII of this book, the takeover of power in 1967 has effectively set a precedent and opened the door for other coups d'etat. This is particularly alarming in light of the strong possibility of the forthcoming power shift to the extremist orthodoxy.

The 1973 (Yom Kippur) War: One Minute to Midnight

Between Two Wars

The inter-belli years between the Six Day War and the Yom Kippur War again heralded for me a period of learning and reflection. The birth of my daughter had solidified my will to expand our horizon in a freer environment.

Most of what started to transpire in the national scene directly emanated from the events of the Six Day War. The mood of the populace was transformed almost overnight. Geographical conquests tripled the national area—from the Sinai Peninsula in the south to the Golan Heights in the north and, most crucially, the capture of the entire area west of the river Jordan. But the crowning achievement was the conquest of the old city of Jerusalem and the holiest shrine to Judaism: The Wailing (Western) Wall.

There was a mood of jubilation and euphoria. In many ways the generals and Moshe Dayan had been vindicated, although their actions and the nuclear assets remained a secret. In the gullible eyes of the populace, diplomacy had failed. It was through the force of arms (albeit conventional) that the threat had been eliminated, and three Arab armies indisputably defeated (Egypt, Syria, and Jordan). The spirit of contentment was also a promise of good times to come, of prosperity and, perhaps, peace with the neighboring countries.

What to do with the immense territory that was added to the nation? A popular discussion ensued, even to the point of a dispute over naming the newly acquired area *conquered* versus *liberated*.[41] Which areas should be annexed and which should remain in limbo, perhaps as an item for peace negotiation?

In time, complacency replaced elation. Old habits of the Bengurionite regime remained unchanged. The Six Day War had helped to alleviate the economic hardship of the recession of 1965-1967. The simple fact of an added market of over a million Palestinians/former Jordanians on the West Bank was sufficient to jump-start the Israeli economy.

But the hefty promises failed to materialize. The elation of the populace could not overturn the trend of continued emigration of the "best and the brightest." The expected massive immigration of talented Jews from the Western Diaspora was no more than a fleeting dream.

The Scientific Administration

In the period between the wars there was much ado about the restructuring of the Israeli nuclear establishment. In his 2006 book, Michael Karpin described the overall aspects of the change.[42] He wrote: "Simultaneously, control over the scientific projects of the defense establishment, including those of RAFAEL, were transferred to a new Scientific Administration that was set up at the Defense Ministry" (p. 266). The restructured entity was "a staff unit and did not contain executive units, all of which remained at RAFAEL" (p. 266).[43]

The Scientific Administration was part of the larger nuclear system. The overall entity continued to be the Atomic Energy Commission. Karpin correctly ascribed to the commission the responsibility for advising the government on all nuclear issues and for representing Israel's peaceful atomic pursuits to the international community. In effect, the commission was responsible for the reactors at Soreq and Dimona, as well as RAFAEL. Professor Israel Dostrovsky was named director general of the commission. He reported to the prime minister.

This restructuring was Levi Eshkol's masterpiece. He hoped to reassemble the nuclear establishment without the early managers and scientists—all ardent Ben gurionites. The emerging duality of units was tailored to his positions as prime minister and minister of defense. Thus, the idea was that the commission was in charge of the *civilian* aspects of the nuclear program (especially with respect to the world community) while the scientific administrator would manage the *military* aspects of the nuclear program. For this Eshkol was severely criticized by the Bengurionites.[44]

Alas, with the coup d'etat of June 1967, the restructuring of the nuclear establishment became the stalwart foundation of political and administrative tools of the defense power brokers. Swiftly, the originally ascribed power of the commission was radically diminished, and the scientific administration, first under Israel Dostrovsky, then Shalhevet Freier, became the true manager of the nuclear program. The Scientific Administration was officially housed in the Ministry of Defense, but reported to the Prime Minister.

After the Six Day War I joined the restructured Scientific Administration as a junior official. My responsibilities included the design of procedures and work processes for the young organization. I was especially intrigued by the interface between this administrative staff and the operational units of the reactors at Dimona, Soreq, and the organization of RAFAEL. Inter-organizational relations was a fascinating area of exploration and a fertile ground for the establishment of effective work processes for exchange and cooperation.

In the meantime, during the inter-belli years, the nuclear cores were stored in a more permanent facility. Located some ten miles from the limits of the city of Tel-Aviv, the facility was a concrete structure built into the slope of a hill. A tortuous road led to the inconspicuous entrance. The building was essentially invisible from the main road, due to the strategic placement of sand dunes that obscured the silhouette of the hill and the structure within it. For several months I "burned the midnight oil" while working the late shift at the facility with a handful of technicians and guards.

One evening the Minister of Defense, Moshe Dayan, paid us a visit. Several officials and bodyguards accompanied him. The staff had resolved to show the minister a "dummy" core. He was not impressed and hinted, "This is not the real thing." The incident was a tension reliever for the staff at the facility. I viewed it as an ominous sign of disaggregation between the technical-scientific people and the politicians in charge of the nuclear trigger. A more disturbing fact was the absence of any oversight from civilian bodies. During my tenure at the said storage facility, not one member of the Committee for Foreign Affairs and Security of the Knesset was ever allowed to visit, or perhaps were never aware or informed of the existence of the weapons.[45]

The Two-Front War

The Yom Kippur War of October 1973 happened to be as much a surprise for us at the Scientific Administration as it was for the remainder of the country. A voluminous literature on this war has since flourished.[46] In this book I limit my contribution to my eyewitness experiences in this war within the organization of the Scientific Administration and the preparations for deployment of Israel's nuclear strike—all this against the background of the early and ominous days of the armed conflict.

For several months since the spring of 1973 there had been a growing tension along the borders with Egypt and Syria. I had to delay my planned departure for the United States. Again, war seemed imminent. The question was: When? This time the cast of characters included Prime Minister Golda Meir, Defense Minister Moshe Dayan, and the newly appointed Chief of Staff of the IDF, Lieutenant-General David Elazar (nicknamed "Dado").[47] On the Egyptian side, President Anwar Sadat and General Hosni Mubarak (who led the Egyptian Air Force) were the architects of the strike against Israel.[48]

On Sunday, the 27th of May, 1973, General Elazar ("Dado") decided—against the advice of his military intelligence—to declare an emergency situation and to call the reserves in partial mobilization. He did so in response to major maneuvers of Egyptian forces near the Israeli border. The country was on alert, but the attack by Sadat's army did not materialize. General Elazar was castigated by his superiors, Golda Meir and Moshe Dayan. Elazar lost not only his credibility among the Bengurionite defense establishment, but also—to the detriment of future events—his flexibility to act decisively. Some historians now believe that Anwar Sadat indeed planned to launch his attack in May, but was persuaded by his Soviet Allies to postpone his strike across the borders.[49]

On Saturday, 6 October 1973, at two o'clock in the afternoon on the holiest day in the Jewish calendar Yom Kippur the Egyptians and Syrian armies launched a coordinated attack across the country's southern and northern frontiers. This was to be the unexpected, bloody, and from the Israeli perspective totally unnecessary two-front war.

Failure of Intelligence: Facts and Consequences

Throughout the summer of 1973 Israeli intelligence agencies received reports that the Egyptians and Syrians were ready to strike. Finally, on Monday, 1 October 1973, Anwar Sadat and his colleagues in Damascus declared a state of alert for both armies. Yet, in the following days there was a shared belief among the key protagonists in the political and military leadership in Israel that war was unlikely.[50]

The military branch of the IDF ("Agaf Modiyin" or Aman) under the command of General Eli Zeira had concluded as early as May 1973 that the Arab neighbors would not risk war. In part this interpretation was based on inadequate analysis, but mostly this was the result of strongly held beliefs instilled by the Bengurionite elite in the leadership ranks of the defense establishment.

Bengurionism had relegated the Arab neighbors to a lower level of national competence. Arab language, culture, history, and technological and educational achievements were not widely studied. Colonel Yoel Ben-Porat was chief of staff to General Zeira at Aman.[51] He described the mood and skills set of Israeli military intelligence as ignorant of what truly transpired in the Arab societies.[52] Ben-Porat argued that Israeli intelligence officers could not fathom a surprise and well-coordinated attack because these officers had a "mental and intellectual barrier…, which, in advance, precludes the possibility that Arabs may have any technological achievements."[53]

In the fall of 1973, this deeply-held disparaging view was not shared by Colonel Ben-Porat and General Elazar. Prime Minister Meir and Defense Minister Dayan had rejected General Elazar's request for full mobilization. The events of the previous decision in May had come back to haunt the Chief of Staff of the IDF. The day before the attack, on Friday 5 October, General Elazar, fed up with the reticence of his superiors, ordered a partial mobilization.

Nevertheless, Elazar's request for a preemptive air strike, planned for the next day, Saturday 6 October, was rejected. He had put the Israeli Air Force on alert for the morning of the 6th of October, but the order was rescinded. The decision to mobilize the IDF was issued by the political leadership around 8:00 AM, some six hours before the massive onslaught of Egyptian and Syrian armor against the ill-prepared Israeli forces.[54] By the time the IDF was fully mobilized, Egyptian and Syrian forces had advanced well into Israel and the cost in human lives began to escalate.

The consequences of this "surprise" were far-reaching. For the first time since the early 1960s, the nuclear option suddenly became operational. The political and military leadership was in disarray. When the October 8th counter offensive of the IDF failed, Defense Minister Moshe Dayan, the declared hero of the Six Day War, became gloomy and desperate. Walter Boyne, a retired American air force colonel, described the behavior of Moshe Daya and Golda Meir in very flattering terms.[55]

He argued that Dayan may have exaggerated Israel's dire position in order to obtain permission to deploy the nuclear option. In fact, Dayan had repeatedly exclaimed during the first three days of the war that the disposition of the IDF meant that there were no forces left between the southern battleground in the Sinai and the heart of the country—Tel-Aviv. His utterance resonates Winston Churchill's meeting in 1940 with the French leadership just before the fall of France to Nazi Germany. Churchill asked the fateful question: Where are your reserves? The French generals presumably responded: "There are none!" Moshe Dayan invariably lamented the destruction of the "Third Temple," a common name for the resurgence of the State of Israel.

Boyne's rationale is faulty. Moshe Dayan did not need, in practice, permission to use nuclear weapons. At that time—since the coup of June 1967—the nuclear arsenal was under the control of the Ministry of Defense. Dayan's finger was always on the nuclear trigger. I overheard Director Shalhevet Freier sadly confide to the senior staff at a meeting upon the arrival of the flood of bad news: "The defense minister ordered us to go on alert. The countdown has begun!" Indeed, the unit overseeing the nuclear option had been mobilized.

One Minute to Armageddon

During the first few days of the 1973 war, the news from the two fronts was not only alarming but also depressing. Syrian and Egyptian forces had broken through the Israeli front lines in the Sinai desert and in the Golan Heights. The Syrians were descending the Golan Heights towards the Sea of Galilee and the City of Tveria along its shore. The path was clear to anyone who could read a map. After Tveria, on to the Valley of Israel, and from there to the lower country and the coast of the Mediterranean Sea. In many respects this was a back door to the highly populated Dan region (Gush Dan) and its prize possession—the metropolis of Tel-Aviv.

The mood at the headquarters of the Scientific Authority was somber. There was the news of the Israeli Air Force flying all its combat aircraft to one front, then another—to the north, then to the south. There seemed not to be enough aircraft to cover *both* fronts with a degree of comfort. There was talk of the lack of ammunition and of tanks stopping dead in their tracks for lack of fuel and armaments. As the situation darkened, the stories began accumulating and gaining a bizarre life of their own.

Occupied with the preparations to move the unit responsible for the nuclear arsenal, I had dismissed these stories as office gossip, regardless of how high the source. The director and his senior staff were visibly upset, uttering some unpleasant remarks, thus adding to the stories. Some of these narratives later became the official line. Indeed, there had been insufficient preparedness. There had been a lack of armaments for the ground troops. Under-investments and a false sense of security had produced a military force not suited for a surprise attack. Faulty intelligence and poor decision-making at the top of the Bengurionite regime had led the country to the verge of Armageddon.

Among the officers in charge of the Israeli military, General David Elazar took upon himself the brunt of the blame for the failure in the early days of the 1973 war. He later took his own life. I met "Dado" when he came to visit the Scientific Authority, as the war was on the horizon. In my capacity as a junior official with the Authority I watched him interact with the director and his senior staff. I was not privy to the actual discussion. I saw in General Elazar a tough soldier, calm and composed. He was destined to take the shame and the blame away from the Bengurionite elite: Moshe Dayan and Golda Meir.[56]

General Elazar was a professional soldier. Born in Sarajevo, then Yugoslavia, in 1925, he emigrated to then Palestine in 1940 and joined Kibbutz Ein-Shemer. He was not part of the Bengurionite inner circle and he had no political ambitions.[57]

In 1976, at the early age of 51, General Elazar took his own life.

During the early days of the war, General Elazar was confident of victory. He expressed this view on Monday, 8 October 1973, on the eve of the counterattack launched by General Albert Mendler's (Magen) 252nd armored corps in the Southern front. Colonel Gabi Amir's brigade, composed of first rate Patton and Centurion tanks, spearheaded the counterattack. The counterattack of the Egyptian positions, recaptured on the eastern (Israeli) side of the Suez Canal had failed, with a loss of over 100 Israeli tanks.[58]

In the midst of the initial setbacks, General Elazar was confident that his forces would turn a near disaster into victory. He allowed his field commanders, General Ariel Sharon (143rd Armored Corps) and Avraham Adan (162nd Armored Corps) in the south, and General Rafael Eitan (36th Corps) in the north ample room to maneuver and to improvise. They succeeded despite the shortages in armaments and munitions.

General Elazar did not recommend or request—at any point in the war—the *total* mobilization of the nuclear arsenal. This confidence did not extend to the other Israeli leaders. The Director of the Scientific Authority commented shortly after the 1973 war that the Authority had overreacted in its preparation and should have kept the nuclear option "secure in its place—not ready to be deployed."

Preparation for deployment meant assembly of the team of experts in radiation safety, meteorology, and nuclear engineering and security. I was part of the team assembled in a clearing in the woods, southeast of Tel-Aviv, near the installation where the warheads were stored. The plan for the deployment of the nuclear warheads was put into operation—in stages one and two of its eight stages.

The Intervention of the United States

The tide began to turn after Tuesday, the 9th of October 1973, when President Richard Nixon authorized a military airlift and promised Israeli leaders that he would replace the losses in tanks and combat airplanes. The conventional wisdom in this matter is that such a promise allowed the Israelis to launch massive attacks with *all* of their reserve of tanks and aircraft. The American airlift was officially authorized on the 10th of October and began that same day when mega transport airplanes, the Lockheed C-5 Galaxy, left Langley Air Force Base in Virginia en route to the Middle East.

The key architect of the assistance to Israel was then Secretary of State Henry Kissinger. The historian Robert Dallek[59] contended that Kissinger initially kept President Nixon out of the loop by delaying the information to Nixon that the 1973 war had started. Instead, Kissinger communicated with Nixon's Chief of Staff General Alexander Haig and assured him that all was under control. For a few hours Kissinger was the sole architect of American policy in the conflict then raging half a world away. Dallek argued that Kissinger and Haig feared that by intervening on the side of Israel, they would challenge the Soviet Union and its leader, Leonid Brezhnev. They decided (without Nixon's knowledge or authorization) to raise the level of readiness to Defense Condition 3—as close to a war condition as possible. Kissinger and Haig in effect had put America on its highest readiness since the start of the Cold War. Since the Soviet Union had become the patron of the Arab world by supplying military hardware to Egypt and Syria, any American intervention on the side of Israel would be perceived by the Soviets as a geo-political challenge.

The strategy of assisting Israel as a counter-measure to Soviet domination of the Middle East—a critical region for America's interests—fits perfectly with the Nixon-Kissinger geopolitical view. This perspective supported the exercise of national interests, while striving to maintain a global state of peaceful coexistence and resultant prosperity. Kissinger, the historian, understood the rationale of the strategic policies of Disraeli and Churchill who steered British policy towards confronting an attempt by one nation to gain hegemony (political, economic, or military) in Europe. He also admired the policies of the Austrian foreign minister Prince von Metternich (1773-1859) who was the architect of the "holy alliance" of the main powers on the European continent (Russia, Austria, and Prussia) to balance the British influence. Metternich was a believer in the balance of power. Kissinger's doctoral dissertation at Harvard University was an analysis of Metternich in the post-Napoleonic era.[60]

But the policy of containment of Soviet expansion in the Middle East may not have been a sufficient reason for Kissinger to risk nuclear war with the Soviet Union. Israel was not yet a full client state of the United States. Before 1973 America's annual military support to Israel amounted to loans of about $500 million. After 1973 Israel would receive over $2 billion, half in grants, and after 1978 over $3 billion per year in military and economic aid.

If Israel in 1973 was not yet America's client state in the Middle East, why would Kissinger, Haig, and later President Nixon himself, use this conflict to challenge the Soviets—while still resolving their own conflict in Vietnam? If Israel had lost the war, there would be no major strategic loss to the United States, except for painful repercussions among Jewish voters at home and a new political reality in the Middle East.

The Nuclear Option: Was It the Trigger for America's Strategic Policy?

Perhaps the bailout of Israel in early October 1973 was based on some internal American politics. The United States had been already deeply mired for an entire decade in the Vietnam War. With the very unpopular conflict and the increasingly insurmountable tide of the Viet Cong and its supporters in communist China, Secretary of State Kissinger began to engineer the peace process with his Vietnamese rivals. Against this backdrop, the conflict in the Middle East was a surprising annoyance to the architects of America's global strategy.

President Richard Nixon was never a strong supporter of Israel. In his more recent attempt to shape historical events in his own description of it, Henry Kissinger indeed combined both events—the 1973 War and Vietnam—in his anatomy of foreign policy.[61] The loss of Israel to its Arab neighbors' victory would have made the Jewish electorate in the United States very upset and unforgiving, but it would not have triggered a "domino effect" that the loss of Vietnam could have engendered. Although Kissinger was warned at the beginning of the 1973 war, on Saturday, the 6th of October, that the hostilities were about to begin, he acted cautiously. His main concern seems to have bee the shielding of his boss, President Richard Nixon, from an early intervention in *another* major world conflict—without having all the necessary intelligence and information to form a considered opinion and to make a reasoned decision.

In the Fall of 1973 the Nixon administration was already embroiled in at least three domestic headaches. The vice president, Spiro Agnew, had been charged with serious financial misconduct and calls for his resignation had emanated from both parties. The presidency itself was increasingly under pressure with the soon-to-become Watergate scandal. The war in Vietnam was progressing poorly with domestic resistance becoming a tidal wave. Revelations such as Dr. Daniel Ellsberg's "Pentagon Papers" (initially published by the New York Times on June 13, 1971) had cast an expanding shadow over Nixon's ability to continue his global strategic policies in Southeast Asia and elsewhere in the world—vis-à-vis the Soviet Union and Communist China.

Kissinger discussed the upcoming Arab-Israeli conflict first with the Soviet ambassador, Anatoly Dobrynin, then a few days later during the conflict itself with Soviet leader Leonid Brezhnev. Kissinger had two key objectives. The first was to engineer a cease fire between the Arabs

(Syria and Egypt) and the Israelis. At the same time he was attempting to avoid a confrontation with the Soviets over the issue of any support given by America to the Israelis. By keeping the president seemingly uninvolved for the time being, Kissinger was able to achieve two sub-objectives: to shield the president from any failure in his dealings with the Israelis or the Soviets and to keep the contacts with them at *his* level, thus keeping open the option for President Nixon to intervene at any point and defuse any conflict between the two superpowers.

For two whole days (from Saturday, October 6, 1973, to Monday, October 8th), as the Israelis were retreating with heavy losses of people, armaments, and strategic space separating their fronts from the heart of their country, Kissinger was playing the diplomatic cards, unwilling to irrevocably commit the United States to the military support of Israel. As of Sunday, October 7, 1973, the second day of the war, Israeli officials had been contacting the Americans, frantically asking for support in the form of massive military supplies. Kissinger describes the following conversation with General Alexander Haig, Nixon's Chief of Staff on Sunday, October 7th, 1973. In response to Haig's question if the Israelis are panicking, Kissinger said:

"They are almost. They are anxious to get some equipment that has been approved. . . If the Arabs win, they will be impossible and there will be no negotiations. . . If we play this the hard way, it's the last time they (*the Israelis*) are going to listen . . . if we kick them in the teeth, they have nothing to lose."[62]

Secretary Kissinger was correct. The Israeli's political leadership was in a state of panic. The "Masada" syndrome was in place. The excruciating painful feeling of the fall of the ghetto—Warsaw or Israel—had taken residence in the hearts and minds of the Bengurionite regime. The nuclear option was now not only "on the table" but put into operation. The plan for the use of nuclear weapons was operational. The weapons themselves had been placed under our team's control, within one hour of mounting them on the specially equipped combat aircraft and within three hours from their intended targets.[63]

Secretary Kissinger and General Haig may not have been privy to the Israeli plan of nuclear attack nor perhaps the exact targets. But it is inconceivable to assume that the American leadership did not consider this possibility in their rationale to risk a nuclear standoff with the Soviets over possible assistance to Israel. The most viable explanation is that Secretary Kissinger and President Nixon were convinced that when felt abandoned, with their backs to the Mediterranean Sea, the Israelis would not hesitate to implement their nuclear option.

Perhaps Secretary Kissinger and particularly President Nixon would have opted to wait a few more days with their military bailout of the Israelis until they could exhaust the diplomatic discussions with the Soviets. But there was no time. Israel, a very small and narrow country, lacked the "strategic depth" that separates the military front from the center of the country. A few additional days of American vacillation would have surely meant that the military situation on the ground would have appeared untenable, hence leading the Israeli leadership to implement their nuclear option. This lack of strategic depth had effectively collapsed the time frame available to the Americans for diplomatic maneuvers. Nixon, Haig, and Kissinger had to act fast, or face a very unpleasant set of events.

The Nuclear Option and Its Potential Impacts

The Americans knew that if Israel would resort to its nuclear option, several damaging consequences would almost certainly occur. The first would be the disruption, perhaps permanently, of the flow of oil from the Middle East. The second would most probably be a very severe political and economic backlash from the Arab and Muslim worlds. Depending of course on the exact targets, the destruction of centers of oil production or of capitals such as Cairo in Egypt and Damascus in Syria would also entail the obliteration of cities and monuments highly cherished by the Muslim global community.

A third damaging consequence would be the political, ethical, and environmental devastation associated with the first nuclear conflagration since the Second World War. It would be abundantly clear, after the fact that America could and should have acted to avoid this catastrophe yet chose not to do it.

The airlift ordered by President Nixon at the behest of Secretary Kissinger was the bailout that the Israel so desperately needed. For President Nixon, a Quaker, it was an act of mercy in addition to a shrewd political move. If not for the Jewish vote, this bailout of a nation in despair satisfied the President's sense of the helping hand that a neighbor extends and that amply represented the American spirit. The clincher was the inevitable conclusion that the president and his secretary of state had reached: if left to its own devices, Israel would be forced to use their nuclear arsenal. This possibility was unthinkable and intolerable.[64]

Although distrustful of the Jews, Nixon the politician must have felt that such a strong support of Israel would bring about some positive feedback from Jewish interests and Jewish voters. This consideration would have been, of course, the "icing on the cake." A shrewd politician such as Nixon, already on a political collision course with the Democrats in Congress, would have welcomed a good deed which could show him as a wise statesman, responsive to the need of a minority yet powerful community.

Once the airlift had begun, the nuclear plan became inoperative. Our unit remained inactive in the vicinity of the installation where the nuclear devices were stored. As the war progressed and the situation in the battlefields became more favorable, some members of the units received transfer orders to other units. The threat had passed. Now it was up to the generals and conventional warfare.

US-Israel Understanding and the Nuclear Policy of Opacity

A curious yet enduring understanding emerged following the Yom-Kippur War of 1973. Since the early 1960s, Israel had established a policy of nuclear opacity. Avner Cohen has written extensively on the peculiarities of this policy.[65] He argued that the policy entailed opacity as the key principle of Israel's discussion, mention, or acknowledging the country's nuclear program, involvement, or capabilities as a military option. For over 25 years the official policy of the Israelis had been cloistered in a "black hole" with a highly restrictive code of disallowing any public discourse of this "taboo." Israeli leaders would engender many misleading explanations. "Israel will not be the first country to introduce nuclear weapons to the Middle East" was the preferred utterance by the Bengurionites.[66]

The problem was always the Americans. After the 1973 war, as the United States became Israel's protector and main supplier of armaments and economic aid, the policy of opacity became an untenable situation between friends. Cohen argued, for example, that Golda Meir, in her capacity as foreign minister, disliked the policy and recommended that Israel should tell the truth to its American friends. Cohen also suggested that Golda Meir, as prime minister after the 1973 war, indeed revealed to President Nixon the "secrets" of Israel's nuclear program and that she explained why the policy of opacity had been necessary, even to the extent that it kept the truth from the Americans.

Cohen also explained that this gesture of Prime Minister Meir laid the foundation of the peculiar "understanding" between America and Israel. This meant that Israel tells the Americans what it is doing in the nuclear arena, and both sides keep the "code of silence" about such activities and Israel's capabilities.

Documentary evidence and comments by senior executives at the Israeli Scientific Authority seem to contradict Cohen's conclusions. Prime Minister Meir did acknowledge in her meetings with President Nixon that Israel had nuclear capabilities but did not reveal its extent or future intentions. This was simply a statement verifying *what the Americans already knew*. Israel gave very little and in return received an "understanding" that America would—as a matter of policy—look the other way and not reveal nor discuss with friends or foes Israel's nuclear story.[67]

However, the understanding led to cooperation. On 12 October 2003, two decades after the 1973 war, the Los Angeles Times reported that the United States provided Israel with technology that allowed it to launch nuclear missiles from its submarines.[68] This American policy with its friendly allies who possess nuclear capability, such as Israel, Pakistan, and India, is primarily based on a cooperative effort and limited transfer of technology. The objectives of this policy are first to maintain a close pulse on where these countries stand and any changes in their capacity, and secondly, to keep the allied country within the American sphere of influence by dependency on American technology.[69]

The Doomsday Plan

The Israeli nuclear plan, like other plans, was a compilation of words, charts, and figures. These coalesced to form objectives, means, and methods. The plan was crafted to answer the following questions: (1) now that we have nuclear weapons, what do we do with them, (2) under what precise circumstances should we employ these weapons, and (3) how precisely are we going to do it?

Although over four decades have past since the drafting of the original plan described here, modifications to its content should not have changed its tenor or its aims. The plan was, and most probably is, essentially unaltered. Changes should have been introduced in the listing of the primary and secondary objectives, the means of deployment, and the set of conditions necessary for the decision to deploy the doomsday arsenal.

What To Do with the Nuclear Weapons?

The original plan was sometimes nicknamed "The Masada Plan," although I disagree with the allegory. In Masada the defenders ultimately perished without inflicting any significant harm to the Roman legions that surrounded and attacked them. This plan was designed to inflict irreparable harm on the Arab countries surrounding Israel.

The overall objective of the plan was to "destroy the enemy." Upon the precise definition of who the enemy is at the time of the nuclear deployment, the nuclear attack would "disrupt and destroy" the enemy's capabilities to continue the war, to mount attacks, hence losing its ability to destroy the "Jewish homeland."

As part of this objective, the differentiation between "tactical" and "strategic" use of the nuclear weapons became irrelevant. *Tactical* deployment is aimed at directly targeting the attacking forces such as armor divisions, infantry concentrations, and forward command posts. The nature of the nuclear weapon—however limited its destructive force—is such that it creates a cloud of radioactive materials. Depending on the winds and atmospheric conditions, the cloud can destroy *both* of the frontline combat formations. Radioactivity does not discriminate based on nationality and color of uniform.

Strategic deployment deep into enemy territory is a more desirable scenario. The nuclear obliteration of major cities, industrial and transportation hubs, and central command and control is preferable to limited battlefield atomic molestation.

In the case of Israel's Arab neighbors and the prime candidates for the mortal enemies of the Jewish state, the strategic use of nuclear weapons was deemed especially appropriate. In the 1970s the potential enemies included Egypt, Syria, Iraq and, to a lesser extent, Lebanon and Jordan. Three decades later, with the fall of Saddam Hussein, Iraq is no longer a viable threat to Israel. The rise of Islamic fundamentalism in Iran and the nuclear ambitions of their leaders have introduced a new and powerful threat.

In all of the Arab and Muslim countries,[70] presumed by the Bengurionites to be Israel's potential mortal enemies, the internal political structure favored the option of strategic nuclear deployment. Each of the aforementioned countries has one major city, usually the capital, with the largest concentration of population which serves as the political, economic, industrial, and military center of the country. These cities also serve as the communication, control, and command hubs for their respective military forces: Cairo in Egypt; Damascus in Syria; Beirut in Lebanon; Amman in Jordan; and Baghdad in Iraq.[71]

Deterrence Versus Deployment

In its background section, the Plan discussed the value of deterrence of Israel's nuclear arsenal. Although the official Israeli policy of not admitting that such capability even existed had the potential of negating possible deterrence, there was an unspoken understanding throughout the Middle East that Israel indeed possessed the ability to inflict a nuclear holocaust on its neighbors.

Deterrence is much more valuable when other countries possess the same capability. During the period of the "cold war," the Soviet Union and the Western powers engaged in a policy of Mutually Assured Destruction (MAD) as the instrument of deterrence. Both sides possessed the ultimate nuclear capability. However, neither of the opposing sides in the "cold war" publicly expressed its desire to annihilate the other. Although sharp, the key differences between the parties were political and economic philosophies—not deep and fundamental religious and ethnic hatred. The West and the Soviets could co-exist, under the deterring umbrella of Mutually Assured Destruction.

In addition to the potential destructive force of a nuclear deployment, Israel's deterrence therefore had to also consist of its superiority over its neighbors as the *only* possessor of nuclear weaponry. Co-existence was impossible, with threats and counter-threats being exchanged intermittently by the opposing leaders. This left little room for anything of a "mutual" nature—including Mutually Assured Destruction.

Although at present Israel and some of its neighbors enjoy a tenuous peaceful co-existence, the policy of deterrence established by the plan of the 1970s continues largely unchanged and unchallenged. A key tenet of Israel's foreign policy remains to prevent any hostile country in the region from acquiring nuclear capabilities. It was Iraq in 1981 and Iran in 2008 and 2013. Once the M.A.D. scenario is declared unfeasible, what remains inevitably is the policy of unchallenged uniqueness as the only native nuclear power in the region.[72] Deployment, therefore, is imaginable only under very dramatic and well-defined circumstances.

Under Which Conditions to Deploy?

The policy of deterrence did not prevent Egypt and Syria from attacking Israel in 1973. The fact that full-scale warfare has not occurred between Israel and its neighbors for the past four decades should be credited to several factors, other than the nuclear deterrence. First, the "cold war" is over, hence the antagonism of client states of the super powers has ended. Second, the United States has feverishly worked under both Democratic and Republican administrations to foster peace initiatives in the region. Third, massive aid from America to all parties to the conflict coincided with the conclusion by leaders of the Arab countries in the Gulf that further funding of the Arab-Israeli conflict is bad for the oil business.

The nuclear plan explicitly provides a framework by which the *political* echelon decides that at least three conditions must be fully met before launching the nuclear strike. The first condition is the failure of the element of deterrence; the second is the irrevocable collapse of Israel's conventional forces in the battlefield;[73] and the third condition is the imminent conquest, occupation, or destruction of the center of the country, including the Jerusalem-Tel-Aviv corridor and its environs.[74]

Key notions of a perilous nature in the plan are "irrevocable" and "imminent." These terms are the result of conclusions by human decision-makers who will act based on information from the chaotic military arena. Such conclusions will be subjective, biased and, to an extent, also speculative.

Another dangerous circumstance, which may be applied to all "fail safe" procedures of all the nuclear powers, is the identity and the characteristics of the decision-makers whose finger is on the nuclear trigger.[75]

The Case for a Preemptive Nuclear Strike

If "war is a continuation of policy by other means" (Von Clausewitz: 1780-1831), then unconventional war and the use of weapons of mass destruction are an extension of war by yet other means. As such, a preemptive strike is a legitimate and justifiable use of these instruments of war. Preemptive action is then warranted once diplomacy has unequivocally failed as an effective mechanism for national security and survival.

The limits to the use of nuclear strikes as a second-generation continuation of diplomacy are the finality of this action and its irreversibility. The conditions that dictate the preemptive strike do not exclude the existence of an intact conventional force. This means that even though the country's conventional military force has not yet been deployed, those who have their finger on the nuclear triggerhead already resigned themselves to the proposition that the conventional forces will be either ineffective or useless to prevent a national disaster.

The plan did not specifically exclude the use of nuclear weapons in a preemptive strike. The fact that in the past forty years the Israelis have not used this option is not a guarantee that it may or will not be used in the near future. With Iran's continuous rhetoric and the rapid progress of its nuclear program, for example, the use of a nuclear strike to neutralize this program appears to be a viable and, in the view of the Bengurionites, a justifiable option.

The plan allowed for exceptions to the conditions under which the nuclear option would be applied. If other means, such as diplomacy and conventional force were deemed ineffective, the decision maker would authorize the nuclear option as a preemptive strike.

There is little doubt that such conditions and allowances described here have not substantially changed since they were written four decades ago. Technology evolves and decision makers are replaced—but principles and the rationale for using the ultimate doomsday weapons are seldom modified.

How Precisely to Deploy?

The targets specified in the plan were in accordance with the preamble describing what to do with the atomic arsenal and under what conditions to deploy this ultimate weapon. There were two categories of targets: *primary* and *secondary*. The primary targets were the capitals of the countries classified as mortal enemies of Israel and who were engaged at the time of the deployment in the struggle to destroy the Jewish state.

The rationale for the deployment of even weapons of the limited magnitude used in Nagasaki (plutonium-based) pointed to the ability of such weapons to cause massive destruction. Since these metropolitan areas were not only military hubs but also very dense population centers, a nuclear strike would certainly create such a chaotic situation that this alone would disrupt communications, transportation, and any vestiges of command and control left in these urban areas, perhaps even in the entire country.

The secondary targets were aimed at the disruption of any surviving economic capability of the attacking countries; chiefly among the secondary targets was the Persian Gulf in the vicinity of the Shat-El-Arab waterway and the oil fields of the region. Such a nuclear strike was designed to achieve two objectives: (1) to disrupt the extraction and transportation of petroleum from the region of the Gulf, and (2) thus to eliminate any economic assistance from the Gulf States to Israel's perceived mortal enemies.[76]

How Soon to the Stormy Night?

> *"Hell begins the day that God grants you the*
> *vision to see all that you could have done,*
> *should have done, but did not do."*
>
> *Johan Wolfgang von Goethe*
> *(1749-1832)*

How possible is the doomsday scenario I described above, as specified in the doomsday plan? Much has changed in four decades, much has remained the same, and some has even become more ominous. The political climate in the Middle East remains volatile. The Arab-Israeli conflict has not been resolved. The hostile environment constantly led by vocal pronouncements of hate, threats, and counter-threats is alive and prospering maliciously.

The secret undertones of the dangerously unstable climate may be even more pernicious than the knowledge in the public arena. In October of 1973 the Doomsday clock of the Bulletin of the Atomic Scientists did not follow the American declaration of Defense Condition 3 by the Nixon Administration. The face-off between the Americans and Soviets and the move of the Israelis ever so closely to a nuclear conflagration came and went so quickly that even the vigilant monitors of the threat to humanity had little time or knowledge to adequately react to the unfolding events.

Many factors are present today as they were four decades ago. The lack of Israel's strategic depth in case of attack by its neighbors, the belligerent rhetoric on both sides, the despair of the Palestinians, and the cloud of the presumed nuclear deterrence are among these factors. The lack of strategic depth dictates Israel's policy of acting with little time to spare in case of a successful attack that would breach its borders. Since the activation of a nuclear response is defined in terms of an act of ultimate desperation,[77] it becomes even more logical and relevant to maintain nuclear deterrence. This translates—today as four decades ago—in a policy demanding that Israel deny, by any means, the emergence of an atomic capability in any of its declared enemies.

Another aspect of the lack of strategic depth and the powerful belief in deterrence by Israeli leaders is the choice between *surgical* nuclear strikes and *massive* nuclear warfare. The limited area between Israel's borders and its population hub dictates the impracticality of a surgical strike against enemy formations. The alternative that remains is a massive strategic nuclear deployment, as specified in the plan.

But, a major development is lurking in the near future. The demographic changes in Israel are an ominous and pernicious "game changer" in the nuclear arena. As the power will certainly be shifted towards Orthodox and Ultra-Orthodox leadership, the nuclear trigger will also be transferred to these decision-makers. As explained later in the book, the policies of reasoned considerations, which animated the Bengurionite decision-makers in over five decades of the history of their nuclear capabilities, will surely disappear. Reason will be replaced with religious fervor. The answer to the question: "How soon to the stormy night?" will be "*very, very soon.*"

Is Nuclear Deterrence Still a Valid Policy?

In the beginning of the twenty-first century some analysts have suggested that the situation in the Middle East has dramatically changed in favor of the Israelis so that a nuclear arsenal as a military option is no longer necessary for the survival of the Jewish state. [78]The argument seems to be that the rationale for unconventional deterrence has been drastically eliminated. Thus conventional military superiority is enough to keep Israel's enemies at bay.

A review by the *Washington Post* of Michael Karpin's book on the Israeli "bomb in the basement" has offered an additional perspective on the need for nuclear deterrent. The review points to Israel's "restrained management of its bomb" which could serve as a prototype, perhaps for a new global nuclear order. After all, Israel has never claimed to possess nuclear weapons and has never used them to enhance its prestige or browbeat its neighbors. For Israel, it is a shield against annihilation.[79] Then the Second Lebanon War of 2006 occurred and many ingrained beliefs were suddenly, perhaps permanently, shaken to their core.

A Crack in the Shield: The Second Lebanon War

In the somewhat unbridled reasoning of the Bengurionite regime still prevalent in Israel, there has evolved a *duality of perception*. First, there is the view that the country's armed forces (IDF) are strong enough at any time to repel any attack by any combination of enemies. This strongly held view has been demystified with the lessons learned from the 2006 Second Lebanon War.

In contrast, yet held as vigorously as the previous, there is the strongly held belief that the country of Israel and its people are totally alone, surrounded, deeply hated, but extremely righteous. These perceptions encourage a view of the world that, although superior with its conventional forces, the country cannot afford but to be ever vigilant. This means the possession, and if need be the use, of weapons that are far superior to its enemies—just in case the superiority of the conventional forces fails. The shield protecting the country must be vigorously and unequivocally reinforced with the ultimate power of mass destructive weapons.

The Second Lebanon War of the summer of 2006 punctured a crack in the shield that the conventional forces of the IDF (Israel Defense Force) had always provided the country. The conflict began in the morning of Wednesday, 12 July 2006. The Lebanese Shia militia group Hezbollah sent an armed contingent across the border and attacked Israeli armored troops, killing eight Israeli soldiers and taking two Israeli soldiers as hostages.

The Israeli government under the Bengurionite Prime Minister Ehud Olmert called the action an "act of war." It blamed the Lebanese government for the attack and requested the return of the two abducted soldiers. The Lebanese government denied any involvement in the affair. Hezbollah leaders refused to abide by Israel's demand.

On the morning of the next day, 13 July 2006, the IDF began mobilizing its reserves, while its regular formations in the northern border began attacking the Lebanese civilian infrastructure. The commander of the IDF, General Dan Halutz, declared: "If the soldiers are not returned, we will turn Lebanon's clock back at least twenty years." In response to Israel's campaign in Lebanon, Hezbollah launched rocket attacks against both military and urban targets inside Israel. On the sixth of August, 2006, Hezbollah rockets hit the port of Haifa, the major city in the north of Israel. Casualties mounted on both sides. Several hundred Hezbollah militias had been killed and the IDF acknowledged 119 casualties among its troops. On Friday, 11 August 2006, the United Nations Security Council issued Resolution 1701 calling for a cease-fire. The Lebanese agreed to it on Saturday the 12th of August and the Israelis on Sunday, 13 August 2006. The war lasted almost a month, with devastating results for Israel's confidence in its leadership and in its armed forces

Painful Lessons, Shattered Confidence

Faced with popular outrage and vocal criticisms within the armed forces themselves, on 11 October 2006 the Olmert government decided to establish a commission of inquiry chaired by the retired judge Eliyahu Winograd. The commission investigated the Israeli conduct of the war and drew some painful lessons from the failures of the Israeli political and military establishments.

The various inquiries and reports on the lengthy military engagement can be summarized as yielding three key lessons. The first called into doubt the *political* reasoning of the government. Acting in haste and with little, if any, strategic planning, the Israeli military, with its overwhelming superiority over a band of guerrillas in a third rate country already ravaged by civil war, failed to win the battle. The political direction of the conflict could not decide whether to destroy Hezbollah, or to punish Lebanon for harboring Hezbollah and for incorporating its leaders into the Lebanese political and economic systems. This lack of a clear strategy also led to the lack of an exit strategy.

Secondly, there were widespread breakdowns in the Israeli military, in terms of its level of preparedness, logistics, supplies, and even reported breakdowns in the command structure. As reserve soldiers and officers returned from the front after 33 days of combat, they described what amounts to a chaotic management of the Israeli military. Elite reserve paratroopers spent a week without water and supplies. Orders for the movement of armored companies were at best confused, with tanks running into each other, and little, if any, allocation by higher officers of territory for the movement and progress of the units. Retired General Gal Hirsch, former commander of a combat group in the war, argued in November 2007 that the political level, and in particular, the senior level of Israel's military had abandoned the troops and had exhibited a total lack of leadership. Worse, General Hirsch also criticized the inquiries of the war as inadequate, biased, and superficial.

The third painful lesson was subtler. The failures of strategy and logistics forced the most powerful conventional military in the Middle East to fight a band of some five thousand paramilitary men for over a month without a semblance of victory, however defined. At the end of the month-long conflict, Hezbollah was back in control of South Lebanon. General Yiftah Ron-Tal, commander of Israel's ground forces, was dismissed after the war because he unequivocally stated that the Israeli army failed to win the war against Hezbollah.[80]

General Ron-Tal and other senior military officers called for the resignation of the political leadership. In the Bengurionite tradition, not even the incompetent conduct of the war could hurt the political leadership. Instead, several military commanders were relieved of their command and the government declared that lessons had been learned and solutions had been implemented to assure the country that such incompetence would not reoccur.

The American Report on Israel's Military Failure

On 14 August, 2008, U.S. Marine General J. N. Mattis prepared a memorandum for the U.S. Joint Forces Command on the subject of assessment of Effects Based Operations (EBO).[81] General Mattis concluded that the concept of EBO was useful when applied to warfare on "closed systems" where the effects or outcomes can be measured—such as attacking military installations, power grids, and transportation facilities. In these instances it is relatively easier to better understand and measure the impacts of military actions.

General Mattis argued that when the concept of EBO is further applied to complex instances of warfare, the inevitable result is confusion—because commanders and troops fail to understand what is required of them and how to accomplish goals that are derived from too much prescription and "micromanagement from headquarters."

The use of EBO by Israel in the Second Lebanon War is the example provided in General Mattis' memorandum.[82] He argued that the IDF's "over reliance on EBO concepts was one of the primary contributing factors for their defeat." This reliance on EBO had led the Israeli politicians and military leaders to believe that: "…the enemy could be completely immobilized by precision air attacks against critical military systems…and little or no land forces would be required since it would not be necessary to destroy the enemy."[83]

Implications for the Plan to Deploy Nuclear Weapons

The plan is to deploy the nuclear arsenal in a preemptive mode or in the "ultimate effects-based operation." If one replaces the assumption that "precision air attacks" would do the job of mobilizing the enemy without the use of ground forces with "precision nuclear strikes," there materializes a justification for nuclear deployment when air power is insufficient and ground forces cannot be deployed for any reason.

As in the case of conventional EBO, such a nuclear strike would require outstanding knowledge of the enemy, centralization of actions, and a high level of predictability of results. The Second Lebanon War had yielded the most discouraging outcome since the Yom Kippur War of 1973. There was a combination of lack of preparedness with poor management of the combat operations. To compound the failure, throughout the month-long war, while the Israeli military pounded Lebanon, Hezbollah continued firing missiles into towns and cities in northern Israel. The war ended because of international pressure, not due to Israeli victory on the ground.

The dire lessons from this war had not been enough of a dramatic outcome to radically shatter the confidence that Israelis had in their conventional military forces. The Olmert government was even able to spin the ceasefire as a victory. But the Lebanon War and its aftermath did produce a new set of circumstances that now allowed for a higher degree of feasibility for a nuclear strike.

The plan for nuclear deployment did not specify the need for a total collapse of the Israeli conventional forces as a fundamental precondition for a retaliatory or preemptive nuclear strike. There was room in the plan to allow for a set of conditions whereby the benefits from such a strike outweigh the cost of not striking at the enemy. The Second Lebanon War provided such a set of conditions. This war was very costly in Israeli lives and treasure.[84] To save the lives of soldiers and civilians and to avert economic collapse, the nuclear strike may seem to be a plausible alternative to a long-drawn conflict. Israel's limited strategic depth, its small population, and the strain of a long war on its economy—all combine to formulate a scenario in which the nuclear option would not be so outrageously incomprehensible or unjustified to the decision-makers.

The key component of an aggressive interpretation of conditions for launching a nuclear strike is the type of leaders in control of the atomic trigger. The lesson from the 1967 confusion on who controls the weapons, the debacle in Lebanon four decades later, and the changing demographics in Israel clearly indicate the rapid movement toward a stormy night.

Part II
The Approaching Calamity

> *"Never, never, never believe that any war will be smooth and easy, or that anyone who embarks on the strange voyage can measure the tides and hurricanes he will encounter. The statesman who yields to war fever must realize that once the signal is given, he is no longer the master of policy but the slave of unforeseeable and uncontrollable events."*
>
> Sir Winston Churchill (1874-1965)

Shattered Hopes

Peoples and countries are distinguished not by color, race, gender, or other innate qualities—but by the leaders they select or tolerate. The tragedy of humanity is that often times we give evil or incompetent people too much power as leaders for some years of their lives, then we all suffer the consequences for many lifetimes after that.

The failed leadership of the Bengurionite regime was but another chapter in the long history of horribly incompetent Jewish leaders and the suffering they brought on their people. In their zeal to grab political and economic power in the new nation, the Bengurionites have left a terrifying legacy with lasting consequences, internally in Israel and externally on a global scale.

The Conflict with the Arab Neighbors

Combined with the forthcoming theocratization of the Jewish state, the Bengurionites have left an indelible mark on the continuing conflict with their Arab neighbors. Power-hungry and ardent socialists, the early Israeli leaders refused to consider contacts or negotiations with the Arab kingdoms that surrounded them. The dissolution of the British empire in 1948 yielded other cases in which territories had conflicting claims based on political and religious differences. The major example was the formation of an independent India and its division between the Hindus and Muslims. This led—by negotiations—to the establishment of an independent India and an independent Pakistan. Many issues of population exchanges and the control of such border territories as Kashmir have persisted for six decades. However, a relatively peaceful arrangement was originally obtained and India and Pakistan have benefited from six decades of relative peace and prosperity.

The Arab-Israeli conflict of 1948 was not more complex or unsolvable than the situation in the Indian sub-continent. Riots and mutual hatred between Hindu and Muslim had become daily occurrences throughout the months preceding the declaration of Indian independence. In the India case, the parties had negotiated with the departing British. In the case of Israel and the Arabs, *both* sides had resolved not to negotiate. The Israelis, for their part, led by the Bengurionites, hurriedly declared independence so that no other *Jewish* party or interest could establish itself and demand even the sharing of political and economic power. The tragedy was that by doing so there remained many legal issues of the validity of such a unilateral action. But the main outcome was the elimination of any possibility of negotiations, discussion, and a peaceful agreement between Jews and Arabs.

Contrary to some myths about the failed effort of the newly established state of Israel to reach an agreement with its Arab neighbors, there were no negotiations or contacts made at the time of the declaration of Israel's independence. There were no attempts on the Jewish side to initiate any contacts with the Arab leaders, directly or through international mediators. There were no attempts to establish contacts with lower level functionaries or through the good services of other countries.

There were elements of understanding, conciliation, and tolerance in the Arab countries and in the Jewish state. Within the business community in the Palestinian portion of the British Mandate there were several influential men who showed an inclination to hold talks with their Jewish neighbors. In the months before May 1948, my father held informal talks with several businessmen in the textiles trade, particularly in the city of Jerusalem. These were members of highly respected families in the city, including the Nashashibbi family—recognized leaders in their community. My father strongly believed that commercial ties between Jews and Arabs would lead to foster political discussions and would ultimately yield tolerance and mutual respect.[85] Even before the declaration of independence in May 1948, the Bengurionites had consistently and forcefully refused any contacts with Arab leaders. They especially abhorred any consultation or discussions with the people they routinely described as "rich Arab capitalists."

The Legacy of Dov Ber Borochov

In addition to the teachings of Berl Katzenelson, another influential labor philosopher who left an indelible mark on the Jewish and Israeli political landscape was Dov Ber Borochov (1881-1917). Borochov was an avowed Marxist. Born in the Ukraine, he died in Russia while fighting for the Bolshevik revolution of 1917.

Borochov believed in the Marxist struggle between the classes and in the conflict between capitalists and workers. He extended these ideas to the Jewish condition in Europe, particularly in Eastern Europe. He believed that the establishment of a *socialist* or communist Jewish state in Palestine would allow Jewish workers to own the means of production, hence to emancipate themselves from the oppression of the proletariat by the bourgeois capitalists. In September 1917, three months before his death, Borochov spoke in Kiev, Russia, to a conference of the Poalei Zion ("Zionist workers") party. "I repeat that we must originate independent activities in Palestine...we must initiate a socialist program of activities in Palestine. Then the Jewish worker, like the rock-bound Prometheus, will free himself from the vultures that torture him and will snatch the heavenly fires for himself and the Jewish people."[86]

The choice of Palestine as a homeland for the Jewish proletariat was based on the practicalities of the socialist-Marxist ideology, not on the emotional attachment of the Jews to their ancient land of their ancestors. Borochov had emphasized "our ultimate aim is Socialism; our immediate need is Zionism. The class struggle is the means to achieve both." The choice of Palestine rested on the premise that "Palestine is a semi-agrarian country, and hence it is adapted to the Jewish city-bred immigrant." Borochov also believed that the Jewish and Arab proletariats would join in the struggle against their capitalist oppressor, and thus would be able to share the Marxist dream and to live in peace.

Dov Ber Borochov concluded, "We do not claim that Palestine is the sole or best territory. We merely indicate that Palestine is the territory where territorial autonomy will be obtained. Our Palestinism is neither theoretical nor practical, but predictive."[87]

Like Lenin and the Bolsheviks in 1917, so did the Bengurionites assume power in a new type of political arrangement. Borochov's ideas of the Socialist agenda influenced the new regime of the Jewish homeland. Any contacts with the feudal lords of the Arab countries would have legitimized their existence. To the Jewish Marxist-Socialists, the kings, emirs, and even the merchant class in the Arab countries were simply an anachronistic anathema and the natural enemies of the Jewish (and world) proletariat. No contacts or negotiations with them would be allowed or conceivable.

Berl Katznelson had advocated the fusion of socialism and Judaism. Ber Borochov preached the fusion of the class struggle of Jewish laborers with nationalism: an independent homeland in Palestine where the Jewish workers would control the means of production. The resulting philosophy of the Bengurionites was a fusion of these two ideologies. Tragically, the realities of the Middle East in the twentieth century had little room for the joining of Jewish and Arab workers in a common struggle for emancipation.

Six decades later it would be presumptuous to claim that negotiations between Jews and Arabs in 1948 would have produced peaceful coexistence, as they had done in the Indian subcontinent. We can, however, indubitably lament that without negotiations there have been six decades of actual war and misery. Since 1948 the region has experienced a consistent array of hatred, killings, sorrow, and the continuing suffering of millions.

The real clash in the region was not one of religion or different political aspirations. It was a clash between two very different economic philosophies of government. The Arab-Israeli conflict started as a clash between Islamic-feudal regimes and the Marxist-Socialists in the newly created Jewish homeland. The monarchies and military dictatorship that ruled the Arab world in 1948 and that largely continues to the present time were perceived by the "progressive" followers of Katznelson and Borochov as evil and oppressive enemies. The Arab middle class was also utterly vilified and ignored.

In the 1990s some economic liberalization has occurred in Israel, but the sentiments of fear and hatred have been well entrenched in the belief system of the Israeli population. For a period of almost half of the country's existence, the Bengurionites controlled the ministries of defense, education, the interior, and the censorship of the mass communication media of radio, and later television. The regime continually and effectively fomented fear in the population of their Arab neighbors. This was compounded by the belief that peace was not only impossible, but also the prelude to the destruction of the Jewish homeland.[88]

One Ray of Hope

Intransigence became rampant on both sides of the conflict. Jewish and Arab leaders characterized each other as mortal enemies, bent on the annihilation of their opponents. The agreements for peaceful coexistence between Israel, Egypt, and Jordan were the result of the brave and rational actions of Israeli Prime Minister Menachem Begin, King Hussein of Jordan, and President Anwar Sadat of Egypt.

Throughout his political life, Menachem Begin opposed Bengurionism and its impacts on Israel's existence, its economy, and its future. Begin attempted to free the Jewish state from the yolk of socialist servitude and the legacy of Borochov and Katznelson. With this in mind, he was able to negotiate with an Arab monarch and an Arab military general, both of whom had fought against his country in past wars.

The Arab leaders were indeed able to put aside their preconceptions of the Jewish state and to negotiate—without pre-conditions—in good faith, bravely in the face of threats from extremists. President Sadat was assassinated. The driving force in Israel and the Arab nations favoring negotiations over war was the *secular* and *business* communities in their respective countries. As these segments of the population distance themselves from the extreme world views of Marxism-socialism and religious intolerance, they are more likely to view the other as a partner around a table of wisdom and reason.

The one ray of hope of the peace agreements that have persisted for two decades shows with abundant clarity that such action is indeed possible in the Middle East. When political or religious extremism yields to reason and when leaders desist from portraying their neighbors as mortal enemies, peaceful coexistence is attainable.[89]

What Happened to the Dream?

Benjamin Herzl had a vision and a dream. He envisioned the Jewish homeland as the shining city on the hill. He envisioned a prosperous nation in peace with its neighbors. He dreamed of a nation that had shed its ghetto way of life. His was also the dream of my grandparents and my parents. My father envisioned a "Switzerland in the Middle East": a peaceful and prosperous country, internationally popular, and a beacon of enlightenment in a troubled region.

Instead, Bengurionism has engendered an isolated nation, surrounded by avowed and uncompromising enemies. The nation thus created is economically dependent on warfare and its only friend in the world, the United States. Internally, the country is cursed with a repressive and belligerent regime.

The dream of a nation that is peaceful, prosperous, popular, and protected has given way to a calamity in the making. Instead of being the Switzerland or Singapore of the Middle East, the nation created by the Bengurionites is mired in constant conflict and has a bleak future.

But, the more disturbing legacy of Bengurionism is the gradual handing over of the country to the religious extremists. Fueled by the teachings of Berl Katznelson and Dov Ber Borochov, the Bengurionites consistently cultivated the religious segment of the Israeli political and economic landscape.[90] This strategy allowed them to control the few political and economic forces who proposed free market philosophies and who opposed the oppressive socialist manipulation of the state. By joining with the religious parties, the Bengurionites had maintained a majority in the Israeli political spectrum for over three decades. The long-term results are catastrophic predictors for the future of the country.

The peculiar brand of socialism and religion adopted by the Bengurionites had evolved from the *unholy alliance* between the two inherently opposite philosophies and political parties. Through a plethora of *economic* exchanges, attractive incentives, and give-and-take pragmatic compromises, the highly divergent groups learned to co-exist. As long as there was a common economic trough at which both could feast and the political power and demographic numbers were favorable to the Bengurionites—all was well and under control. But, the effects of six decades of benefiting a dormant power are starting to unravel. The *unholy alliance* is starting to fall apart, and the approaching storm is at the gates of the beleaguered state.

The Demographic Storm: The Making of the Jewish Theocratic State

The trend is unmistakable. The demographic composition of the Jewish segment of the state of Israel is undergoing a radical change. There is a dramatic increase in the religious segment of the Jewish population and a much slower growth of the secular segment of Israelis. The reasons behind this trend are various and in some instances unrelated.

The Growing Religious Population

In a revealing article on the role of religion in Israel, the German magazine *Der Spiegel* stated, "the demographics, however, favor the religious groups. Birth statistics suggest that the number of ultra-orthodox Jews, who traditionally have larger families, will double over the next 15 years, reaching 20 percent. As Juli Tamir, Israel's education secretary, recently projected, the country's elementary school classes would soon comprise three evenly balanced groups—one third secular, one third ultra-orthodox and one third Arab."[91]

The Spiegel article correctly pointed out that the vision of the Jewish state, as Benjamin Herzl had dreamed it, was to be a secular state. Herzl wrote: "We shall keep our priests within the confines of their temples." This part of his dream, to have a secular nation, has also been demolished by the Bengurionites.

The growth of the religious population can be attributed to six causes. The first is the rate of natural birth, estimated to be four to five times that of the secular Israelis. The second cause is the fact that religious men are insulated from service in Israel's military, hence are much less likely to die in the country's armed conflicts. Religious men are also insulated from the daily stress that so violently affects secular Israelis. The religious community receives a plethora of economic and financial support and incentives. Many spend their early life studying in Yeshivas, with the community fully or largely funding their daily existence.

The fourth reason is the nature of religious life in their communities, ensconced in self-established ghettos. There are good healthcare services and a blanket of security with social services unique to the community. This and the previous conditions contribute to a rapid growth in the numbers and in the longevity of the religious population.

The fifth cause is the growing number of Jewish immigrants to Israel who are not only religious but also ultra-orthodox. This flow of immigrants comes primarily from the United States. The religious organizations sponsoring such immigration are much more sophisticated and effective than the official Israeli agencies promoting immigration. In contrast with the masses of secular Jews who immigrated from the former Soviet Union and other countries, the ultra-orthodox Jews are readily absorbed into the religious community. They are seamlessly integrated into the social and economic structures of the community. They share the same values, attitudes, beliefs, and wishes as the natives.

62 *Shattered Hopes Magnificent Failure*

Finally, the religious community in Israel receives substantial contributions from their counterparts in the world, particularly from North America. These financial contributions are in addition to the economic incentives and the hefty tax advantages the community receives from its own government.

The ultra-orthodox community in Israel has thus created a "state-within-a-state." This community has established a shadow economy, alongside the government controlled secular marketplace. This economy is based on the diamond trade and other commercial activities closely linked to their counterpart communities in Europe and North America.

Political Aspirations and the Rise of the Religious Bases of Power

As their numbers rapidly increase, the younger ultra-orthodox Jews in Israel are nurturing political aspirations beyond the confines of their community. The less orthodox religious youth are already joining the Israeli military within units that conform to their needs and specifications. With their control of the interior ministries and of the civil services of all Israelis, such as marriages and naturalization rituals, ceremonies and procedures, the ultra-orthodox are increasingly extending the reach of their power to other aspects of Israeli society.

The ultra-orthodox are a unified community, economically powerful and under the centralized command of their rabbis. This community has very strong beliefs, opinions, and convictions. They see themselves always on the side of righteousness. Thus when the younger generation is increasingly convinced of their growing numbers and influence, they tend to flex their political muscle to bring about the "right" solutions to the management of the country.[92]

The rise of the religious base of power will be manifested in three complementary areas. The first is the *social* domain of the country. Internal legislation that imposes strict Mosaic laws will be rapidly enacted and implemented. All aspects of religious, social, and legal life in the country will be strictly subjugated to the strictest interpretation of Jewish orthodoxy. The immediate and longer-term result will be a sharp increase in emigration of secular Israelis. Squeezed by what they consider to be unreasonable and pervasively restrictive legislation, large segments of the secular component of the population will be faced with two unpleasant alternatives. One will be to stand and fight. This option will not be feasible, since the secular population is fragmented and politically as well as economically diverse. They will be faced with a highly determined, unified, wealthy, and uncompromising adversary. Their position is hopeless.

The only other options are to become a subservient minority or to emigrate. A similar scenario could be seen in the Iranian revolution of the 1980s in which religious leaders assumed control of the country's bases of power. Emigration of Israelis to Europe and North America will decrease the numbers of secular Israelis and increase the power of the theocracy. Many of the secular Israelis who will emigrate will be knowledge workers, professionals, technical experts, scientists, and engineers. Their exodus will weaken the Israeli economy and the Israeli military. The latter outcome will also mean a sharp reduction in the available reserve troops who are needed by Israel to fight traditional wars with their neighbors. Faced with a shrinking military, devoid of its past superior technical advantage, the ultra-orthodox regime will be driven to the reasonable conclusion that the next conflict with the Arab world will have to be by the use of nuclear weapons.

The second area is the *military* domain. The new regime will revamp the armed forces to strictly conform to orthodox doctrine. This trend has already begun with the pronouncements of the former chief Rabbi of the Israeli military, Shlomo Goren (1917-1984).[93] Born in Poland, he was a graduate of a Yeshiva, and in 1948 he became the chief rabbi of the newly formed Israeli Defense Forces. Rabbi Goren became a Brigadier General and has served as chief military cleric till his retirement in 1972, and for the following decade served as the Chief Ashkenazi rabbi of Israel.

In various appearances on Israeli television and radio, Rabbi Goren consistently urged Israeli military personnel to disobey their orders and to obey the commands of their religion—as he, Rabbi Goren, had interpreted them. He forbade soldiers from dismantling illegal settlements in the occupied territories. He issued a religious command to assassinate foreign leaders such as Yasser Arafat. In the name of Jewish orthodox rulings by rabbinical authorities, he urged his fellow citizens to ignore and aptly disobey civilian authority.

Rabbi Goren was a precursor of the future orthodox leaders. He participated in civilian institutions and lived in both worlds: the secular and the religious. He exemplifies the new breed of military commanders whose allegiance is to their religious doctrine and orthodox rabbinical authorities—not to a civilian, albeit legal military authority.

Rabbi Goren personified the "Jewish paradigm" of strict adherence to the religious codes of behavior and morality in striking antagonism with secular authorities. Control over society and the military will eliminate this incompatibility between government and orthodoxy as both come together as they did in the Iranian revolution since the 1980s and in the Taliban regime in Afghanistan in the 1990s until their collapse in 2002.[94]

The third area is *international relations*. A takeover of Israel's foreign relations by the ultra-orthodox regime will start a terrifying period of intense diplomatic hostilities. The ultra-orthodox perspective of isolationism is much stronger than the Bengurionite philosophy of "The whole world is against us." Among the possible effects, the most pungent impact of the ultra-orthodox control of diplomacy will be in the relations between the Arab world and Israel.

Theocratization and the Arab-Israeli Conflict

The Middle East is heading toward the emergence of an orthodox Jewish state. The uncompromising, eschatological, and determined regime that will take over the Israeli base of power will undoubtedly create a new dynamics in its relations with the Arab world. This scenario is not only terrifying but also highly possible.

Dr. Israel Shahak (1933-2001) was a survivor of the Nazi concentration camp of Bergen-Belzen. He immigrated to Israel at the age of 12, soon after the liberation of the camp. Shahak served in the Israeli military and was a professor of chemistry at the Hebrew University in Jerusalem. In his writings he lamented the emergence of Jewish fundamentalism in Israel.[95] Shunned by his contemporaries in Israel and in the Jewish Diaspora, Shahak nonetheless presented a coherent insight into the nature of Judaic extremism. He strongly criticized the rabbinical teachings, especially with regard to the treatment of nonbelievers, Gentiles, and secular Jews alike. The inevitable conclusion that Shahak derived from his analysis was that with the growth of religious fundamentalism in Israel, any rational negotiations of peaceful agreements with the Arab world would be utterly impossible, thus leading to the inevitable final conflict in the Middle East.

Similar critics of Jewish fundamentalism in Israel have concentrated on the nature of rabbinical teachings. They correctly argued that Jewish ultra-orthodoxy is anachronistic, practicing ideas, concepts, and rituals that are frozen in the sands of the Sinai desert for over 35 centuries. These practices never evolved. This segment of Judaism is unable to function in modern society within mechanisms that call for interaction, sharing, and a fair exchange of ideas and resources.

The Perfect Storm

The Middle East in general and the Israeli scenario in particular will soon experience the perfect storm in the Arab-Israeli conflict. The emergence of the theocratic Jewish state will be up against the already awakened Arab and Muslim extremism. Faced with years of conflict and frustration, the Palestinians are at a point where extremist ideas and a fatalistic course of action seem the only solution to their suffering.

These two forces of extremist ideologies are emerging to face each other in an atmosphere of determined and uncompromising clash of ideologies. This is not only the clash of religions. This is a clash of two camps entrenched in their immutable beliefs that they own not only the title to the disputed parcel of land, but also, perhaps foremost, the title to absolute righteousness.

When one adds to this mixture the possession of nuclear weapons and over a century of conflict and mutual hatred, the only possible outcome would be a perfect storm of a bellicose future. There are several factors that dictate the possibility of such a horrific forecast. First, for the forthcoming ultra-orthodox regime in Israel, peace with the Arab world is not a viable option. The advent of peace would entail a radical change in the economy from a military to a civilian base. The international isolation of the Jewish state and the rule by a religious dictatorship make this transition impossible. When, after the Second World War, the former dictatorships of Japan, Germany, and Italy transformed their military economies to civilian uses, they did so because their regimes had also changed to the democratic form of government.

Secondly, the forthcoming ultra-orthodox rulers consider the conflict with the Arab world, even a final military confrontation, as the prelude to the arrival of the Jewish Messiah. There are no incentives to motivate these rulers to seek, or even to negotiate, peace agreements with their neighbors.

If the final confrontation does not hasten the coming of the Jewish Messiah, the ultra-orthodox are ready and willing to continue their centuries old waiting in the Diaspora. Those who may survive the nuclear holocaust of the final confrontation between Israel and its Islamic enemies will leave for Europe and North America to continue in the diamond trade and other traditional enterprises that have sustained this element of Judaism for many centuries.

A third factor in bringing about a nuclear war is the inexperience of the ultra-orthodox leaders with military affairs. In the many wars of the Jewish state, since its inception in 1948, this religious segment of the population has been the least affected by the misery and the carnage of war. Few of their sons have been killed or maimed in actual battle. Once they take hold of the reigns of power, their leaders will be much more likely to accept war as a viable option.

Dictatorship of the self-declared righteous, fatalism, eschatology, and the possession of weapons of mass destruction—all combine to draw a terrifying scenario of a bleak and deadly end to the Arab-Israeli conflict. This perfect storm will consume all those in its path.[96]

The Prospect of Civil War

A different scenario is possible. As the ultra-orthodox seize power in Israel, the internal situation may become intolerable for secular Jews and other minorities. The level of intolerance and almost paranoia of the new regime will make daily life extremely difficult for those Israelis who have not yet left the country or, for any reason, are not able to flee.

The secular political parties in Israel are in disarray even as early as the first decade of the twenty-first century. The Bengurionites under the mantle of its Labor Coalition are confounded with lack of leadership and a coherent sense of direction. Their counterparts, successors to the patriotic movement established by Menachem Begin, are scrambling to establish a clear identity and a social and economic agenda. This party has changed its name from "Herut" (Freedom) "Likud" (Union) to "Kadima" (forward), with little to show for as a viable political alternative to traditional Bengurionism.

In many respects, the confusion and weaknesses of Israel's political parties resemble the disintegration of political entities in the German republic of the 1920s. The scenario unfolding in Israel offers a golden opportunity for an extremist movement to take over the state—as the National Socialists under Adolf Hitler had done eight decades ago. The ultra-orthodox and other religious factions are already immersed in Israeli politics, its society, and its economy.

The disintegration of the Israeli political spectrum in the near future, coupled with the takeover by the religious extremists, may well force the remaining secular Israelis to oppose this radical development—

by force if necessary. As reservists, most of the secular Israelis own military weapons and other gear. On a moment's notice they can be called to active duty. Although, in the case of an internal conflict, the reservists only have light armament and their access to heavy military equipment may be barred by the religious authorities, they nonetheless possess enough military skills and training to offer serious and bloody resistance to the ultra-orthodox regime. The outcome will inevitably be a civil war. This is not unique to the twenty-first century. Several times in their history the Jewish people have been engaged in civil strife identical to the forthcoming struggle: religious extremists against secular or less orthodox factions. The prospect of an internal confrontation is very high. In June 1948 a civil war between the Bengurionite regime and the followers of Menachem Begin was narrowly avoided when the anti-Bengurionite forces decided to step down in the "Altalena" affair.[97]

The Arab Response

If the Israelis find themselves immersed in the nightmare scenario of civil war, the response of their Arab neighbors may take one of two paths. The Arab leaders may well decide to "wait and watch" the Jewish state internally self-destruct. Alternatively, the Arab leaders may decide to join in and attack the tormented country.

In the first instance, the ultra-religious regime may resort to the tensions with the Arab world as an excuse to disarm the civil secular revolt. Failing an internal solution, the ultra-orthodox regime may find it uniquely reasonable to use nuclear weapons against the Arab neighbors with the clear intent to divert the internal conflict to an external enemy. But, lacking the domestic unity necessary for the deployment of massive forces composed mainly of reservists, the only viable military option will be the use of weapons of mass destruction—even without Arab provocation.

In the second instance, where Arab forces attack Israel, the ultra-orthodox leaders will call upon all Israelis to stop their civil revolt and divert their collective energies to repel the attacking enemies. It is highly unlikely that such an appeal will prevail, or that an effective turnaround of forces—from internal strife to external warfare—can be seamlessly attained. The ultra-orthodox leadership will therefore find itself faced with a very grave situation that will require the only possible solution: massive nuclear retaliation.

However the prospect of civil war plays out, the outcome may be the same—a takeover by religious extremists of the Israeli base of power that will result in a horrendous war with the Arab world. In this instance, however, unlike the Jewish experience with the Babylonians and the Romans, the Jewish state will set the region afire.

The Changing World and the Middle East

Several trends dominate the twenty-first century. We are witnessing a changing world order, manifested by significant changes in the global economy, the cultures of nations and regions, the political spectrum of alliances, and the composition of the world's nuclear club.

Globalization

Much has been written about the phenomenon of globalization. Spurred by dramatic innovations in information technology and the more efficient movement of goods, services, and skilled people, the global economy is rapidly taking shape. From India to Ireland and from China to the Greek Republic, Brazil and Russia, there is a movement toward relaxing international commerce and the liberalization of government controls. Outsourcing by major companies worldwide is becoming the norm rather than the exception. Transnational companies now dominate the global economic spectrum. Capital and knowledge flow freely between countries, even continents.[98]

Globalization in trade and communication has also engendered radical changes in cultures. Geography is no longer a separator of peoples, their preferences, their ideas, and their uniqueness. Many scholars argue that the relatively free flow of goods, people, and ideas is contributing to a global surge in technology, innovation, and creativity. Peoples across the globe have a much better understanding of other cultures, to the extent of assimilating many aspects of their distinct products, behaviors, fashions, and ideas. Brand names such as Coca Cola, Toyota vehicles, Amstel beer, Siemens equipment, and Indian software, to name just a few, are household names in countries all over the globe.

In some respects, analysts contend that the world of the twenty-first century is becoming the "post-American" world. Fareed Zakaria, who writes for Newsweek Magazine and hosts a television show in the United States, has argued that his book on the post-American world "is not about the decline of America, but rather about the rise of everyone else."[99] The emergence of countries such as Brazil, Indonesia, and

India—until recently considered to be "developing economies"—to become powerhouses of commerce and prosperity is a robust indicator of the globalization phenomenon. The special case of China has shown the emergence of a "sleeping giant" to become the second largest economy in the world. Wealth and free trade ideas are being rapidly spread throughout the world. Regardless of whether the United States continues to dominate the world's economy, the effects of globalization are already too entrenched to be scaled back or diminished by any ideology or leaders who oppose it.[100]

Yet the more fundamental change brought about by globalization is the diminished role of national boundaries and nationalistic ideology. The multinational or transnational corporations now operate across national boundaries. They have little need or respect for artificial limits on the free flow of goods, services, people, funds, and knowledge. As the financial difficulties of the credit crunch in late 2008 in the United States have shown, problems as well as positive developments presently flow with utmost speed across national boundaries. Financial markets around the world react without delay to events that happen half way across the globe.

Formation of Global Groups and Coalitions

Another aspect of globalization is the formation of groups and coalitions of nations. Some are regional, such as the European Union, the North American Free Trade Agreement (NAFTA), and the Association of Southeast Asian Nations (ASEAN), while others are ad-hoc groupings of countries with similar interests, such as the G-8 (group of eight richest countries: The United States, Germany, Japan, Russia, Great Britain, France, Italy, and Canada).

The main purpose of these global groups and international coalitions is to facilitate trade and to resolve issues of mutual interest, such as political, cultural, and social policies. The European Union is by far the most striking example of a group of nations in the same region with a common currency, very few border restrictions, and a free flow of capital, goods, and people among the countries in the union.

The United States and the emerging groupings of nations are intricately tied by strong links of trade and the ideology of freedoms for the individual citizens and the exchanges among nations. The leadership and preeminence that America offers the world in the twenty-first century is less the military super power and primarily the architect and leader of the new era of knowledge and enlightenment.

Is Globalization Working?

Although the concept of globalization has become a widely accepted cliché for worldwide progress, there are several critics who point to the shortcomings of this phenomenon. The economist Joseph Stiglitz has contended that globalization with its support of free trade and the work of international institutions has failed to benefit millions of the world's population.[101] He criticized the working of international institutions such as the World Bank.[102] Professor Stiglitz argued that officials of these international organizations made decisions that were "a curious blend of ideology and bad economics, dogma that sometimes seemed to be thinly veiling special interests."

In a later book, Joseph Stiglitz offered suggestions for improvements in the management and processes of international institutions.[103] He proposed improvements in lending procedures (from the rich to poor countries) and more useful international legislation. Although Stiglitz, as other critics have done, acknowledged the benefits of globalization, his solutions are focused on financial, economic, and accounting procedures. These solutions to the management of international allocation of resources ignore the behavioral and organizational issues as well as the shortcomings of individual countries.[104]

Much of the failure of globalization and the formation of regional groups of nations to produce significant economic and social benefits all across the globe can be attributed to corrupt leaders and the lack of responsible governments in many developing countries. William Easterly, also a former economist at the World Bank, had argued that providing aid to poor nations and simply asking in return that they adopt market economies is a failed strategy.[105]

Paul Collier has echoed Easterly's analysis.[106] He has forcefully argued that in the battle between reformers and current corrupt leaders in the developing world, the corrupt leaders are winning and the billions they receive in aid are engulfed in their bottomless ineptitude rather than in helping their populations. Collier lists the traditional causes of underdevelopment: civil wars, overdependence on exports of selected natural resources such as minerals and food crops, and the corruption and incompetence of the leaders of these poor countries.[107]

Yet, although there are national barriers to the sharing of the benefits of globalization throughout the developing world, the majority of economists and policy-makers indeed believe in the positive outcomes from globalization on the world's economic, political, and social welfare.[108]

The New Enlightenment and the Age of Knowledge

The twenty-first century had effectively started in the 1980s when U.S. President Ronald Reagan and British Prime Minister Margaret Thatcher unveiled their march towards global market economy. In their groundbreaking book on this remaking of the global landscape, Daniel Yergin and Joseph Stanislaw traced the evolution of enterprises, ideas, and industries that helped to forge the making of the new century.[109] The demise of the Soviet Union and the liberation of its Eastern European satellites, combined with the transformation of China into a less restrictive society, were the key *political* changes that occurred in the first decade of the twenty-first century.

At the same time these political and social transformations were happening, there was a stunning array of developments in science and technology. The information age has arrived at maturity. The world of the twenty-first century is highly connected, drastically more mobile, and more interdependent than ever before. The convergence of the demise of communism and the arrival of a world characterized by unparalleled connectivity and mobility has been the basic drive of the revival the world is experiencing in its third millennium. This revival is similar to the phenomenon of European Renaissance of the seventeenth and eighteenth centuries. It is the *New Enlightenment*.

Instead of the age of reason, the world is experiencing the irreversible triumphal emergence of the Age of Knowledge. This new age is characterized by the proliferation of several forms of freedoms; the fight against intolerance, ignorance, and other manners of inhumanity. Specifically, the new enlightenment is based on (a) cooperation—not conflict among nations and within countries; (b) trade—not isolation or tribalism; (c) freedom of sharing and exchange—not tariffs and barriers to the flow of goods, people, and ideas; (d) transnationalism—not chauvinistic enclosure within borders; and (e) measured approach to problems with rational moderation—not extremism and intolerance.

The United States, together with its allies in Europe, Asia, the Americas and Australia, has taken the lead in the new enlightenment.

In a mode similar to its Marshall Plan after the Second World War, the United States exports and supports the emergence of freedoms and market economies all over the globe. It also led the growth of the information revolution by establishing fiber optics, the Internet, and the watershed of innovations of information technology in commerce, health care, transportation, agriculture, and education.

While having to rely on international organizations to bring this new age of knowledge to all corners of the globe, the United States and its allies had to endure and confront the malaise of indifference, tribalism, ineffectiveness, corruption, and the remaining vestiges of nationalistic tragedies, poverty, intolerance, and inhumanity.[110]

In the second decade of the twenty-first century, there are signs that some political and social forces in the United States and other countries have been attempting to challenge market economics in favor of increased government intervention in the economy and social affairs of nations. These events and the persistent conflicts with religious and nationalistic aspirations in many parts of the globe cannot and should not undermine or even detract from the positive effects and the global benefits of the new enlightenment and the age of knowledge.[111]

The Changing Middle East

In this new enlightenment, the Middle East plays an important part. This troubled region was the cradle of civilization. Traditional rulers in Middle Eastern countries are concerned about the changes heralded by the new enlightenment and the age of knowledge. But they are also weary of the religious extremists in their midst.

The modern Middle East was born after the First World War by design of the European victors: France and the United Kingdom. National boundaries were promptly drawn, monarchies established, and national identities thus emerged—all this in the aftermath of the disappearing Ottoman Empire of Turkey, which was defeated by the Western powers. Insufficient attention was given to the religious diversity of the population (Sunni versus Shia Muslims), tribal allegiances, and historical trends of Arabs and Muslims.[112]

Almost a century later, many of the countries in the region have established their unique way of life, albeit besieged by social, political, and ethnic issues. But their leaders are increasingly resigned to the idea that their system of government is being challenged by globalization and the new enlightenment. They recognize that the alternative to their system of government will not necessarily be a religious orthodoxy. The case of Iran, where the Shah was replaced in 1979 by the Ayatollahs and where an Islamic Republic replaced the autocratic monarchy, cannot be viewed as the model for the region. Different circumstances, distinct historical development, and the unique nature of the Iranian people make their transformation the exception in the Muslim world.

Globalization has begun to have its impacts on the Middle Eastern countries.[113] Arab and Muslim students travel throughout the world, are educated in the United States and Europe, and return to their countries with knowledge, ideas, and different perspectives on the social and political make-up of their homelands. This new generation views their economies in the post-petroleum world and their political systems as an anachronistic remain in the global economy. Increased openness, more freedoms of expression and commerce are increasingly being sought. The ruling regimes have no choice but to defer to the new forms of changes in their countries. They understand that these transformations are far better than the isolation of the countries taken over by religious extremists. These circumstances have led to the "Arab Spring."

Within a generation most of the Arab and Muslim countries in the Middle East will join the global economy. They will be full partners in the new enlightenment and the age of knowledge.[114] The road to a distinct version of democracy will be taken, leading to transitional modes of government that de-emphasize authoritarian regimes and promote openness and a variety of freedoms.

The United States and its allies will closely work with these revitalized and transformed countries. A parallel trend will be the diminution of Islamic extremism and terror. The United States must, and will, develop its policies in the Middle East to accommodate and to boldly support the move to democratization. This scenario is highly probable with or without the forecasted transformation of the global economy from dependence on fossil fuels to energy independence.[115]

The new Middle East will be characterized by a rejection of extremism, abandonment of regional and national uniqueness, and membership in the global economy.[116] This phenomenon will also result in friendly and cooperative relationships between the United States and the Arab world.

Israel and The New Middle East

The Jewish state stands alone in the watershed trends that are reshaping the new Middle East. Against the fray, the political and social make-up of the country and its leadership is moving away from the new enlightenment of the twenty-first century Two key developments mark the approaching conflict between Israel and a rapidly changing world: the move toward theocracy and the loss of the unprecedented support of the United States.

Jewish Theocracy and the Arab Israeli Conflict

As Israel drifts toward the rule of the religious extremists, any hope for sustained peace agreements with its Arab neighbors essentially disappears. But religious orthodoxy also assumes another role in the internal affairs of the country. The modified theme of former Prime Minister Levi Eshkol will be "we want knowledge without Jews and Jews without knowledge." In the Bengurionite tradition, the ultra-orthodox will prefer Jews without independence of opinion, without the knowledge to govern, and without the zeal to achieve accommodation with the Arab world.

The ultra-orthodox regime in Israel will lead the country toward isolation from the global community. The emphasis will be on the nationalistic aspects of the country and its uniqueness, instead of integrating it into the world's freedom of the global existence. While its neighbors become active players in the new enlightenment, Israel is moving toward a status of anachronistic vestige of failed historical events and a political and social form no longer in favor by most nations.

There is a painful irony in these developments. As a people, Jews had been the original "globalists." Dispersed throughout the known world, they transacted across countries, without much concern with borders and national interests. They shared cultural values, an ancient yet unifying language, and a shared sense of community regardless of geography. Now that the world has adopted these same attributes, it is the Jews in their own country who succumbed to the irrationality of the Middle East and are becoming the isolationist unit in a unified world.

Losing Foreign Support

The United States, the European Union, and other regional alliances will nurture and develop close relationships with the Arab and Muslim countries, all within the evolution of the new enlightenment. The staunch support of Israel as a bastion of democracy in the Middle East and an ally in the war of terror will rapidly evaporate. The Israeli descent toward the dictatorship of the orthodoxy will be widely characterized as an estranged, even intolerable, impediment to peace and prosperity in the Middle East.

The resulting impacts on the Israeli leadership will be devastating. Already convinced of their isolation and the enmity of their neighbors and the world's nations, the religious leaders will be utterly assured, in their own mind, that their backs are against the wall and that the day of reckoning has arrived. The time for reconciliation will have passed; the time for war will have arrived.

The Approaching Calamity in the Levant

The "Levant" is a term that largely describes the region that includes all the countries between the valley of the Nile and the valley of the Tigris and Euphrates. It is somewhat synonymous with the term describing the Middle East.[117]

With the takeover of the state of Israel by religious extremists and their unaltered conviction that the Jewish nation is all alone, besieged by enemies, and devoid of global support, they will opt for war and the use of the nuclear option.

The question is not whether the nuclear option will be applied, but when and how. The results will be calamitous. According to the plan devised by the Bengurionites and undoubtedly perfected by the orthodox leaders, the death toll in the region will be over 20 million within the first hour of the conflict. An additional 20 million will perish within a few days from radiation effects. These will be inhabitants of large metropolitan areas and industrial and military centers. Another 40 million will die within the next twelve months following the war because of famine, rampant infections, and neglect.

An extremely high price, an unbearable price to pay for a conflict that could and should have been resolved. All because of the greed, intolerance, and personal ambitions of misguided leaders and their sheepish followers.

The Irony of History

Compare two historical events. Around 1500 B.C. a prophet (Moses) led his desert tribes to their destiny. He gave them a religion and a sense of unity. Thirty-five centuries later the descendants of the Jewish tribes are again a troubled minority, heading toward disaster.

Around the seventh century another prophet in the same region (Mohammed) led his desert tribes to their destiny. He gave them a religion and a sense of unity. Fifteen centuries later the descendants from these tribes and their adherents number over a billion people and are a growing and productive force in world affairs.

What Can We Do?

Since the arrival of globalization, the international community has been relatively effective in mitigating certain national and regional conflicts: Bosnia and Darfur are examples of relative successes. But, this same community has been quite ineffective when dealing with countries that possess nuclear weapons or those who aspire to belong to the atomic club.

The main instruments of international acts of persuasion have been baskets of sanctions, ranging from diplomatic pressures to restrictions on trade. This strategy was used by the United States and the European Union in the case of North Korea and Libya and, with much less success, in the case of Iran.

However, the Israeli-Arab conflict is a very different affair. Virtually every American president since Harry Truman in 1948 has attempted to mitigate the conflict, to bring the parties together for negotiations, and to seek a peaceful solution. Yet, for the past six decades the conflict has grown in complexity and the intransigence of the parties. The question of a Palestinian homeland has not been resolved. Four major wars and countless incursions and mutual killings have occurred. As new generations replace the original leaders, the conflict assumes a life of its own. Deeply rooted hatred, mistrust, and unbending hopes and requirements color the dreams of both sides to the conflict.

There is very little that the global community can do to resolve the conflict and to prevent a nuclear holocaust. Barring extreme economic and political pressure backed by military intervention, there are no reasons for the parties to act rationally and responsibly. Any forceful action by the international community will likely achieve the effect less desired: war. The more pressure is exercised upon the Israelis and the Arabs, the more the extremists on both sides will revolt and resort to desperate actions. On the Israeli side, the ultra-orthodox leaders will definitely feel vindicated that "the whole world is united against us because we are Jews." This sentiment will add to the circumstances triggering a nuclear response.

The forecast is gloomy. The nuclear war will precipitate a "nuclear winter" in the Middle East. If the industrial world still consumes petroleum and depends on fossil fuels, its economies will undergo an extremely painful period of economic shocks.

In addition to the loss of human lives, the nuclear holocaust will also generate a religious nightmare. The holy cities of Mecca, Medina, and Jerusalem will be utterly pulverized. This will lead to many years of grief and strong religious sentiments of mourning, resulting in explosions of sorrow and violence all over the Islamic world. A similar reaction will grip the Jews and also many Christians.

The international community by and large is unable or unwilling to believe in such a catastrophic scenario in the Middle East. If we have learned one lesson in this troubled and irrational region, it is that anything—even the most outlandish prediction of an unbelievable scenario—is not only possible, but also highly probable.

Part III
Reinventing a Homeland: The State of Israel

Too Little, Too Late

In the fifty years between the first Zionist Congress (in Basel on August 25, 1897) and the establishment of the State of Israel (May 15, 1948), over one third of the Jewish world population was extinguished. The establishment of the Jewish state, although heralded in the Jewish Diaspora as a uniquely magnificent event, was nevertheless too little and too late. Only about a third of the remaining Jews in post-war Europe immigrated to the new state of Israel. The majority found homes in the Americas and other countries in the English-speaking world. In 2004 the Institute for Strategy of the Jewish People, an organ of the Jewish Agency, published a report on the state of the Jewish people worldwide. It concluded that in the period 1970-2003 the global Jewish population had increased by 2% whereas the world's population grew by 70%, over 65% of world Jewry lived outside the state of Israel, and 92% of these Jews lived in highly developed countries after the massive Jewish emigration from the Soviet Union in the 1990s.

The Jewish state had not been the desired refuge for European Jews during and after the holocaust, nor the dreamed-about homeland for the masses who escaped communism in Eastern Europe. Over 60% of Soviet and other Jews who left in the late 1980s and 1990s emigrated to North America and countries in Western Europe. Many Russian Jews who did come to Israel later left for a better life in the United States and Canada.

Six decades after the founding of the State of Israel, the dream of two millennia of the Diaspora has not yet crystallized. A more disturbing fact is the constant emigration of Israelis—many natives to the Jewish state—to other countries in the Diaspora. Natan Sharansky, the Russian immigrant who served as Minister in the Israeli cabinet, wrote in 2004: "There are hundreds of thousands of Jews, not millions, who once lived in Israel and who now live in the Diaspora. I would not however call them disenfranchised since all of these people can vote merely by showing up at the polls."[118]

However much admired by Jews and Gentiles in the world, the state of Israel is hardly the "shining city on the hill" as envisioned by Theodore Herzl and the Zionist movement of the nineteenth century. Since its establishment in 1948, the Jewish state has been one option for immigration for world Jewry—not *the* option. In the 1990s, when thousands of Jews from the former Soviet Union arrived in Vienna, Austria, as the gateway to other destinations, they routinely considered several choices for their new homeland, one of which was Israel. To the consternation of many Israelis, a considerable number of immigrants chose Israel because of economic incentives in housing and other material things. Then, after a short period, they would sell their property and emigrate to the United States or Canada.

The Holocaust and the State of Israel

No other event has left such a tremendous mark on a people's consciousness as did the holocaust on the Jewish psyche. This pivotal and horrific page in the history of the people was followed by another event: the birth of the Jewish state of Israel. The proximity in time of these unprecedented punctuations of history have led many scholars and politicians to link these two events as being strongly related or even as "cause and effect."

After two millennia of Diaspora and the sudden appearance of a cataclysmic genocidal event followed so closely by the reinventing of a Jewish political homeland, there was clearly a widespread desire to link the two events. Yet, as much as this was the general attempt, the relationship between the holocaust and the establishment of the state of Israel is largely a myth.

Historically, the establishment of the Jewish homeland in the British Mandate of Palestine was the subject of discussion during the period following the First World War. In November 1917, the Foreign Secretary of the United Kingdom, Arthur Balfour, sent a letter to Lord Rothschild. The letter, known as "The Balfour Declaration," stated: "His Majesty's government view with favour the establishment in Palestine of a national home for the Jewish people, and will use their best endeavors to facilitate the achievement of this object...".

Secondly, the withdrawal of the British colonial forces from Palestine in May 1948 was part of a global retrenchment of the British

Empire. Within the few years following the Second World War, several key components of the Empire had been given independence. India, the "Jewel in the British Crown," gained independence in August 1947. Burma became an independent country in January 1948. Ceylon (now Sri Lanka) was given independence in February 1948. In the Middle East, the Kingdom of Jordan was established in May 1946. Other members of the Empire included Pakistan (1947), and later in Africa: Ghana in 1957, Nigeria in 1960, and Uganda in 1962.

The Jewish population in Palestine during the Second World War was known as the "Yishuv" (The Settlement). Due to a combination of factors, it could not receive, absorb, nor settle the many thousands of Jewish refugees from Nazi Europe in the period 1939-1947. In part, the British authorities in Palestine had imposed strict limits to Jewish immigration into Palestine, in order to avoid confrontation with the Arab inhabitants. Several ships with Jewish refugees from Europe had to be turned back to their ports of origin. Some ships managed to break through the British blockade and their human cargo then interred in camps in the neighboring island of Cyprus.[119] Another reason for the impotence of the Jewish settlements in Palestine to aid its displaced people in Nazi Europe was a combination of the small size of the population and their seemingly unwillingness to "go the extra mile" for the victims of the Holocuast.[120]

In part due to a conscious decision, the leaders of the "Yishuv" had opted to separate themselves from the remainder of the crumbling Jewish population of Europe. This phenomenon is further explored in the following pages of this narrative, in particular as a component of the description of the legacy of David Ben-Gurion.

The decision to distance the nascent state from the decimated European people has since then animated the cultural and psychological makeup of modern Israel. Several examples will illustrate this complex perspective. The forging of a new, reformulated Jewish person was a paramount factor in the rejection of the stereotypical European Jew sheepishly led to the slaughter in the death camps. The reinvented composite of the Israeli Jew was a fearless, uncompromising man who possessed knowledge in the martial arts and sciences and in the production of food from working his land. This image stood in utter contradiction to the skeletons of a depressed people who survived the Nazi camps. This was not the acceptable platform—historical, psychological, ethnic, or otherwise—on which the followers of Ben-Gurion planned to reinvent the Jewish homeland.

The results of this dilemma permeate the key aspects of Jewish-Israeli life. Elite units of the Israeli Army hold their swearing ceremony for recruits in the ruins of Masada, the mountaintop fortress destroyed by the Romans in 73 C.E. Instead of uttering the words "Auschwitz will never happen again," the soldiers are sworn in with the words: "Masada will not fall again." Although over 1,000 defenders of Masada committed suicide and the fort fell to the Roman legions, at least these Jewish zealots faced over 15,000 Roman soldiers, fought a magnificent battle, and fearlessly engaged a superior enemy. Masada was all in the distant past, thus it can be glamorized and the bravery of its defenders can be easily cherished. Conversely, the Nazi death camps are a recent memory, and many survivors still walk among the Israelis.

Although Ben-Gurion's Israel had negotiated reparations with post-war Germany, many holocaust survivors live in poverty in the state of Israel. In April 2006, the Associated Press reported that about 90 thousand holocaust survivors in Israel live in poverty. This number is a third of the total of holocaust survivors in Israel.[121] Such a national disgrace, whether a failure of the hideous Israeli bureaucracy or as a conscious indifference, clearly demonstrates the ambivalent feelings of Israelis towards the survivors. These poor souls, battered both physically and mentally, are nevertheless a constant reminder to Israelis of the horrific failure of their people to save itself from disaster. Moreover, in their search for modern heroes of Jewish strength and power, Israelis found no heroes in the holocaust.[122]

For contemporary Israelis, the holocaust and its survivors constantly remind them that they exist in a modern form of a ghetto. Surrounded by hostile Arab countries, with very few friends, and a malignant psyche of isolation, they are enthralled in the cold embrace of a belief that such a fate as the holocaust is indeed a possibility, albeit hopefully, remote. Thus, the search for heroes of the distant, rather than the recent, past.

The state of Israel was not established because of the holocaust, or as a refuge and asylum for its survivors. It was created independently of the fate of the Jews in the Second World War, although its creation had been an integral part of the process of the breakup of the British Empire after 1945. The state of Israel was established by the Jews who already inhabited the land, not by a massive immigration of refugees from the ashes of European Jewry. The British had won the war against Nazism, but were not in a position to maintain their global empire. The pieces of the empire began to fall apart in Asia, Africa, and the Middle East. The exigencies of major historical events had led to the partition of Palestine and the creation of an independent Jewish state. The holocaust was but a note in the margin of these global trends.

Jews and Germans

The German obsession with the Jews and the tragic and barbaric slaughter of European Jewry was in essence a conflict between two groups of people who believed in their superiority, based on one criterion or another. This of course does not excuse nor explain the horrific acts of the holocaust. It does, however, fall within the framework of those historians and social scientists that explains and comprehends such major human phenomena in their broader configurations across the journey of human existence.

Both groups believed that they were chosen, for theological or racial reasons, to be not only different but also much better than any one else. Their philosophies were not so different, as both abhorred diversity and considered themselves the select few. This conflict was of course asymmetrical, since the Germans had the resources of the mightiest nation in Europe and the Jews were a divided group of tribal congregations, spread over large territories and multiple countries, deeply involved in self-defeatism and in internecine struggles and led by sectarian orthodoxies.

This conflict was not a coincidence of the actions of one lunatic with barbaric ideals, such as Adolf Hitler is customarily portrayed even in well-documented historical studies. The genocide perpetrated by the Nazis on the Jews in Europe was different than similar documented genocides perpetrated in Bosnia or in Darfur in the Sudan. The German genocidal barbarism against the Jews was not based on religious differences, geographical or political aspirations, or on economic needs. Rather, it was based on a deep-rooted conflict between what the German Nazis described as "racial" differences, in which one group declares itself superior and wishes therefore to do away with another group that is also considered superior. The German Nazis did not covet Jewish geographical territory nor were they threatened by the Jewish religion. The German Nazis were not religious people and, in fact, routinely persecuted their own religious organizations and the religious beliefs and leadership of their own population. What the German Nazis could not tolerate were the Jewish people as competitors in the quest for superiority over other groups of human beings. This was the core of the Nazi philosophy, and any group that posed a threat to such "superiority" had to be eliminated. The Nazis emphasized the international aspects of the Jewish people and their superior abilities in literature (most books burned by the Nazis were of Jewish writers) and in science (physics had been declared a Jewish science). This struggle was seen by the Nazis as a struggle between the two groups who received the gift of superiority over all others.

Connecting Jewish influence over events which led to World War I and its aftermath was also a Nazi exercise in distorting historical facts. Although there were a few well-known Jewish financiers in Europe (such as the Rothschilds), the First World War was the internal rivalry of the European monarchies over territories and their national interests, and the unexpected implosion of a complex network of national security agreements.

As much as the Germans tried to coat the reasons for hating the Jews with nationalistic xenophobia embedded in a distorted perspective of the modern history of Europe, the viable motive that animated their ideology was the Hegelian-type struggle against another entity of self-proclaimed superior attributes.

The hatred of the Jews by the Germans did not necessarily fit the philosophy of George Friedrich Hegel (1770-1831), nor the sequential line linking his ideas to those of the Nazi ideology. Hegel's "speculative or pure reason" and his conception of the dialectic of history culminated in the *political* entity of the state. History is a succession of these political struggles. The superiority of the state as the ultimate form of logic invariably leads to its dialectic competition with similar forms of political entities—rather than the rag tag groups of dispersed tribes who lack an organized form of polity. As the personification of pure reason, the German state had no issues with this puny agglomeration of individuals called "Jews."

However, this group of a political people had several practices which seemed similar to those advocated by German-Nazi philosophy. Both believed in the purity of their membership, thus practicing a form of eugenics, in which the leaders strongly opposed reproduction outside the group. This "purity" of the group, long practiced by the Jews, has produced genetic repercussions, such as the hereditary diseases and malformations that are primarily found in the Jewish populations.

Paradoxes of Isolation and Superiority

Both ideologies also catered to the notion of xenophobia and the sense of isolation, as well as the constant fear of being threatened with extinction by neighbors and enemies. In the Jewish tradition this view of the world ("weltanschauung") produced the "Paradox of Jewish Isolation."

This paradox was the incongruence between the perceived need to isolate their people from harmful foreign influences and the realities of the Jewish Diaspora. If isolation (into the ghetto-like enclaves, by choice or by external requirement of the Gentile leadership) is the means to maintaining one's *unique* religious and social existence, then the formation of a manageable geographical entity is a workable solution. But the reality of the Jewish dispersion attested to the existence of Jewish communities in many continents, living under different rulers, political systems, and religious practices.

How can such a dispersed group of people manifest itself to the world as very unique and, in many ways, superior to *all* other countries, peoples, and communities in which it resides? This paradox of isolation yet dispersion produced some unintended consequences. The dichotomy of what the Jews perceived themselves to be and what appeared to the Gentiles engendered a perception by the Gentiles of the Jews as an organized *international* entity, acting as a power with centralized direction and control.

Another consequence was the reaction of many rulers and leaders of the various countries and societies where Jews resided in their isolation. These rulers considered the Jewish community as "their" Jews with all the privileges that such a classification provided the host countries and smaller social and political entities. Thus, the rules of behavior for the Jews and their treatment varied dramatically by location and by ruler. This sometimes-tragic differentiation in treatment indeed enhanced the paradox of Jewish isolation. The harsher the treatment in one community, the more there was the need for even more isolation along national lines—by empire, or kingdom, or city. This localized isolation added to the empowerment of the local leaders of the Jewish communities and to a heightened sense of isolation.

The Germans experienced a similar process. Nestled in the middle of Europe between France and the Slavic countries, the Germans suffered from a "paradox of superiority." They considered themselves superior to their neighbors—first by virtue of their history, organization, and force of arms, and later by transforming these attributes into a theory of racial superiority. Yet, they also experienced a compelling and irreparable sentiment of being "squeezed" between powerful neighbors who exhibited, throughout their history, overt animosity. Like the Jews, the Germans by and large felt themselves to be the victims of others who disliked them because of their superior qualities as a people, and who continuously strove to cause them some form of harm. These sentiments became imbued in the German psyche, just as similar sentiments animated the Jewish persona.

The savagery of the holocaust may be attributed more to commonalities between oppressors and victims than to their differences. In fact, after the war there had been a movement of *rapprochement* between post-war Germany and the post-war Jewish state of Israel. Both countries considered themselves to have emerged from the ashes of a horrific catastrophe. Both considered themselves standing alone in the face of the neighbors who surround them and who, to varying degrees, seem resentful of their achievements in industry and in culture. The warm relations between the two countries transcend their historical bond of the Second World War. There is a shared commonality in their perceived existence as different, unique, and superior peoples— yet controlled with a painful history and forced by geography to face unpleasant neighbors. This has resulted in on-going cooperation in the military, financial, economic, and cultural arenas.

Reinventing A Homeland: Inside The Bengurionite State

The horrific events of the holocaust helped to shape the nature and the psyche of the reinvented homeland of the Jewish people. Although not a cause for the establishment of the state of Israel, the holocaust created a mentality of both "siege" and fear of even the appearance of being gullible, frail, vulnerable, or a dupe.[123] The modern Israeli thus strives to establish the image of whatever his ancestors failed to be: no longer the victim, never again the lamb being led to the slaughter. Even a minor incident tends to evoke images of planned extermination such as those of the historical events of Masada and the Nazi death camps.[124]

Another factor that shaped the new homeland and its people was the reinvented mentality of siege or ghetto existence. Whereas the "macho" image controlled overt behavior of the citizens, the ghetto mentality became inculcated in the culture and psyche of the society and had far-reaching implications in Israel's domestic and foreign policies.

The ghetto mentality stemmed from two main sources: the traditional behavior of Jewish communities, extended to the reinvented homeland, to live in a secluded environment with little contact with others (magnificent isolation), and the result of the policies of the early governments of Israel.

Ebbtide of the Light to the Nations

The opportunity to create an old "new" homeland was a "once-in-two-millennia" event for the Jewish people. The people who had suffered so much and whose pride rested on its abilities to produce great minds in so many areas of human endeavors had finally reached the end of a painful journey. The Jewish people were ready to establish a homeland with political, economic, religious, social, and cultural independence.

Here a golden opportunity presented itself to create what early Zionist idealists had imagined as "the city on the hill": a shining example to other nations of what the Jews could achieve as an independent people in their own country. This promise, like the promise of the successful and happy Jewish existence throughout recorded history, never materialized.

Visitors to Israel, particularly Jews from the United States, always marvel at the modern country nestled among less developed Arab neighbors. These tourists are impressed with the ability of Israelis to work the land, to maintain national institutions, and to own and operate a military force—all the activities that Jews in their Diaspora had been unable to accomplish.

Yet, underneath the apparent successes of an independent homeland lurks the realities of a promise unfulfilled, a dream tarnished, and the ideal left unaccomplished. As of the writing of this narrative, the reinvented homeland of the Jewish people is mired in a plethora of unflattering shortcomings.

The State of Israel is surrounded by neighboring countries, all of which are its sworn enemies. It maintains seemingly normal relations with two neighbors (Egypt and Jordan), but there is tremendous hatred simmering in the populations of these two countries. The dream of a Middle Eastern commercial and cultural network or union—encompassing Israel and its Arab neighbors—remains just a dream.

Israel is isolated within the world community of nations. Diplomatically and in other areas, Israel can count on the United States as its *only* ally and benefactor. Repeatedly, the United States vetoes

United Nation's resolutions against Israel, and often the United States is the lonely voice for Israel among all the nations of the globe.

Although some immigration of Jews to Israel has taken place, particularly after the demise of the Soviet Union, the country has a low growth rate when compared with its neighbors. Since the early years of the Jewish state, there has been a continuing outflow of Israelis, emigrating to other countries in North America, Western Europe, Australia, and South America. Instead of being a true magnet to Jews in the Diaspora, Israel has absorbed only a small number of them and has been severely hemorrhaging its own people who have chosen to live in other countries.

In addition, the internal rate of growth for the Jewish sector of the Israeli population cannot outpace the rate of natural growth of its Arab component, nor that of its Arab neighbors.[125] The combination of the low rate of immigration, the continuing waves of emigration of Israelis, and the low birth rate for the secular Jews in Israel is considered by many to be a "demographic time bomb," threatening the future viability of the country and its Jewish character.

In addition to its diplomatic isolation, Israel is the object of hatred by much, if not all, of the Muslim world. Even in the United States, where public discussions were held on such topics as the war on terror and the wars in Iraq and Afghanistan, many speakers and commentators insert the "Israeli question" into the discussion, however marginal the connection. In many debates and political interactions, the state of Israel has replaced the Jews of yesteryear as the focus of hatred.[126]

An objective observer who would engage even in a brief assessment of the status of the Jewish homeland would undoubtedly find it in a constant state of upheaval, turmoil, and belligerency. Every five or six years the country is engulfed in a state of minor or major conflict. Its borders are in constant ebullience, with danger lurking at every border crossing and with the classification of the military forces of its neighbors. The people of Israel have not experienced a true period of peaceful existence since the founding of the State in 1948. They are always at war, always on alert, and never have the comforts of friendly surroundings or the benefits of a relaxed and peaceful life.

A different shortcoming of the reinvented homeland of the Jewish people is an internal configuration of a disturbing cultural legacy from the founding of the state in 1948. This is a legacy of favoritism, political corruption, and harmful divisiveness, all of which have helped to stimulate the waves of emigration. This was the legacy of Bengurionism, as detailed in the ensuing pages of this narrative.

How did a dream of a Jewish homeland that would be a "light to the nations of the world" turn into a reality of a struggling and isolated contemporary "ghetto-nation"? How has the dream of Herzl's reinvented homeland descended into the unenviable position of sorrow, constant struggle, and the agony of a people under a life-long siege? Some answers can be found in the events of the founding of the Jewish homeland in 1948, the first three decades of its existence, and the forming of its institutions under the leadership of David Ben-Gurion.

David Ben-Gurion: The Man and His Legacy

David Ben-Gurion (1886-1973) is credited with the creation and establishment of the State of Israel to an extent that rivals all the American founding fathers combined. He chaired the hastily gathered convention on May 14, 1948 in Tel-Aviv and single handedly proclaimed the independence of the newly established country.

Who was this man and what was his legacy? Historians and politicians have written extensively about his beliefs and accomplishments. Much of this work tells the story of his political career and the Israeli-Arab wars that he commanded as Prime Minister.[127] Israeli writers who had close liaisons with the regime tended to depict Ben-Gurion with adulation and to profusely excuse his shortcomings.[128] Some biographers indiscriminately linked Ben-Gurion's life to the Jewish struggle in modern times. Dan Kurzman (1983), for example, referred to Ben-Gurion as a man who encompassed the biblical attributes of a Moses, Isaiah, and as the ultimate redeemer of the Jewish people.

This narrative focuses on the disastrous implications from Ben-Gurion's philosophy and actions during the first three decades of Israel's existence. In addition to the military outcomes of his tenure in Israeli politics, this narrative explores his influence on the culture, institutions, internal and external policies, and the economic framework of the Jewish state.

Born David Gruen in June 1876 in the city of Plonsk in Russian-occupied Poland, he adopted in 1910 the name Ben-Gurion. In 1915 he went to New York for a few years, where he met and married Pauline (Paula) Munweis. In 1920 he immigrated to Palestine and was instrumental in the founding of a socialist-Zionist workers organization. He traveled to Moscow in 1923 to discuss with the Communist rulers of the Soviet Union the possibility of cooperation but his effort was unsuccessful.

Ben-Gurion was a short man, five feet four, who lacked the gift of oratory of his contemporaries, such as Churchill and Hitler. Although some historians grandiosely compared Ben-Gurion to the American founding fathers, he was neither Washington, nor Jefferson, nor Franklin. He lacked the erudition of a Thomas Jefferson, the strategic conception of a Benjamin Franklin, and the sense of public service of George Washington. He was first and foremost a union organizer and a life-long political being, dedicated to the tribal tenets and interests of his trade union and political party, at any cost, and as a life-long employment opportunity. He was first and foremost a socialist and an ardent anti-capitalist.[129]

Ben-Gurion referred to himself as a "farmer," yet he did not engage in agricultural work until his retirement to Kibbutz Sdea-Boker in 1953 and again in 1963 at the age of 77, where he presumably helped with the agricultural chores of his fellow residents. Ben-Gurion also considered himself a scientist and a writer, perhaps on a level of Benjamin Franklin. However, Franklin stood for tolerance and virtue, the excellence of merit, and the exaltation of small entrepreneurs and businessmen. Ben-Gurion stood for the supremacy of the party and union functionaries, for a distorted view of socialist ideals, and for the suffocation of the middle class, of small businesses and business people, and for intolerance to all those who held different views and different political ideologies.

Ben-Gurion, like his contemporaries Joseph Stalin and Adolf Hitler, lacked formal education but was a voracious reader. Like the two great dictators of his time, he considered the political party he led to be an integral part of the nation and the country. He also considered himself to be the "father" of the nation and extended the rule and influence of his party to the culture and the institutions of the nation. Like Stalin and Hitler he was concerned with establishing national institutions that would mirror his beliefs and his party's philosophy.

The Nature of Bengurionism

The blending of Zionism and socialism that Ben-Gurion developed during his youth became the guiding philosophy of the newly established state of Israel. In this narrative this cultural, political, and economic framework is described as "Bengurionism." It may be further defined as a national state of mind, penetrating every echelon of Israeli society.[130]

Bengurionism introduced a special brand of socialism and a "worker-paradise." Ben-Gurion was fascinated with Joseph Stalin and his rule of the Communist Soviet Union. As a socialist and a trade union organizer, Ben-Gurion understood the advantages of having power over both the military and the civilian institutions. The ministries of defense, education, treasury, foreign affairs, and interior have always been considered "sacred" possessions of Bengurionite political followers. Ben-Gurion and his party cronies were extremely disappointed and dismayed at the purge that the Soviets perpetrated against Jewish doctors in the early 1950s. Accusations of false crimes targeted Jewish physicians in the major cities of the Soviet Union. The dream of cooperation with the Soviets on the basis of common beliefs in socialism died with these waves of Soviet-style anti-Semitism. Thus, the Bengurionites turned their fury against the Israeli middle class, its business people, and its intellectuals.

The Bengurionites were initially an army of party and trade union functionaries.[131] With the establishment of the country in 1948, a host of institutions and national companies were created, thus offering employment to the politically-connected in the population. This created the "economy of dependence," characteristic of the former Soviet block in Eastern Europe.

Bengurionism was never about social justice or Zionism—it was always about raw political power and the grabbing of resources for the party and the trade unions. Those in the population who were politically connected to the party or the trade union received varied benefits and incentives in housing, employment, and education. The remainder of the population was simply tolerated as a necessary resource to staff the armed forces and the economy.

Abraham Lincoln once said: "There are a few things wholly evil or wholly good. Almost everything, especially of government policy, is an inescapable compound of the two, so that our best judgment of the preponderance between them is continually demanding." The absolute evil and absolute good are perhaps only a figment of our nimble imagination. Yet, was Stalinist Russia such a figment? Is Bengurionite Israel?

Perhaps the answer is in the details, rather than in a sweeping generality. It manifests itself in the experiences of individuals and their life stories. The evil of regimes and political systems is also reflected in the damage they leave behind, in the form of broken lives and tragic memories.

Lincoln's perspective was influenced by the American political tapestry of the separation of powers and the balancing act that each branch of government maintains in restraining, monitoring, and assessing the performance of the other branches. Lincoln's admirable perspective was also ingrained in the American Constitution and Bill of Rights—both created as a shield against the excesses of government and the overbearing power of its leaders. Such documents did not exist in Stalinism or in Bengurionism.

How It Started: Usurping the Lead

On the afternoon of Friday, the 14th of May, 1978, in the Museum of Art in Tel-Aviv, David Ben-Gurion and a carefully selected group of 35 mostly political functionaries declared the independence of the Jewish population in Palestine and the establishment of a new country, "Mediant Israel" (State of Israel).[132] The land between the River Jordan and the Mediterranean Sea was part of the British Empire. The League of Nations in 1922 gave the British government a mandate to administer the lands of Palestine and Transjordan (east of the Jordan River). At that time there were about 84 thousand Jews and 590 thousand Muslims (as well as 71 thousand Christians) occupying the land of Palestine. The British Mandate was scheduled to be terminated on 15 May 1948. This was in accordance with the United Nations Resolution 181 of November 21, 1947, which authorized the partition of Palestine into two independent states: a Jewish homeland and an Arab state.[133]

The day before the last high commissioner for Palestine, General Sir Alan Cunningham, was scheduled to officially terminate the British Mandate, Ben-Gurion declared the birth of the Jewish State. It was a sudden declaration, based not on general elections or another form of the "will of the people," but on a vague promise of "the establishment of the elected, regular authorities of the State in accordance with the Constitution which shall be adopted by the Elected Constituent Assembly no later than the 1st of October 1948...."[134]

Thus, the self-proclaimed "People's Council" declared itself the Provisional Government, with David Ben-Gurion as its leader and future Prime Minister.[135] Several other political groups had been excluded from this "people's" council.[136] The followers of the Jabotinsky movement, led by Menachem Begin, were not invited to participate. Neither were business leaders or commercial interests of the Jewish population. The "Yishuv" (Settlement), the "people's council," was composed of representatives of Ben-Gurion's socialist organizations, the trade unions, and some religious organizations. This became the trademark composition of future Israeli governments: a narrow coalition of "workers" (mostly left of center trade unions) and orthodox religious parties.

The sudden and unilateral declaration of independence by Ben-Gurion and the highly selected group of his cronies was carried out without consultation with or the knowledge of the other parties in the region: the British and the Arabs. There was no attempt to coordinate any of the political actions with other organizations—Jewish or Gentile.

The Illegitimacy of Bengurionism

This action by Ben-Gurion and his cronies represented a grabbing of political and economic powers of the nascent country. It contributed to the precarious situation of the continuing conflict between Israel and the Arab countries. Although it is impossible to ascertain that the armies of the Arab neighbors would not have attacked the newly established Jewish state (as they did on the 15th of May, 1948) had Ben-Gurion not unilaterally proclaimed the birth of his socialist "country-paradise"—this act nevertheless undermined any possibility of an orderly transfer of the British Mandate to both Jews and Arabs in Palestine. It undermined the possibility of negotiated borders and the establishment of some form of bilateral relations. It effectively and forcibly contributed to the constant state of war that has lasted six decades.

The takeover by the Bengurionites of the reigns of the future government of a state had also made it impossible to negotiate with the departing British authorities. Although Ben-Gurion brazenly presented himself to the British as the leader of the "Ishuv," he never intended to parlay with them, or to enter in negotiations with them and with Arab leaders in the region.

The two parallels that historians tend to make between the birth of Israel and the American revolution and India's independence are striking examples of contradictions, The American founding fathers had been elected by the constituencies they represented. They came from a variety of geographies, economic interests and political and ideological beliefs. Their actions and guiding documents had been constructed after extensive consultations and debates. Careful consideration was given to all parties, in particular to smaller states, and to the various geographical regions.

In the case of India, the Mahatma Gandhi and Jawaharlal Nehru had declared independence after a lengthy process of negotiations with Lord Mountbatten, the last governor of India, and with Muhammad Ali Jinnah, the leader of the All-India Muslim League. These discussions resulted in agreements about the partition of the Indian sub-continents into two separate countries, differentiated by religion and customs. The Indian reality was much more complex than that of Palestine, As Gandhi clearly stated, there were Muslim and Hindu living in almost every city and village of the country. In Palestine the geographical division was much more demarcated, except for some coastal cities such as Haifa and Jaffa, where Jews and Arabs cohabitated.

No attempts were made by either side to come to the negotiating table. The Bengurionites were pleased with this situation, because they planned to undertake their planned unilateral declaration of independence. The British probably believed that by just leaving without negotiations—as they had conducted in India—they could spare themselves the trouble of being a party to another rancorous exchange of demands by the parties. Similarly, the Arabs in Palestine lacked a unified position, so that even if they had been invited by the British to such deliberations, they would have been hard-pressed to assemble a representative delegation.

These circumstances led to the Friday, 14th of May 1948, "one man show" in which David Ben-Gurion singlehandedly established a country, molded after his convictions and in his image. The people who gave humanity Moses, Maimonides, Spinoza, and Einstein descended to the level of a Ben-Gurion.

In a way, this power-grabbing action by Ben-Gurion and his selected group of cronies has also contributed to the origins of the current Palestinian problem. The unilateral and mostly homogeneous group of leaders assembled in Tel-Aviv on the 14th of May 1948 had little interest in, and little knowledge about, the neighboring Arab countries and the Arab population in Palestine.

The abrupt and unilateral power grabbing by the Bengurionites also contributed in large measure to the selection of the system of government of the new country. Ben-Gurion would have preferred a political regime similar to that of the socialist republics of Eastern Europe, then under the occupation and influence of the Soviet Union. He also held in high esteem and admiration the dictatorships of the African and Asian countries that had at that time gained independence from their European colonial powers.

Ben-Gurion had to abandon these ideas because of two reasons: first, to create new political and administrative structures which would depart from the existing British colonial institutions would have been very difficult in the first months and years of the newly established state. His abrupt and unilateral action needed some form of legitimacy, and this was to an extent supplied by the continuation and preservation of British colonial institutions, customs, and many legal frameworks. One such immediate benefit was the effect on the newly formed Jewish/Israeli military force. Established along the lines of the British armed forces, the young army was also manned by many Jewish officers who had served in the British Army and its Air Force during the Second World War.

Secondly, although Ben-Gurion and his cronies had established the only viable Jewish institutions in Palestine (the Histadrut and ancillary labor/"workers" organizations), the large Jewish immigration in the post-war period of 1945-1948 was not favorable to the Bengurionite ideals. Most of these immigrants loathed any form of authoritarian regimes, be it from the right or the left. Even though they were not asked to participate in the effort to declare the independence of the Jewish state, this segment of the population would certainly have opposed an extremist regime of socialist ideals. Ben-Gurion and his cronies understood this, and since they badly needed the immigrants to administer the new country and to fill the military vacancies, the new leaders thus reluctantly opted for the British model of democracy. This model was adopted with many of the constraints that the Colonial regime had imposed on the country during the Mandate. This included censorship, restrictions on the rights of the citizenry, and a plethora of "emergency" legislation that allowed the government to suspend basic rights for an unlimited period of time.

The existence of democratic institutions in Israel today is not the product of the democratic ideals that might have animated the Jewish people or its leaders. Nor is it the result of the freedom-loving spirits of Ben-Gurion and his cronies. Rather, democratic institutions exist today in Israel because the British institutions of the Mandate in Palestine were transferred, at first almost unchanged, to the new and hastily created Jewish state. By seizing power on the afternoon of that critical day of May 14th, 1948, the Bengurionites locked themselves into the system of government that they knew well and in which they had built their own institutions. In time they would convert the economy of the country into a socialist model of centrally directed activities, and the political system into a model of socialism, opposing the middle class, the entrepreneurial spirit, and any ideals that contradicted their "workers"-run country.

And so it came to pass that after two millennia of Diaspora, the Jewish people once again added another disastrous stitch to the tapestry of selecting poor and unqualified leaders. On the eve of independence from the British colonial rule, people of mediocre intellect, lacking in vision and in political and economic foresight, hijacked the new state. The leadership of the new state had been taken over by a trade union organizer and a bunch of political functionaries, ready to serve at any capacity at his pleasure as long as political power and economic benefits were involved. Many luminaries of the Jewish settlements in Palestine (such as Haim Weitzman) did not participate in the inaugural ceremony and did not sign the declaration of independence.[137]

The Background: The Influence of Berl Katznelson

Ben-Gurion's socialist ideology had its origins in several left-wing Zionist philosophers, but mostly he was influenced by Berl Katznelson (1887-1944). Born in Belorussia, he emigrated to Palestine in 1909. Berl (as he was known in Jewish circles and the Labor movement) brought to the movement a spirit of affability and a structured ideology that combined Judaic tenets with socialist and collectivist imperatives. Berl was instrumental in the founding of several labor organizations, among them the health care fund "Kupat Holim" and "Bank Hapoalim" (The Workers' Bank).

But above all, Berl's influence emerged in his post as editor of the daily newspaper of the workers' movement and their union: "Davar" (The Word). He envisioned the establishment in Palestine of educational institutions that would train leaders of the workers' movement in the Jewish-socialist amalgam. He also wrote commentaries and editorials on a variety of topics, hence he assumed the role of spiritual leader of the movement. Unlike so many of his colleagues and followers, Berl was unpretentious and modest. He was a true ideologue, with a passion for visionary concepts and a deep dislike of power and its trappings.[138]

Berl's ideology was challenged by two distinct yet powerful paradoxes. The first was the spiritual and structural co-existence between "true" socialists and Judaism's strict rules of daily life. He was a proponent of the interjecting of basic Jewish religious customs, rituals, and festivals into the life of the socialist agricultural and labor collectives and institutions. This ideology of "fusion" of radically distinct views of the world was not well received by many quarters in the labor movement but had a durable impact on Ben-Gurion's thinking.

There was an inherent, seemingly irreconcilable conflict between socialism as a secular and egalitarian belief system and the exclusionary sectarian belief system and orthodoxy of the Jewish view of the world. Berl attempted to reconcile this conflict by proposing a total labor or socialist system of national existence—beyond the agricultural collectives.[139] He considered the labor movement to be the foundation of the reborn Jewish state. Therefore he strongly advocated the establishment of powerful labor institutions as the dominant instruments of economic and social services in the Jewish state. He co-founded the laborer's bank, a distribution company for commercial goods (Hamashbir) and similar enterprises.

Within such a total state dominance of the socialist movement, Berl could now insert the Jewish religious component without directly offending the basic principles that led to the departure of the Zionists-socialists from their religious shackles: the return to working the land as a collective where socialist/collective ideals replaced Jewish orthodoxy and festivals. Berl attempted to attenuate the rift by interjecting a flavor of Judaic customs, such as circumcision and the observance of the Sabbath.

Although Berl's model of blending socialism and Jewishness did not resolve the inherent conflict between secular and religious ideologies, it appealed to Ben-Gurion's conception of the Jewish state. The dominance of socialism and its control of political, cultural, and economic life (beyond agriculture) gave Ben-Gurion the ideological framework he needed to obtain as much power as possible in the reborn Jewish homeland. This ideological platform also permitted him to rally the labor movement behind him—as the successor to the venerated Berl Katznelson.

The far-reaching consequences of the adoption by the Bengurionites of Berl's model included the coveted blessing of this ideology to the unholy alliance between the socialists and the Jewish orthodox parties. This alliance gave the two different and extremist ideologies the means to maintain control over the state. The socialists received *political* control; in exchange for *economic* and other benefits they gave to the religious parties and to their leaders. This strange, yet highly effective coalition remained unchallenged in the Israeli political and economic climate for almost three decades and, in spite of many changes since then, is very much alive today.[140]

Setting the Stage and Molding a Nation: The Rise of Bengurionite Israel

Although over forty years have passed since the death of David Ben-Gurion, his ideology and management of the country's affairs during the first half of its existence have left an indelible mark on Israel's condition—past and present. The failures of Bengurionism in almost every category of government have contributed to the sorry state of the internal and external existence of the Jewish state.

In the early years of this century, Israel has engaged in multiple offensives against Lebanon. By many accounts, these operations have failed to achieve their stated objectives. An intense debate began in August of 2006 inside Israel. The leaders of the government were accused of incompetence to the point of putting the security of the nation at grave risk.[141] Prime Minister Ehud Olmert and the Minister of Defense Amir Peretz were the primary recipients of the harsh criticism. In Bengurionite Israel such failures of management are more of a norm than an exception. Like Ben-Gurion, Amir Peretz was a labor organizer, whose sole skills and training for the post of Minister of Defense were his political affiliation and political ties.

Ben-Gurion and his followers have shaped a country whose political culture is enmeshed in a world in which personal connections are the sole criterion for leadership. This type of culture rejects merit as a criterion for preference and selection along the entire spectrum of government. Incompetence, inappropriate training and education, and an inherent lack of depth of ideas and judgment are endemic throughout the country's institutions. The failure of the Israeli military to achieve its mission in Lebanon in the summer of 2006 is indicative of the spreading of such culture of incompetence to the Israel Defense Forces.[142]

In the Bengurionite state, the public trough is the exclusive domain of those who have close connections to the leadership. While maintaining the socialist tenets of punily compensating hard work and enterprise, the ruling class enjoys almost unlimited access to the country's treasury. There are virtually no controls or regulations constraining or limiting this practice. The State Comptroller General simply audits the expenditures, not the underlying circumstances of their existence.

Life In Bengurionite Israel

Bengurionism is a way of life in the Jewish state. Formed as a bureaucratic reality as well as a peculiar state of mind, Bengurionism affects almost every facet of life in Israel. Its characteristics are a mix of the traditional Jewish failures of the Diaspora. The key features are the existence of a small group of the leadership elite—many of whom are the direct descendants of the cronies who surrounded Ben-Gurion during the first two decades of his rule. This self-selected elite cuts across political ideologies and its purpose is to perpetuate its existence to gather power and to control as many of the nation's resources as possible.[143]

Bengurionism and the Economy

Winston Churchill once said: "The inherent vice of capitalism is the unequal sharing of blessings; the inherent virtue of socialism is the equal sharing of misery." Ben-Gurion chose the latter. In the first two decades of his rule as Prime Minister of the Jewish homeland he scrupulously enforced the ideology of Berl Katznelson of concentrating as much economic power as possible in the hands of the government, the trade unions, and the orthodoxy.

Ben-Gurion's economic outlook and policies had kept much foreign capital out of Israel. He had effectively driven away such companies as Philips, the electronics giant from the Netherlands, and Parker, the American maker of writing instruments. His economic ministers demanded control over foreign investments, including control over daily decisions on production and human resources. His ministers of economic affairs were grey, uneducated, and meek individuals. Levy Eshkol (1895-1969) served as Finance Minister from 1952 until 1963.[144] He brilliantly summarized the economic philosophy of Bengurionism with the declaration: "Israel wants money without Jews and Jews without money."

In conjunction with Eshkol, the Ministry of Trade and Industry was the powerful instrument of economic policy. In the crucial decade of 1955-1965, the post was held by Pinhas Sapir (1909-1975). Born Pinhas Koslowski in Suwalki, Poland, Sapir once boasted that he managed the Israeli economy with a "little black book."

While in the years after the Second World War European and American companies began a global expansion with investments in each other and in many developing countries, the policies of Ben-Gurion and his henchmen, Eshkol and Sapir, effectively excluded Israel from receiving a fair share of such investments. The massive flow of Jewish donations and loans from North America and Europe was used to create an indigenous military industry, as well as a fledgling textiles industry that supplied low paying employment to unskilled Jewish immigrants from the Arab countries.

Ben-Gurion himself was ignorant of economic theory and indifferent to economic matters. The ministers he appointed to this critical area of government shared his ignorance. They also shared his ideology of the socialist economy, characterized by high income taxes, public control of economic activity, and a campaign to combat and to suffocate the middle class, entrepreneurs, and private businesses.[145]

Although since the 1980s there have been some attempts at the "liberalization" of the Israeli economy, the results of the failed economic policies of Bengurionism are still entrenched in the Jewish state of the twenty-first century. The Israeli economy largely relies on a continuing state of conflict with its neighbors. The economy is a "war economy," to an extent that even the recently created high-technology industry is based on military and security applications, such as weapons, airport security, and radar and laser applications in weaponry and rockets.

The dream of transforming the newly established Jewish homeland into a shining example of an economic powerhouse has never materialized. In the 1980s, the Israeli economy was on the brink of collapse. Instead of becoming a "Switzerland of the Middle East," its economy is plagued by socialist incompetence and the lack of the work ethics that has made similar nations such as Singapore, Taiwan, South Korea, and Ireland economic success stories.[146]

For the Bengurionite philosophy of economic dependency this state of affairs is a welcome situation. Poverty, incompetence, and political connections are the guiding principles of the Bengurionite economic tradition. It allows the small political elite to exercise its power over the population by providing basic economic goods such as government-supplied or directed employment, housing, education, and other economic opportunities—at the discretion of the *political* elite. Alongside this elite, in the six decades of Israel's existence there has emerged a small but powerful "*economic* elite" within Israeli society.

Composed initially of people who worked alongside Ben-Gurion and his political associates, this group of economically endowed Israelis has gradually incorporated members of the opposition, particularly the

"Herut" party and other center and right-wing smaller parties. The Bengurionite government had consistently showered these individuals with *economic* favors, although they were ideologically opposed to the socialist agenda. Such economic give-aways helped to keep the opposition to the Bengurionite rule under control and to drastically lower the level of their *political* activism.

In 1952 Menachem Begin (1913-1992) vigorously protested the arrangement that Ben-Gurion was negotiating with the Federal Republic of Germany on the payment of reparation for Nazi atrocities and for restitution of the confiscated treasuries of European Jewry. Begin was suspended from the Knesset and there were rumors of attempts to bomb the Knesset building. The Bengurionites diffused the situation by offering Begin's associates a plethora of economic favors, thus ultimately gaining support for the agreement with Germany.[147] This policy of providing political opponents with economic incentives has been so effective that it essentially silenced any opposition to Bengurionite rule. In June 1967, Menachem Begin and other political figures from both parties approached the then retired Ben-Gurion and pleaded with him to return to power!

Ben-Gurion considered economics to be a tool of political maneuvering. He instinctively understood that a prosperous and active middle class would soon divert its economic power into the political arena and exercise political influence that could weaken or even destroy his regime and his cherished socialist agenda. He therefore focused the economic program of the nascent country on the grinding of the class of economic entrepreneurs, professionals, and small businesses. The subjugation of this highly productive component of any national economy resulted in a massive exodus of immense productive energy. About two million former Israelis and their first-generation foreign-born descendants live outside Israel today, primarily in the English-speaking democracies. Among these exiled Israelis were and still are the "best and the brightest."[148]

Bengurionism and Foreign Policy

The legacy of Ben-Gurion's tenets of foreign policy has been more devastating to the fortune of the Jewish homeland than his economic misadventures. In the economic arena, Bengurionism vanquished the commercial prowess of the Jewish people in favor of an alien philosophy of socialism imported into Palestine by the strange amalgam of Zionism, religion, and socialism concocted by Berl Katznelson and his disciples. By so doing, Bengurionism also destroyed the global outreach of Jewish commercial linkages in the Diaspora. These were the strengths of the Jewish people which had greatly contributed to its ability to survive over the centuries in exile and which had also become the benchmark of criticism and hatred by many anti-Semitic groups.

The economic war on private enterprise carried out by the Bengurionites somewhat subsided in the late 1980s and even more so during the 1990s. But this slow reversal of the "economy of dependence" inside Israel and of the antagonistic treatment of global and private enterprise was "too little and too late" to help reverse the damage on foreign relations and the global standing of the reinvented Jewish homeland. *Commerce makes good foreign policy*. The European nations had proven this axiom by setting up the treaty of Rome in 1957 in which *commercial* ties afterward contributed to the *political* organization of the European union.[149]

But the most compelling and harmful effect of Bengurionism on Israel's standing in world affairs has been the implacable desire of Bengurionites to fulfill the socialist dream as a world bastion of this new religion of the twentieth century. To this end, the Bengurionites navigated Israel's foreign policy in the direction of "socialist" countries—both the established and the newly created nations in Asia and Africa. Warm ties were established with U-Nu, the first Prime Minister of the newly independent Burma (1907-1995). In 1955 the Burmese leader visited Israel, as the *first* state leader to visit the Jewish homeland.

Israeli leaders of the Bengurionite regime participated with vigor and enthusiasm in conferences of the socialist countries of the world, and also consistently attempted to join the non-aligned movement of nations. This group, originally composed of 25 countries that were former colonies of the European powers, was co-founded by Jawaharlal Nehru of India and Gamal Abdel Nasser of Egypt, the latter being an enemy of the State of Israel. The first meeting of the group was held in 1961. Like a kid who is socially rejected in the schoolyard, the Bengurionites continued to try to join the group and to actively participate in its activities and its agenda. Several of the leading nations in this group did not even recognize the existence of the State of Israel and did not maintain diplomatic relations with it. Yet, their judgment clouded by the socialist ideals, the Bengurionites hoped that their unwavering belief in socialism would be something they had in common with the nonaligned nations.

Such an implacable yet myopic adherence to the group, post-colonial, socialist, and emerging nations came at a very high price. The Bengurionites sacrificed their relations with the democracies in Western Europe and with the United States. To the present time there is a gap between what Israelis believe they and their country represent and what the Europeans, particularly the young and educated citizens of the European Union, believe that Israel represents in world affairs. To a growing segment of the population in Western Europe, Israel is the target of hatred, considered a warmonger and a destabilizing force in the Middle East. Ironically, this trend in public opinion is fomented and led by socialists and left wing politicians and thinkers in Western Europe.[150]

A visitor in 1948 to the creation of the State of Israel as the Jewish homeland would have been impressed by the euphoria and the promise of this new country and its potential to be a guiding light to other nations. This same visitor returning today—when these lines are being penned—will find a very different scenario. The State of Israel is undoubtedly a pariah state, perhaps the most isolated and hated country in the world. It counts on only one friend, the United States.

Ben-Gurion's misjudgments of the world in the post-war era resulted in a confused and misdirected foreign policy for the State of Israel. The first three decades of missteps in the short life of the country had been so overwhelming that those who succeeded Ben-Gurion, of all parties, were unable to reverse the course of such a calamitous trend toward global isolation. The Bengurionites consistently misjudged the growing influence of the international community through the United Nations.[151] There was also a consistent, unpardonable misjudgment of the trend of the noncommunist block to step away from the control of the state over the national economies and the formation of economic and political groups. Israel's foreign policy was at times led by intelligent, yet feeble functionaries. Abba Eban (1915-1992) was an excellent example of the able yet misguided diplomats of Israeli foreign policy. He was an erudite scholar of the Middle East. Born in South Africa and educated at Cambridge University, he served as Israel's ambassador to the United Nations and as Minister of Foreign Affairs. Eban understood the way the world was being transformed, but could not stand up to the mercurial temperament and obstinate ideals of his boss and patron: David Ben-Gurion. Abba Eban worked long and hard to improve relations with the United States, the United Nations, and the Arab world. He was the darling of the American Jewish community because of his enchanting accent and his brilliant scholarship.

Bengurionism and America

A keystone in Bengurionite foreign policy was the deep disdain and mistrust that David Ben-Gurion felt toward the United States and the English-speaking world.[152] In this perspective he was supported by two strong women in his life: his wife Paula and his political associate, Golda Meirson (Meir). He was deeply disappointed by his failed trip to New York during the First World War. Paula Ben-Gurion had been active in the Jewish socialist movement in New York when she married David in 1917. She strenuously disliked the capitalistic nature of her country and never relented in fomenting her husband's disdain for all things American.

Golda Meir (1898-1978) was born in Kiev, in Russian Ukraine. Her family emigrated to the United States in 1906 and settled in Milwaukee, Wisconsin. Golda worked as a teacher in the Milwaukee public schools, married Morris Meirson, and in 1921 emigrated to Palestine.

Although growing up in two different cities in the United States, both women experienced the hardships of Jewish immigration to America in the early part of the twentieth century. The socialist ideas of Jewish workers and social justice were a common cause widely embraced by both women. Such zeal, laced with frustration and the impacts of the stark economic realities of their communities, had inflamed in them the views that America represented the epitome of social and economic evils, and that only a Jewish homeland, based on socialist ideals of what they perceive to be justice and equality, would be the solution to the Jewish problem.

As they rose to power on the coat-tails of David Ben-Gurion, these women were unable to shed the image of the evil America, a champion of what they perceived to be social and economic injustices, lust for money, and the anathema to the socialist experiment so marvelously established in the Soviet Union, and later in the post-colonial developing countries. It is not surprising that Golda Meir was a catalyst in fomenting Israel's warm relations with the nascent African nations throughout the 1950s and even through the 1970s.[153]

Egged on by these powerful influences in his life, Ben-Gurion viewed American Jewry not as partners in the building of the Jewish homeland but as wealthy and misguided products of the corrupt economic American system of government. At best, he viewed America as the home of those wealthy Jews whose dollars he desperately needed to build his ideal socialist country. He could unashamedly utilize the favorable, even enthusiastic sentiment of American Jews for Israel so that they could influence the foreign policy of the United States in Israel's favor, and lavishly fund the Jewish homeland where "Jews without money" were being settled and indoctrinated in the Bengurionist principles of the socialist agenda of "truth" and "justice." Ben-Gurion's stance toward America and American Jews was the application of what Lenin once described as "useful idiots"—those unsuspecting citizens of the Western democracies who support the socialist agenda to the delight of the "true" socialists.

Ben-Gurion's dislike of the United States received a boost during the 1956 war in the Sinai, in which the United Kingdom and France joined Israel in an attempt to oust Egyptian dictator Gamal Abdel Nasser and to occupy the Suez Canal. This military misadventure was foiled by stiff resistance from the United States. President Dwight Eisenhower was not ready to start another global conflict for what he believed to be one final attempt of the European empires to delay the loss of their foreign possessions. The leaders of France, Britain, and Israel felt betrayed by the Americans.[154] Ben-Gurion never forgave what he considered to be the perfidy of President Eisenhower, his foreign secretary John Foster Dulles, and America in general. In his anti-American sentiment he met the new French leader, General Charles DeGaulle, who became president of France in 1958. The Francophiles in Ben-Gurion's inner circle, led by Shimon Peres, thus became the commanding force in shaping Israeli foreign policy away from the United States.

When John F. Kennedy replaced Eisenhower as president, Ben-Gurion went to meet the new American leader. Their encounter in May 1961 was a crucial development in Israeli-American relations. Ben-Gurion considered the meeting to be a major disappointment, and the new president as a young, shallow product of the American media. He discounted Kennedy's intellectual skills and his strategic outlook on the world. Although President Kennedy did not exercise much pressure on the Israeli Prime Minister to allow more transparency in his nuclear initiatives,[155] the meeting with the new American leadership team convinced Ben-Gurion that his contempt of America had been wholly justified and vindicated.

When Ben-Gurion met President Kennedy in Vienna on May 30, 1961 he considered Kennedy as the embodiment of the vacuous Americans who ascended to power because of his family and its treasure. The naval hero of the Second World War perhaps reminded Ben-Gurion of Lieutenant Monroe Fein (1923-1982), a decorated Jewish-American naval officer who served with distinction in the Pacific theater of war. Fein commanded the *Altalena*, the ship shelled and sunk by the Bengurionites on June 20, 1948. He was one of the most loathed people in the nascent state. Following the sinking of the ship, he was arrested by the Bengurionites with other political figures of Begin's organization aboard the ship, such as Eliyahu Lankin.

Arthur Schlesinger's account of the Kennedy presidency (*A Thousand Days*, Houghton Mifflin 1965, pp. 104-106) had described the evolution of Kennedy as an intellectual, An analysis of what transpired in the meeting between Kennedy and Ben-Gurion indicates that Ben-Gurion—like other dictators before him, such as Stalin—completely misjudged the makeup of what the United States stood for and its power, not only as an economic and industrial giant, but also as a fountainhead of ideas, innovation, justice, and progress.

Ben-Gurion lacked the intellectual capabilities to understand the meaning of America's standing in the world. He considered America to be a country of cowboys and playboys, of a people whose main interest in life was the maximizing of pleasurable activities, at the expense of all else, In contrast, leaders like Hitler, Stalin, and Ben-Gurion were busy building a nation, armed with deep ideological foundations of patriotism and fear and hatred of all enemies, internal and external. Ben-Gurion seemed to have failed to grasp the qualities of American presidents as men of integrity, peace, ideas, and good will for their country and for other people.

Both Kennedy and Ben-Gurion disliked each other on a basic, almost primeval level—with grave consequences for the Bengurionite state. Kennedy saw in Ben-Gurion a medieval leader, detached from the modern era, which Kennedy espoused and represented in the Post World War II period. To Kennedy, Ben-Gurion must have appeared to be a socialist ideologue with implacable and unmovable opinions and an innate ability to compromise, even to negotiate, while clinging to his power at all cost. As Schlesinger concluded, Kennedy had mastered the ability to inhabit both sides of an issue and to approach politics and power with the humility of a decision-maker who possesses much less information that he desperately needs for a reasoned decision. Ben-Gurion seemed like a leader who had all the answers, and who is irrevocably on the right side of every issue. It was not until Ben-Gurion's successor, Levi Eshkol, visited Washington in June 1964 to meet with President Lyndon Johnson that Israeli-American relations began to defrost and a true cooperation began to emerge.[156]

Ben-Gurion despised America not as an Israeli or a Jew, but as a socialist. Since the 1920s Ben-Gurion viewed the Soviet form of government as the "great spiritual influence on our movement and our work in Palestine." It is hard for today's citizens in the United States and in Israel to imagine a period when such animosity toward America inhabited the corridors of Israel's political and economic powers. While American companies were heavily investing in Western Europe and in Asia, there were hardly any economic ties in Israel, except in some segments of military cooperation, and mostly in the American companies desire to use Israel's wars on "Beta" testing grounds for their new weapon systems

In the end, Ben-Gurion's foreign policy was a disastrous failure. Over sixty years after the founding of Israel, virtually all the "friends" sought by the Bengurionites among the nations of the world—and the non-aligned countries in particular—have abandoned the Jewish state. Ironically, only the United States, the target of Ben-Gurion's aversion, is today the sole supporter of Israel in world affairs and the predominant force animating the economic well being of the Jewish state.

Bengurionism and the Arabs

Bengurionism was never about peace. As a political being, Ben-Gurion instinctively understood that a peaceful and prosperous country would undermine his regime. Such a country would naturally become more liberal in its economy, which would lead to a more relaxed grip of the government over its economy and social fabric. This was an unacceptable trend. Ben-Gurion had to maintain the sentiment of crisis and the continuing belief that the country stood alone, against a coalition of mortal enemies, In this scenario, he alone was the savior; he alone was the supreme expert on national defense; he alone was the father and the benefactor of his nation. The Soviet dictator Joseph Stalin was his prime example of such a leader. Bengurionism was shaped accordingly.

From the beginning, in his days as a labor organizer, Ben-Gurion despised and ignored the Arabs who lived in Palestine and those in the neighboring countries. His personal contempt for them was instrumental in making Bengurionism an impediment to relationships between Jews and Arabs in Palestine and after 1948 in Israel.

Ben-Gurion's political views again clouded his judgment with respect to the Arabs. He considered them a remnant of feudalism in its worst form of inequality and social injustice. The socialist ideals of the ultimate battle with the forces of capitalism had infused his policies toward the Arabs. The confrontation between Jews and Arabs in Palestine would be not only a clash of religions, but also a conflict between the forces of socialist enlightenment versus the evil of the Arab societies ruled by emirs, kings, and tribal chiefs.

This ideological persistence manifested itself in two related phenomena: neglect in foreign affairs and, internally, the abandonment of regionally-targeted education for generations of Israelis.

In the area of foreign affairs, Bengurionism kept to its implacable socialist ideology that resulted in neglect and avoidance of its neighbors and its own Arab minorities. Since declaring the new state without due process, for the next three decades the Bengurionites avoided all contacts with the *governments* of their neighboring countries. Generations of Israelis were raised and indoctrinated in this policy of insane isolation.[157] The Arab countries had indeed reacted following the 1948 war by declaring an economic embargo on Israel. Yet, throughout Ben-Gurion's years at the helm of Israeli power there were no attempts to seriously open diplomatic channels to the neighboring Arab governments.[158] By acting as if the state of Israel existed in a regional vacuum in the Middle East, the Bengurionites, and even their successors, have consistently exalted the uniqueness in the nature of the Jewish state as the "only democracy in the Middle East" to the "beacon of Western values and modernity" in the region. These terms served merely as an aphoristic description of the conditions of regional isolation of the country.

Even more seriously, the Bengurionites thus abrogated the decisions on the security of their nation to the unstable leadership of armed groups rather than to the governments of the Arab nations—however dictatorial, monarchial or, to the Bengurionites, distastefully unsocialistic they might have been. In the absence of channels to the Arab governments, political and religious "movements" and their armed bands began to emerge and to fill the void of discourse—albeit radicalized and violent—with the Israeli presence in the region. First it was Yasser Arafat and his Fatah movement, followed by a variety of armed groups, initially marginalized, thereafter becoming mainstream parties led by middle-class and well-educated Palestinians and other Arabs.

In their zeal to accumulate and to solidify their internal power and the economic prowess of the state, the Bengurionites inadvertently cooperated with the radical factions in the Arab world to erect a virtual wall around their nation, separating them from their neighbors, without any possibility for diplomatic exchanges.

Internally, the abandonment of any relations with the Arab world manifested itself in the Bengurionite approach to education. The study of the Arab language, Arab culture and customs, and the learning about the Muslim world were not compulsory courses in the curricula of the primary, secondary, and even higher educational institutions in Israel. For the first thirty years of the nation's existence, school-age children could not and did not learn about their neighboring countries. The Ministry of Education had been closely held by the Bengurionite political cronies and his party. Party officials scrupulously determined the curriculum, so the government officially sanctioned the exclusion of all material about the Arab world that surrounded them.

In the traditional universities established before 1998 (the Hebrew University and the Technion) there were no formal studies or departments of Arab language or Islamic culture. The universities of Tel Aviv, Bar-Ilam (a religious college), and Haifa were established in the 1950s and 1960s. There was no concerted effort to found research centers or degree programs on Islam, the Arab world, Arab language and traditions, or the history, economics, and political histories of the Arab countries surrounding the Jewish state.

Since Arabic was not offered as a second language, nor was there any focus on the Arabs and their culture in the Israeli educational system, the vast majority of Israelis had been, and are today, ignorant of their neighbors, their language, and their culture. Their encounters with Arabs have always been limited to the Israeli Arabs and, after June 1967, to the Palestinian Arabs in the territories. Ignorance led to disdain and a lack of respect for the ancient civilization of the Arab world, its achievements, and its contributions to culture, the sciences, mathematics, medicine, and philosophy.

The more the Bengurionites isolated their youth and themselves from the neighboring nations, the more they declared all Arabs to be mortal enemies of Israel and the more they continued to ignore the need to gain knowledge—from a very early age—of what this enemy was like—their language, customs, strengths and weaknesses.[159]

Such a clear policy to exclude Arabic studies from the Israeli educational system can only be explained by the Bengurionite conscious effort—at least in the first three decades of Israel's existence—to limit the nature and the amount of information and knowledge distributed to the Israeli population. With their zealous control of the national media outlets (radio, then television), their application as a powerful censor of the printed press and their furious control of the national educational scene, the Bengurionites were able to foment at least two generations of Israelis who are shamelessly ignorant of their neighbors. The more ignorant the populace about another nation and another people, the more they will accept the pejorative definition of such a people—however outrageous and wrong—that is offered by their controlling government.

After 1967, when a million Palestinian Arabs suddenly became economically intertwined with the Israelis, there was perhaps an opportunity to gain "rapprochement" with the Arabs. But, as usual in Jewish history, it was too little and too late.

Although economic relations between the two populations had begun to bring them together, on the Israeli side the indoctrination of three decades had accomplished its objectives. Israelis viewed their neighbors as an inferior people, enslaved anachronistically to an aggressive and outmoded system of religion and bound by an odious feudal regime of the privileged over the masses.[160]

Bengurionism and the Control over Information

David Ben-Gurion did not understand nor did he wish to understand the power of mass media. Unlike other leaders of his generation, such as Roosevelt and Churchill, he lacked experience in his youth and earlier career to gauge the impact of the media. Roosevelt had been an editor of his university's paper, *The Harvard Crimson,* and Churchill served as a war correspondent in South Africa. Ben-Gurion's central theme was to gain *control of the media* in the country and to limit exposure of his people to means of mass communication. He openly persecuted those elements of the media who displeased him, or those close to him and to his party.

Raviv and Melman (1990) in their book "Every Spy a Prince," although highly impious and obsequious to Ben-Gurion and his associates, described the attempts by the Israeli intelligence apparatus, the Shin Bet ("Security Services") and its leader, Isser Harel, to discredit and ruin a weekly publication *Haolam Hazeh* (*The Current World*). In 1956 the news magazine published reports of corruption in the national police whose chief had been Ben-Gurion's son, Amos Ben-Gurion. The Prime Minister and his cronies never hesitated to use the country's services, military and civilian, even its intelligence agencies, to spy upon those citizens they did not like and to vigorously act to destroy them.

An illuminating example of the Bengurionite policy of restricting the flow of information in the country is the striking absence of public libraries and bookstores in the homeland of the "People of the Book." The concept of the public library never took hold in Israel. Almost every American town has a public library with access to books, newspapers, and other means of information. University towns in the United States, such as Evanston, Ann Arbor, and Berkeley, each have more book stores than the large metropolis of Tel Aviv,[161] although they have a fraction of the population.[162]

The Bengurionites did erect a "Museum of the Book" in the vicinity of Jerusalem, the capital. This is a cold, sterile, unimpressive and useless structure. Its contents are references to past achievements in the generation of books throughout Jewish history. One cannot borrow any of the books in the exhibits. In another venue, universities have their libraries but unauthorized people cannot check out their books—one has to be a student or an employee.

Ben-Gurion was not interested in fomenting culture or libraries. In fact, he considered the diffusion of knowledge via learning and the reading of books by the general populace to be a menace to his ideology and to the aims of his party and the trade unions.

In addition to the absence of libraries, the Bengurionite regime was also in control of the radio and other telecommunication venues in Israel. This control continues today by means of the Broadcasting Authority— the agency in charge of both radio and television broadcasting in the country. The authority was set up originally as a copy of the British Broadcasting Corporation. Over time it acquired additional powers to exclude any private use of the airways and to control and censor the contents of broadcasting.

Ben-Gurion himself strenuously opposed the introduction of television in Israel. He instinctively understood the power of this medium to shape and influence political ideas, careers, and discourse. Only after his total retirement from political life were Israelis allowed to entertain the establishment of television stations—albeit under the strict ownership and control of the government.[163]

Perhaps the most telling example of the control of information is the story of Israel's history of the establishment of the telephone network in the country. Aware of the Jewish tendency to excel in person-to-person communication, Ben-Gurion devised the most ingenious method of limiting such exchange by imposing extraordinary constraints on the diffusion and use of telephones by Israelis. During his twenty-year reign the telephone was considered and officially declared by the government a "luxury item" and an instrument of frivolity and sheer self-indulgence—hence necessarily only for important government functionaries or emergency personnel such as physicians. This was a marvelously devised euphemism for the Bengurionite control of the telephone as a means of rapid communication across distances.

The resulting situation was immensely detrimental to the operation of the country's modern army. One outcome was that while the Western world was awash in telephones, in Israel this device was severely limited and scrupulously budgeted, to be allocated to the deserving few by indisputable government criteria of worth. This also led to the unbelievable reality of how Israel called to arms its army of reservists. As a military force that relies primarily on its rapid mobilization of reserve officers and soldiers, during the first 30 years of its existence, the Israel Defense Forces (IDF) relied on an antiquated system of communication which was originally developed by the French resistance to Nazi occupation during the Second World War.

As an emergency arose, the IDF would use radio broadcasts to alert its personnel. Each unit had been assigned coded messages such as "Red Sheet," "Long Horn," or "Green Valley." Israeli radio stations, under the control of the government,[164] broadcast news every hour on the hour. The messages would thus be continuously broadcasted, as did the French resistance in its broadcasts from London to its cells of resistance in occupied France. Since it was utterly impossible to reach most Israelis by phone, this antiquated system of broadcasted messages was deemed necessary and effective. As late as on the eve of the 1973 war, when there was little time to mobilize and to face a war on two fronts (Egypt and Syria), the IDF had to resort to the system of coded messages.

But, despite the effort by the Bengurionites to limit and control the flow of information, there was in the Jewish state a continuous *informal* network of information gathering and sharing. The small size of the population, its life of dangers and constant security, threats, and the influx of Jews from Western Europe and principally from the United States—all have contributed to the desire for more transparency in the flow of information and ultimately, in the late 1980s, to the softening of restrictions on the ability of the larger population to own and use telephones. Yet, as long as Ben-Gurion was in power and as long as he was alive, the means of telecommunication remained a government-controlled resource, to be allocated to party officials and to those in the favor of the ruling functionaries—even if the consequences of such restrictions were detrimental to national security and to the Army's ability to quickly and massively mobilize its troops.

Bengurionism and Life in the "Promised Land"

The Jews in 1948 Palestine had allowed an uneducated and megalomaniac leader to assume political and economic power without representation, consultation, elections or deliberations. He forged a country and its institutions according to his distorted views. Ben-Gurion considered himself a genius in military affairs, institution building, foreign affairs, literature, even the correct usage of the Hebrew language. He copied all that was lacking in the formation and life of the Soviet Union and none of the greatness of the West. He also continued some of the failing traditions of Jewish isolationism and tribal discord, internecine hatred, and rabbinical control.

The fall of the Hebrew monarchy, when King David and his son Solomon focused on the tribe of Judah and ancillary tribes, they sidelined and discriminated against the Northern tribes, particularly Ephraim and Menashe. To these Hebrew monarchs these tribes were simply a source of income through increasingly harsh, even intolerable taxation, and also a source of manpower for their armies. This was precisely what Ben-Gurion had done to the business community that he now controlled, and how he viewed the population, except for those citizens who were party members or at least supporters of his ideals. Bengurionism was and remains the essence of the country.

In the mode repeatedly seen in the history of the Jewish people, the choice of David Ben-Gurion and his cronies as leaders of the newly created homeland resulted in a country in which daily life has become a difficult and unenviable existence. Bengurionism has created two very distinct economic and social divisions within the small country of Israel. The first is a striking distinction between a tiny group of very wealthy families and a large majority of under-employed citizens (primarily immigrants from Arab countries and North Africa), many of whom live below the poverty line. The Bengurionite ideals of Berl's philosophy of a socialized government economy run by trade unions and dispensing economic favors to the larger population have terribly soured under Bengurionism. The numbers are painfully revealing.

Sixteen families own over 20 percent of all the business revenues in the country through 500 companies that employ over 100 thousand workers. Many of these companies receive government subsidies.[165] By contrast, foreign companies account for only nine percent of total revenues and employ 84 thousand people.[166] This makes the Israeli economy one of the most concentrated economies in the world.

Side by side with public enterprises, privately held companies, highly concentrated in the hands of the very few, exist in a marvelous exchange of favors and benefits. In 2005 the public sector accounted for some 40 percent of leading companies, but these included much of the infrastructure of the nation, such as the utilities and heavy industries. As the country evolved, the Bengurionites began transferring much of the public sector to very selected private owners through politically animated maneuvers. At the same time, unemployment in 2005 reached 10 percent and over 20 percent of families lived below the poverty level.

More recent studies paint an even darker picture. A 2013 study by the Israel National Council for the Child showed that 33.7% of Israel's children lived in poverty, and that this number had quadrupled since 1980. In 2013 a poverty study by the highly-respected Organization for Economic Cooperation and Development (OECD) showed that Israel leads the developed countries as the country with the highest poverty rate. This report found the poverty rate of 21%, almost double what it was in 1995 (13.8%), and the income gaps between a small set of rich families and the rest of the population continued to widen.

Bengurionism and the Culture of Favoritism

Over four decades have passed since David Ben-Gurion relinquished power and died in 1973. However, his legacy, "Bengurionism," has lasted and is present today in nearly every aspect of Israeli society, economy, and its government. Although several individuals have assumed the leadership of the Israeli government since Ben-Gurion's departure from political life, his imprimatur on how daily life transpires in the Jewish state has remained unchanged and barely challenged over the years.[167]

In the early years of the Jewish state, affairs of the government were conducted via the culture of the "Petek" (a written note). Government services—from allocation of housing to jobs—all depended on a government functionary or a union operative sending a note to the respective bureaucrat. With the passage of time the system has evolved to rely on complex processes of selection and allocation of government favors—but even today all depends on the approval by government officials whose key selection criterion is political clout. This has led to the strengthening of a "culture of corruption" and cronyism.

In the Bengurionite system of government, true facts, simple justice, the proud history of a citizen, and the provisions of orderly ministered procedures are by and large subordinated to political connections. Unless the citizen has such connections, and few do indeed belong to this privileged group, there is virtually little recourse and few means to rectify the government's flexing of its internal political muscle.

A major illustration of this phenomenon was the uprooting in 2006 of the settlements in the Gaza Strip. After providing incentives for settlers to inhabit these parcels of land, the government ordered their evacuation, an action that led to violence and scenes of emotional disconnect between citizens and their government. A year later, Benjamin Netanyahu, the former Prime Minister and an ardent advocate for the privatization of the Israeli economy, called for the abolition of the Authority of the Land of Israel. This is a government body, uniquely created by Bengurionism, which owns and controls 93 percent of the land of the State of Israel.[168]

A minor illustration of the power wielded by such government organizations over home ownership in Israel is the case of an elderly widow and her painful experience with the Bengurionite regime. In the early 1960s, the Israeli government provided incentives for its citizens to move into housing hastily constructed in the Negev desert. The widow had rented a small apartment in the city of Beer-Sheba where she resided for over two decades. She maintained the apartment in immaculate shape and always paid her rent to the government authority, via deductions from her salary, as she managed a municipal day care center for the blind and the elderly. In the early 1980s she traveled abroad to visit with her children and grandchildren. A neighbor in the building coveted the apartment and filed a false report with the housing authority that the resident had abandoned the apartment. Because of the complainant's political connections, the regional office of the housing authority immediately and without due process or investigation issued a notice of eviction to vacate the apartment within 90 days. Terrified and bewildered, she hurried back to salvage her decades-long residence, but to no avail. The Bengurionite Byzantine bureaucracy of the housing authority had made its decision and stuck by it.

The family intervened and various meetings were arranged with officials of the government. In one such meeting, the following exchange took place.[169] Family: "She has done nothing wrong, why don't you investigate the facts." Government official: "She will be evicted and if she does not vacate, we will use force and throw her things onto the street." Family: "Where will she go?" Government official: "Not our problem. As far as we are concerned, she can go live with relatives." Family: "But she lived in the apartment for twenty years, all her friends and her job are here." Government official: "None of our business—we don't care."

The family then consulted several attorneys, who expressed severe doubts that there would be any legal recourse. After weeks of despair, the family turned to a cousin who was a reputable journalist and a former comrade-in-arms of Menachem Begin during the struggle against the British Mandate in Palestine. He journeyed to Jerusalem where he met with a senior official of the housing authority. In his report of the meeting, lasting only twenty minutes, the cousin explained to the official the *political* implications from this case and the damage that this could cause to the officials in the government. By the end of that business day the order of eviction had been rescinded.[170] This incident illustrates the troubling working of the Bengurionite regime.[171] The cold, callous, and Byzantine behavior of the omnipotent government officials is typical of the congruence of the legacy of the Ottoman rule in the Middle East and the Jewish tradition of Rabbinical undisputed power over their subordinates. These traditions had coalesced within the Bengurionite formulation of the Israeli regime.[172]

To the officials in the Bengurionite regime, it did not matter that the elderly widow they were about to callously evict was a member of a family who resided in the land for several generations, and whose men and women were veterans of all the wars of the Jewish establishment, first in Palestine, later in Israel: from the struggle against the Turkish Empire, the British Mandate, the War for Independence in 1948, and all subsequent conflicts. It did not matter that her husband fought in the War of Independence, her brother had been wounded in that war, and that her son was a veteran of the 1967 and 1973 wars. None of this mattered; what counted and what truly animated decision making in this regime was political clout.[173]

Scared, bewildered, and angry because of these Byzantine practices of an indifferent bureaucracy that practically dominates all aspects of the economy, Israelis react in several ways to ensure their survival and to facilitate a sensible navigation through this maze of government agencies. They find ways to bypass the system; they resort to violence and intimidation in government offices; they form new fringe political parties (such as the party of the "retirees"); and, finally, they act dramatically by leaving the country altogether.[174]

The Bengurionite legacy has generated several cycles of transformations in the economic, political, and social tapestry of Israeli life. Although some initiatives for change have been introduced by the new generation of leaders, the core of the Bengurionite failure has remained largely untouched. Four alarming trends can be identified, leading to the possibility of a potentially calamitous event in the foreseeable future.[175]

There is a trend of decline in the social and economic position of the Jewish state, both at home and in the international scene. Israel is the least preferred country in world opinion for investment, travel, and the desire to learn about its history, people, and culture.[176] Inside Israel there is a dangerously alarming sentiment in the population of despair. Almost 1/3 of university students have some form of depression requiring psychological or psychiatric treatment.[177]

Israelis are also showing a decline in the sentiment of pride they feel for their country. In 1948, during the war for independence of the Jewish state and before the advent of Bengurionism, all able-bodied citizens had volunteered to serve the emerging country in its military conflict. My father, my uncles, and my cousins all served with distinction. In 2006 almost one in five young Israelis said they would refuse to fight in its wars, and almost *half of them* would seriously consider emigrating if they could have a better life in another country.

From the beginning, the Bengurionite social agenda has been a fascinating amalgam of socialist charity and the merciless flexing of government power. By controlling the citizenry's housing and land ownership, the Bengurionites did not necessarily execute their prerogatives of taking properties away from residents by evicting them as a measure of perverse pleasure of almighty bureaucrats. Rather, this constituted the means to exercise immense impact over the most precious and most coveted asset in the Middle Eastern tapestry of politics, religion, and economics—the land. Government ownership of the land satisfied the strange combine of socialism and Orthodox Judaism, which was Berl Katznelson's core principle and became the enduring ideal of Bengurionism.[178] The lack of the orderly succession to Ben-Gurion's powerful reign over Israeli body politic has also contributed to this trend. After David Ben-Gurion the political elite at first accepted his lieutenants (Eshkol and Meir), followed by Menachem Begin and his underling (Shamir). The following string of Prime Ministers consisted primarily of retired generals (Rabin, Barak, and Sharon). None of them has been able to form or create an alternative to Bengurionism—hence the continuing influence of this system of government, regardless of the crop of leaders and their ideological affinities.

The second trend, to an extent the result of the Byzantine decadence of Bengurionism, is the continuously endemic corruption in the political and economic aspects of Israeli government. In 2006, for example, there were indictments of bank officials, treasuring officials in the tax departments, senior police commanders, and even the Minister of the Treasury was being investigated. Allegations against the President of the country and another Minister (Haim Ramon) resulted in the trial of the latter and his conviction for sexual assault.

The alarming aspect of this massive array of indictments, investigations, and convictions by the obsequious courts of the country is the sentiment among the elite and in the general population that "those at the top" are immune from any prosecution and that they effectively "own" the country.

In many ways the climate of decadence and corruption is the norm rather than the exception in the Middle East. Although Israel proclaims itself to be the "only *true* democracy" in the region, a closer observation of its Byzantine form of government and its ubiquitous climate of corruption and undeterred exercise of power leads one to the conclusion that such a system is hardly a "true" democracy.

The Bengurionite period of the early two decades of the reinvented Jewish homeland can be described as the "Dark Ages" of the country. During this period the roots of decadence and corruption had been established. The Palestinian problem was created and, as a consequence, there emerged the militant revolutionary branch of the Palestinians, led by Yasser Arafat (1929-2004). This was also the period in which Israel's isolationist stance in world affairs began to emerge. In this period there was a continuous exhaustion of the positive emotional capital felt by the world community towards the Jewish people and their sufferings during the years of the Nazi Holocaust. Current crises in the region are a direct result of this Bengurionite age.

In contrast with European history after the Middle Ages, there was no period of Renaissance in the short history of the country. The trends begun in the Bengurionite "Dark Ages" continued, some have even alarmingly intensified. The meeting between David Ben-Gurion and President John F. Kennedy exemplified this pattern of the Bengurionite rule in darkness. The American president represented a new and re-energized country. His call to his people still echoes: "Ask not what your country can do for you, ask what you can do for your country." The Bengurionite motto had always been: "Ask your country what it can do for you, and obtain as much as you can with whatever political connections you can muster." During Ben-Gurion's "Dark Ages," the notion of "Zionism" in Israeli culture had been radically transformed from self-sacrifice for the homeland to merely the means to improving one's material existence. The American president was a messenger of revival and a bright future, while the Israeli Prime Minister was the tired, dark, and incompetent leader with only his union organizer credentials at his disposal. Ben-Gurion was a sorry figure, much like King Herod (73-4 B.C.E.), the unpopular ruler of Judea, a decaying vassal state wholly dependent on the good will of the Roman emperor.

Perhaps the most alarming and potentially calamitous trend of the Bengurionite legacy is the rapid descent of the Jewish homeland toward the realities of a theocratic state. The core of the country's being is rapidly, dramatically, and irreversibly changing.

The Rise of Jewish Orthodoxy and Extremism: Toward the Theocratic Jewish Homeland

Several factors have contributed to the phenomenon of the rise of religious orthodoxy in the reformulated homeland of the Jewish people. This reverses almost two centuries of the enlightenment movement of European Jewry with its many progressive ideals that the movement had engendered. Even the ideal of the independent homeland as a *political* entity for the Jews in the global landscape is irrevocably being challenged by the growing orthodoxy.

The first factor is the direct consequence of Berl Katznelson's philosophy "gone bad"—when applied by the Bengurionites as the state's political, social, and economic policy. Berl's dream aspired to merging religion and socialism. Its application in a real-life platform of the country and its various and conflicting segments of the population resulted in the nightmarish situation of offering the religious minority the "keys to the store."

Following the Berl Katznelson philosophy, the Bengurionite regime gave the religious parties and their various organizations a plethora of economic, political, and social favors. They were allowed to establish their own "state within a state," complete with their own laws and customs and free of the obligations of all other secular Israelis, in particular military service and crucial forms of taxation. The religious minorities, orthodox and ultra-orthodox, were allowed to live their lives as they had done in the European Diaspora: on the fringes of the political regime, with few links to the world outside their ghetto-like existence.

However, the more ominous outcome of the Bengurionite catering to the isolationist wishes of this estranged community of orthodox Jews in the state of Israel is the degree to which their influence far exceeded their numbers or contributions to the welfare of the state. In the misguided quest for the semblance of the Jewishness of the country, the Bengurionites gave the orthodox minority the power to manage the cultural and personal lives of *all* Israelis, however secular they may be. Personal life is managed according to the strictest rules of the Jewish religion, orchestrated and run by orthodox rabbinical courts and judges. Thus, all affairs of marriage, divorce, administration of religious sites, citizenship rights, births and deaths, and a host of favors and rights (such as allocation of resources for religious education and exemption from military service) were left to the discretion of these rabbinical institutions.[179]

The Threat of Demographic Trends

Jews in Israel generally consider the growth patterns of their Arab countrymen and neighbors a threat to the "Jewishness" of their state. In recent years, however, the demographic trends of Jewish orthodoxy have been discussed as "the *other* demographic threat" to the identity of the secular Jewish homeland.[180] There are four distinct categories of Jews in Israel, classified by the level of religious observance. The first is the group of non-observant or totally secular. In 2007 they comprised about 25 percent of the country's five million Jewish inhabitants. The second category consists of the semi-secularists who observe the high holidays and other festivals such as Passover and Hanukah. They comprise about 40 percent. The third category comprises traditionally observant-orthodox Jews (10 percent) and ultra-orthodox (20 percent).

This segment of about a third of the Jewish population, particularly the 20 percent ultra-orthodox, is the subject of the hidden threat to the future of the reinvented Jewish homeland. The menace of this segment of the population lies in the set of their beliefs and in their very high rate of demographic growth.

This unique growth is fueled by a fantastic birth rate. The "Haredi" or ultra-orthodox average over 7 births per woman, or a growth rate of about 6 percent per year for this segment of the population. This birth rate is three times the rate for the entire Israeli population, and about 50 percent higher than the Palestinian natural growth of about 4.4 percent per year. There is, however, a crucial difference between the two segments. Palestinians also have a high rate of infant mortality as compared with the ultra-orthodox community.[181]

This trend of unparalleled natural growth is reflected in the country's educational system. According to Israeli government statistics, in 1995 one in ten Israeli pupils was enrolled in the religious educational system. In 2009 the ratio was estimated at one in four. In 2009 the number of pupils in the national (non-religious) system of compulsory education (K-12) had actually decreased by over 70 thousand children.

From a negligible and estranged minority that openly opposed the creation of the Zionist State of Israel in 1948, the ultra-orthodox community has grown to almost a quarter of the population in sixty years. Its political power has also grown to the point where it currently dominates the issues it considers of critical impotence to its set of religious beliefs. In the next two decades this community may be more than half the population, overtaking the secular majority—all with unimaginable and menacing consequences.[182]

Setting the Stage for Disaster

The menace of the ultra-religious segment in Israel is perhaps one of the key elements of the approaching disaster in the future of the reinvented homeland. The decline of secularism and the emergence of extremist religious power in Israel politics was a direct consequence of the failures of Bengurionism. By and large Israeli leaders were petty politicians with little education and, in the Bengurionite tradition, puny in their quest for power and resources. These attributes contributed to the facility with which strong ties were established between the Bengurionites and the religious extremists in Israeli politics. The last Israeli leader to directly oppose the religious factions was General Ariel (Arik) Sharon.

The stage was thus set for the unholy alliance between the two factions for the grabbing of power and resources. The only victim is the country whose future is wrapped in the nebulous blanket of impending disaster.

Why Is This Scenario So Alarming?

An important thesis of this narrative is that the decline in Israeli secularism and the rise of the religious orthodoxy promises a potential overtaking of the nuclear arsenal by the religious authorities of the Jewish state. In previous chapters it was clearly described how relatively easy it can be to get hold of the nuclear weapons of a nation. As I stood with a few men, poorly armed, against an organized military force whose sole aim was the control of the weapon of mass destruction, it became abundantly clear to me that this scenario can repeat itself in years to come, in any country, and with even more determined and more ardent and committed a group than Colonel Yaakov and the generals who sent him.

In the first decade of the 21st century there has been much discussion and deliberations among the world's powers concerning the perils of smaller nations led by zealous dictators acquiring weapons of mass destruction. These concerns continue into the second decade of this century, and undoubtedly will continue and will intensify into the future. In the case of orthodox Jewish leaders taking control of the state of Israel, as well as of its nuclear arsenal, there is a heightened possibility that the apocalyptic perspective of such leaders in which is embedded their desire to hasten the coming of the Messiah will facilitate their willingness to deploy these weapons against their Arab neighbors. This is indeed an extremely frightening scenario—and a very possible one.

The Notion of the "Jewish" State of Israel

There is a continuing debate in Israel regarding the notion of the state as a "Jewish" state. The country lacks a constitution, hence there is not a coherent definition of what the "Jewishness" of the state means to its inhabitants as well as its neighbors. The Bengurionite government has generally referred to this notion in terms of a "nationality", so that the political entity named "Israel" is the nation of the *Jewish* people, characterized by a unique culture, tradition, history, language, and religion.

This definition is not received favorably by Israel's neighbors, particularly the Palestinians. Although the Balfour Declaration of 1947 has defined the land as a "Jewish State", the Palestinians argue that such a definition established the *legal* control of the land by the Jews—at the expense of the Palestinians, especially in contested parcels of land such as Jerusalem, religious sites that are sacred to Muslims, and other areas of the West Bank. These conflicting definitions of who "owns" the land have been a strong impediment to agreements needed in the peace process between Palestinians and Israelis.[183]

However, the lack of clarity of what constitutes the "Jewishness" of the state of Israel is more troubling in its *internal* implications, rather than as a problem in the peace process. Whatever the definition, it clearly includes the religious aspect of the Jewish people inhabiting this parcel of land. The Israeli government has argued that Israel is to the Jews what, for example, France is to the French, Ireland is to the Irish, and Japan to the Japanese. However, these comparisons do not include a religious component that France and Ireland are members of the Catholic, Apostolic, and Roman Church. Ireland, for instance, is divided among Catholics and Protestants. There is no inherent definition of Japan as a country of a people practicing a mix of Shintoism and Buddhism. Thus, as the religious attribute is introduced, it becomes a "slippery slope" of a discriminatory instrument to be applied by the orthodoxy *within* the country.

The Test To Determine "Who is a Jew"?

Once the definition of the political entity is imbued with the notion of a "Jewish" state, this invariably brings about the issue of "Who is a Jew?". This issue has been debated in Israel for several decades, but it is intensifying as the influence of Orthodox Judaism takes over larger chunks of political and economic power. Initially designed to facilitate the integration into Israeli society of Jews from many different countries, customs, and religious practices, this concept has evolved into a dangerous component of the selection of people for legal, ethical, religious, political, and economic purposes.

Specifically, this concept entails a "test" of *Who is a Jew to* determine the viability of the person to be labeled as a "Jew".

Any evaluation scheme, whereupon an individual is categorized according to certain criteria, positions the individual in a certain group and separates the individual from other groups. This leads to a stereotyping effect. When widely applied across the population in Israel, this test will lead to the generation of distinct groups of citizens, some of whom will be privileged (those who pass the test) and some of whom will lack certain privileges (as determined by the government agencies responsible for the test).

As an evaluation scheme, the key criterion of *"Who is a Jew?"* is religious. The simplest criterion used by Jewish religious authorities has been the proven fact that a person is born to a Jewish woman. Since in the past it was difficult to prove the identity of the father, the best evidence was the identity of the mother as Jewish. However, in the present state of improved technology and the increasing integration of the Orthodox Rabbinical rule into the political and economic affairs of the state of Israel, the criteria that can and will be used for the test will dramatically change to go well beyond the religious identity of the mother. The test can and will rely on the following criteria: 1) the traditional background check of the mother and father as belonging to the Jewish faith. This criterion will have measures such as the number of generations which can be certified as having been Jewish. For example, were the grandparents and great-grandparents Jewish? 2) Use of DNA testing of the person and comparing it with the DNA of his/her ancestry. But, the most vexatious and terrifying criterion will be 3) the person's *behavior* as a Jew. This criterion will measure the behavior of the person as an observant Jew. Does the person practice Judaism as dictated by the rabbinical authorities? Does the person observe the festivals and the rituals as specified by the orthodox authorities?

Once implemented, this test will require Jews in Israel to be vigilant with the daily behavior of their neighbors and to continually inform the authorities of any deviation from the orthodox practice of the religion. Any pejorative talk or negative discussion of the religion and its rituals must be reported to the authorities. The key to the harmonious existence of the community is absolute *conformity*. The history of the Jewish people in its Diaspora has numerous examples of the rabbinical insistence on absolute obedience and conformity. The rationale for such demand has been the peril in which the community always found itself, hated and threatened by external forces. This same argument is alive and well in today's modern Bengurionite state.

The result will be a climate of forced adherence to the most extreme tenets of the religion and of social behavior and political beliefs. Any difference of opinions will not be tolerated and will be severely punished, not only with the denial of services and rights but also with the ultimate weapon of religious excommunication, which, in this scenario, will be akin to social, political, and economic excommunication. Moreover, a non-practicing Israeli Jew will be punished not for what he/she has done, but for what he/she has *not* done—namely, the failure to practice the Jewish religious rituals in a manner acceptable to the orthodox rabbinical authorities.

The implications of the test in daily life are many. In the *economic* arena, government benefits can be denied to secular Jews and to Gentiles who reside in Israel. Since Bengurionism already consists of a tight grasp over the economy, it will be a very easy transition to allow the capability of the orthodoxy to control the flow of government grants, goods, and services to the populace. A religious "clean bill of adherence" will be required for state services such as licenses to operate businesses, social security and health care insurance, and housing benefits. The latter is already being practiced in the settlements around Jerusalem. Some of these settlements are funded by wealthy American ultra-orthodox Jews. These settlements only accept individuals as residents who abide by the most stringent criteria of religious observance. All other Jews need not apply. These settlements are, for all practical purposes, "ghetto-like" enclaves, highly selective in who can and cannot join them.

In the *employment* impacts of the application of the test, the orthodox authorities will restrict government employment to citizens who are acceptable orthodox Jews. In certain government agencies and ministries in today's Israel this is already the case. The ministries under the control of the orthodox and ultra-orthodox parties already apply discriminatory practices in the hiring of their functionaries.

The *legal* and *judicial* implications of the test are even more troublesome. The orthodoxy-controlled government may deny *documents* to those citizens who fail the test. Currently, most of the legal instances in a citizen's personal life are controlled by the religious authorities. Marriages and divorces are notable examples. With the results of the test at their disposal, the orthodox authorities may deny the citizen who fails the test such documents as: a passport to leave the country, and permits to marry and to divorce and remarry. The children of these citizens will become pariahs in their community and in their schools.

Secular Israelis will now face the challenge of a choice between two options: conform to the rule of the state and practice the rituals of the religion, albeit one is opposed to such behavior, or rebel against them and be forced to become a second-rate citizen and be forced or encouraged to leave the country—with the sad proviso that the state may deny them the issuance of a passport, or any other travel documents.

In so many ways, this regime will be doing to selected segments of its Jewish population what others have done to the Jews throughout the centuries. Antisemitism has always been a scourge on the human experience. But, Jew-on-Jew hatred and discrimination for the sake of orthodox zealotry is unimaginably terrifying in the context of Jewish history. If this is the next face of the "Jewish Homeland", and those who refuse to practice its orthodoxy are forced to leave,[184] where will the non-orthodox Jews who failed the test go? Where will *their* homeland be?

The discrimination against secular Israelis will ultimately lead to another wave of massive emigration. A similar episode in Jewish history was the emigration of Jews from Catholic Spain. One of those who emigrated was Maimonides (1138-1204) who left Cordoba for Egypt, where he and his followers contributed their immense skills to the Cairo caliphate. When secular Israelis will leave Israel, they will take with them their technical and entrepreneurial skills—as many have been doing since the birth of the State. The result will be a continuing descent into economic downturn and increased poverty. Recently, the OECD has already issued a damning report on the level of Israeli poverty. This trend will intensify and the more the economy falters, the more stringent, unbending, and isolationist will be the orthodox authorities.

The Teacher and the Rabbi

This is a case of an American teacher who was a secular Jew. In the 1980s he filed a lawsuit in an American court for the right of visitation with his two children. He had divorced his wife and she had custody of two of the couple's three children. The former wife, who had been secular, converted after the divorce to ultra-orthodox Judaism. Upon refusing to allow visitation, the teacher decided to sue. Within a month, the teacher's lawyer had a message from the former wife's lawyer that a local rabbi had volunteered his services in this case, to try and persuade the former wife to allow visitation. The lawyer recommended that the teacher agree to this gesture. The rabbi was a known figure in the city, had a law practice, and had dabbled in municipal politics. But, his intentions were not to assist, but to take over the case. Instead of assisting in the case, the rabbi interjected himself into the case as a third lawyer, with the pretext of caring for the welfare of the children. He convinced the teacher's lawyer that he would be named "attorney ad leitem" in order to convince the former wife that he was acting on behalf of the children.

This was a ploy. An attorney ad leitem in the American legal system is a lawyer who acts on behalf of children and who represents their interests. As very quickly the matter unfolded, the rabbi/lawyer had not the interests of the children in mind, but the interests of the former wife and his perspective of the nature of Judaism. Although the teacher hired a different lawyer to represent him, the court refused to vacate the order, which made the rabbi the attorney for the children. The rabbi then proceeded to interview the teacher and the other child of the couple whom the teacher was raising under his custody. By applying a variety of legal maneuvers, the rabbi, who was also a good friend and collaborator of the attorney of the former wife, had gained control over the case and was able to extend it for five long years for a case which should have ended in a few weeks. Six different judges were sequentially assigned to the case or had some input into it.

Although the teacher had impeccable credentials as a family man, a devoted father and husband, and was a highly respected member of the community, the rabbi insisted that because the teacher was not a religious Jew, the teacher should be denied visitation, in any form, even with supervision. In the interviews he held with the teacher the rabbi said: "I'll do everything in my power to prevent you from seeing your children. I don't care if you pay for their support or that you are a good man. You are not a religious Jew, therefore you have no right to see your children."[185]

The teacher responded that he was a Jew and that he had a distinguished Jewish family tree. The rabbi replied with contempt: "I interviewed your daughter and she told me that you do not celebrate most of the important festivals in the religious calendar. She said that you celebrate Hanukah, which is hardly an important festival. You do not keep a total "kosher" household, and you don't practice the daily routines of a Jew. How can I allow the children to spend any time with you? In my eyes you are less than a Gentile. You are nothing; you are not a person. You will never see your children! Never!"

The teacher asked: how could a rabbi utter these words four decades after the Holocaust, and how could he exhibit such hatred for a fellow Jew? The rabbi was adamant: "You are nothing to me! I cannot allow true Jewish children to be associated with you or with their sister who has been influenced by you. To me and to true Judaism you don't exist, so you don't have any rights."

"But you are a lawyer in America. How can you talk about taking away a person's rights?" asked the teacher in his despair. The rabbi quickly replied: "I am not talking as a lawyer. The law is not as important to me as my role as defender of true Judaism. If not for the order of the court, I would not even waste my time talking to you or to your family. To me and to Judaism, you are a non-entity." The teacher ended the interview and walked toward the door. He paused at the door and just before he left, said: "These words are exactly those used by the Nazis as an excuse to exterminate a large portion of my family and the Jewish people. They did not ask how many important festivals each Jew celebrated. They just killed them all. I am glad to see that you are a more refined and discriminating person".

This case illustrates the nature of rabbinical Judaism, its intransigence and its intolerance. One should reflect upon the possibility of entrusting to these leaders a country armed with nuclear weapons. Admittedly, dictatorial regimes and those led by a monolithic single political party tend to be intolerant. However, there are exceptions whereby even ardent followers of a *political* or *economic* fundamental credo will behave in a rational and compromising manner. The Soviet leadership during the Cold War exhibited such behavior and, although armed with weapons of mass destruction, chose peaceful and deliberative means to resolve conflicts with the West. As this case illustrates, this may not be the case with the ultra-orthodox takeover of the Bengurionite state and its arsenal. Gentiles and secular Jews will initially be treated as second-class citizens, and then will be asked to permanently leave the orthodox enclave that will thus be "purified" of any external influences.

Where Are The Secular Israelis?

The Bengurionites and the orthodox leaders in Israel were able to form an enduring alliance partly because both had similar key characteristics. Although inhabiting opposite sides of the social and philosophical spectrum, both are content in their isolationism and in their belief that their way of life is superior to all other. Bengurionism had its origins in the agricultural communities patterned after the Soviet communist "Kolkhozes". These collective farms were small agricultural enclaves, highly segregated and very selective of their membership. The Bengurionite experiment with the "Kibutzim" was very similar to the Soviet model. A Kibutz ("collective") is a small agricultural enclave, highly segregated and very selective of its members and their political affiliation. These collective enclaves are very similar to the ghettos of the ultra-orthodox Jews in Israel. Both have stringent rules of conduct, a virulent distrust of foreigners and foreign entities and, despite their proclaimed aversion to capital and its ills, both pursued the accumulation of wealth with unflinching resolve. Both consider their communities superior to all others and, in many ways, above the secular laws.

Over time, secular Israeli Jews considered the orthodoxy as merely a nuisance and the price to pay for being Jewish. Rabbinical control over their personal lives had been grudgingly accepted. As this form of control has increased, some conflicts arose, including a small political party whose sole aim was to reverse the trend of religious takeover of the state. In Bengurionism any form of dissatisfaction with the regime is severely punished. When young orthodox students rioted in Jerusalem and other cities, they were let go with a slap on the wrist. When secular Jews exhibit any behavior that is critical of the regime, they are brutally punished. In time, secular Israelis have given up. Many of them understand the ramifications of the demographic time-bomb and the bleak future that awaits them once the orthodoxy gains control of the resources and the arsenal of their state. But most of them prefer to adopt the attitude of wait-and-see and to hope for the best. Their opposition effectively ceased to exist.

Part IV
How It All Began: The Origins

In The Beginning

Who were the Israelites and where did they come from? This is the title of a very interesting book by the archaeologist William Dever.[186] He authored several books on the ancient near East and ancient Israel in particular. Dever focused on the conflict that invariably exists whenever one relates the events of the antiquity of the Israelites: the account given by the Bible versus archaeological findings. How accurate are the stories of the Bible when compared with dates and conclusions supplied by archaeology?

The origins of the nomadic people known as "Israelites" or "Hebrews" are enmeshed in the migrations of tribes from pastures to greener pastures.[187] Although there is no archeological evidence for the existence of the Biblical story of Exodus from Egypt, there is mention in some findings in Mesopotamia of names similar to those of Abram and Jacob. There is agreement that the "patriarchal period" in which clan of the Abraham[188] would have wandered from Mesopotamia occurred around 1900 before the Common Era (B.C.E.). This was the Middle Bronze era. In this era there were migrations of Semite people into Canaan, and they were probably related to the Canaanites. About two hundred years later, circa 1700 B.C.E. until about 1550 B.C.E. a branch of these semi-nomads, known as Hyksos, invaded Egypt and started a new (16th) dynasty in lower Egypt, in the Delta region. To put this in context, King Hammurabi of Babylon reigned around 1778-1686 B.C.E. The Hyksos were expulsed from Egypt in the 16th century B.C.E. leading to the establishment of the 18th dynasty of pharaohs in the city of Thebes.

Two facts seem to emerge from what we know about the origins of the Israelites. The first is their origins in the region of Mesopotamia and their relation to the Amorites and to the inhabitants of Canaan. There are scholars who suggest that the period of the "patriarchs," as described in Biblical accounts, is a compilation of several traditions and stories. Much of our knowledge of this period remains nebulous.

The second fact seems to be the strong link of the story of the ancient Israelites to the events in the life of the kingdoms in Mesopotamia and in Egypt–the two major forces in the Bronze Age. The Biblical stories of the migrations from Canaan to Egypt during the life of Jacob and his sons may reflect several centuries of such movement of nomadic tribes to and from the green pastures of the two deltas, particularly that of Egypt.

The Israelites and the Exodus

There is a wonderfully powerful motif and a vibrant message in the story of the Exodus of the Israelites (or Hebrews) from Egypt. Two questions are key to this event: Did it *happen* at all, and if so, *when* did the Exodus occur?

The story of the Exodus is composed of three interrelated events. The first was the tenure of the Israelites in Egypt for about four centuries, as slaves to the Pharaohs. The second event was the liberation of the Israelites, by means of the work of Moses and the "Ten Plagues." Finally, the Exodus also includes the wandering of the Israelites in the desert before their incursion into Canaan–their promised land. Did this compound story happen?

There are three main scholarly explanations to the story of the Exodus. One view suggests that the Exodus did not occur at one time. Rather, small groups of Israelites within different tribal arrangements had transited in Egypt, entering and leaving over a period of several centuries. Another explanation suggests that perhaps Moses left Egypt with a small group of followers, after a conflict with Egyptian rulers. The third approach suggests that the story of the Exodus is a complex narrative made up of various traditions and stories of the early Israelites, but it could not have happened as described in the Bible. Archaeological excavations and ancient Egyptian and Canaanite texts have failed to substantiate such an extraordinary event.

Perhaps the question of the timing of the Exodus may help us to gain a better perspective of the story. Archaeologists today generally agree that the Exodus, if indeed it occurred, happened in the 13th century B.C.E. This coincides with the reign of Ramses II (about 1290-1224 B.C.E.). Conversely, Jewish tradition computes the Exodus as having occurred 480 years prior to the fourth year of King Solomon's rule–which would place the Exodus at 1446 B.C.E. Archeologists generally agree that the appearance of the Israelites in Canaan can be traced to around the end of the Bronze Age (1250-1150 B.C.E.), so that the Exodus could not have occurred two centuries before this period. This computation also discounts the possibility that the story of the Exodus coincides with the expulsion of the Hyksos around 1550 B.C.E.

How did the Israelites find their way to Canaan? Did they wander in the desert, and did they fight their way, under the command of Joshua, into Canaan? As in the story of the Exodus and liberation from Egypt, the conquest of Canaan is also composed of a variety of oral traditions– woven across times and events– into a magnificent narrative.

Wandering through the desert was not such a difficult affair. The route between Canaan and Egypt was well traveled and Egyptian records tell the stories of Egyptian military campaigns in Canaan and beyond. After the expulsion of the Hyksos, the pharaohs (such as Thutmosis III) had subjugated Canaanite cities and moved military forces from Egypt to Canaan. In terms of numbers, historians and archaeologists agree that the Sinai desert could not have supported so many Israelites, as listed in the Biblical account. William Dever (2003), for example, suggests that of the sites mentioned in the Bible, only "Kadesh-Barnea" has been excavated at the oasis of "Ein Qudeis" in the northeastern point of the Sinai Peninsula. Although Israeli archaeologists extensively researched the area, they found no evidence that a large group of Israelites occupied this site during the era when the Exodus is said to have occurred.

A summary of the current knowledge suggests that perhaps the Exodus was a combination of oral histories of the journeys of the Israelites to and from Egypt. Written many centuries later,[189] the account was combined into a magnificent story. The objectives of such a larger-than-life story may have been to strengthen the Hebrews' historical roots in the land they now inhabited, and to collect the various oral accounts into a cohesive story, with a strong emphasis on the unity of the tribes and the central role of the Lord, the God of the Patriarchs.[190] There is little concrete archaeological evidence to any component of the Biblical account of the Exodus. The picture that seems to emerge is that of groups of semi-nomads, originally belonging to a mix of Amorites and Canaanites, who for several centuries traversed the region into and out of Egypt. They ultimately settled in Canaan, on both sides of the river Jordan, and formed a distinctive community. When, much later, their historians sat down to chronicle their origins and the story of their people, they combined the assembled oral stories into an embellished and comprehensive narrative that emphasized their native links to their land ("promised land") and the tortuous road of their ancestors in their effort to inhabit such land–all with the constant help from their mighty God.

Creating a Religion

The Biblical account of how the Israelites received the religious commandments is a magnificent story of miracles, the direct link to God, and a story of human emotions and human frailty. Regardless of one's belief in the Bible as a sacred description of events, there is a marvelous allure of the story and the manner in which it is chronicled. The Bible has such an attraction because the historical chronicles are laced with human stories and with fundamental human emotions, such that any person can understand and can identify with in comparison with her/his own life and experiences.

Unlike Greek mythology, where the Gods take on human traits, the Biblical stories are those of shepherds and kings alike. Human emotions described in the narrative are raw, fascinating, and widely understandable. There are stories about love, greed, jealousy, friendship, intolerance, vengefulness, avarice, and forgiveness. The Biblical narrative is a combination of dry historical facts with the effervescence of stories that could be the script for any modern popular novel. There are stories of sibling rivalry, as in Cain and Abel, Jacob and Esau, and Joseph and his brothers. There is the sorrow of a couple's inability to conceive, as in Abraham and Sarah, and their recourse to surrogate motherhood, as in the story of Abraham and Hagar. There is the tale of love that conquers all, as in the story of Jacob and Rachel, and love and lust, as in David and Bat-Sheva. There is deep friendship as in David and Jonathan, and treachery and ingratitude as in the story of Absalom, son of King David.

These stories of the human condition overshadow the dry historical narrative. They are therefore ageless, and even modern readers are captivated by the psychological depth of the narrative, and the writer's understanding of human traits and human frailties and strengths. Moreover, to the contemporary reader who is versed with the working of complex organizations, there are "real-life" accounts of events that are very familiar to modern employees and their managers.

For example, how one mistake led to the "firing" of an old and faithful employee. This was the case of Moses, who was not allowed to cross over to the promised land. In another account, an aging and fairly incompetent king (Saul) is replaced by a younger and dashing candidate (David).

But, the Biblical account was written at least several centuries after the Israelites coalesced as a nation in the land that stretched both east and west of the river Jordan. The complex and detailed set of rules described in the Biblical books such as *Leviticus* contains references to a people living in permanent residence and working the land–not an assembly of former slaves wandering through the desert.

The story of the ten commandments has a very different flavor and seems to better fit the conditions surrounding the Israelites in their sojourn through the Sinai desert. These commandments are a marvelous summary of rules of civilized behavior. They are similar to the code enacted by the Babylonian King Hammurabi (about 1728-1686 B.C.E.).

As Moses was presumably leading a ragtag group of former slaves on their way to a new country and to self rule, he had to provide them with a semblance of a code of behavior that would allow them to lead a somewhat civilized existence. It is highly conceivable that very few, if any, of the Israelites who marched with him knew how to read and write. Their language skills were probably a combination of their ancestral Aramaic, Akkadian, and Canaanite dialects–mixed with the Egyptian language spoken by the common folks in the Kingdom of the Nile.

Recent research into cognitive abilities has shown that people of nearly all cultures collect stories we call "myths." They have done so especially in antiquity because in those nonliterate societies it was impossible to transfer information in large quantity–such as codes of ethics, behavior, and morality–due to the limited capacity of human memory and the limited ability of the human mind to process and to analyze vast amounts of knowledge.[191]

Regardless of the size of the group of Israelites that followed Moses out of Egypt, they needed a very concise code of behavior they could remember in order to abide by it. These "commandments" had to be clear, to the point, and had to carry a punch, both in the form of incentives to those who abided by them and a threat to those who disobeyed them. The most appropriate means to assure compliance was to wrap the commandments in the mantle of religious significance, and even make them a direct command from the God of the Israelites.

Who was this God and how was he reintroduced to the people who had been reentering the land of Canaan–whether as refugees from Egypt, or in a lengthy process of tribal movements? There are two issues to be considered. The first is the monotheistic idea, and the second is the unique form in which this idea was presented to the Israelites by their leaders of that time.

The monotheistic idea was not an original invention of the ancient Israelites. The pharaoh Akhenaten (ca. 1370-1353 B.C.E.) believed in one god–in his case the Sun-God.[192] But, as we further explore the role that belief in deities played in ancient civilizations, the picture that emerges is paradoxical. On the one hand there was a need in ancient societies to relate to natural phenomenon–beyond the impacts of "magic." Life in those times was precarious, violent, and dependent on the forces of nature. It was only obvious that such unexplained natural phenomena be represented in the form of powerful deities. By giving these deities a somewhat human form, the ancient people felt closer to the unexplained powers of nature, hence having some measure of control over their lives. Prayers to these gods and gifts in the form of sacrifices provided a measure of interaction with the gods and a channel of communication with them.

Major events in human existence, such as procreation and the yield of agricultural activity took the form of, for example, the goddess of motherhood, the earth, and the bounty of life. The Babylonians named this goddess "Ishtar," the Egyptians "Isis," and in Canaan she was "Anat," later named "Aphrodite" in Greek mythology and "Venus" in the Roman pantheon.

On the other hand, the belief in one god, omnipotent and omnipresent, is therefore unnatural. It requires a conceptual acceptance of a hidden and mysterious being, and a disconnect from the representation of the forces of nature. In the case of the one-God-Sun, at least there was a visible representation in the sky of the supreme being. But, an *invisible* god requires a considerable cognitive leap fueled by a strong belief in its existence and in its powers.[193]

Yet, consider the story of the wandering Israelites on their way to becoming a people with permanent residency and a more intimate relationship to their future land–that is, getting involved in agriculture and industry, in addition to sheep and donkey herding. The people Moses was leading or even the tribes commuting between Egypt and Canaan were essentially different from both the Egyptians and the Canaanites. They were detached from a permanent land. Which gods should they follow?

If they chose the traditional pantheon of gods of either the Egyptians or the Canaanites, or the Assyrians, they would need to relate them to the land and to activities in farming and small industry which they did not possess. As semi-nomads on their way to settlement, the Israelites under Moses needed a deity that would serve at least two purposes. First it should be commensurate with their current life-style as nomads, roving between the rivers Nile and Jordan. They could not carry with them idols nor portable temples or housing for their gods. The Biblical story of the construction of the "Sacred Cow" as an idol demonstrates the impracticality of hauling such a contraption–in addition to the religious outrage of defying the laws of God, which is the key lesson of the story. In this sense, a single god who is not necessarily related to a specific country and its practices, would be more appropriate.

Secondly, this god would have to serve as a link to the history of this people, so that a common background could be established for the various tribes which were coalescing into a unified people. Thus, such a god would be unique, differing from the gods of neighboring countries, but omnipresent so it would be powerful wherever the Israelites went and from wherever they originated. The god of the patriarchs was a perfect choice for a shared history of the various households and tribal groups who were about to inhabit the land of Canaan.

The monotheistic idea fits a band of nomadic or semi-nomadic people herding sheep and donkeys. The idea of the omnipresent and omnipotent deity may have been an innovative idea. In addition to the link to the land, this one ethereal god had to follow the people wherever they went and have superior power over *all* their enemies. The invisible omnipotent god had to replace the functional gods of antiquity: those responsible for *war*, the *home*, *procreation*, *food* or *agriculture*, and *nature* (the sun, the moon, the rivers and the sea, and the rain, storms, and lightning, among many other feared and ferocious forces).

This single omnipotent god had to intervene in the affairs of his believers. To the primitive mind of nomadic tribesmen, the concept of an invisible and inaccessible god would have been wholly unacceptable, particularly when the neighboring cultures had pantheons of visible gods represented in a variety of forms and shapes. However and wherever the idea of the single, omnipresent, omnipotent, and invisible god was introduced, it also had to abide by at least two conditions in order to even remotely gain acceptance by the people.

First it had to be mobile, accessible, communicable, and responsive to its people's requests. There had to be some form of communication with this god and the ancient procedure of offerings had to be reincarnated. But, why would such an omnipotent and spiritual god need the meager sacrifices of his followers? To the primitive mind of the ancient nomads, there had to be some form of barter, or quid-pro-quo. In modern parlance we would say: "There is no free lunch." The people in antiquity believed that their gods needed an offering of something of value to the petitioner in order to make an exchange, or barter, and satisfy the request. The more critical the request, the more valuable the offering had to be so that the exchange would be acceptable to the gods.

Such "transaction costs" and procedures required a set of rules and the intervention of specialists in the knowledge-base of what constitutes fair barter and what would appease or displease the gods. The emergence of a priestly profession was a natural outgrowth of the relationship between gods and believers. The Israelites adopted a similar configuration, albeit the transactions were geared toward the single and invisible god.

The contacts with this god were in the form of specific missions, commanded by the deity but executed by selected emissaries. They were plenipotentiaries–that is, they were authorized to apply supernatural power over the human and physical world. This particular means of interference in human affairs and the mode of applying such interference was indeed a radical innovation of the new religion.

In the pantheon of gods represented by idols, the communication with the god was a direct appeal to the god (by the petitioner or through the services of a priest) and the outcome or result appeared in the form of the satisfied request. In the case of an invisible god, however, when the intervention required divine appearance, how would such a god appear and act? Consider the stories of Lot and the doomed cities of Sodom and Gomorrah, or Abraham and Sarah in their anguish over Sarah's inability to conceive. The idea of *angels* as emissaries of the invisible god helped to maintain intact the concept of invisibility, and also made it possible for this god to actively participate in the mundane lives of his believers.

Another condition for acceptance was some form of proof of God's existence. Stories about emissaries and their "miracles" were insufficient tools in the difficult task to allay the primitive mind in his need for material proof. This brings us to the story of Moses, the two tablets, and the ten commandments.

The Biblical account of this event is complex and open to many interpretations. Throughout history scholars of three religions (Judaism, Christianity, and Islam) have carefully studied the event and have developed diverse and often contradictory analyses. Within the context of this chapter, the tablets and their content of commandments served not only the function of giving the people rules of civilized behavior, but also *material proof* of the existence of their invisible god.

The only evidence of the existence of such a powerful yet invisible god was the "burning bush," but it remained a story told by Moses. The physical phenomena in the desert, such as the columns of smoke and fire leading the way, as well as manna from heaven could have been explained, and they were only temporary. The tablets, written by the hand of the Lord, would be a permanent proof of his existence. Thus, in addition to the content of the commandments,[194] the tablets served several purposes in the difficult task of endowing the semi-nomadic tribes with a new religion.

One problem, however, remained unsolved and would hound the Israelites not only in the desert but also during their tenure in their land. This was the problem of enforcement of the commandments. In other cultures and other religions in antiquity, there was generally unity between the king or ruler and the country's religion. The pharaoh in Egypt was also the religious leader, and similar arrangements are found in Mesopotamia, Assyria, Canaan, and Phoenicia. Even in these countries where there was a duality in functions and the king did not perform the duties of the high priest, he had the authority and the incentives to enforce both the secular and the religious laws.

The ten commandments and the hundreds of rules of behavior that came to be afterwards (and are carefully listed in the Biblical narrative) deal with a mix of secular and religious rules of behavior. As a universal God, omnipotent and omnipresent, He could not intervene in each individual case and punish each offender. Instead, the Hebrew tradition had devised an innovative and genial solution. Trespassing the Lord's commandments became a *people's* offense, not an individual act of defiance. Only kings and very prominent people were directly punished by God–whereas with the remainder of Israel the sum total of sins over a long period of time would trigger a negative reaction from the Lord, and this would be translated into disasters and bad fortune for the *whole of Israel*. Moses, David, Solomon, and other leaders had been directly punished for specific infractions, but the remainder of Israel were treated as the entire people straying from God's word.[195]

There was one source of power, which could have retained the authority to enforce the laws of God: the tribal leadership. As the Israelites later settled the land, they remained strongly attached to their tribal traditions and highly divided along tribal lines. But, here is the paradoxical situation that has emerged. As a single, omnipresent God, the God of the Israelites was a central figure, and His reign was centralized, beyond and above the divisions of the tribal traditions. He was the God of "All of Israel" and His benefits as well as punishments were global and, in the case of the Israelites, given to the *entire* people–regardless of their tribal affiliation. The ethereal deity was linked to the Mesopotamian origins of Abraham, the patriarch, as well as to the exodus from Egypt, and finally to the land of Canaan as the promised final destination of the Israelites. The only link to this land was the promise He had given to the patriarchs and to their descendants. Therefore, this universal God was not specifically a God of a geographical location, but a God of a people, wherever destiny would take them.

In this framework, the tribal leaders had very little, if any, power to enforce the religious laws, nor did other civilian leaders such as the judges and the kings. The emerging system became a losing proposition of a tripartite organization: the tribal structure; the central rulers such as the kings; and the religious entities such as the priesthood, the prophets, and the religious sages in their organizations and conclaves. With an ethereal God and a religion which was dynamic and open to interpretation, this power arrangement would lead to strife, chaos, and, ultimately, to disaster.[196]

The Divine Promise to the People and the Promising Beginning of the Israelites

The seeds of destruction of the Jewish homeland, both in ancient times and in the present, are not in the external enemies but embedded in the traditional and ferocious division of opinions and direction that is so endemic to the religious makeup of the Jewish people.

The unique religious arrangements of the Israelites began with a "bang." Here was a people ready to embark on a wondrous adventure of history with the backing of the ultimate venture capitalist: the God of their ancestors–the omnipotent and omnipresent benefactor.

The Biblical account tells of an agreement made between the Israelites and their God. This contract became known as "The Covenant." But, as any lawyer would agree, it was a poorly designed construct. The Covenant lacked specificity. It was a very general pact, declaring that if the Israelites would follow in the path of "righteousness," they would conquer and inhabit the land of the Canaanites and Amorites and Moabites, and live there happily ever after.

The Covenant lacked a clear and workable definition of what was and was not "righteous." It lacked measures of performance and non-performance. When would deviations from the laws of God be serious enough to warrant a retaliatory strike by the Lord? Such judgment was entirely up to the God of the Israelites–without any inkling to the other party for an agreement of what constituted minor or grave infractions. At best, this pact was impractical because in order to avoid punishment, the Israelites had to obey *all* the rules imposed by their God–since any infraction may be serious enough to trigger the Lord's punishment.

But the Covenant also contained an innovative idea, hitherto unprecedented in the ancient religions. The omnipotent God of the universe made a personal pact with one specific people, the so-called "chosen people." Many scholars have examined this unique event, but all possible explanations are based on religious beliefs, faith, and myths. None of these explanations answers such simple questions as: why would the God of the universe bother with making a deal, and why with the people of Israel? Why would the omnipotent God enter into a pact with fallible humans?

Assuming, for the sake of argument and a rational discussion, that such a Covenant indeed came to pass, its existence and its terms engendered two critical outcomes that forever shaped the character of the Israelites and, later, the Jewish people. The first outcome was the Covenant as a descriptor of a people. Unlike other peoples and cultures in antiquity, the Covenant was a *unifying concept*, similar to a modern document of articles of incorporation of a company or a declaration of independence of a nascent country. The Covenant, under the tutelage of a religious instrument of God's plan and desire, gave the Israelites a sense of unity and a justification for being.

Even if we assume that the Covenant was conceived and developed much later, when the Hebrews inhabited their land, it gave them a justification for their history and for the ownership of their country. Unlike other ancient countries where unity was enshrined in a ruler or in geographical proximity, the Hebrew Covenant was an independent document registering a bond with the supreme being, without any dependence on people or institutions, which tend to be temporary residents of the world. This bond was eternal and indestructible, and could not be challenged or even copied. As such, the Covenant was a marvel of design and imagination of the ancient mind. Regardless of its flaws as an agreement, the Covenant was the ultimate contract any people could have created or desired.

More importantly, the second outcome was the provision that offered divine power to assist people in their hour of need. This gave divine intervention the potential to solve problems of the Hebrews (and later the Jewish people) and to extricate them from danger and from the hands of their enemies. The application of this intervention was down to the operational level of selected "miracles," such as actions in the battlefield. The conquest of the Promised Land was possible because the Hebrew general Joshua was able to stop the clock and to make the mighty walls of Jericho fall–all with the help of divine power.

In the relationship between parent and child, when the parent keeps bailing out the child who is constantly in trouble, the child has little incentive or experience to exercise self-reliance and to act on his own. In a later time period, this outcome produced the concept of the "Messiah" who is charged with saving the people of Israel and restoring them to their days of glory. The radical implications of this outcome were the extension of the reliance from purely religious to political considerations and the formatting of the Jewish psyche as a people always waiting for the intervention of their God whenever hard times and disaster occurred. As we shall see, this state of affairs ultimately led to political and national paralysis.[197]

So, the promise *to* the people is also the promise *of* the people of Israel. Here is a collection of tribes, starting their history as an emerging nation. They are a people united by a divine Covenant, joined by a common heritage and language; united by uninterrupted geographical expanse; and endowed with a unifying religion that advocated a unique and special standing among other nations.

These were very powerful assets with which the emerging nation could start its ascent into history. Never in the chronicles of antiquity had one nation started its existence with so many gifted assets and with such a magnificent promise to eventually become a shining star on the stage of human affairs. Nevertheless, never was such an exalted promise so brutally broken, as we shall see as this story unfolds in the promised land.

In summary, the Israelites, or Hebrews, initially appeared on the stage of history sometime during the 19th century B.C.E. and coalesced as a distinct people in the land of Canaan in the 13th century B.C.E. This was also around the time the Philistines settled along the coast of the Eastern Mediterranean. The Israelites were probably part of the movements of semi-nomadic tribes from Mesopotamia to the land by the River Jordan. They were related to the Canaanites and Amorites, and shared with them aspects of their language, their religion, and their culture. Sometime in the period between the 19th and the 12th centuries B.C.E., the Israelites developed a unique form of religious belief in a single, universal, and omnipotent God. They settled in the land that lies between the two great valleys of the ancient world: Mesopotamia and Egypt. A plausible mode might have been the long-term settlement of the different tribes and large households of Israelites rather than one coordinated military incursion. Thus, in this "promised land" began the next chapter of the Israelites' adventure.

Part V
The People and Its Land: What Went Wrong and Why

Creating A Nation

Perhaps the unity of the Israelites as a people cited in the previous section as a driver of their promising future was more of a wishful thought than a crude reality. Unity may well have been the creation of chroniclers who composed the story many centuries later. The sense of unity and purpose that reverberated in the covenant may have been the wish that later writers *hoped* it should and would have been. A more plausible history would have been the settlement of the land in dribs and drabs by the various tribal units in several geographical concentrations, thus creating regional differences that would play a decisive role in framing the nation during the period of the kingdom.

The history of the Israelites in their ancient land (in the 500 years between about 1200 B.C.E. and 721 B.C.E., when the kingdom of Israel was destroyed by Sargon II) was a constant search for a workable formula that would have allowed them to form and to maintain a stable political entity. The Kingdom of Judah was conquered in 587 B.C.E. and the first temple was destroyed by the Babylonians. In the year 70 A.D. the second temple was destroyed by the Roman Emperor Titus. Altogether the Hebrews or Israelites (later also called Jews) maintained a political nation in their ancient land for a period of over 1000 years.[198]

During this long period the Israelites left a mark on history. The nature of this mark and the degree to which it was equivalent to the expected performance of this extraordinary people are the topics of this chapter. Based on the Biblical narrative and on archaeological findings, the story of the Israelites in their land is one of a magnificent failure.

But, how do we define "failure"? Some historians have theorized that in light of the concept of the rise and fall of civilizations, the modern Jews, as descendants of the ancient Israelites, are an historical anomaly. Arnold Toynbee (1889-1975) suggested that once the ancient Hebrew civilization had been destroyed in 70 A.D., its people should have dispersed among other nations and essentially "disappeared" in the annals of history. He commented that: "Civilizations die from suicide, not by murder."[199] More recently, Jared Diamond (2004) also examined the collapse of societies such as the Anasazi Indians of the Southwestern United States, the Viking colonies of Greenland, and the Maya civilization of Central America. Although almost half a century apart, Toynbee and Diamond view historical events as tidal waves of changes, in which some societies are able to persevere, while others collapse and perish.[200]

This approach leads me to believe that we are engaged in a discussion of two distinct yet perhaps related modes of failure. One such mode is the failure of a society in its struggle to survive. This, it seems to me, is the mode of failure that historians such as Toynbee and Diamond espouse when they examine the collapse of societies and civilizations. This is mainly the collapse of the society as a political entity with an independent (or semi-independent) nationhood. The society or civilization of the Maya in Central America did not entirely disappear. Its people blended into the immigrant conquerors of European descent. Their unique physical characteristics are vividly seen in today's population throughout Central America. But, the Maya failed as a political entity, as a nation, and as a society who maintains political, geographic, and cultural control over its destiny. The language of the Maya, their customs, religion, and political statehood had been replaced by the Spanish/European alternative.

The second mode is the failure to perform per the expectations of the society. This may be a step in the direction of final failure and collapse—as described above. The difference is that the failure to perform as a society or a nation has the connotation of trailing other peoples and societies in demography, biology, economics, technology, or ecology.

As Toynbee and Diamond had documented, the Israelites were not the only society to fail and collapse. The peculiar characteristic of the Jews (as professed descendants of the Israelites), and an anathema to Toynbee's framework, was their resurgence as a culture with ties to the ancient land and to their failed civilization.[201] Other civilizations rose and fell in antiquity, but in most cases the conquering society either merged with its former enemy and absorbed its culture (Rome and Greece), or imposed its culture and norms on the vanquished. However, in most of these cases the vanquished remained a *physical* presence, albeit culturally transformed. Similarly, the barbarians transformed the Roman Empire but did not eliminate the citizens of the empire.

In the case of the Israelites in their land, both types of failure occurred. Historians are usually concerned with the collapse of the Israelites and their deportation to the Diaspora. This was a clear failure to survive as an independent nation and a failure to remain a society in its land; thus, it was no longer identified with a geographic expanse or a political authority. In the view of historians like Toynbee, this society would be practically extinct.[202]

In this book I will initially focus on the second mode of failure: underperformance of the Israelites to their promise and their potential. Indeed, in the period leading to the emergence of the kingdom and centralized government, the Israelites had begun to create a distinct nation. For almost two hundred years after their settlement in Canaan and its vicinity, the Israelites had made several attempts to engender unity among the tribes and large households. This began around 1200 B.C.E. and culminated with the ascension of King Saul circa 1000 B.C.E.

The Israelites were primarily an agricultural society. They did not follow the example of the Canaanites or the Philistines who built and maintained several city fortresses and a vibrant urban life. The Israelites remained predominantly a primitive agrarian people, whose economy was based on native crops such as dates and olives, and the herding of livestock, particularly in the hills of Judea, Samaria, and in the lands east of the River Jordan.

Linked by a common language, history, and religion, this cultural bind was sufficiently strong to foster a cohesive national identity. Differences by tribal affiliation, geography, and economic activity were set aside by a wish to energize a common mode of government. This led to the emergence of the "judges" as a temporary solution. They were roving arbiters of inter-tribal disputes, but fell short of any centralized authority. The political and economic powers remained within the tribes and their elders. Not until David, son of Jesse, ascended Saul's throne (and ruled circa 1000-961 B.C.E.) was there any serious attempt to form a national system of government.

So, as a predominantly agrarian society composed of a dozen different tribes settled throughout the land, the binding force was the shared religion. In the case of the Israelites, the religious framework had been a mix of history and myths as well as a code for behavior and for worship. There was a very little in common between, for example, the tribe of Reuben who settled east of the Dead Sea by Moab—and the tribe of Asher, who settled in the northwestern corner of the country, north of today's Haifa. The Asherites had perhaps more ties with the Phoenicians (their neighbors to the North), and hardly any incentives to transact with their brethren in the southeast. However, the tribes had a common history and a shared religion.

But was this enough to create a nation? Some historians contend that the Israelites formed a confederation of tribes. Because of the incomplete conquest of the land, there were Canaanite cities in the midst of the geographic expanse of the tribes who settled west of the River Jordan, as well as the Philistines who controlled the southwestern portion of the coastal areas.

The religious bind then as well as in the 3000 years that followed was not sufficiently strong to maintain a sustainable national entity. A united nation, embracing all the tribes and with a central government, emerged around 1000 B.C.E. and ceased to exist in 922 B.C.E.—after a period of only 100 years. The Kingdom of Solomon's heirs were shattered circa 922 B.C.E. by the division into two separate entities. This event was not caused by any external enemy. It was due to internal strife and the inherent differences between the various groupings of the tribes.

The Promise

What was the promise of the Hebrews or Israelites in the land they inhabited? There are two modes by which one can interpret the events of the Israelites in antiquity. The first is based on faith and on the account given in the Biblical narrative. Here was a people chosen by its creator above all the peoples of its time. The historical narrative of the Bible describes several instances in which the Hebrew God intervened on behalf of His people, by helping them win battles and subjugating the land. Thus, a band of semi-nomadic and disorganized tribes were able—with divine assistance—to conquer well-entrenched people in their fortified cities.

With divine power at their side, the Israelites conquered the land of Canaan. They had a marvelous initial advantage over other tribes and peoples of the region. They were united by their unique religious beliefs and the unifying concept of having received the promise of their God to choose them among others and to offer them the land that they had conquered. Their existence was therefore blessed and protected by divine power. Jewish scholars in antiquity and afterwards have reiterated that divine assistance was contingent upon obeying the divine laws as given to Moses; the result of non-obedience would be the removal of divine help but would still leave the Israelites with their initial advantage. Never in the history of nations has a people had such a promising head start on a glorious path, with all the aid and comfort of the Almighty, only to magnificently fail at every juncture of time and by every yardstick known to humankind. They were twice expulsed from their land, their temple was twice destroyed, and the people were scattered in an unending Diaspora of blood and tears.

Thus the story of the Israelites all started in antiquity, in the land of the Amorites and the Canaanites, so gloriously conquered and inhabited with the active support of the Almighty. The Biblical account describes the Hebrew God as the "General in charge of the armies of Israel"— so involved was the Almighty Himself in the bellicose affairs of His conquering people.

Another mode of interpretation of the events of the Israelites in their land is a multi-disciplinary analysis with modern tools and unambiguous answers. The Israelites had several advantages that offered them a strong position in their region and a very promising start. The first was their *location*. Some historians have considered the position of the country inhabited by the Israelites in a negative light. Schindlin (1998), for example, argued that the location of the country in the region between the Mesopotamian Kingdoms and Egypt was detrimental to the Israelites. He contended that "much of the political history of the Israelite kingdom is the history of the rivalry between Egypt and Mesopotamia....The Israelite kingdom could enjoy a modest prosperity under the patronage of one or the other of its neighbors, but it could also become caught up in their rivalry. It was finally destroyed when it chose the wrong one as its protector" (p. 3).[203]

A much different viewpoint can be advocated. It can be argued that the location of the Israelites in the region that served as the passageway between the kingdoms of the great river basins of the ancient world offered the Israelites countless advantages of geography. The land of the Israelites was largely a terrain that was difficult to traverse, with fortified cities that could easily protect the main roads and passages. As a stronghold guarding routes of commerce on land between Egypt and Mesopotamia, the Israelite country could have achieved an enviable position in which the neighboring kingdoms would have sought their favor as an ally in order to maintain open avenues for trade. The advantages of geographic location that the Israelites potentially enjoyed are similar to those of the Italian cities of Genoa and Venice, situated between the Western and Eastern empires of Rome and Byzantium.

A second and related advantage was *ecological* control. The Israelite tribes had occupied both sides of the river Jordan and its resources. They controlled the river and other smaller fluvial outlets that punctuate the geography between the river Jordan and the Mediterranean Sea. They also controlled the higher ground in the hilly country of Judea and Samaria. Translated to a military-strategic perspective, the Israelites occupied the key positions in their country, which made any attempt to invade and to conquer them a very costly and uncertain proposition.

The third advantage, and a strong contributor to the set of elements that offered such a promising start, was the host of *opportunities to learn* from their neighbors. Bordering the most advanced cultures of antiquity, the Israelites absorbed some knowledge from their surrounding neighbors but could have learned much more. They did adopt writing from the Phoenicians, military tactics from the Hittites, and a political form of monarchy from the centralized states of Egypt and Mesopotamia. They also adopted social, religious, linguistic, and other cultural practices from the Canaanites and other peoples they had conquered and which whom they shared the land. However there was also a vast pool of knowledge on technology, weaponry, maritime and commercial abilities, and military and civilian organization that the Israelites had ample opportunities to learn. The promise turned into failure; the failure into disaster.

The fourth element of the promising start was the sense of *unity* as a religious and historical people. Even before King David established a capital city in Jerusalem, there was a religious center in Shiloh where the tribes maintained the Arc of the Covenant, the symbol of their heritage as a unified people. Festivals and ceremonies were performed during the year and annual gatherings of pilgrims from all corners of the land were instrumental in fomenting this sense of unity of the people.

In summary, we have a magnificent beginning of a people endowed with the potential to shine and to prosper. Nestled on the shores of the Mediterranean, the Israelites had the potential to rival or exceed the Phoenicians and the Philistines who inhabited the coast to the North and to the South. They occupied the strategic passageway linking the great empires of the time. The potential for commerce, economic, and political gains was substantial. They had a common culture, a unifying religion, and a shared history—enshrined in the belief that the creator of the universe had bestowed upon them a special blessing as a chosen people destined for greatness.

The Hypotheses of Failure

The Israelites inhabited their promised land from the thirteenth century B.C.E. till the fall of Jerusalem in 587 B.C.E. and the beginning of their exile to Babylon. For six centuries they lived and documented their history in a series of narratives, some of which were assembled into the text of the Old Testament. Later, the Israelites returned to Judea under the auspices of the Persian kings. In 525 B.C.E., Darius I of Persia conquered Egypt and installed Zerubbabel as governor of Judea. The second temple was established in Jerusalem in 515 B.C.E., thus starting the restoration of the Israelite existence in their land. This lasted for almost five centuries until the destruction of the second temple in 70 A.D. by the Roman emperors Vespasian and Titus.

The two epochs in the Israelite existence in their land will be analyzed separately. The first period began with the conquest of the land of Canaan and ends with the exile to Babylon. There are six elements in the hypothesis of utter failure that greatly contributed to the weakness and ultimate destruction of the national being of the Israelites.

The hypotheses of failure suggests that, as a nation, the Israelites failed to utilize their strengths and to apply the skills that were so aptly used by other peoples in antiquity in order to survive and to prosper. They certainly had the potential to excel in the various areas, which I enumerate below, and to avoid the disastrous consequences of their weaknesses, which invariably led to their exile and to the destruction of their country.

Commerce and Trade

The first element of failure was their inability to exercise their capabilities in commerce and international trade. The Biblical account of King Solomon transacting with his neighbors to the north and with exotic lands in the horn of African is an acute exception—if indeed the story reflects historical facts of his reign or was written centuries afterwards with the objective of embellishing the king's achievements. In general, throughout the era of the kingdoms of Israel and Judea, the commercial and international trading effort was limited to selected caravans with little support from the government. Nestled in the passageway between the Nile and the Euphrates, the land of the Israelites was a natural haven for active commerce and trade relationships. There was very little. The Biblical account of the period fails to mention the emergence of a trading elite or the existence of well-established commercial activities of the Israelite settlements in their country.

The modern reader, Jew or Gentile, will express disbelief at this analysis, due to the long-standing view of the commercial abilities that are said to be ingrained in the Jewish character. Yet, whatever modern circumstances have led the Jews in the Diaspora to heavily engage in commerce and international trading, this trait was not present in the life of their ancestors in the land of the ancient Israelites.

Some historians have expressed a different view and have attempted to demonstrate that the Israelites engaged in active commerce with their neighboring countries. Isserlin (1998), for example, relied on Biblical narratives and archaeological findings. He argued that the life style of the ruling classes and the ritual needs of the priests and the kings required imports of precious metals as well as spices (such as myrrh and cinnamon). But Isserlin admits that much of the trade in and with the Israelite kingdoms was carried out by foreign merchants. Furthermore, he also concluded that many goods produced by the Israelites "featured little among exports" and that "most textiles produced in Israel do not seem to have appealed to foreign customers" (p. 182).

A prerequisite for active trade would have been the establishment and maintenance of a system of roads with a provision of security for the caravan routes through the lands of the Israelites. For such an infrastructure of transport to exist and to persist, there would be a need for centralized power, vested only in a monarchy. Josephus Flavius (Joseph Ben-Matytianhu) in his book on the antiquity of the Jews tells the story of King Solomon who constructed high-quality roads around his capital city of Jerusalem.[204] With the partition of the country into two kingdoms around 922 B.C.E., the kingdoms lacked the power of a larger and unified central authority with taxing capabilities that could have been applied into an aggressive program of the construction and maintenance of roads.

The Israelite country was a passageway for merchants from the lands of the Ishmaelites, the Midianites, and the Amarites who conducted caravans from and to Egypt and Mesopotamia. They were the engines of trade and, perhaps due to their activities, archaeologists are finding articles from surrounding countries in their excavations throughout Israel and ancient Israelite goods in other countries. Isserlin (p. 188) sadly admits that "evidence about Israelite traders and their activities is tantalizingly incomplete."

A possible explanation to the paucity of Israelite trading and commercial activities is the location of the country alongside powerful trading nations such as Phoenicia, the Philistine cities, traders of Arab descent, and the empires of Egypt and Mesopotamia. However, there is no evidence that the Israelites actively attempted to learn from their neighbors or to compete or cooperate with them. Perhaps the inherent characteristics of the ancient Israelites as a loose conglomerate of semi-nomadic tribes prevented them from exercising such potential capabilities. Nomadic practices involve moving cattle and possessions rather than establishing routine trading relations. The Israelites in general seem to have been highly provincial, regionalists, and divided in their tribal traditions of isolation.

William Dever (2003) suggested that the period of the "proto-Israelites" (the 12th-11th centuries B.C.E.) was the period of Iron I, whereas the monarchy (10th-7th centuries B.C.E.) was Iron II. In the first period the economy was primarily agro-pastoral, with limited industry and trade. In the second period of Iron II, there was more intensive agricultural activity, as well as additional activities in industry and trade. Even during the period of the monarchs in both Judea and Israel, there was minimal trade and only enough commercial activity to accommodate the foreign caravans and foreign traders who traversed the land. The Israelites failed to promote and engage in active or aggressive commercial effort on a national level, or even at a level that would have contributed to their national wealth and their relative standing in the region.

Shipping and Seafaring

The land of the Israelites was on the eastern shores of the Mediterranean Sea, south of Phoenicia and north of the Philistine cities. Although the Israelites did not possess high quality ports such as Tyre, there is hardly any evidence that they had seafaring capabilities, commercial or military. Archaeological findings such as ancient seals and Biblical stories of maritime activity were probably the result of the Israelites participating in voyages aboard Phoenician ships, since there were friendly relations between the Israelite kings and Phoenicia.

The Phoenicians inhabited the northern coast of the region, presently Lebanon and parts of Syria. Their civilization was based on maritime commerce, shipbuilding, and seafaring. They were industrious, particularly in the manufacture of dyes and wood products, and were the inventors of a simple and usable alphabet. Their name comes from the Greek word for the color crimson or purple—a dye produced by the Phoenicians and much coveted in the ancient world. Another special invention of this enterprising people was glass.

The Phoenicians embarked on long range voyages throughout the Mediterranean Sea and established colonies in North Africa, in the great city of Carthage, later destroyed by the Romans during the Punic Wars. Other colonies were also established by the Phoenicians as commercial and military outposts in Cyprus, Malta, Sicily, Corsica, and Spain. Their colonies thus surrounded the Italian peninsula, in direct threat to the emerging Roman sphere of influence in the Mediterranean Sea. This led to the several wars between Rome and Carthage, and finally to the destruction and obliteration of the Carthage and the Phoenician culture.

Although the Phoenicians were culturally very similar to the Canaanites and the Israelites who also lived in the coastal areas, there is a theory that perhaps they were descendants of a maritime people from the Greek Islands. This legacy would explain their interest in the sea and their extraordinary maritime capabilities.

Whatever their origin, the Phoenicians developed maritime power and probably shared some activities with their southern neighbors—the Israelites. Yet the Israelites failed to learn and to imitate their neighbors. The Israelites had access to trees and wood to build ships but lacked the will and the knowledge to do so. They ignored the opportunities that maritime power provided for trade and military capacity. In this aspect of economic life the Israelites lacked leadership, entrepreneurship, and scholarship. They did not master the various disciplines of seafaring. In addition to the small tribe of Dan, who inhabited the region of the modern port of Tel-Aviv-Jaffa, the larger tribe of Asher lived in the northern coastal region, along the shores of today's Acre and Haifa—two natural seaports.

Patai (1999) argued that since Noah's voyages, the Israelites and later the Jews had been a seafaring people. His argument is based on biblical and other religious stories. He proposed that in the Jewish literature, the sea was a projection of the powers of the Israelite God. Noah was a skilled navigator and in Jewish history of the antiquity there were always seamen. He also argued that the literature contains references to the rabbinical rules of conduct and diet, which apply to Jewish sailors in long seafaring voyages. Even if one accepts Patais thesis, the fact remains that these were perhaps instances of individual Israelites who joined, in various seafaring capacities, other peoples' ships. There was no national or tribal enterprise in ancient Israel regarding navigation and the use of the sea as an important venue for commerce, transport, or military uses.

As a conglomerate of tribes whose economy rested mainly on agro-pastoral and limited home industry occupations, the Israelites could not comprehend nor adopt a seafaring culture. They had at their disposal all the ingredients that made the Phoenicians, the Philistines, the Greeks, and later the Romans, effective maritime nations. They had the raw materials to build ships, the coastal shores and the natural ports, and the example of great neighboring seafaring nations with their pool of knowledge, experience, and entrepreneurial spirit. It is highly conceivable that the Israelites saw the benefits and the wealth that these maritime nations gained from their seafaring activities. Some of them may have sailed on Phoenician ships. None of them became a Marco Polo and none of the Israelite kings turned into a Henry the Navigator.[205]

Political Structure and Organization

A major failure of the Israelites during the period from the conquest of the land until the fall of the first temple was the lack of an effective political structure and a very poor organization of government and its institutions. Throughout these centuries, the dominant political framework was the tribal arrangement of a loose confederation. The diversity of regions and geographical and cultural differences made it difficult to centralize power and to govern the country from a single location.

During the tenure of the Israelites in their country there was never a *political* elite, as was found in ancient Greece and certainly in Rome. Israel (a term I will use to include the kingdoms of Judea and Israel), then and today, was a house divided with tribal leaders constituting the political caste of the nation. This divisive arrangement continued after the destruction of the first temple, and more so after the fall of Jerusalem to the Romans in 70 A.D. and the expulsion of the Jews to their Diaspora.

In ancient Israel the monarchy was a political illusion. The political power rested with tribal leaders, whereas the moral authority was assumed by the "prophets" who claimed their calling to be directly endowed from God. The kings ruled in a superimposed and superficial manner, hence the facility with which the country was torn apart into two realms after the death of King Solomon in 922 B.C.E.

The Biblical story of the ascension of David as king and the genesis of the "House of David" in Jewish history is a very detailed account of the life of this monarch and his accomplishments. In Samuel II, 18, King David initiated the reorganization of his kingdom and, in particular, his armed forces. He conducted a census of the population and established a hierarchy of units and commanders in his forces with the objective of creating a professionally-skilled standing army. The census also allowed him to impose a centralized system of taxation that would pay for the central bureaucracy, the expenses of palatial life, the construction of the new capital city, and military campaigns.

In effect, King David instituted a three part political reorganization. The first was the creation of a centrally-controlled army. The second comprised the concentration of political power in the office of the monarch, with the help of "ministers" of his court and centrally-appointed roving judges.[206] The third and inevitable step was the establishment of a *political* capital to replace the religious center of the country in Shiloh.

King David was an astute administrator and a politician of international stature. He was able to negotiate treaties with his neighbors to the east, southwest, and north. The reorganization he imposed on the country was a sound plan, aimed at concentrating power in the monarchy and creating conditions that would allow his kingdom to live in secure borders and to engender wealth.

But the king failed in his entrepreneurial actions in two key aspects of his administration. He was, and continued to be throughout his life, a product of a rural or "small village" heritage and upbringing who suddenly was catapulted into the highest post in the land. He relied on a few intimate advisers, drawn from his tribe of Benjamin and from the tribe of Judah that inhabited the land around his native Bethlehem. For his personal guard he relied on soldiers from his tribe of Benjamin.[207] Although he envisioned a unified nation of all the twelve tribes in the south as well as the north, King David remained a simple shepherd who could not entirely comprehend the role that the northern tribes would play in his unified country.

The other aspect of his failure to secure a stable centralized monarchy was the pace and the scope of his reorganization. King David acted too fast and made too much of a change in the lives of the Israelite tribes. I emphasize these failures because they laid the foundation to the division of the country during the reign of David's grandson. This division was the cradle of the subsequent downfall of the Israelite presence in their land. After the breakup of the unified realm in 922 B.C.E., the Israelites, and later the Jews in history, never recovered, and would never again rule a country of the size and importance as that of their second king—David.

Perhaps the paramount action by King David that was influenced by his provincial upbringing and the hurried pace of change he engendered was his choice of the new capital city: Jerusalem.[208] The selection of Jerusalem, nestled in the hills of the tribe of Benjamin within a short distance from Bethlehem, was a very poor choice. From a national viewpoint, David had declared the conquered "city of peace" as both the political *and* the religious capital of his kingdom. With pomp and circumstance he moved the religious symbol of the Israelites, the Arc of the Covenant, from Shiloh to the new capital.

As a soldier, David was perhaps impressed with the resistance of the Jebusites, the city's original inhabitants, and the inaccessible location of the walled city, making it an excellent fortress. From the narrow viewpoint of security, this city was a much better choice than Shiloh to be the center of religious life and the harbinger of the Arc. Having both the religious and political centers in Jerusalem also guaranteed economic progress to the region, particularly to the tribes of Judah and Benjamin.

But security and apparent impregnability came at a price of distance from a stable water supply. In later periods of the monarchy, a siege upon Jerusalem required complex engineering effort to transport water into the city to avoid a catastrophe of thirst and disease. Other shortcomings included the need to build a network of roads that could be guarded and maintained for both religious pilgrimage and for military and commercial uses. The treasury of the monarchy, first in the days of David and Solomon and certainly later during the smaller kingdom of Judah, was insufficient to fund such a task.

Such considerations of selective regional benefits did not escape the northern Israelites. They openly complained. In Samuel II, 42-44, the Biblical account describes the argument by members of the northern tribes that they were ten to the two tribes of the south, yet were at a disadvantage where the allocation of favors was concerned. The north provided the bulk of human resources and the greater part of agricultural and industrial production. Much of the land of Judah and Benjamin was semi-arid and could only support sheep and goat herding and a limited array of agricultural products, such as olive oil, dates, and inefficient vineyards.

The capital city of Jerusalem thus became a symbol of the power of a select group of southern Israelites. Although led by the king who had been anointed by the prophet, his ministers, the court, and his bureaucratic organization were not the preferred children of the Almighty. Most northern Israelites were now subjected to the collection of taxes that would be directed toward the embellishment of David's city and for the economic benefits of his associates and tribesmen. This was a disaster in the making. It needed an incident or a major event that would ignite the flame of revolt and would thus destroy the unity of the nation. The event at hand was the outlandish construction project devised by David's son and successor, Solomon, to build a magnificent temple in Jerusalem.

King Solomon (961-922 B.C.E.) was not as wise as we have been led to believe. He inherited a unified country with an expanded territory and a well-trained and respected military force. He took over a realm with a good treasury for a small agricultural nation. But Solomon built the temple and bankrupted the country. His taxes were exorbitant, paid in large measure by the northern tribes with their agricultural and industrial products. Solomon outsourced the construction of the temple to builders from Phoenicia because the Israelites lacked the skills and the knowledge to design and to build such a structure. The king ruled for forty years, yet his reign—besides the building of the temple—did not excel in any other area. Unable to establish an adequate system of succession, the reign of Solomon was the last to include all the tribes of the Israelites.

The king was also unable to assuage the spirit of discontent and the ebullient revolt of the northern tribes. In effect, he ruled over a political system where the religious center and the seat of government were located in the south, whereas the economic powerhouse and the major concentration of population were in the north. This inevitably led to the unfolding, within a generation, of the "great partition," thus erasing the benefits of David's reorganization and his conquests.

Rehavam, son of Solomon, was the last king to briefly rule over the whole country. With the partition, Jerubaam became king of the ten tribes in the center and the north of Israel, whereas the house of David was left with Jerusalem and with the tribes of Judah and Benjamin.

There were three disastrous consequences of the "great partition." First, the size of the newly formed monarchies was about half of David's country. Hence, the political power and influence of both monarchies had been drastically reduced. Secondly, David was able to make political alliances with his neighbors and to engage the two empires of the Nile and the Mesopotamia in relationships based on the power and size of his realm. After the partition, the monarchy of the south was "allocated" to its closest neighbor, Egypt, whereas the northern realm of Israel was now inexorably linked to the Assyrian and Babylonian rulers. The two distinct monarchies now developed their own interests and political alliances with the inevitable consequence that both had a weakened standing in the region.

Thirdly, internal arrangements were such that the sects of religion and actual power were separated—the religious center in Jerusalem and the political muscle in the kingdom of Israel. The coveted unity of the people with its shared religion and festivals was shattered. For a while the pilgrimage to Jerusalem continued unabated for two centuries until the fall of the northern kingdom to Sargon II in 721 B.C.E.

The Israelite leaders had failed to establish and to keep a functioning political system and organization that would keep the country unified and that would take into consideration the political and economic aspirations and interests of all the tribes. Instead they allowed their regional differences and petty special considerations to outweigh and to destroy the national objectives and institutions that make a country function and prosper.

Scholarship and Learning

Although much has been written about the scholarship of the Hebrews in the form of the Old Testament, the performance of the Israelites in scholarship and learning during the era of the first temple was negligible. There are no conclusive archaeological findings of any centers of learning or of the production of works of intellectual curiosity or imagination.

The priesthood in charge of the Arc and later the temple was a self-centered elite whose traditions, myths, and rituals were scrupulously kept as oral learning. If there were any documents of scholarship from this group, they were lost or destroyed.[209] The prophets who roamed the land spoke of moral issues and religious adherence to the teachings of the Israelite Almighty. There were no texts or traditions of which we know that reflect any substantial secular knowledge.

The poetic outputs of King David and the literary outcome of his son Solomon (in the book of Proverbs) are the exception to an otherwise nonproductive society. Although the Biblical account attributes the Book of Songs to David and Proverbs to Solomon, there is a strong possibility that they were composed or assembled much later, during the era of the Second Temple (in the third to the first centuries B.C.E.).

Besides the monarchical outputs, there are no historical or archaeological findings of other intellectual contributions of the kings or others in the Israelite society. The rules, procedures, and historical accounts of the Torah, later assembled by Ezra circa 445 B.C.E., continued to be oral traditions throughout the period of the first temple. The priesthood kept their rituals and traditions to themselves, and there is no evidence that learning was a public affair.

It seems without doubt that the Israelites did not excel in the arts or sciences when compared with their neighbors and with other nations and cultures of the time. They were perhaps typical of the Iron Age and, in some respect, less productive and imaginative than their neighbors. The driving force for the establishment of some form of intellectual activity and schools for the young, which began in the Babylonian Diaspora, was the Diaspora itself. The need to preserve the traditions, the unique rituals, and the history of the people of Israel led to the development of interpretations of the rules and historical accounts and later to their codification in the Talmud. It is ironic that while the Israelites inhabited their land and enjoyed political sovereignty, they did not feel the need to cultivate intellectual activities. Only after their expulsion from their native land did such a need arise, and then religious writings and schooling began to emerge.

Technology

Perhaps the most glaring example of the paucity of accomplishments of the Israelites was their poor performance in the area of technology. Derry and Williams (1961) suggested five major areas in which we can pinpoint technological achievements in human history. The Israelites failed to perform in all of them.

The first area was the *production of food*. There was enough output from agricultural activity to feed the tribes. The country was geographically diverse, allowing for a variety of crops in the fertile valleys and even in the hills of Judea and Israel. Some agricultural products were even used for exports (such as wines to Egypt), but none of the products gained distinction as an item of export. Part of the answer lies in the fact that the Israelites lacked the technical skills to produce high quality olive oil and wines, among other crops that were desirable in the region. Their regional and tribal isolation had worked against cooperation and the profitable exchange of agricultural goods.

The *extraction and working of metals* is another area of technological achievement. Although some mining of bronze is mentioned in historical accounts, the Israelites lacked the technological know-how to fabricate iron utensils and, especially, iron weapons. The Biblical narrative explicitly detailed the ban imposed by the Philistines on the secrets of forging iron weapons. The Israelites lacked the skills and knowledge for technology transfer and "reverse engineering" by which they could have copied the methods and techniques used by the Philistines. This weakness in the extraction and fabrication of metals represented a disadvantage in comparison with neighboring countries. In the course of large public projects such as the construction of the temple and the reorganization of David's army, the Israelites imported experts from Phoenicia, Assyria, and Egypt. These experts possessed the knowledge necessary to use metals in the construction of buildings, including the fabrication and use of precious metals such as gold and silver. The Israelites failed to learn from these foreign experts and to establish their own industries. Such technological deficiencies, combined with the division of the land into two separate and smaller kingdoms, greatly contributed to the weaknesses of the Israelites and to their defeat and expulsion from their native soil.

A third area of technology includes *modes and methods of transportation*. With the lack of building skills, regional and tribal differences, and provincial petty interests, the construction and maintenance of roads in ancient Israel was merely a dream. I already commented on the paucity of naval skills and the fact that the Israelites never achieved any useful mastery of the sea. A similar weakness was also present in the development of transportation by land.

The fourth area is the *generation and usage of energy*. Because of the temperate climate of the country, the use of wood for heating and for cooking would have been sufficient. Furthermore, there are no accounts of the construction of a network of irrigation channels or of attempts to artificially link the few rivers that traverse the country as was the case in Egypt. Again, the lack of central authority, regional and tribal interests, and provincial agriculture were practices that inhibited such irrigation projects.

Finally, *methods of communication and record keeping* are the fifth area of technological achievement. In this area the Israelites fared somewhat better, although still lagging in comparison with their neighbors. In Egypt and Mesopotamia, a wide array of commercial and military records has survived in the form of tablets and other inscriptions. The Israelites produced few such records. There are, however, some archaeological findings of records in ancient Hebrew and Aramaic that depict commercial, religious, and military life in the ancient land, particularly during the monarchy.[210] Perhaps due to the decentralized form of government, there was no urgent need to establish and maintain an elaborate system of communication and record-keeping, except in the collection of taxes.

Historians seem to agree that the Phoenician alphabet of 22 characters had widespread usage in the eleventh century B.C.E. The Hebrew language was influenced by the Canaanites and the Phoenician advances in writing. Archaeological findings from the period of the first temple include pottery, seals, and weights depicting writing in ancient Hebrew. The development of their own language and writing are marks of achievement of the ancient Israelites. But with the dominant role of religion and oral communication, the production of routine records and documents was severely curtailed.

After the fall of the kingdom of Israel, many northern Israelites fled to the south. Their preferred destination was Jerusalem and the city thus vastly expanded. This flow of refugees contributed to the merging of dialects and to the development of a more unified form of the language and its documentation.

Warfare and the Military

Some historians have suggested that the Israelite military during the period of the first temple and the monarchy was organized along the principles of the other nations in the region. Based on biblical account there is a futile attempt to describe events in which the Israelite military seemed to have excelled. The overall picture is quite disappointing.

During the monarchy, the kings had developed a system of recruiting necessary forces from the various tribes. Israelite forces included many foreign fighters and commanders and there was a specific bureaucratic organization of the military. Yet, the Israelites failed to defend their territory and were resoundly defeated and expelled.

When the Israelites went to war, their God (the Lord of Hosts) was a companion to their armed forces. In antiquity armies fought a military as well as a religious battle. Army confronted army and one God confronted other deities. In the case of the Israelites, the Almighty was a universal God but Israel was His chosen people. Hence He protected them and did His best to destroy their enemies. When battles were nevertheless lost, the priests and prophets had to account for God's failure and provide a strong religious explanation. Often this explanation rested on the sins of the Israelite king or the people leading to God's displeasure—hence to the Almighty's withdrawal from the battlefield.

Although the monarchy was able to organize a viable army, it nevertheless lacked central power that could overcome the division among regions and tribes. Neighboring nations, such as Assyria, Moab, Egypt, Babylonia, and Edom, continually attacked Israelite cities and villages. Particularly after the partition, the two kingdoms were unable to protect all their inhabitants, first in the TransJordan, later in the main regions of Israel and Judea. These constant incursions contributed to the erosion of economic life and the personnel needed for military recruitment.

In ancient times (as perhaps even today) military prowess, skills, and abilities were paramount to the survival of a national entity. The Israelites failed to secure a constant military force that could defend its country. They failed to develop the necessary technology for making armaments. They failed to learn from their foreign military advisors. They failed to capitalize on the achievements of their early kings in their territorial expansion and the reorganization of their military. While the religious leaders instilled in the people the notion of divine retribution for their sins, which meant being abandoned at their time of need, the secular leaders failed to equip the people with the martial tools that would guarantee their survival and security. The average Israelite farmer in the hills of Judea or in the valley near Meggido in the northern region felt twice abandoned by those he most trusted in his culture.[211]

Hypothesis of Failure During the Second Temple

The era of the second temple began after the fall of Babylon to Cyrus, King of Persia, circa 539 B.C.E. The expansion of the Persian Empire westward in the sixth century B.C.E. would bring it into conflict two centuries later with the Greeks under Alexander. The Persians procured to undo some of the conquests of Babylon and to restore stability to their western frontiers. They chose to reinstate Babylon's former enemies, such as the people from Judea who had been driven out of their country and into "Diaspora" in Babylon.

In 525 B.C.E. the Persians conquered Egypt and in 520 B.C.E. appointed Zerubbabel governor of the new province of Judea. He chose as his capital the city of Jerusalem and in 515 B.C.E. dedicated the site for the second temple.

The hypothesis of failure during the period of the second temple (515 B.C.E. to 70 A.D.) is predicated on four circumstances that did not exist during the previous periods in the history of the Israelites in their country. These circumstances engendered a unique revival of life in the part of the land now called Judah. Built in concentric expansion from Jerusalem, the revised nation now existed first as a province of the Persian empire, then as a province of the Greeks and later the Romans until the fall of the Second Temple in 70 A.D.

A Community of Exiles

With the expulsion of the inhabitants of the kingdom of Judah to Babylon, there emerged a community of exiles in Mesopotamia and in neighboring countries. The revival of the idea of return to Judea began soon after, when Cyrus conquered Babylon. The second temple in Jerusalem was dedicated only sixty years after the destruction of the first temple and the expulsion of the people. But much had changed in almost three generations.

Not only the political and military landscape in the Near East had been dramatically altered, but there were also changes in the composition of Jewish life.[212] The exiled had established a community with strong historical ties to their ancient land. By doing so, they addressed two problems: first, how to keep their people involved in the ancient traditions so they would not convert to the Babylonian way of life, and, second, how to balance the ordinary daily life in exile with the idea of a distant politically-viable homeland. These two problems they solved with the ingenious engineering of religious institutions, a religious-historic book, and the genesis of the idea of a "messianic" concept.

By the time the colony in Babylon was established, a similar Hebrew settlement was taking roots in Egypt. This was Elephantine, where the exiled from Judea even built a temple (later destroyed in 410 B.C.E.). These settlements on the shores of the Euphrates and the Nile marked the beginning of the Jewish Diaspora that would last for two and a half millennia and continues to the present day.

The Changing International Landscape

During the five centuries of the existence of the second temple in Jerusalem, the political and economic landscape of the Near East underwent dramatic changes. With the conquest of Mesopotamia and Egypt by the Persians, there began the occupation of the Near East by imperial interests from *outside* the region. While previously the land of Judea and Israel had been the piece of real estate coveted by its great neighbors, with the arrival of the Persians, then the Greeks and finally the Romans, this land became simply a province at the edge of the empire of a distant country.

To these empires the land of the Israelites or Jews resembled a territory along the intersect of tectonic plates. The last thing one wants is the eruption of a fault at the intersect and the arrival of earthquakes. Similarly, the successive empires recognized the importance of the land of Judea as a passageway at the frontiers of their possessions. They now had a different set of interests and requirements than the previous contenders—Egypt and Mesopotamia. The main concern of these new imperial powers was to maintain the peace at the borders and to abide by imperial needs for taxation, passageway, and resources.

The Persians, Greeks, and Romans had very few historical ties to this region and no history of conquests in the region. Their economies did not depend on this territory. Their interests were strategic and imperial.

The Greek Empire of Alexander was divided in 323 B.C.E. upon his premature death among his generals. Ptolemy I ruled Egypt and Seleucus I became ruler of Syria. Initially Ptolemy I conquered Judea in 301 B.C.E., and a century later Antiochus III of Syria conquered the land from the Egyptians. This turn of events engendered a situation similar to that of the period that led to the twilight of the first temple. In an usual act of interference in the internal affairs of the Jews in Judea, Antiochus IV entered Jerusalem in 172 B.C.E., proclaimed it to be a Greek city (renamed Antiochia), and essentially outlawed Judaism as a religion. This led to the revolt of the Maccabees in 166-160 B.C.E. and to the conquest of Jerusalem by Judah Maccabee in 161 B.C.E.

But on the horizon loomed the new power of the Roman expansion into the hitherto Greek possessions in the Eastern Mediterranean. Almost a century later the Romans, led by Pompeii, added Judea to their eastern provinces in 63 B.C.E.

Although the intervention of Antiochus IV left an indelible mark on Jewish traditions and its history of the era, it was quite different from the behavior of the Assyrians and Babylonians some four centuries earlier. His adventures in Judea are an aberration, whereas the political landscape before and after Antiochus IV was one of different empires safeguarding their frontier provinces in search of calm and peace.

Entrepreneurs and Visionaries

The story of the return to Judea after the Babylonian exile is one of a few visionary individuals who devoted their lives to the revival of Jewish life in the ancestral land. At the heart of this story are the personages of Nehemiah and Ezra.

Nehemiah was a member of the court of the Persian King Artaxerxes I who ruled during the period 465-424 B.C.E. Nehemiah was an entrepreneurial leader who sought the establishment of a *political* entity in Judea—at that time part of a Persian province. He described his effort and the difficulties he encountered in a book that bears his name and is today one of the later books in the Old Testament. Nehemiah received a commission from the Persian monarch to rebuild Jerusalem. His hope was to improve the poor condition of the city so as to attract Jewish pilgrims who later would want to become settlers in the revived capital of Judea. He immersed himself in the task of building consensus among his fellow Jews and among the Persian bureaucrats who ruled the imperial province. But principally Nehemiah's task was to build the city, re-erect its shattered walls, and make it a livable and defensible capital city.

Ezra had a similar vision but his means to getting there were different from Nehemiah's. Ezra had obtained in his native Babylon a permit from the Persian authorities to revive the Jewish religion and its traditions in the land of Judea and especially in Jerusalem. Ezra, son of Seraiah, was an accomplished scribe and a scion to a distinguished family of the Jewish priesthood.[213] His accomplishments were narrated by a contemporary historian in the book of Ezra, which precedes the book of Nehemiah and follows the book of Daniel.

Some fourteen years before the arrival of Nehemiah in Jerusalem, Ezra had started his task of rebuilding the Jewish religion (circa 459 B.C.E.). As the book bearing his name describes in the first few chapters, there had been a movement of immigrants from Babylon to Judea. Ezra observed the somewhat chaotic flow of Jews from Mesopotamia into Judea in an unregulated manner, with little common ground in the pilgrims'/immigrants' motives for their journey. He understood that a tacit approval by the Persian monarch was hardly enough to forge the revival of the Jews in their ancient land. Ezra then embarked on a project that perfectly matched his abilities as a scribe and his background as a priest.

Ezra searched for the glue, or the unifying concept and framework, around which the Jews could rally and which could serve as the principle guiding the national revival in Judea. He found it in the work of Jewish sages in Babylon who had compiled the ancient stories, myths, rules, and religious rituals and practices into a comprehensive volume of history and laws—the five books of the Torah in the Old Testament.[214]

As an accomplished scribe, Ezra recognized the value of the written document and its significance as an instrument that described the history and the religious rules of the people. He then proceeded to read portions of the book to the crowds in Jerusalem and instituted formal readings of the Torah as an obligatory part of prayers and sacrifices.

In effect, Ezra's endeavor, though sensible, laudable, and effective as it was at the time, set the tone for the next two millennia of Diaspora. The religious aspect of Ezra's unifying principle was at the heart of the failure of the political and national rebuilding of Judea. Together with the emergence of the Messianic idea during that period, the religious institutions and the religious attributes of the restoration of the country created by Ezra had in effect condemned the *national* aspirations of the returning Jews to utter failure.

All of the conflicts of the Jews in Judea with the ruling monarchies that followed Ezra's entrepreneurial project had become religious in nature. The nationalistic spirit and interest gave way to religious fervor. The revived country was thus perceived by both Jews and Gentiles as a *religious* people that happened to occupy the land rather than as people of the nation of Judea (later Palestine in Roman time) that happened to espouse the Jewish religion. Even when native rulers were appointed by foreign powers (such as Agrippa and Herod) to rule over the Jews, they were never again able to view themselves, nor have others view them, as a nation and a country first, and a religion second.

To the Romans in particular who were deeply trained in legal thinking and in national characteristics of social and political life, it was extremely difficult to understand this strange entity based on a religions framework.

Unintentionally, yet with consequences far-reaching into the future, Ezra created a mold for Jewish existence in Judea and in the Diaspora that would be scrupulously maintained by all Jewish future generations. Instead of giving strength to a unifying framework of Jewish revival, Ezra's endeavor created a situation whereby Jews could now rationalize their life outside Judea and Jerusalem by merely adhering to their religious practices and by obeying the rules and rituals ascribed in the Torah. The *national imperative* of the return to the native land became lost forever, giving rise to the "Duality Paradox."

The Duality Paradox

From the fifth century B.C.E. and the return of Jewish religious life to Jerusalem, Ezra's endeavor has engendered what I call the "Duality Paradox." This paradox is the quest for the identity of the Jewish people, those returning to Judea and those who remained in exile. There was no blueprint or viable master plan for the revival of Jewish existence in the native land. True, the temple in Jerusalem was rebuilt after 515 B.C.E., the walls of Jerusalem were re-erected after 545 B.C.E., and Jewish settlers began their return to various cities and regions of Judea and Samaria. But the notion of national identity as a people and as a political entity was not achieved. Instead, fueled by the mix of history and religious mandates and the emergence of the Messianic idea, the Jewish identity became a *religious* existence. Even today Israelis and Jews in the Diaspora are haunted by the questions: "Who is a Jew?" and "What makes a Jew?" An underlying problem engendered by Ezra's work was the limbo in which nation and religion had been placed. The revival of Jewish presence in the land of their ancestors was a patchwork of settlements and reconstruction. On the one hand there was not a *union* of religion and national identity nor, on the other, was there a *division* or separation of nation and religion. Driven primarily by the Messianic idea, the ethereal form of Judaism took over and became the framework that identified Jewish existence anywhere in the world.[215] There emerged a disconnect between the "facts on the ground," namely, the routine existence of the settlers in Palestine[216] and the universal-local attributes of their religion. The outcome was a tension-filled construct in which universal notions of an omnipotent and omnipresent almighty conflicted with the concept of the promised land and the complex history, folklore, and festivals that composed this concept.

The Messianic Idea

It would be highly presumptive of me to offer in this book a comprehensive historical review of this topic. Over two thousand years of Jewish and Christian scholarship has been devoted to the study of the Messianic idea in Judaism, and later in its interpretation in Christianity, and to an extent also in Islam.

Professor Joseph Klausner (1874-1958) has written a fascinating book on the origins of the Messianic idea.[217] There are several hypotheses as to the external influences on the eschatological thinking of the Jews in that period. Some scholars have suggested Persian influences through the interaction of Babylonian Jews with the Persian conquerors of Zoroastranian faith.[218]

But the unique characteristics of the Jewish belief in the "redeemer" suggests, as Klausner had argued, a process of integration of specific Jewish experiences and their maturation during special times which offered an auspicious background for such an intellectual development of the idea. Klausner (1955) interpreted the Messianic idea as "fundamentally the idea of redemption from exile" (p. 48). The driving scenario was the traditional narrative of the deliverance from slavery in Egypt and the subsequent occupation of Canaan, which led to an independent nation (among the nations of the world) with the freedom to fully practice their religion. This story that became an integral part of the Torah was delivered by Ezra and his partners to explain and to justify the project of renewal and reconstruction of the land promised to the people, as when they were delivered from Egypt.

In modern vernacular of the age of telecommunication, television, and the Internet, this would be a marvelous public relations "spin." The enterprise of the return to Palestine as advanced by Ezra was now anchored in the comparison with a similar occurrence some 800 years before. In addition, the hand of the Almighty was also present in this story through the services of His "anointed" leader, as He had done with the selection of David son of Jesse and his appointment by the prophet Samuel.

For those Jews who could not or would not join the project of reconstruction, the leaders of the project had to offer an alternative rationale that would fully justify the reconstruction while also giving hope to those who stayed behind—thus gaining their approval and their moral and financial support.

The idea of the Messiah or Redeemer perfectly fit this requirement. The reconstruction of the land of David and Solomon would be incomplete as long as the "true" leader had yet to emerge. Thus, in a complex manner, the ultimate *political* concept of nationhood for the Jews became enmeshed in the idea of the redeemer. The project of the redemption from exile and the reconstruction of the ancient homeland was therefore defined in a constant template of "work in progress." The pressure on the Jews in the Diaspora to return was greatly reduced and the evaluation of how well the reconstruction was proceeding also received a tremendous reprieve. Ezra and Nehemiah could then issue (in modern terms) a press release which would state: "We are doing the best we can, but the final success of this program can only be judged when the redeemer completes his work, with the mandate that he has from the Almighty. As you know, he is a righteous person—without reproach—and has an impeccable background as a scion to the house of David—all at his own pace, in good time, and when and if the conditions are propitious for his actions."

As it evolved in Jewish tradition, the Messianic idea encompassed the merging of the glorious past of the Israelites with an even brighter future. It became an open-ended conception of good things to come, of redemption from bad fortune, and the full return to the ancient homeland. It also became an umbrella for hope and trust in an uncertain future.

Unfortunately, the Messianic idea did not require any action on behalf of the people, nor could it be put to the test and either disproven or its veracity declared. It was also not related, nor did it advocate or reject any enterprises related to the renewal or reconstruction of the ancient homeland. Most of all, combined with religious aspects of the reconstructed Jewish identity, the Messianic idea became an eschatological and universal view of the world—without the elements of nation-building or a national identity in the independent homeland.

Historical Events and The Hypothesis of Failure

The four circumstances described above (community of exiles; changing international landscape; entrepreneurs and visionaries; and the

Messianic idea) greatly contributed to the failure of the reconstruction of the Jewish homeland during the period of the Second Temple (515 B.C.E.–70 C.E.). In essence, the revival of Jewish national life in Palestine never fully materialized. Other centers of Jewish life and Jewish religious learning emerged and prospered in Babylon, in Egypt, and later also in other cities and countries throughout the Persian, Greek, and Roman territories.

A tempestuous and melancholic set of events marked the five centuries of Jewish resettling of their homeland until the fall of the Second Temple in 70 C.E. Without an adequate national identity, major *political* actions by the Greeks who ruled Syria, and later by the Roman governors, were considered by the Jews of Palestine to be intolerable *religious* interferences. The revolt of the Maccabeans in 166-160 B.C.E. and the Jewish revolt against Rome in 66-70 C.E. are two major episodes representing the disastrous consequences of religious fervor at the expense of national and political existence.

There are four major historical events that punctuated the period of the Second Temple: the revolt of the Maccabeans, the revolt against Rome, the codification of the Jewish religion, and the rise of Christianity. Many historians of Jewish life in this period are almost apologetic when they describe the destruction of the temple and the exile of the Jews by the Romans. When combining the revolts against the Greeks and later the Romans, historians have attributed the blame for these events on the intolerance of the conquering forces. Josephus Flavius, a contemporary of the revolt against the Romans, has attempted a more even-handed analysis, but was largely criticized due to his well-known effort to appease the Romans and to cater to their interests. Yet, this trend of blaming others for one's inability to survive has become ingrained in the Jewish perspective upon the world for the two millennia that followed.[219]

The revolts against the Greeks (166 B.C.E.) and the Romans (66 C.E.) cannot be classified as national uprisings. Although triggered by different sets of conditions, they had in common elements of both the causes of the revolts and the nature of the uprising. In both cases, although two centuries apart, these revolts were carried out in the form of guerilla warfare of bands of lightly armed, yet very courageous, believers. The immediate cause for both uprisings was the rulers' desecration of Jewish sacred places and beliefs.

The revolt of the Maccabeans resulted in relative success. However, the leaders of this revolt failed to capitalize on their victories and to exploit them in order to establish a durable and viable national entity. In part this was due to the fact that the Maccabeans were not national leaders with a clear political agenda for their people. Rather, they were temporary solutions to a dire crisis. They were called to arms to lead the rebellion, without a strategic outlook on what to do afterwards.[220]

Codification of Judaism and Duality of Traditions

Hailed by Jewish scholars as one of the pivotal achievements of the period of reconstruction, the codification of Judaism produced major unintended consequences. Religious authorities and scribes in Babylon and in Palestine began a major project to assemble and codify the various oral traditions and surviving written documents. Ezra's effort to combine the codified Torah and the revival of ancient festivals was part of this project.

In addition to assembling the historical-religious documents, the codification also included the beginning of assembling procedures, legal opinions, case studies, and rulings on many religious issues. This effort produced the scholarly volumes known as the "Talmud" (learning). In the five centuries of this period (from the dedication of the second temple to its fall to the Romans in 70 C.E.), there emerged two parallel projects in the development of the Talmud. One was by the exiled community in Babylon, the other by the Jewish community in Jerusalem. This created the "duality of traditions."

The importance of such duality is not in the differences in content or in the authoritative aspect of the volumes—these were minor—but in the impacts on the viability of Jewish life in exile. The fact that Jewish scholarship and religious authority could be developed in an exiled community provided a very strong justification for the feasibility of a *complete* Jewish life outside the Promised Land. Jerusalem and the ancient homeland ceased to be the religious center of Jewish life. With the continuing absence of an adequate or respectable political center in Palestine, the diffusion of religious centrality to the far reaches of the Mesopotamian land has irreparably contributed to the erosion of the importance of Jerusalem and Palestine in Jewish existence. Even more so, it contributed to the suffocation of the urgent need to rebuild and to re-establish the Jewish nation in Palestine.

In the centuries to come, other centers of learning and Jewish religious scholarship emerged in Europe where Jews established large communities in major urban areas. Centers of rabbinical excellence existed in Spain, Russia, Poland, France, and Germany. They overshadowed the religious activities in Palestine. Their interpretation of the Torah and the teachings of the Talmud became the guiding light of Judaic wisdom. This trend had begun with the duality of traditions in Babylon and Jerusalem.

The initial duality in traditions had fostered the mold in which the Jewish religion was transformed into a "religion *with* a people," rather than a "religion *of* a people." By codifying the rules, traditions, myths, and historical accounts, and by making these documents the heart and soul of the religion, the scholars of this period had in effect accepted the condition of the Jewish people as an exiled entity. This would be an entity of a people bound by shared religious beliefs—as codified in the documents created to serve as key instruments of worship—exiled in the four corners of the ancient world and lacking political shape or any vestiges of control over their nationhood and national destiny.

Religion alone, as predicated in these documentary instruments of worship (the Torah, the later books which completed the Bible, and the Mishna-Talmud), could not become substitutes for nationhood. Rather, they irrevocably established a theocratic framework for the exiled Jewish people, in which there was a *past* and a mythical *future*, laced with messianic promises—but *no present*.[221]

The identification of the Jews with their religious beliefs, rituals, and the written essence of the faith—instead of a people with national characteristics—has also initiated a pattern of hatred and violence. In 38 C.E. during the reign of the Roman emperor Caligula, anti-Jewish violence erupted in Alexandria. This Jewish community was established during the Greek rule of Egypt under the Ptolomid kings following the death of Alexander the Great. The fate of this colony of Jews in a foreign land was illustrative of the fate of hundreds of similar Jewish communities worldwide in the next two millennia.[222]

Traditional historians describe the events as a conflict between the Romans and the Jews regarding the status of the community in the Egyptian province. The Romans were very sensitive to issues of citizenship and the Prefect of Egypt, Flaccus, refused to recognize the special status of citizenship that the Jews enjoyed under the Greek rulers. This portrays a very early instance in which civil authorities in a country began to classify a community of Jews as a separate religious group, but without a special status of a unique people. This was akin to recognizing a *faith* as a characteristic of the community, rather than their *civil* or *national* status as a *political* group. The consequences were disastrous for the Jews of Alexandria, as they were for Jews throughout the history of the Diaspora. In 66 C.E. the Jews in Alexandria protested the dilution of their rights and the violence exhibited by the local population against them a generation earlier. The revolt failed and many Jews were massacred and their community was decimated.[223]

By codifying their traditions and beliefs, the Jews of that epoch had created a religion that can be characterized as "portable." Rules and procedures were carefully crafted and tweaked to allow festivals and rituals to be practiced anywhere in the world where Jews could congregate—even temporarily. The concepts of nationhood and of a sovereign political entity were abandoned to be replaced by selectionism and isolationism.

Selectionism was the concept of the "chosen people." Converts and newcomers were discouraged from joining. The past—this incredibly artificial mix of historical figures and events, myths, and theological constants—became the determinant of the Jewish existence. It could be shared—most preferably—by birth, transferred from parents to children. In this way they could maintain the lineage to the . and to the early-anointed monarchs in the promised land. In a sense they were similar to the caste of patricians in Roman society—privileged by birth and superior to others because of their lineage to the founders of the city.

Such a quest for purity and inward looking had led to the emergence of isolationism. In order to adequately practice the faith, Jews had to congregate in tight-knit communities. This made it very difficult for them to expand—demographically and geographically. It also prevented them from being inclusive—as the other religions of Christianity, Islam, and Buddhism had become in their quest for universal manifestations of their beliefs.

The seeds of the fate of the Jewish people as being small, isolated, and disliked for believing in its superior standing in the world were sown during the period that began with the return to Judea after the exile to Babylon. These were the seeds from which grew the tree of tragedy, destruction, persecution, and national suicide. Although Jewish historians and scholars—starting as early as in that period of antiquity—have developed an extensive literature of the "blame game," the events of this period can be interpreted toward a conclusion that much of the ill-fated history of the Jewish people from that time on was self-inflicted. Blaming external forces and the indifference, even cruelty, that animated behavior toward the Jews for the ill-treatment accorded to Jews in so many countries throughout history is a highly injurious exercise in self-deception.[224]

The Loss of the Golden Opportunity

The six centuries between the beginning of the return from Babylon and the destruction of the temple in 70 C.E. is the time space in which the Jewish people lost a golden opportunity to restore its national existence. This was a unique period in history—as if the relevant stars were aligned and conditions were right—for one, and one time only.

What were these conditions? First, the initial movement of return began only a few years after the exile to Babylon. The country—Judea and Northern Israel—was largely uninhabited. Secondly, from a geopolitical standpoint, the region was under political unrest. The Persians were replaced by the Greeks, who were then replaced by the Romans. Thirdly, for the first two centuries, there was active support from the Persian rulers for the reconstruction and establishment of a strong Jewish state in the outpost of the Persian empire. Finally, in the aftermath of the rebellion of the Maccabeans, Judah Maccabee had negotiated an agreement with the growing power of the Roman republic. The agreement was later broken only when the Romans intervened in the Jewish civil war in 63 B.C.E.

The period in question started with the support of a mighty empire of the Persians and ended with the initial support of the Roman republic. The opportunity was there to rebuild the nation and to bring it to the point where it would be strong enough to negotiate diplomatic ties with the changing rulers in the region. Instead, as described below, the reconstruction was carried out haphazardly, with internal strife preventing adequate leadership from arising. The Greeks and the Romans who followed found a land inhabited by a strange collection of cities and rural areas, with Jerusalem as its religious center. They also found political and social divisions in the population, lack of national leadership, and the continuing inability for self-government. Although this is a speculative scenario of a lost opportunity, it was during this same period that the cities of Greece rose to prominence and the city of Rome became a global power.

What Went Wrong?

Some of the key reasons for the failure of the Jews to reconstruct their ancient homeland have already been discussed. To recapitulate, there was a very damaging lack of certain national attributes, skills, and characteristics that were highly conducive to internal instability.

Beginning with this period and continuing thereafter throughout the Diaspora, the Jews lost the refined skills of the discipline of civil commitment, self-government, and the creation and careful maintenance of political and national institutions. Self-reliance and self-government became attributes of small community, whereas on a national level the trend was shifting toward reliance on others, specifically, a string of foreign benefactors.

There was a constant lack of civil and secular leadership whose interests extended beyond self-enrichment and the pursuit of power. Civic commitment on the part of such leaders never materialized.[225] During the Greek period and particularly during the brief role of the Romans there emerged two elite groups within the Jewish population in Judea and northern Israel. The prosperity of the Roman period (63 B.C.E. to 70 C.E.) gave rise to an aristocracy of wealth in Judea and Galilee. Alongside it there was the religious or rabbinical elite whose main concern (in addition to its own survival) was the strict adherence to the newly codified rules of the faith, and avoiding the actual, or even the appearance of, divergence from the teachings of the religion.

What political scientists would later call "the other estate," namely the political elite, never materialized. Thus, there was a lack of civic and national sentiments of nationhood and loyalty to the country as they existed in the Greek cities and in Rome. Besides a religious attraction, Jews in exile had no persuasive reason or justification to emigrate to the reconstructed land of their ancestors. As soon as the codified books of the faith offered them a universal justification for worship anywhere in the world, the religious attraction to the promised land lost much of its luster.

The religious or rabbinical elite lacked the strengths of political officeholders yet possessed their shortcomings. Its members exercised authority and made rulings but could not muster the civic entrepreneurship and enthusiasm that contribute to a vibrant secular regime. This elite later became a universal group. Its members were interchangeable in geography. They were not bound by secular rules and rulings and they were not responsible to any specific order or territory.

The Roman Period and The Final Collapse

The Romans ruled the land of the Jews for a relatively short period. Their government of Palestine began in the middle of the first century B.C.E. and ended toward the end of the first century C.E. with the exile of the Jews and the destruction of their temple in Jerusalem.

This period in the history of the ancient Middle East was one of economic prosperity and relative peace. Among the innovations of the epoch were the introduction of the saddle on horses and the domestication of camels for transportation in the harsh desert lands. Judea and Galilee enjoyed the proliferation of commerce, trade, and the prosperity encouraged by Roman peace and security. In addition to the economic growth in Jerusalem, other cities in the country also flourished. One example is the vibrant and prosperous city of Sepphoris ("Zippori" in Hebrew) in lower Galilee near Nazareth. The site of this city has been recently excavated, revealing its extensive construction.[226]

Thanks to contemporary historians such as Flavius and chroniclers of early Christianity, the Roman period and the fall of Jerusalem have been amply documented. In the year 73 C.E. the desert fortress of Masada was finally conquered by the Roman legions. The inhabitants of this last stronghold in Judea took their own lives. The Romans exiled most of the Jews from Judea and Galilee.

After the Roman exile there remained only a small number of Jews in Palestine. For the second time the Jewish population was expulsed and its center of religious and political life was annihilated. There were four key differences between the Roman and the Babylonian exiles.

First, the Roman empire endured for five more centuries. Any organized return—as carried out by Nehemiah and Ezra—would not have been possible without the permission and support of the Roman emperors. Second, the Roman exile was much more dispersed than the previous expulsion to Babylon, because of the vastness of the empire. Thirdly, at the time of the Roman destruction of the country there already existed Jewish settlements throughout the empire, even in Italy itself. Finally, soon after the Roman exile a new religion emerged from Judaism and from the land of Palestine: Christianity. Promulgated initially to the Jewish settlements in the Roman empire, the Christian faith grew in numbers and importance and constituted in many instances a substitute religion to traditional Judaism.

In his study of the emergence of Christianity, Professor Joseph Klausner proposed a similar scenario. He argued that "among these 'converts' were Hellenistic Jews of the Diaspora. These Jews provided the basis for Christianity as a religion. If it had not been for them, Christianity would have remained a Jewish sect like the Essenes. Detached Jews, not rooted in the soil and traditions of Palestine, spiritually suspended between Judaism and Hellenism, they were the very best material for a new religion...."[227] He further argued that this new religion had the following attributes which distinguished it from traditional Judaism: "...a definite depreciation of the ritual requirements in favor of the ethical; a definite exaltation of blind belief in a personality and in miraculous deeds at the expense of the study of Torah; and, along with this, an indifferent attitude toward political life and the political future of the nation, and a covert inclination to put a higher evaluation upon the individual than upon the nation and a stronger emphasis upon humanity than upon Jewish nationality" (*ibid.*, pp. 275-276).

Professor Klausner's text evokes his passion and his frustration at the historical developments of the first and second centuries C.E., in which the Jewish decline was accompanied by the rise of Christianity. But, in contrast to the conclusions from his analysis, the departure of early Christianity from Jewish nationality toward more human and universal values was not uniquely Christian. It was a trend also found in Judaism. There was hardly any "political future of the nation" in the Jewish existence in Palestine during this period. Some cities and settlements and even the temple in Jerusalem do not make a nation or a Jewish nationality. The choice made by the Jews of the Diaspora was not between a national Jewish entity and a new universal religion. It was a choice between two distinct ways of worship, different rituals, and a set of commonly shared beliefs and basic tenets.[228]

Sic Transit Gloria Mundi

"Thus the glory of this world passes away"—supposedly the last utterance of the Roman emperor Nero (15 C.E.-68 C.E.).[229] This is also an illustrative description of the lost opportunities of the Jewish people to establish a national entity in Palestine that could withstand the geopolitical and social changes of the millennia. First under the Persian rule, upon the initial return from the Babylonian exile, the Jews failed to exploit the opportunity offered to them by the favorable set of external circumstances. Ezra, Nehemiah, and the other leaders of the time tried to get the job done in any way possible—mostly by emphasizing the religious aspects of the reconstruction rather than the national revival.

During the early years of the Roman conquest another golden opportunity was utterly lost to incompetence, to greed, to division rather than unification, and to adherence to religion rather than to people and nation. The Roman annexation of Palestine heralded a period of peace and prosperity, thus offering a unique chance to cement a strong Jewish presence as an outpost of the empire. Revolts against Roman rule were not an exceptional occurrence, mostly due to the excesses of the provincial regime and its procurators. What made the Jewish revolt such a disastrous affair was its fragmented explosion and the internal discord of its participants, combined with the excessive religious fervor of an impoverished part of the population.[230]

Yet, Roman prosperity did benefit a small class of the Jewish elite in Palestine. This group was composed of an alliance between merchants and members of the priesthood. The Romans at that time had already gained considerable experience in governing colonized people and were thus able to exploit the local shortcomings. Their governors encouraged the divisions among the various factions of the elite and the religious parties. They took sides and used their power to administer harsh penalties on those who would not play by their perverse rules. The Jewish sects and religious parties were continually engaged in a type of "gang war" at the expense of the population. Instead of looking inward to their own foibles, all sides to the internal upheaval blamed the Romans for the discontent within the larger population. Poverty and religious fervor combined to incite the populace, whereas Messianic dreams fueled this movement.

Throughout their empire the Romans looked for the merging of local customs and their laws, rules, and structures. In many instances they had opted for compromises and native rule of internal affairs. Why was Palestine such an exception? It was hardly a crucial part of the empire. The harshness with which Rome extinguished the revolt was more to serve as an example rather than a strategic necessity that endangered Roman security. Personal glory of Roman generals notwithstanding, it was expensive and disruptive to send the legions to the outposts of the empire to quench some uprising of the local population. These legions could be better used for additional conquests of richer and more promising territories, such as those in western and northern Europe.

A unified people with strong internal government and a civic-minded leadership would have gained the respect of the Romans and would have led to an accord with the empire for honorable co-existence.

Such was not the case in Palestine. Then, as in the Diaspora, the Jewish people were divided, internally chaotic, uncompromising, and a threat to the peace and order so desired by Rome in its empire.

The thesis that Judea or Palestine could not succeed or survive because of its location between major powers and the paucity of its natural resources is, in my view, untenable. The following citation is illuminating: "It had none of the resources of the others. Its land was barren and bereft of minerals. The population was small. There were no large towns, no industry, and little culture. Even the nobility was poor and the landless peasants lived like cattle. Yet, by a supreme act of will and a genius for organization ... and ... Machiavellian diplomacy of temporary alliances with whatever power seemed the strongest brought constant additions to its territory."[231] This was not a description of Palestine— it was William Shirer's portrayal of Prussia in the eighteenth century. Other examples of small countries situated alongside or between larger powers and who managed to excel and to prosper are the Netherlands, Switzerland, Portugal, and, in present times, Singapore.

In a way the relationship between the Jewish religious institutions and core beliefs and the Jewish people in Palestine and later in the Diaspora resembled that of the Prussian state and its people. It is usually accurate to say that the Prussian state, anchored in the philosophy of the divine establishment of its rulers, demanded from its people unquestioning obedience and sacrifice. Prussia was not a state for its people. Rather, it was a state with a people, who were supposed to suppress their feelings, individuality, and desires in favor of an ethereal idea of the goodness and the absolute superiority of the "state."

After the reconstruction in the post-Babylonian era, and culminating with the development of the Jewish religious institutions under the Romans, Judaism became not a religion *of* a people, but a religion *with* a people. Similar to the ideal of the Prussian state, it became an entity in itself. Its tenets and basic ideology were uncompromising, wholly concerned with its own survival as a besieged faith, run by ruthless priests with absolute power and indifferent to the individual.

These developments in the structure of the religion and the role it was beginning to assume in the lives of the believers naturally led to the emergence of dissatisfied factions and a tendency to create movements aimed at protecting the poor and the disadvantaged—that is, rebelling against the organizational supremacy and ideology of the religion. Blind obedience to strict rules of behavior had now become enmeshed—in popular beliefs—as a revolt against organized religion and simultaneously against the Roman rulers. Finally, the bloody and protracted revolt that ensued was as much an internal struggle against division and corruption and religious indifference as it was against a foreign oppressor. This aspect of the rebellion may explain its exceptional fury and the inability of the parties to reach a peaceful conclusion. The war brought in its wake the destruction of the country and the exile—again—of its population.

What were the conditions during the period of the Roman rule that may have facilitated the building of a strong Jewish presence in their homeland? The experience of other Roman provinces had been a mix of Roman attempts to keep the peace and encourage economic prosperity and commerce and at the same time deal with discontent and selective uprisings of dissatisfied populations. The Romans employed a method laced with harsh punishment and delicately woven diplomacy. Complete destruction of the province and exile of the population were not the preferred mode of dealing with grievances.[232]

Secondly, the Jewish community in Palestine had grown in size and wealth since the reconstruction began four centuries earlier. There was a sufficient stock of population and assets to build a powerful presence in the region. There was also sufficient talent and human resources to build a credible and effective military—within the bounds of Roman legal constraints.

But the reality was disastrously different. As was the case with the monarchy before the exile to Babylon, the Jewish population in Palestine during the Second Temple did not excel in any technological or social-economic areas. Increasingly the nature of the interface between the people and their religion led to a tendency to become isolated, and distant from the world around them with a mentality of a besieged population. The fate of the fortress of Masada is telling, as it exemplifies the character of what Judaism and the Jewish people had become. Besieged by Roman legions, the citadel was finally destroyed. It was built by King Herod as a royal refuge in the Judean Desert in the vicinity of the Dead Sea. The citadel sat on a barren rock with difficult access. Upon the Jewish revolt in 66 C.E., several hundred zealots escaped to Masada under the command of Eleazar ben-Yair. The Roman Tenth Legion attacked the citadel. Facing defeat, ben-Yair ordered a massive suicide of the defenders and their families. In 73 C.E. this last outpost of Jewish resistance was finally conquered.[233]

Thirdly, there was already a history in the Jewish psyche of revolt, defeat, and exile, as during the Babylonian period. The reality under the Roman rule was a different approach of an empire toward its distant province. Jewish leaders of the epoch had not learned from the experience of the First Temple, nor did they draw any conclusions on how to deal with the new rulers of the ancient world. The Roman reality was indeed the last opportunity for the Jews to have and to keep a viable land of their own in their ancient homeland. However, the Jewish leadership was so embroiled in petty conflicts of selfishness—cloaked in the masking of religious integrity—that they remembered very little of their history.

Thus, although conditions were generally favorable for the survival and prosperity of the Jewish province, the stage was nevertheless set for failure and ultimate perdition. The destiny of the Jewish people to be exiled into a Diaspora for two millennia was not written in the stars. Then, as throughout the remainder of the Jewish history, it was the result of incompetence and indifference on the part of the civil and especially the religious leadership of the Jewish people.

Promising Beginning and A Failed Ending

The "antiquity of the Jews," as Flavius called it, began with a bang as a promising start of an exceptional people—then ended with a subdued failure of the nondescript inhabitants of an impoverished and war-torn province of the Roman empire. If one believes in the assistance that the Almighty provided His chosen people during their settlement in Canaan, such help ceased to exist during the period of the Second Temple. Such a gap in credibility of the existence and power of the Almighty and His unfulfilled promises requires a solid explanation. Jewish sages have been engaged for two millennia in developing complex explanations and reasoned arguments as to why the Almighty turned His back on His chosen people. In a blending of punishment for horrific sins, and the concept of the "Messiah" as redemptor of His people (as Moses had done in Egypt), these scholars composed a marvelous justification for Jewish suffering and for the failed destiny of the chosen people.

This justification and the emphasis on strict adherence to religious tenets and rituals formed the cornerstone of Jewish existence in their Diaspora. Life was composed of reliving the past in daily prayers and periodic festivals, and hoping for and believing in the day of salvation when the Messiah would restore the glory of the past.

Readers who are familiar with the achievements of Jewish communities in North America and in Western Europe may be appalled at reading my analysis of the incompetence and the overwhelming failure of the Jewish people in antiquity. Are we even examining the same people? As my narrative on the Diaspora will show, the accomplishments of Jews in commerce, science, technology, the arts, even politics and government were due to the fact that so many of them had rejected the shackles of their religion. Unfettered from the constraints of their past as a religious burden, they considered the past merely as an historical narrative. Similarly, they began to view their future in light of their own effort, without the immobilizing waiting for the Messiah. In turn, they channeled their energies to their present and the outstanding challenges and opportunities it provided in all aspects of human endeavor.

But this was a very late development. In most of the two millennia of the Diaspora, the Jewish people carried on a painful existence, the direct result from the failures in their antiquity. The religious and philosophical accomplishments of their scholarship would have been confined to their isolated communities but for the emergence and rise to prominence of Christianity. Although Jewish scholars had labored in Palestine and in the Diaspora during the era of the Second Temple, their outputs constituted refinements of the Torah, rules of behavior, and codes of laws for the Jewish believers. This effort continues in the early centuries after the Roman exile. The scholarly activities of rabbinical sages in Palestine during the first to the fourth centuries C.E. became the guiding learning material for Jews in the centuries that followed. Yet, by adhering to the formal aspects of the religion and its codex of tenets, they instituted an irreparable disconnect between the religion as a companion to a living people and the people themselves. The main outcome from this failure in antiquity was the transformation of Judaism into a religion that happens to have a people (albeit fragmented, exiled, and battered) rather than a people who have a religion.

However historians and Jewish scholars have tried to justify, explain, and even celebrate the story of the Jews in their ancient homeland, the outcome of an incisive analysis is irrefutable. The grand beginning of the Jewish people has ended with a colossal failure. They lost the land of their ancestors and were exiled to the four corners of the ancient world. They lost the structure and the semblance of civic and national existence. They were now at the near total control by others. They were now doomed to twenty centuries of a sorry existence in their Diaspora.[234]

Part VI
The Diaspora: Recreating A Religion But Losing A People

Never in the recorded annals of human existence did so many hold such deep hatred of so few, for so long, for so little, and with horrifying consequences as in the Jewish Diaspora.

Weaving a Tapestry of Twenty Centuries of the Lost

The story of the Diaspora is a tapestry of human history of two millennia, laced with the Jewish experience, which was generally of intense but mostly unnecessary misery. How does one tell such a complex story, intricately woven through several epochs, many historical events of tremendous importance in human history, and in so doing, highlighting the role of the Jewish experience? How can one explain the phenomenon of the Jewish people who persevered throughout all the transformations that two millennia had engendered?

But why would we want to highlight this peculiar experience of a displaced people? What is so important or fascinating about the Jewish people in their Diaspora?

Firstly, the Jewish people had assumed a *global presence*. From the Atlas mountains in Northern Africa to the Indian sub-continent to Eastern and Western Europe and the Americas—the Jewish people had found a home in all the continents and under all types of political, economic, and religious regimes. Was such presence the result of a pervasive need to always adapt to changes in their environment, or perhaps an inherent capacity to withstand different systems of government and religious influence? Perhaps a combination of both reasons has made the Jews such an *omniglobal* people, adept to living under all and so different circumstances.

Secondly, unlike any other people in human history, the Jews were the staple of hatred throughout the two millennia and practically everywhere they lived. The persecution of the Jews was limited to major events, particularly in the history of the Christian and Muslim countries.

Consider the events of the Crusades, the "reconquista" of Spain from the Moors in the fifteenth century C.E., and the decline of the Russian monarchy in the nineteenth century. These historical milestones were punctuated by the persecution of the Jews and even to their expulsion (from the Iberian peninsula).

Thirdly, as the Jews were able to somehow unfetter themselves from the shackles of their total and oppressive religious mandate, they began to contribute to the social and political environments that they inhabited. When given citizenship rights and relative freedoms, Jews in various countries in the nineteenth and twentieth centuries C.E. unleashed dormant energies. They excelled in the arts, the sciences, and in the economic welfare of their countries. These contributions became particularly noticeable in Western Europe and in the Americas.[235]

Unique among other peoples and races, the Jews are of acute general interest due to their ubiquitous global presence and their participation—albeit mostly as a victim—in critical junctures of world history in the last two millennia. In most countries, Jews inhabited primarily large urban areas, so that the majority of the rural population was unaware of their presence. Nevertheless, the Jewish presence in large metropolitan conclaves had them rubbing shoulders with the elites of their respective countries. Hence, for better or worse, Jews left their mark on the decision-makers and the urban classes of note.

The story of the Jews in their Diaspora is also a cogent instrument I employ in this narrative to address the five myths of the history and performance of the Jewish people.[236] The narrative itself revolves around the general thesis of this part of the book: how the Jewish religion evolved during the Diaspora at the expense of the progress of the Jewish people. The narrative contains selected events and individual cases that illustrate the thesis and provide examples of the concepts I advance in this book. Unlike methods used by other historians, such as Moore (1966), I am not collecting events to build a theory and to generalize from them. Rather, I believe that the events described in this part of the book strongly support the thesis I espouse—however uniquely argued and irreverent it may appear.

What was the Jewish Diaspora? Many peoples in the course of history have been living outside their native lands. The English, the Poles, the Irish, and the Italians have emigrated to the Americas, to Australia, and to other countries. The flow of masses of migrants is a staple of historical events of transitions and settlements. The migrations of the Nordic tribes into Western and Eastern Europe, and the massive movements of the Mongols and the Huns are examples of historical relocations of vast human hordes.

The Jewish Diaspora is different from other movements of peoples across geographical expanses. The differences are the basis for the myths about the Jews in their Diaspora that this book addresses. These myths and deeply ingrained beliefs in the Jewish collective psyche have created a unique mentality that has been nurtured for two millennia. This book is, in part, a result of an analysis by a twenty-first century person who is simultaneously a product of this mentality and a rebellious consequence of it.

The differences of the Jewish Diaspora are also its characteristics. These are attributes of not only a state of the Jewish people over two millennia but also their "state-of-mind."

Firstly, the Jewish Diaspora did not create or engender a nation. It was simply a state of affairs in which Jews existed in "pockets" in almost all the continents. They never established a *national* identity—as we understand it nowadays in the twentieth and the twenty-first centuries. There were, of course, some unifying elements that tied the Jews together as a people, but not within a national identity. As national movements emerged in Europe during and after the Middle Ages, the Jewish pockets were left behind. They were aware of these movements and their consequences, both political and economic, but they chose not to participate in them, primarily because it meant assimilation and adherence to a belief system that departed from the religious structure into assuming a secular model of existence.

Secondly, the Jews in their unique Diaspora, by and large, did not mix with the local populations of the geographical area they happened to inhabit at any particular time. This phenomenon of creating a closed enclave became the hallmark of two millennia of diaspora living. It was based on almost complete separation, not only religious but also economic and social. Separation led to exclusions that then led to rules and regulations to tighten up the separation.

The term Diaspora originated from the Greek and its meaning is "dispersion." The Jewish term is "Gola" which translates as "exile." The difference in the terms is meaningful, in that the Greek term describes a reality from the non-Jewish perspective, whereas the Hebrew term describes an event in the life of the Jewish people (or a series of events) where they were exiled by others from their homeland and made to wander for centuries of misery and loss.

The description of the "Exile" as a wrong perpetuated by Gentiles has greatly contributed to the institutionalization of the need for and justification of separation. How could the victims of such a wrong mix with the perpetrators of this injustice? The more the Jewish enclaves lived separate lives, the more they maintained a purified life which served as a clear demarcation between good and evil, between criminals and victims.

A complementary attribute of the Diaspora was the ingrained belief that the state, or political entity within which the Jewish enclaves existed, was the "enemy." At best it was a distinct, separate, alien, and unfriendly institution whose purpose and actions had very little to do with the enclave. This separate existence and such beliefs gave rise to the reality of the Jewish ghetto.

The original version of the ghetto began in 1509 when German Jews were allowed to live in the Italian city-state of Venice. They were allowed to live in an enclave known as Ghetto Nuovo (the new foundry). The enclave was surrounded by a wall and the Jews were ordered to reside only within its confines. Other Italian towns adopted a similar policy (in 1555 the Pope allowed Jews to live in a segregated enclave along the river Tiber in Rome). The term "ghetto" became synonymous with a Jewish quarter, where the Jews not only sought an enclave for protection and a segregated existence, but also where they were *ordered* to reside by decree of the state.[237]

The Jewish Diaspora was also different because the Jews had permanently lost their homeland. This led to subsequent attempts to reinvent their identity and their cultural and religious existence. The Diaspora became a permanent way of life, not a transitional state of affairs. Paradoxically, however, the concept of the Diaspora was consistently framed by Jewish leaders as a temporary condition, until the return to the ancient homeland ("The Promised Land"). Yet, the longer the Diaspora continued, the more permanency had been injected into its reality, and the less attractive the transitional form of it became to the masses of the displaced Jewish people.

The Diaspora was a *concept*, not simply a set of conditions that described the Jewish existence. It became a religious concept, as well as a social and cultural idea. Its peculiar attributes created a special reality that in essence defined the Jewish people: who they were, what they were doing, even what their future would be. This concept became the embodiment of the Jewish experience.

Images of Tenacity and Abandon

In reality the total period of the Jewish Diaspora extended for 25 centuries. The first was the expulsion by the Babylonians, known in Jewish history as "Galut Bavel" (the exile to Babylon). Even during the Roman occupation of the revived Jewish homeland there were Jewish settlements throughout the Greek and Roman possessions in the Eastern Mediterranean basin. These were the remnants of the Babylonian exile.[238]

Before the Roman exile of 70 C.E. there were lines of communication and commercial ties between the Jewish Diaspora of the time and the Jews living in the ancient homeland (named "Palestine" by the Romans). Following the fall of Jerusalem, many Jews joined their former countrymen in these established settlements in Syria, Egypt, and other Greek and Roman territories along the shores of the Mediterranean. Within a few centuries Jewish settlements flourished throughout the ancient world and, as the Roman Empire continued its expansion to the east and the west, Jewish settlers followed this geographic pattern.

Mostly these settlements were a Jewish minority within the more urban form of life in the Greek and later Roman dominions. In the several centuries before and after the fall of Jerusalem, the patterns that later would dominate the Jewish Diaspora began to emerge. These included minority states, segregation within a conclave, religious leadership that assumed the political and social control of the community and, not the least, the maintenance of on-going relations with similar communities in other cities and provinces, while keeping a low level of interaction with the majority population and its institutions.[239]

Any endeavor to cover the journey of a people over 25 centuries would be not only difficult but almost by definition a study in selectivity. The images that emerge over this enormous period of human history are generally of the Jewish minority subjected to continuous persecution, forced to abandon its homes and move about across provinces, later countries and continents. This image principally conjures the concept of the victimized people whose only sin was its tenacious holding on to its ancient religious traditions. Such tenacity of existence is generally viewed by historians and modern observers as an admirable quality of a proud people, victim to circumstances well beyond its control. Similarly, a religious approach by Jews and Gentiles views the centuries of oppression as divine retribution for a favorite people who had sinned, but whose turn shall certainly come in an unspecified time in the future.

Both approaches to the phenomenon of the Jewish Diaspora seem to disregard several factors that are inherent in the Jewish experience in at least twenty centuries. These factors are the explanation provided in this narrative. It is difficult to weave an account of over twenty centuries of a people's wandering throughout the world. So, to make it more concise, this narrative concentrates on dispelling two basic myths. One, the concept of Jews as victims—either of divine actions or by the cruel hand of their Gentile persecutors. The second is the idea or concept that the Jews had no choice but to remain in the captive state of a people in its Diaspora, forced on them by inhospitable and unwavering external forces. The narrative then will focus on the factors that help us to dispel these basic myths.

The Prejudice and The Passion

The images conjured by the Jewish Diaspora are misleading. They are particularly tainted by the horrific occurrences of the "Pogroms" in Russia during the nineteenth century, culminating with the holocaust of the Nazi regime in the twentieth century. Yet, there were 18 prior centuries of Jewish history among the nations of the world, and the images that these other centuries conjure are both as a people of tenacity and a people resigned to its destiny of being a victim of prejudice and persecution.

During this long stretch of history, the Jewish people in its Diaspora had ample opportunities to affect its liberation and to return to its ancient homeland, thus ending the painful dispersion of its members. In this period of almost two millennia, there occurred several transformations, rebellions, and revolutions that brought about dramatic changes in the maps of the world, its political, religious and cultural landscape, and in the distribution of nations and governments. Yet, almost by design, the only constant in this utterly dynamic scene of history remained the pathetic presence of the Jewish people: captive in its Diaspora, pitifully moving from one spot to another, while appearing to maintain a granite-like tenacity of existence under all possible odds. If even half of this tenacity and a quarter of the passion it took to maintain this miserable existence had been directed toward a national resurgence and a political and cultural reawakening of the people in its ancient land, the history of the Jewish people would have been totally different.

Throughout the twenty centuries of the Jewish Diaspora, the land between the River Jordan and the Mediterranean Sea lay scarcely inhabited. Following the emergence of Islam in neighboring Arabia, the Muslim conquerors established their rule in several urban dwellings, including Jerusalem. The long battles with the Crusaders left much of the country in a state of a wasteland, denuded of trees, villages destroyed, and the parties to the conflict ensconced in their forts and several cities. Both Christian and Muslim rulers had little interest in the land besides their religious fervor to keep it as a place for pilgrimage and to make sure that the other side would not monopolize access to the holy places, particularly in Jerusalem, Bethlehem, and the Galilee region.

Even as the Jews maintained a modest presence within the population of Jerusalem and other cities ever since their exile by the Romans, there was never a serious attempt to execute a massive return to the ancient home. There was never a "Jewish Crusade" or an organized and consistent "counter-exodus" or pilgrimage with the intent of settling the land. Many Jews did visit their holy land and brought news of its desolation to their respective communities in the Diaspora, but that was the extent of the attempts to ever return to the land they considered their homestead.[240]

Shabbetai Zvi and the Failed Redemption

One attempt to create a movement that would direct common Jewish folk towards settling the ancient land of Judea and Jerusalem in particular was the adventure of Shabbetai Zvi.[241] A much vilified character in the Jewish tradition, his life was a noted chapter in the Messianic movement. Shabbetai Zvi was one of a few Messianic leaders, known in the Hebrew vernacular as "Mashiach Sheker" (false Messiah).

He was born in 1626 in the Turkish city of Smyrna. He studied Jewish mysticism and at the age of 36 traveled to Egypt and to Gaza, where he met a young rabbinical student named Nasan Ashkenazi (born in Jerusalem in 1643). This young scholar considered himself a prophet and soon had revealed to the world his spiritual apparitions in which he saw Shabbetai Zvi as the long-awaited Jewish Messiah. They traveled to Jerusalem, where Shabbetai Zvi proclaimed himself the Messiah, and made announcements of both a reformulation of religious rituals and a rebirth of the national identity of the Jewish settlements in the Holy Land. For example, he abolished several days of fast that commemorated tragic events and announced the re-establishment of sacrificial ceremonies at the Temple Mount where, according to tradition, Solomon's Temple once stood and where the second Temple was destroyed by the Romans.

Many Jews in Palestine and the neighboring countries, even as far as Rome, were electrified by the news of the daring self-appointed Messiah and joined his movement. But the core of Shabbetai Zvi's appeal was his religious reinterpretation of Jewish existence and its future. There was very little political or national undertone to his movement. He and his associate Ashkenazi soon found themselves entangled in a conflict with rabbinical authorities in Jerusalem. In 1664 the rabbis excommunicated them and banished them from Jerusalem. The rabbis declared Shabbetai Zvi a false Messiah and sent missives to other rabbis in neighboring communities warning them of the unauthorized actions by the false Messiah.

Shabbetai Zvi left Jerusalem and for almost two years wandered throughout the Turkish Empire.[242] He appeared in Istanbul (Constantinople) in 1666 and was brought before the Sultan on charges of rebellion. Given a choice to save his life, he converted to Islam, while declaring that his conversion was merely another stage in the Messianic road to redemption. Many of his followers followed him into conversion to Islam.

The fiasco of the Messianic adventure of Shabbetai Zvi exemplifies not only the failure of the Jewish movement to return to its homeland, but also the power exercised by the rabbinical leadership. It was not by chance that the Shabbetai Zvi attempt was brought down by the rabbis of Jerusalem, Gaza, and Egypt. These religious authorities merely exercised their powers of leadership of the Jewish Diaspora.

This religious leadership and the lack of any other leaders, especially civil and secular leaders, are at the heart of whatever reasonable explanation one might advance for the length and the tremendous and disastrous story of the Jewish Diaspora. It was all a question of leadership or lack of it.

Reinventing a Religion: The Disastrous Failure of the Religious Leaders

Throughout the history of the Jewish people, even when it inhabited the promised homeland, there was never a time when a sustained civil and secular leadership took hold to exercise its positive influence, as it did in other countries and with other nations. During the few years of the monarchy, there was little that the Jewish kings could or did accomplish as secular rulers. David and Solomon ruled over a bunch of tribes, in a culture imbued with religious influences in every aspect of civilian life. David reorganized his ragtag army, but failed to structure a centralized civil authority. His son and heir, Solomon, accomplished very little besides the construction of the religious building: the Temple. The Jewish state in the time of the early kings resembled the Germanic tribes in the few centuries before and after the Common Era.

Following the partition of the Kingdom into the Kingdoms of Judea and Israel, all was lost for any ruler to attempt a centralized structure that could rein in not only the tribal but also the religious leaders. The city of Jerusalem was a religious center much more than the seat of the civil and secular government. After the exile of the Jews by the Romans and the actual beginning of the Diaspora, Jerusalem never regained even the vestige of any secular importance or power. It was all religion.

But what kind of religion? The people were banished from the land, and all the practices and rituals that incorporated events that emanated from the land had ceased to exist. The rabbinical leaders of the Diaspora were thus faced with a difficult problem: how to reinvent or restructure the religion, its principles and practices, so as to make it survive the new set of conditions of the Jewish existence among the nations of the world.

The rabbinical leaders confronted a reality in which Jews were dispersed in many different communities, first the Greek and Roman empires, then in the territories conquered and ruled by Islamic monarchs. These Jewish conclaves spoke the local language and were subjected to local rules with great variability in customs, culture, and belief systems. The only possible unifying link would be the religion of their ancestors, to be reconstituted so that it would play a new role in the life of a diverse and highly dispersed people.

Reconstituting the religion was an endeavor based on four key principles. The first was to continue and vigorously reinforce the ethereal link to the land of their ancestors. This link offered a material, albeit unattainable, dreamlike connection to "Eretz Israel" (the Land of Israel). There was a growing emphasis on stories and myths about the period in which Jews lived in their land, and the feats and accomplishments of their great leaders became the essence of embellished folk tales.

In a sad paradox, the more this link to the land became a foundation of the reconstituted religion, the less attractive was any attempt or movement to return to the land and to reoccupy and resettle it. The idea of the Land of Israel as the ancestral homeland thus became a purely *religious* concept, devoid of any political or national and secular attributes. It was a concept to be revered, the essence of hope, and the one—larger than life—element that linked all Jews like an umbilical cord, wherever they lived and in whatever culture or country they currently resided. The resulting logical extension of this was the inadequacy of any attempt to reconquer the land—except by the divine act through the good services of the redeemer, or "Messiah." This event would be a purely *religious* event.

With the passage of time, as centuries went by and the history of the Jewish Diaspora became a plethora of suffering and disastrous persecutions, the idea of the distant land of the ancestors gained in prominence. The concept had turned into a dream, and the dream into a powerful hope that often acted as a sedative to ease the pain of the suffering Jews. The dream of again living in the land of the patriarchs became an integral part of such ceremonies as the Passover "seder," in which the folks gathered around the dinner table would proclaim: "Next year in Jerusalem."

This strong link to the ancient homeland reverberated throughout Jewish communities. Many poets have composed passionate poems on the theme of the longing of a distressed people to its roots, its glorious past, and the land of its ancestors. It was the glue that held together a dispersed people and also offered an unquenched glimmer of hope.

A most noted poet who composed in Hebrew, the ancient language, was Yehuda Halevi, born Abu Elhassan Yehuda Ben Shmuel Halevi, in 1075 in the city of Toledo, in what was then Muslim Spain. In 1140, at the age of 65, he ventured a difficult maritime travel to Egypt with the intent of settling in Jerusalem, but a year later he died in Alexandria, Egypt. Yehuda Halevi wrote passionate and uplifting poems. His mastery of the Hebrew language enchanted his contemporaries and all generations since then. He lamented the sufferings of the Diaspora and dreamed of the return to the land of Canaan, with all its mythical beauty. His poems equated the Jewish Diaspora to slavery in Egypt, and his hope for the return to the land of his ancestors as another exodus, from shackles of serfdom to freedom and bliss.

In a collection of poems on the topic of "Zion," poem number 71 is a cry and a prayer:

> "My heart is in the East and I am at the edge of West—
> How will I ever enjoy my food?

> How will I ever render my vows and promises
>> while Zion is in the province of the desert and
>> I am in the Arabian shackles?
> It will be better for me to leave all the goods of Spain,
>> as it will be more precious for me to see the charred
>> earth of the destroyed city."[243]

In another poem, number 72, Yehuda Halevi directly addressed the land of his dreams:

> "Zion, should you not inquire the welfare of our prisoners, those who wish you well and they are the remainder of your flock?
>
> From West, and East, and North and South we greet you,
>
> Those from afar and from near, from all sides
> And the weeping prisoner of your desire, crying like the dew on Mount Hermon, desirous to pour over your mountains?
>
> The cry of your suffering I am the venue,
> and while I dream of my return to you—I am the violin to sing your songs."[244]

By creating the bond between the dispersed people and the land of their ancestors, the rabbinical leadership had transformed the natural longing of an exiled population to its native soil into a religious concept and an unattainable dream. The only possible (and religiously permissible) venture of return to the land of Israel would be by divine intervention, through the good services of the appointed Messiah. This action effectively destroyed any vestige of political, national, and secular effort on the part of the Jewish people in its Diaspora. It also condemned the Jews to an indefinite exile without any concrete hope for an earthly redemption.

The Calendar of Rituals and Festivals

A different mechanism used by the rabbinical leadership to reinvent the Jewish religion and to consolidate their own power was the "packing" of the religious calendar with an inordinate number and variety of festivals, each with its own assembly of busy rituals and ceremonies.

An urgent problem faced by the rabbinical leadership was how to maintain the Jewish religion and how to ensure that Jews would not succumb to the attractions of rival religions in their Diaspora. One answer was the "packing of the calendar." Jews were kept very busy with many frequent religious obligations and festivals. The outcome was an annual calendar effectively dictated by the religious festivals and events.

When the Israelites had engaged in agricultural activities in their homeland, there existed several yearly festivals that were linked to events such as the harvest of crops. These festivals were now considered religious obligations. The rabbinical leaders endowed them with the aura of sanctity. In addition, there were new events of historical significance. These added ceremonies celebrated or mourned events such as the fall of the Temple in Jerusalem.[245]

Jews were thus kept so busy with religious observances that they had no time to contemplate any other spiritual endeavors. They had barely enough time to engage in their daily routines to make a living. They effectively existed from one festival to the next. With the passage of time the rabbinical leadership added rules and rulings, making each festival more precise and burdensome. The purification of the Jewish home from any leavened bread before the festival of Passover was transformed into a very elaborate activity that required much effort and dedication.

Strict adherence to such rules of behavior and the exact performance of rituals of each festival became implacable obligations that carried stiff penalties when disobeyed. In effect, the Jewish religion had become a set of festivals and rituals sewn together under a few principles of the interpreted will of the divine creator and the Promised Land. The Jew in his Diaspora had become merely an observant practitioner of rituals and ceremonies. In the absence of the land and a national identity, the creators of the reconstituted religion had substituted the core national values of the Jewish people with the periodic onslaught of rituals and religious events.

Several rabbinical leaders have, throughout the two millennia of the Diaspora, arrived at this conclusion. They understood the implications of abandoning the core values of being a person and a people for religious rituals aimed at the interaction between man and God and the mere celebration of historical events. Early in the era of the Roman Empire, Rabbi Akiva is quoted as answering the question, "Can you summarize Judaism with one sentence?" with "Don't do to others what you don't want done to you." Similar orations frequently emerged as pious rabbis attempted to inject a more personal and humane touch into the fanaticism of the rituals-based religion, as it unveiled to them, albeit a product of their own doing.

One such pious individual was one of my direct ancestors, Rabbi Levi Itzhak of the city of Berdichev in the Ukraine. Born in 1740, he became a passionate advocate of Israel. Although he delved in Jewish mysticism as an adherent of Hasidic teachings, he routinely broke with tradition to pursue his personal relationship with his divine creator.[246] Rabbi Levi Itzhak died in 1809. Several stories about his unusual behavior are now a permanent part of Jewish folklore.

In one such story, the people gathered at the temple on the eve of Yom-Kippur (Day of Atonement), the holiest day in the Jewish calendar. This is the day when the Almighty stamps the fate of each and every individual for the coming year: who will live, who will die, who will be ill, who will keep his health. The evening's prayers are the last chance for the faithful to atone for their sins and to ask for forgiveness before sentence is passed on them.

The congregation waited for their revered Rabbi to appear and, as darkness fell and he failed to show up, there was consternation bordering on panic: Where is our rabbi? After much consideration, the city leaders decided to send a party to scout the city and to look for the rabbi. Later, into the night, they found the rabbi. He was in the yard of a modest house at the outskirts of town, chopping wood in the cool September night. The house belonged to an old widow who fell ill and could not attend the services at the Temple. She was also cold, so the rabbi was making sure that she had enough wood burning in the fireplace to keep her warm for the remainder of the night. "Rabbi," asked the panicked men of his flock, "what about the prayers and the atonement?" "There is no greater way to atone and to grab the attention of the Almighty than one simple act of kindness" answered the Rabbi.

The fact that such a story of defiance of tradition and the established rituals captivated the minds of common Jewish folk speaks volumes to the rigidity of religious life imposed by most rabbinical leaders. A succession of rabbis acting as religious scholars added complexity and interpretation to the existing body of religious practices. Rebellious acts, such as that of Rabbi Levi Itzhak, captured the imagination of the common folk as defiant acts of special and heroic figures. They appealed to the imagination of the multitudes that were captives of an extremely rigid way of life, punctuated with ceremonies and a constant barrage of rituals and festivals.

The Overwhelming Rabbinical Authority

In the absence of a Jewish national identity and a Jewish system of secular institutions, the rabbinical leadership filled the vacuum of power with their overwhelming presence. The Diaspora was characterized by the existence of Jewish communities living in the midst—yet separated from—the peoples, cultures, and political nations in which they resided. In this respect, there were very few differences between the Jewish communities living in Western and Eastern Europe and those in the world of Islam. The Jews generally kept to themselves, while always at the mercy of the political and religious authorities of their host countries.

Rabbinical power and influence replaced civil authority in all aspects of Jewish life. Rabbis served as counselors to the perturbed and offered advice to families and business partners. They also served in the capacity of a judicial system by setting up rabbinical courts to resolve civil conflicts and complaints, and to make decisions on religious uncertainties, questions, and controversies. They created an elaborate system of educational facilities, including control over the curriculum and the rules and regulations that governed learning and the authorized acquisition of knowledge. They also served as ultimate arbiters in all other aspects of the life of the community, including ethical judgments of acceptable behavior, allocation of physical and monetary resources, and the establishment of rules as to what constitutes Judaism and who is a Jew.

But the most important role of rabbinical authority was in the dispensation of their ceremonial duties in the key events in the life of every member of their communities: birth, coming of age, marriage, and death. Defined by religion, devoid of civil and national institutions, and isolated within their country of residence, the Jews in the Diaspora were left completely at the mercy of their rabbinical authorities. In every facet of their life they depended on their religious leaders, who thus assumed absolute power over their communities.

The influence of these leaders has been highly injurious to the fate of the Jewish people. It is utterly impossible to understand the Jewish Diaspora without clarifying the disastrous influence of the rabbinical authorities. They effectively and mercilessly confined the Jews within isolated enclaves, forcing upon them the curse of exclusivity and confinement in the harshest of conditions. Assimilation with the Gentiles was definitely prohibited, as the rabbis struggled to keep the purity of the people, genetically as well as religiously. Such purity was never achieved in the genetic pool. Jews in Europe have similar physical characteristics as their non-Jewish neighbors, whereas Jews in India and in Ethiopia, for example, resemble their neighbors and fellow countrymen.[247]

It was in the cultural and religious observances that the rabbis had the most success. The religious leadership accepted nothing less than absolute obedience and total conformity to its rulings. In the absence of any civil authority or policing powers, the rabbis had to resort to instruments of enforcement that had profound religious and social implications. The most important was the "Herem," a ban or excommunication from the community. This meant that the Jew was denied the rituals that made him Jewish and access to the educational, social, and cultural activities of the community. Unable to effectively function outside the Jewish enclave, the person excommunicated was forced to either repent or cease to be Jewish. Although rarely applied, the mere threat of such an instrument was enough to keep the flock obedient.

Another aspect of rabbinical authority was the creation of a unique caste of rabbinical leaders whose source of power emanated from their purported scholarship. They possessed the power to interpret the written word and the rulings of previous authorities. But they also established familial dynasties. They inter-married in a mode similar to that of kings and monarchs. This practice was instrumental in consolidating their power across geographical boundaries.

As a consequence, some of these leaders were endowed by their followers with extraordinary attributes including mythical abilities to perform magic and miracles. Religious schools, such as the Hassidic movement, started in Europe and lasting for the past several hundred years, emphasized the figure of the rabbi and his close followers as the center of religious life. The "Rebbe" became a royal figure, venerated and adored by his many followers.

Reinventing the Economic and Social Order

Led by the class of religious scholars with unlimited authority, the Jews of the Diaspora had to recreate their economic and social realities. Two key attributes characterized their existence. They were disengaged from all activities related to agriculture. Jews had been prohibited in many countries from owning or working the land. Secondly, they were also confined to an urban existence and disenfranchised (by force or by choice) from civic institutions of their cities, provinces, and countries.

As they were concentrated within the confines of their conclaves (by choice and by force), their economic activity had to be focused on commerce, particularly among themselves. They became artisans and merchants of commodities. The latter was also due to their desire to engage in economic activities that could be easily transported to other provinces and countries—if and when they would be again expelled by a ruthless ruler. Transportability meant concentration on such commodities as precious stones, money (when it became ubiquitous after the middle-ages), and crafted objects. They chose professions such as medicine and other knowledge-based skills because those could be transported with the body of the Jew to other destinations. Any investment in property or business that depended on real estate was subject to expropriation by the civil authorities at the discretion of unscrupulous rulers.

The basis for Jewish religious practice was the prayer and the public reading of the "Torah" on the Sabbath and during holidays. This meant that every Jewish man had to learn how to read and write, at times when most of the inhabitants of Europe and the Muslim world were illiterate. But the rabbinical authorities prohibited the use of Hebrew as the commonly spoken language. Hebrew was the language of ancient times and the language of the holy texts—not the idiom of everyday life. In Europe, for example, the Jews developed a dialect ("Yiddish") as a refurbished form of German, and in the Middle East they developed the dialect of "Ladino," as a form of a mix of Spanish and Portuguese. In communicating with others across geographical distances, they used concepts from their holy texts and their rituals and festivals, and often utilized Hebrew writing as a mode of "Jewish" correspondence.

The emphasis on "transportable skills" based on knowledge and education made the Jews a very distinct minority. Many rulers who needed to expand their centralized power found themselves lacking competent civil servants, such as tax collectors, scribes, and other skills in the organization of their government and finances. Often they turned to "their Jews" and offered them such positions, knowing that the Jews depended on the rulers' good will to remain in their domain, hence they would be trusted agents and employees.

Unfortunately, these forms of employment were not favored by the population that was oppressed under heavy taxation. Often the only contact many peasants had with the government of the ruler was the Jew in charge of collecting taxes or the "books" of the estate. The general population could not comprehend the existence of this strange group of people, relatively highly educated, practicing a different and mysterious religion, and having access to other such communities in far-away provinces or cities. To the peasant in bondage on the land, the mobility of this group of strange people became an economic and social anathema. Envy and deep odium became the prevalent sentiments towards the Jews.

Economically and socially, being Jewish had become an *identity* that encompassed all aspects of life: private, professional, public, physical and, of course, spiritual. The religious content with its rituals, ceremonies, and packed calendar of obligations and procedures had become the essence of "Jewishness."

Unlike other major faiths, where religion is but a *part* of life (albeit an important one), Judaism had become the defining nature of the person. It determined his domicile, his profession, and his fate in life. Often this meant suffering and humiliation with no end in sight and no alternative to the life his religious identity had imposed on him and his family. His personal identity as an individual had collapsed into the religious community.

A most unwelcome result was the definition of Judaism as a set of religious practices and rituals. Individual behavior of the Jew as a person towards others had been severely discounted in favor of practicing the required religious rituals. Some, albeit too few, religious leaders recognized this dangerous phenomenon. They interpreted the practice of rituals as communication between the individual Jew and his creator, whereas a different set of ethical rules would apply to his relations with other people. It was therefore unacceptable to behave unethically or immorally towards others and hope to be pardoned by praying and by observing the rituals of the faith.[248]

Anatomy of Absurd Reality

How could this have happened? How could a few rabbinical leaders usurp the power of leadership and exercise such tremendously injurious authority over the Jewish people for over two millennia? By monopolizing the power structure of the people, these religious authorities prevented the emergence of any other secular leadership with influence and consequence. The answer resides in the historical makeup of the Israelites and later the Jews, and the very early abandonment of all vestiges of national unity.

The Israelites never coalesced into a nation. They started their history and then remained a bunch of loosely connected tribes, linked by a common religion and a vague promise of a real estate transaction that was promised to their mythical patriarchs by the Almighty. Sadly, from the start, religion played a divisive, rather than a unifying role in the life of the Jewish people. The first attempt to unify the tribes and to create a national entity had been the selection of Saul to be king. The elders of the tribes had made the choice. But the religious selection of the king by the prophet Samuel, disregarded the *political* desires of the tribal elders, and anointed David as the new king. David proceeded to organize a national army, but his choice of a capital was a political and national blunder. He failed to heed the desires and interests of the powerful northern tribes, and thus created a political rift with disastrous consequences for his successors.

King Solomon then failed to continue the national buildup initiated by his father. He invested whatever resources existed in his impoverished realm in the construction of a *religious* structure: the Temple in Jerusalem. He taxed the Northern and Western tribes for a mega project in which they had no economic interest or benefits. After Solomon's death, his son Rehavam continued his father's practice of heavily taxing the powerful tribes of Northern Israel, which led to their cessation from his kingdom and the establishment of two smaller and weaker kingdoms.

From the early conquest of the Northern Kingdom by the Assyrian King Shalmaneser V in 722 B.C.E., there vanished any political or secular force that could unify the Jewish people. Religious authorities—who bore much of the blame for these events—hastened to fill the leadership vacuum and then reigned as unchallenged leaders for over two millennia.

Losing a People: The Jewish Being and Being Jewish in the Diaspora

The tapestry of the Jewish experience in the Diaspora extends over several continents and many centuries. Nevertheless, it is possible to weave a coherent picture across the barriers of time and geography. By reinventing a religion, in separation from the Promised Land but in a strong link to it, the Jewish people became an anachronistic entity. Whether in Europe, Asia, or the Middle East, the Jews became dispossessed of a political identity, existing in inglorious separation from their host nations and countries. Worse, they were disengaged from the major historical events that helped to shape their world.

Judaism, as shaped by the Rabbinical authorities, has undergone incremental changes. Until the mid nineteenth century when the "emancipation" movement liberated many Jews from the burden of their religion, there had been mostly an effort to clarify and to continue to interpret the tenets of the religious practice. Thus, Judaism did not endure the conflicts that shaped Christianity in the Middle Ages and afterwards. The conflict between church and emperors, also known as the "Investiture," helped to define the scope of the influence of the church in the lives of its believers. This conflict also helped to clearly chart the political, social, and economic spheres of influence of monarchy and the clergy.

Since antiquity and throughout the Diaspora, there was not any separation of religion and secularism. During the monarchy in ancient Judea the kings had been anointed by the prophets who did so in behalf of their God and who alone interpreted God's will, His pleasure, and His anger. This issue also emerged during the life of Jesus Christ when he emphasized in his teachings that his message was not a secular message but referred to the "kingdom of Heaven." In the gospel of Luke (20:25) in the King James Bible: "And he said unto them, render therefore unto Caesar the things which are Caesar's, and unto God the things which be God's." However, the separation of the secular from the religious world never materialized in the history of the Jews. The Investiture in Europe of the Middle Ages and later the emergence of Martin Luther and the protestant revolution had no effect on the Jewish concept of their world. They viewed these developments as internal affairs of the papacy and the kings, as the internal strife for power between the lords of the land and *their* religious leaders. The philosophical foundations of these watershed events were never considered or absorbed by the Jewish leadership, and were utterly dismissed by the rabbinical leaders.

By contrast, Judaism remained an overwhelming religion that encompassed all aspects of the lives of its believers. Judaic practices became a substitute for political and social institutions. As Jews disengaged themselves—within their conclaves—from the national institutions of monarchy and other forms of lay government, they totally surrendered to the dictates of the rabbinical authorities. There was no process of determination of boundaries or a definition of where religion ended and civil authority began.

Judaism also failed to undergo the schism that occurred in Christianity, from which the Protestant movement emerged. Such religious upheavals served as "release apparatus" for dissatisfied believers who were either disenchanted with the current religion and its practices or disenfranchised by it. In the Jewish Diaspora there were no monarchs or other secular rulers who could lend their support to rebellious factions or to the movement to reframe the existing religious structures.

Islam had also been the subject of refinement and delimitation. In the continuing conflict between secular and religious rulers, there emerged compromises that helped to establish boundaries to the spheres of interest and influence of both sides. Religious Islamic leaders would join secular rulers in their "holy wars" by supporting these ventures and by offering religious justifications to them. After periods of "trials and errors," an acceptable compromise was achieved, following several centuries of conflicts and resolutions.

Besides some failed attempts at messianic ventures, Judaism remained an ossified and implacably rigid framework. Over the centuries, some rabbinical authorities attempted to provide the believers with a more "populist" version of rules and procedures that would guide their lives. These unique efforts helped to temporarily demystify the power of rabbinical authorities and to make available to the masses some form of popular reading of the complex system of rules.

Two such authorities come to mind. The first was Rabbi Shlomo Yitzhaki (known by the acronym of "Rashi"). Born in France in 1040 C.E., he died in 1105. During his life Western Europe was caught in the grip of the first Crusade. Strong religious sentiments had animated Christian communities in France and elsewhere in Europe. These also led to massacres of the Jews and generally to an increased climate of religious persecution. Concerned about popular religious education, Rashi composed an enormous scholarly work: commentaries and explanations of the text and concepts of the "Talmud" and the Old Testament. His style was based on the use of a few words for each commentary, written in a populist approach that endeared him to subsequent generations of Jews. Rashi's commentaries to the "Torah" and the "Talmud" simplified the difficult language and the legalistic style of this major work.[249]

Rashi's contribution for Judaic scholarship was in his simplification of the ancient texts. His work made them more accessible to the masses and, in a way, somewhat discounted the role of the rabbinical authorities. His impact was similar, although not as powerful to that of the invention of the press in Europe and the proliferation of religious texts, a phenomenon that had contributed to the Protestant movement.

Rabbi Moses Ben Maimon ("Maimonides," also known by the acronym of "Rambam") was born in Spain in 1135. He fled to Egypt to escape the conquest of Spain by the Moors. He practiced medicine and rose to the position of physician to the Sultan of Egypt. Maimonides wrote a major code of law, the "Mishna Torah" (Second to the Torah). This book made it possible for common folk to arrive at opinions concerning behavior without deep study of the "Talmud." Maimonides also wrote a more controversial book: "Moreh Nevuccim" ("The Guide to the Perplexed"). He generally opposed the interpretation of the written word as literal manifestations of God's desires and will.

As Maimonides' reputation spread throughout the Jewish Diaspora, many traditional rabbis rejected his interpretation of Jewish laws. They went to the extreme of denouncing him and his books to the Inquisition. Maimonides' books were then publicly burned. But to the Jewish common folk he was a hero, one of the few religious authorities endowed with the skills and the courage to bring the complexities of Jewish laws and customs to the level of the simplest members of the community.[250] Maimonides died in 1204 and is buried on the shores of the Sea of Galilee, in Tiberias.

On Being Jewish in the Diaspora

To understand Jewish life in the Diaspora is to live a life wedded to three basic companions: never-ending hope against all hope; never-ending despair; and a gnarled sentiment of permanent uncertainty, as if one is confined to or shackled by the unknown. Life was a harsh reality for everyone, Gentile and Jew alike. Except for the few privileged strata of society, poverty, disease, and a short and miserable life were the norm for most people.

The Jew in his Diaspora lacked the attachment to the land that he inhabited. He also lacked a folklore of heroes and a tradition of events, which were part and parcel of his present dwellings. Rather, his heritage and his heroes were all protagonists of a nebulous, albeit glorious, past in a far away land. Being Jewish in the Diaspora was wishing that you weren't living here and now, but centuries ago, or centuries hence. The present was a very busy religious calendar of events commemorating what had occurred centuries ago, without any actual link to the reality of the here and now.

With constant hatred and persecution by his fellow countrymen, the Jew in his Diaspora had to employ several defense mechanisms—psychological as well as social. He had only his religion for support so his devotion to its practices and rituals became the absolute key to his daily and earthly life. Propelled by the teachings of his rabbinical authorities, he gained a sentiment of superiority over his fellows, often inimical Gentiles. This was a psychological outlet that allowed the Jew in his Diaspora to partly justify the constant persecution to which he was subjected.

"They hate me because I am better, more educated, more able, and very different" became the rationale for his curious existence, as an island within a sea of different nations and faiths. The more he differentiated and isolated himself from his surroundings, the more his individual and collective frustration increased, and the more refuge he procured in his religion.

There were no recorded acts of rebellion in the Jewish communities to this nefarious state of affairs. Muslims and Christians had ample opportunities to vent their frustration in wars of conquest, internal revolutions, and political, social, and religious changes. The Jews lacked all these mechanisms of emotional and physical release. Instead, they were driven by a potent sentiment of acceptance and resignation to their miserable fate. Religious authorities enhanced these sentiments to the point where they became cultural icons of a lost people.

There emerged in the Diaspora a unique Jewish mentality. Unable to exert pressure outward, Jews turned upon other Jews. To the consternation of some well-meaning religious leaders, Jews tended to use civilian authorities to punish and to police their own brethren. This meant taking the issue *outside* the enclosed community and involving non-Jewish organizations in the affairs of the Jewish community. Reactions against such behavior consolidated the norms of isolation. A "ghetto mentality" came into existence. It contained internal strife and led to a people in limbo. All that was of earthly nature conjured a state of transition. The only continuing factor was the Jewish religion, its practices, and its rituals.

As they continually reinforced isolation and the inward perspective of existence, the inevitable course of action for the Jewish religious authorities was to emphasize the value of the written documents. Protestant reformists adopted a similar course, but these religious leaders had something to rebel against: the existing structure of the Catholic Church. Jewish authorities and their followers had no clear enemy or rival against whom they could rebel and fire the arrows of their discontent.

There was the Almighty, but He had undisputed reasons for allowing such conditions to exist. There were the rabbinical authorities, but the community indelibly needed them for the conduct of any social, judicial, educational, and institutional life. There were the tormenting or, at best, indifferent Gentiles, but they owned the land, the power, and the institutions of government. Consequently, Jews in their Diaspora developed the mentality of the "hopeless victim," resigned to its fate and subservient to an implacable destiny.

Survival and Preservation

Jewish existence in the Diaspora consisted of two complementary and often conflicting strategies. One was the physical or earthly survival in the face of constant and relentless adversity. The strategy of survival was based on several elements—family, ceremonies, policing dissent, education, and a sense of a common destiny. Family life became the focal point of attention. The continuation of the people as a physical entity had been translated into the strong desire for large families and very strong familial ties. Whereas in agricultural societies the extended family had a specific economic function, Jewish families in the Diaspora had acquired an overarching goal of the survival of the people, hence the overwhelming focus on marriages within the Jewish people and an aversion to assimilation among the Gentiles.

Ceremonies that marked life's milestones had been transformed into religious events that signified the survival of the people. Weddings and the coming of age of the Jewish male ("Bar-Mitzva") had been redesigned to include references to Jewish history. More than family events, they marked the steps taken by the Jewish family unit to contribute to the survival of the Jewish people.

Similarly, the Jewish family and the larger community engaged in effective policing of any signs of dissent. This included ideas and options that diverged from the conventional wisdom of the rabbinical authorities and the Jewish "way of life." Thus Jewish philosophers such as Baruch Spinoza (1632-1677) incurred the ire of Jewish leaders. Spinoza was excommunicated, partly because his writings had made an initial step towards the enlightenment. He offered a rational approach to Biblical research and his philosophy had a perilous aspect of dissent. It contained more questions than absolute answers. Such implacable policing of any dissent also extended to *political* or rational thought that might undermine the Jewish way of life as subservient victims of their surroundings. Any thought or attempt to invoke the return to the Holy Land and a political solution to the Jewish condition were immediately and ruthlessly squashed. Religious and civic leaders joined forces in a relentless policing and punishment of even minor offenses of dissent from the "status quo."

Educational institutions and the Jewish learning curriculum became a powerful instrument in the constant struggle for survival. From the tender age of three, Jewish children gathered in the "Heder" ("room")—a one room pre-school. They began their studies of religious tenets, ethics, and practices. Their studies also contained a strong curriculum of indoctrination. This method was very similar to the practice of military training: unquestioned obedience combined with pride in belonging to the elite group of comrades, and a strong sense of purpose and necessity for survival against potential enemies.

A sense of a common destiny imbued the Jewish community. As a result of extreme conformity to the ideas and rules of the people—all for the sake of survival, there emerged a sense of "us versus them," albeit in the form of "us" being eternal victims of misfortune and cruelty by others. Survival was therefore much more than the daily grind of human beings. It became an obsession of an entire people, passed along from generation to generation. How else can one explain or justify the proverbial threat of Jewish mothers that they would "kill themselves" if their children ever strayed outside the community and married a Gentile?

The Jewish Diaspora was a long and tortuous road: from agricultural communities of family farming and sheep herding of the tribes of the Israelites to the concentration of religious enclaves in their "ghettos." As they began to coalesce from a bunch of bickering tribes to a real nation with political identity, the Israelites had been exiled never to achieve their coveted union. The Jewish Diaspora contained a veiled attempt at survival of a unique and cohesive people. This attempt failed. Jewish survival was at best a mitigated disaster. The number of worldwide Jewry never rose to a point where demographically it should have, considering the high birthrate used by the Jewish people to ensure their survival. Persecutions, "pogroms," and finally the Holocaust in Europe in the twentieth century decimated their numbers. Today there are fewer Jews in the world than the populations of cities such as Sao Paulo, Brazil, Tokyo, Japan, and Calcutta, India.

The Jewish Predicament: Physical Survival Versus Religious Preservation

Jewish existence in the Diaspora depended on the convergence of physical survival and the preservation of the Jewish faith. The continuing predicament was anchored in the paradoxical coexistence of these crucial objectives. In both the Christian and Islamic worlds, Jews had been under constant pressure to convert and to change their disengaged way of life. Periodically such pressures became more pronounced by means of increased persecutions. Notable examples are the blood baths during the Crusades, the Spanish and French inquisitions, and the "Pogroms" in Eastern Europe. For the inevitable choice between preserving the religious practices and the physical well being of the people, rabbinical authorities established a set of rules. These were assembled under the rubric of "be killed but don't trespass."[251]

The paradoxical concept of resisting "evil forces" ordering the Jew to trespass his religious beliefs with one's life had produced the horrific notion of "Kidush Hashem" (sanctity of God's name). Under this rule, Jews would choose death over the loss of their faith. This was a choice between survival of the people and the preservation of the religion—all in the name of the Almighty.[252]

Perhaps the most chilling account of the predicament is a short story by I. L. Peretz (1851-1915). Born in Poland to an orthodox Jewish family, he became a lawyer and a supporter of Jewish enlightenment. The short story relates the tribulations of a physically strong Jew who chooses to be burned at the stake rather than relinquish his beliefs. He commands his body to the Almighty and happily cries that his extraordinary physical strength will allow him to burn longer, hence to have more time to sanctify the name of his creator. The acute symbolism of this narrative offers a striking image of the Jewish dilemma and the constant struggle between physical survival and the preservation of religion.[253]

The notion of "Kidush Hashem" contained the ultimate sacrifice of the Jews in their Diaspora. The Jewish religion was viewed by the rabbinical leadership not as a religion of the people, but as a detached conceptual framework, perhaps a Platonic idea that can and will exist outside and without the corporeal being of its people. Justification for such a horribly repugnant and degrading indifference to the lives of the Jewish people became a matter of dispute, yet persisted throughout the centuries. Corporeal life was but a transitory state, towards the day of redemption when the Messiah would return and the dead would be brought back to life. In Judaic terminology, cemeteries are "houses of the living," since at the appointed time life will spring from the remains of the dead.[254] The practical outcome of the Diaspora was the incremental and cumulative destruction of the Jewish people.

In all of this, the religious and civic leadership of the Jewish people continued unchanged and unchallenged. It bore no responsibility for the continuous decimation of its followers. These leaders ferociously and blamelessly clung to the futile notions of the "chosen" people of moral superiority—above all others. In practice, while other nations had begun a process of continuous improvement and enlightenment, the Jews remained in their stagnation, an ossified island of an anachronistic system of beliefs.

A Different Analysis of Survival

With continuous threats of physical extinction and consequently the containment within the secrecy of the Jewish conclave, there is seemingly a mystery in the survival of the Jewish religion and its impacts in modern times. After the fall of Jerusalem to Roman legions, Judaism had become one of the many religions in the Roman Empire. It had to compete with other faiths from Egypt, Mesopotamia, Persia, India, and the various religions of the barbaric tribes of Northern Europe.

Paradoxically, Jewish beliefs, some of its customs, and several notions and concepts were passed into modernity not because of the effort of the Jews, but due to the emergence of two other major religions: Christianity and Islam. The remarkable feat is that the Judaic tradition had not vanished into the dust of the Roman Empire, as did so many other religions of that era. Notions such as monotheism, a belief in an invisible God, redemption, and messianic salvation were handed down into Christianity by a group of Jewish dissidents. These apostles and their disciples vigorously exported their new religion, first to Jewish communities in the Graeca-Roman world, then to all corners of the globe. They based the tenets of their new religion on the foundation of the old. Thus the Judaic heritage is incorporated in the fabric of Christianity.

The Prophet Mohammed had great respect for the major religions of his time: Judaism and Christianity. He espoused several tenets and principles from these religions and incorporated them into his teachings. Some Judaic traditions found their way into Islam.

Although Jewish religious leaders have scrupulously attempted to keep their exclusivity of the faith and to avoid any unnecessary contacts and influences from external sources, the propagation of some lay principles of Judaism was due to the other major religions. Instead of being a secluded sect of mysterious practices, Judaism has remained, in the eyes of the modern world, a major religion. It is evidently not because of the number of its followers—that was very small even before the European Holocaust. The place of Judaism as a major religion can be credited to its influence on Christianity and Islam, and also on the role played by numerous Jews who had left the confines of their world community and had dramatically increased their participation in the societies of their host countries. This was the result of the movements of enlightenment and emancipation that swept the Jews in their Diaspora in the past two centuries.

Enlightenment and Emancipation

After the Middle Ages with the fall of Constantinople in 1453 and the defeat of the Muslim armies in Vienna in 1683, there began a period of consolidation of the two major political and religious world blocks. In Europe, Christendom had solidified its relations with the political structures of the emerging nation states. Two camps, Catholic and Protestant, had taken shape, with each side forming alliances with kings and nobles. Several wars, such as the 30 Year War in the seventeenth century were necessary to establish a lasting arrangement between the Christian factions.

In the East and North Africa there was a period of growth and consolidation of the Islamic institutions and their political counterparts. Defeated at the gates of Vienna, Islam nonetheless had expanded its reach into India, southern Russia, and further east into Indonesia. In North Africa the consolidation of Islamic countries had taken place after the loss of the Iberian peninsula in 1492.

The Jews of the Diaspora found themselves in the midst of these tremendous events. As centuries of living in exile had come and gone, the rabbinical authorities continued to accumulate increasing amounts of power. They became the sole arbiters and the recognized and accepted leadership of Jewish communities in both the West and the East. Persecutions became a way of life. In the Muslim world there was less persecution of the Jews than in Christian lands. Jews in Islamic culture had earned a measure of respect because of their commercial activities, which were highly regarded by the Muslims.[255] But isolation and exclusion from social life were the practice everywhere, regardless of the faith of the realm.

The reaction of the rabbinical leadership to the major events around then became increasingly more extreme. They opted for more seclusion, less compromise, and a strict adherence to religious practices, ceremonies, and rituals. As the world around them was engulfed in torrents of tumultuous changes, their response was to resign, acquiesce, and fervently hope for divine salvation. They called these momentous events the preparatory stages for the coming of the Messiah. Their convoluted logic argued that the harsher the persecutions, the more unstable the times, and the darker the horizon as a hopeless future—the more conditions are becoming ripe for the coming of the savior—son of David, the long-awaited Messiah. In such a climate of resignation to the cruel fate of the victim, any political discourse or national ideas were considered radical, revolutionary, and utterly heretic. Any attempts to consider the possibility of a Jewish movement by *the people* from the ground up led by secular leaders towards a national solution were considered heresy and ultimate treason to the ideals and principles of Jewish existence.

The solution had to have *religious* dimensions and a religious rationale. Hence the Messianic adventures of people like Shabbetai Zvi. These adventures were certainly destined to fail. They lacked rabbinical support and they could not link the populist uprising with a sound religious agenda of Messianic salvation. They could not employ the powers of the Almighty in their services. There were no miracles, and certainly not the appearance of the armies of the heavens. Thus, these ventures became the subject of ridicule and served as examples of the futility of *any* kind of uprising designed to hasten the coming of the Messiah.[256]

The "Haskalah" Movement (Jewish Enlightenment): Origins and Consequences

As centuries progressed, the Jewish Diaspora had become more desperate and certainly more disillusioned. Rabbinical control had scuttled any effective attempts to release the anger over persecutions and misery. The energy enclosed in common folk in the Jewish community had to be directed towards making a living and the strict observance of religious mandates.

The Jewish communities in Europe consisted of two main groups. Those in western Europe, France, Germany, the United Kingdom, and the low countries had many restrictions, but since the eighteenth century also a decrease in state-sponsored persecutions. They also enjoyed a better standard of living. In Eastern Europe, particularly in Poland and in Russia, there was a higher degree of poverty and a constant barrage of persecutions.

In all of Europe there was a sense among the Jews that they lacked any type of power. Due to the self-imposed segregation and the restrictions by the civilian governments, the Jewish existence had been painfully fragmented. They lived in constant fear of their surroundings, their neighbors and, above all, the future. Their religion dictated that the future is in the purview of divine providence, so that human actions to obtain a national identity would equal an attempt at salvation—and this is not the province of the people but of their creator. Fragmentation, inaction, and resignation animated the Jewish person.

Such a sorry state of affairs was bound to yield resentment and perhaps even revolt. This would have been the natural way. But the rabbinical hold upon the Jews had been so constant and overwhelming that any and all dissent was not allowed to sprout. Yet a few bright Jews had the audacity and the intellectual prowess to question their heritage, their religion, their leadership, and their standing in the countries they inhabited. What were the factors that contributed to this movement, and what were its consequences?

Several events in world history seem to have contributed to the emergence of a Jewish movement of enlightenment. Chronologically, the first was the European movement of enlightenment, with its concepts of the "age of reason," the rise of scientific advances, and the persistent separation of reason from religion. The truth could and should be explored outside the confines of religious tenets— such was the key notion advocated by the philosophers and scientists who shouldered the enlightenment in the European nations.

As some Jews began to absorb these notions, they also descended into the profoundness of doubts. Until that point they had been indoctrinated that Gentiles were the religious zealots whose mission was to persecute Jews for no apparent reason but their hatred, inspired by unscrupulous clerics and a vengeful host of the combined cabal of civic and religious leaders. Many Jews had daily interactions with Gentiles, particularly in commercial and professional activities. On such a personal basis of daily contact there was less animosity and an improved capacity to exchange pleasantries and to discuss other, more elevated subjects, if and where they did not contain religious significance.

The "age of reason" provided the perfect platform for exchange among people from different faiths who had finally discovered a common ground for conversation about intellectual issues that precluded—by design—inferences to religious methods or "external truths." Some Jews found this set of ideas extremely attractive. It provided them with two key instruments that would help them change their existence and ameliorate their unnatural and painful sentiments: a framework to separate themselves from rabbinical control and a bridge that would allow them to start an effective integration into the secular society.

Reason, empirical science, and the humanistic approach of the Enlightenment became an ideal framework for some Jews to make a case for their separation from rabbinical control. Aided by the much publicized experience of Galileo Gallillei who had defied the Catholic Church, these Jews could now justify their departure from the constraints of their implacable faith by raising reasoned arguments and models which better explained their misery and hopelessness.

This framework of reason also served to catapult these rebellious Jews into the secular society. They found common interests and a common terminology with their Gentile counterparts. As religion was pushed to the sidelines, they had more to share with one another. Their Christian fellows had come to appreciate the devotion of these newcomers to the ideas of the enlightenment and pleasantly welcomed their contributions to society, the new philosophy, and to science.

Among the other factors contributing to the Jewish movement of enlightenment were the momentous events in European history. As Jews avidly observed the French and American revolutions, they keenly learned that the revolutionary leaders had eloquently and vociferously extolled the virtues of liberty, human rights, equality, and dignity. The Gentile world was changing. It drifted away from the religious shackles of the Middle Ages into an era of secular notions of societal coexistence.

Rational Jews quickly and valiantly compared their own deleterious conditions with the exciting new world unfolding before their eyes in the Gentile communities. These Jews increasingly saw themselves as the prisoners of a bygone era of religious strife and rabbinical control—in the same vein as the Christian churches had controlled European societies. The *political* and social aspects of the French and American revolutions offered a glimpse of hope into the Jewish notion of community, albeit not as far as kindling the torch of nationhood.

Other factors were the concentration of the Jews in urban communities and their primary occupations in commerce and banking. Although largely confined to the ghettos, many Jews had intense interactions with the more privileged urban Gentile families and organizations. To effectively conduct commercial activities, Jews had to learn the language of the land and be well acquainted with its laws, rules, and norms of behavior.

The "Haskalah" movement produced two key outcomes: "coming out of the ghetto" and the secular study of Jewish traditions and knowledge. The movement was led primarily by Moses Mendelssohn (1729-1786) and Aaron Wolfssohn (1754-1835) in Germany and, in his own way, also by Baron Maurice Hirsh (1831-1896). These men of letters and commerce shed the traditional appearance of the Jew in his ghetto. They dressed, spoke, and acted like their Gentile countrymen. They "came out of the ghetto" and pursued a pressing way to become integrated and assimilated into the larger society of their countries.

"Coming out" of the ghetto meant not only in person, by living among the Gentiles and assuming their physical appearance, but also by changing their outlook upon the world. This mental transformation included thinking of themselves first as citizens, then as Jews. Religion had thus been relegated to a secondary role in their lives. Perhaps more than any other changes, the act of distancing themselves from their religion in favor of a reasoned perspective on life was the hardest to accomplish.

But the exodus from the ghetto and the attempts to assimilate within the larger secular community were particularly mitigated by the formation of a special identity for the followers of the "Haskalah" movement. Full integration did not appear to be a viable possibility, leaving the ghetto did not signify abandoning their Jewish ancestry and their Jewish being. The "Maskilim" (followers of the Haskalah movement) continued to cling to their past. Their brave act of distancing themselves from their implacably immobilized leadership was not powerful enough to completely sever their Jewish ties to their heritage.

Although the "Maskilim" could not and would not venture all the way towards establishing a political and national identity, they did progress halfway towards some kind of a unique entity. They ultimately chose to assume the more salient characteristics of their ancestors, so as to create the appearance of equality with the nationalistic institutions of their Gentile counterparts. Simply put, if they were unable to form national unions of statehood with independence and a unique way of life (such as they saw in Prussia, Bavaria, France, or Flanders), then the next best thing would be a community endowed with a unique set of *national* characteristics. They opted for "different but equal." The difference was in a new form of Judaism: nonreligious, with the distinct attributes of the ancient language (Hebrew) and the possession and practice of secular knowledge accumulated by centuries of Jewish philosophy.

As a movement of separation from religious dogmatism and intransigence, the "Haskalah" has been a momentous occasion in Jewish history. Yet, it was a movement that attracted only the Jewish intellectual and commercial elite. The majority of the Jews in the European Diaspora failed to join. They could not comprehend the rationale behind half-baked measures of integration into the civic society, nor the effort required of them to reinvent their identity by adopting Hebrew as their daily language and by leaving the bosom of relative security of their ghetto.

Hebrew: Resurrecting the Language and Identity

Hebrew had been the Jewish language of prayer and religious documents. Rabbinical authorities had consistently condemned its use in daily secular parlance. In the vast Jewish communities of Middle and Eastern Europe, "Yiddish" became the vernacular of Jews from different countries. Yiddish began as a mix of German dialects spoken by Jews of the growing German cities of the Middle Ages. As Jews moved eastward to Poland and Russia, they created a more diverse blend of the language by adding Hebrew and Slavic words and concepts[257]

The revival of Hebrew as the national everyday language was an essential component of the "Haskalah." The person most responsible for this revival was Eliezer Ben-Yehuda (1858-1922). Born in Lithuania, he was deeply impressed during his studies in Russia with such historical events as the national liberations of Greece, Bulgaria, and Italy. He harbored ideas of national revival for the Jews of Europe, but during his visit to Palestine in 1881 he came to the realization that such an endeavor was beyond his reach. Instead, he took upon himself to revive the national language of ancient Judea and Israel, and to make it the current language, first in Palestine, then throughout the Jewish Diaspora.[258]

The revival of the Hebrew language served as a unique identifier of Jewish existence and a reminder of its past. The language also unified the diverse communities of Jews throughout the Diaspora. Hebrew became the link between religious practices and everyday secular living. To Ben-Yehuda and many of the followers of Jewish enlightenment, this act was the first true milestone on the way to emancipation of the Jews and the revival of their long-lost national identity. But, reality had its own convoluted agenda. A unique language does not a nation create, and Jewish revival emerged only as a paltry extension of the movement of Jewish enlightenment. The so-called "Emancipation" of European Jews has been gravely exaggerated as an instrument for a true revival of Jewish national awakening.

The Shattered Dream of Emancipation

Much has been written about the events of the Jewish emancipation in Europe in the nineteenth century. Upon its revolution, France emancipated its Jewish population in 1791, Germany in 1871, and Great Britain in 1890. The Russians emancipated their considerable Jewish segment upon the Communist revolution of 1917.

The concept of "emancipation" meant the official abolition or removal of state-mandated discrimination against the Jews. They were now allowed to travel, to become citizens, and to fully participate in all economic and social activities. Although these acts of emancipation appear close in time to the height of the movement of Jewish enlightenment, it would be impossible to determine whether there is some sort of a cause-and-effect relationship between the two phenomena. They are definitely closely related. European governments would not have lifted centuries-old restrictions unless there were considerable numbers of Jews who were already contributors to the economic, social, and intellectual life of their nations. In Germany, these were the notable poet Heinrich Heine (1797-1856) and the politician Johann Jacoby (1805-1877) elected to the Prussian National Assembly. In the United Kingdom several Jews had arisen to positions of national prominence. Lionel Nathan Rothschild (1808-1879) was a member of the British House of Commons. Sir Moses Montefiori, knighted by Queen Victoria, was a successful banker and a known philanthropist. Perhaps the most famous was Benjamin Disraeli (1804-1881), later knighted as the Earl of Beaconfield, who served as the only Jewish Prime Minister of Great Britain, several times, from 1852 till his latest election in 1874. He was instrumental in the expansion and consolidation of the British Empire and, to his credit, he was the effective founder of the Conservative Party in the United Kingdom.

Yet, as in the case of the intellectual enlightenment, only a relatively small number of Jews could fully benefit from the removal of political, social, and economic constraints in their country's legal system. The Rothschilds, Montefiori, and Disraeli became indistinguishable from their fellow Gentiles—in appearance, education, career choices, and accomplishments. But even these few, the fortunate product of the changing times, had to continually engage in the reactionary backlash of non-Jews who reviled in their opposition to equal rights to their Jewish neighbors and fellow citizens. The majority of European Jews remained in urban ghettos and in the small towns and villages, under rabbinical control. Largely unaware of the potential benefits of emancipation and unwilling to assimilate and to change their religious existence, especially in central and Eastern Europe, they formed the bulk of the Diaspora: unmoved, unchanged, prisoners of their perverted miserable existence.

The Jews in Europe had missed the opportunity to join their Christian brethren in rising up to establish or reclaim their national aspirations. Emancipation was nothing more than a "mirage": the formal recognition by a few governments of the reality that some Jews had carved a prominent niche in their culture, political arena, economy, and intellectual life. The great political movements in Europe and America in the late eighteenth century and throughout the nineteenth century did not make a significant impact on Jewish fortunes.

Emancipated Jews in their Diaspora were concerned with integration and assimilation into their countries' societies. There was no interest in establishing their own revolution to achieve nationhood. Who would lead such a movement? The Jewish enlightenment produced only a handful of "liberated" Jewish professionals, intellectuals, and merchants. Who would follow? The vast majority—the people who would follow the leaders to form their own nation and obtain political identity—were huddled in their ghettos, living under conditions that had suffocated their ancestors for centuries. There were no people, no masses, no followers, no leaders.

Baron Maurice Hirsch and the Fiasco of Jewish Colonization

Born in Munich, Germany in 1831, Baron Hirsch was a practical man of considerable intellect and financial means. After marrying into a Brussels banking house, he was able to multiply his fortune through major ventures with the Turkish Empire. He was an entrepreneur in the modern sense of the term. He could identify a problem, define it, and apply to it plausible solutions. In 1891 he founded the Jewish Colonization Association, with an initial capital of 2 million pounds. The charter of the Association was simple and straightforward: "to assist and promote the emigration of Jews from any parts of Europe or Asia, and principally from countries in which they may for the time being be subjected to any special taxes or political or other disabilities, to any other parts of the world, and to form and establish colonies in various parts of North and South America and other countries for agricultural, commercial, and other purposes" and "to establish and maintain or contribute to the establishment and maintenance in any part of the world of educational and training institutions, model farms, loan-banks, industries, factories, and any other institutions or associations...to fit Jews for emigration and assist their settlement in various parts of the world, except in Europe."

Emigration "to any part of the world!" This was an ambitious plan, an entrepreneurial effort by a very wealthy and influential Jew, a product of at least two centuries of Jewish enlightenment. In addition to his plan for colonization, the Baron also established various charitable foundations to help Jews in Russia, Poland, Palestine, and wherever they needed assistance, not only from persecution but also to improve their poor economic conditions.[259]

The most ambitious and also most cohesive part of the effort of Baron Hirsch was the attempt to colonize Jews in Argentina. In 1891, land around the capital of Buenos Aires was purchased by the Colonization Association. Following incidents of persecution of Russian Jews in the Spring of 1891, the Baron decided to send several hundred Russian-Jewish families to Argentina, with the purpose of establishing agricultural communities.

Unlike other emigrations such as the Puritans in America or the Mormons in Utah, the colonization of the Jews in Argentina was a resounding failure.[260] Many colonists were not suited for agricultural enterprises. The harsh conditions of working the Argentine land discouraged the colonists. Some moved into the cities to reenter life in commercial activities, while other colonists abandoned the enterprise altogether.

Baron Hirsch established other Jewish colonies, with similar outcomes to the Argentine venture. In the end his fund was largely used to assist Jews who had emigrated on their own—to the United States and Palestine. The fund supported projects in education, commercial lending for small businesses, and generally helped the poor and the unfortunate.

Baron Hirsch's initiative of colonization had lacked an underlying theme, be it a religious platform or a political framework of aspirations and dreams. Faced with strong rabbinical opposition, Jews in Russia, Galicia, Poland, and other countries in Eastern Europe failed to rally to the Baron's call for emigration. The rabbinical authorities had ably explained the suffering and the hardships of poverty and persecution, so the vast majority of Jews preferred to wait for the Messiah rather than embark on a difficult journey to other lands—even when funded by a few well-meaning and wealthy Jewish aristocrats. After centuries of resignation and acceptance of their miserable destiny, the "fire in the belly" which propels people to emigrate and start new lives in other continents had been extinguished in the Jewish psyche. The rabbinical leadership had seen to it. Instead of religion being the driving force for enterprising ventures (as was the case with the Puritans in North America three centuries earlier), Judaism became a stifling force that kept the masses of the followers chained to their pitiful and merciless existence.

The Emergence of Jewish Political Movements

Thus passed another chapter in the attempts to free the Jews from their wretched existence. But not all was in vain. Once unshackled from the control of their religious leaders, many Jewish intellectuals, dreamers, and those who arrived at positions of influence in the secular world had begun to question their fate and the misery of their condition. The Jewish enlightenment, coupled with political emancipation in key

European countries, finally resulted in the establishment of *political* movements led by some Jewish personages of power and free will.

These movements gained impetus and further traction when events at the end of the nineteenth century made a turn for the worse. Political persecutions in Russia in the 1800s awakened many younger Jews, already influenced by the age of reason and Jewish enlightenment. The political movements led to European conferences and congresses of the Jewish intellectuals. They were bolstered by poets who dedicated their talents to developing powerful images and slogans. Abram Ber Gottlober (1811-1899) was a member of the movement "Lovers of Zion" whose aim was to create agricultural settlements in Palestine. He composed a resounding verse: "Awake! Israel and Judah arise! Shake off the dust, open wide your eyes."

Another poet and a prolific supporter of Jewish enlightenment was Yehudah Leib Gordon (1831-1892). He was born in Vilnius, Russia. He served a prison term for allegedly participating in anti-government conspiracy. Gordon wrote these fervent and inspirational verses: "Arise my people! It is time for waking! The night is over, and daylight is breaking."

Gordon's writings had a certain evolution in his support of various ideas. Such changing focus mirrors the basic issues that Jewish intellectuals were facing in the nineteenth and the beginning of the twentieth centuries. There were two possible avenues of action for those Jews who desired to "leave the ghetto." The first was assimilation into the society in their country of residence. Russian Jews argued for integration into Russian society and German Jews into German society—with or without conversion to Christianity.

A second course of action was emigration. Here there were several possibilities. Emigration from Central and Eastern Europe to Western Europe and the New World, or emigration to Palestine, the land of Zion and of their ancestors. Those who supported the latter option were called "Zionists," thus the movement towards establishing an independent Jewish homeland in Palestine was created and institutionalized. All other options meant a Jewish existence as a minority within the larger Gentile community, be it Russia, Germany, or Poland. The Zionist movement was different. Its ultimate objective was the establishment of a *political* solution to the Jewish problem, in the form of a *Jewish country*, owned by the Jews, and governed by the Jews.

Y. L. Gordon initially lashed out against the rabbinical authorities in his native Russia. He blamed them for preventing their followers from assimilation into the Russian society. He avidly supported the use of the Hebrew language and denounced the widespread use of Yiddish. But, with the decay of Tsarist Russia, political events in the 1880s produced popular uprisings against the regime, accompanied by bloody persecutions against Russian Jews. Gordon realized that Russian society was not willing or able to accept a massive movement of Jewish assimilation. He then refocused his poetry on supporting emigration to Western Europe and to the New World.

The 1800s had been an era of dialectics among the Jewish of the enlightenment. There were countless debates, arguments and counter-arguments, and lengthy discussions in Congresses on the course of action available to European Jews, then under continuing waves of persecutions. Scholars and writers of that era expressed their often extremist views, immersed in their emotional depression and disbelief in the fate of their people. Y. L. Gordon had said: "Be a human being outside and a Jew at home" as a mode of assimilation into Russian society. This was a call for a dual-personality syndrome, by playing two distinct, largely conflicting, roles. The inevitable outcome from this famous advice would have been role-conflict, anxiety, and mental anguish.

The reaction from rabbinical authorities was swift and uncompromising. They considered all of the options, such as emigration or assimilation, as sinful and diabolical enterprises. They viewed any venture not anchored in the religious texts as an unwelcome influence of the ravaging and destructive Gentile world. Unable to persecute and eliminate the Jews in the physical sense, they argued that the non-Jewish world had begun operating on the spiritual level by enticing Jews to abandon their traditional ways.

Many Jewish writers of the era were incensed at the notion that the Jews were destined to a life of misery. These writers could not accept the idea that theirs was a people without a political or social structure, and without a rational ambience of existence. Joseph Brenner (1881-1921) was born in the Ukraine and emigrated to Palestine in 1901, where he was killed during the Arab uprising of 1921. He summarized the insignificance of the Jewish existence as simply biological organisms without the semblance of a people: "We have no inheritance" he proclaimed, and lamented that Jewish generations handed down nothing of value to its children. He argued that all that is transferred is the religious tenets. "We are better off without them" he forcefully exclaimed.

All the movements clamoring for separation from the unbearable, abnormal, and miserable situation of European Jewry (emigration, assimilation, or Zionism) lacked in both leadership and followership. None of them became a truly popular movement. The Jewish intellectual elite was overly fragmented. There was no overarching theme that would convince and electrify the Jewish masses. The only justification and the rallying slogan employed by these movements was the wretchedness of Jewish existence in the ghettos and the constant barrage of unprovoked persecutions and pogroms.[261]

The Religious Opposition

The reaction of rabbinical leaders to the Jewish political movements is also illustrative of the landscape of ideas of the era, and the intellectual drivers of the religious opposition. Across the main Jewish communities in Europe, the rabbinical counter-attacks flourished in brutal and uncompromising expressions of fear laced with calls for action. These counter-attacks consisted of three key strategies: (1) disprove the concept of a political or national solution to the Jewish existence; (2) expose the potentially disastrous consequences to Judaism and to the Jewish people from those ideologies, and (3) discredit those who spread such infamous ideas.

The attack on the concept of Jewish nationalism was particularly directed at the Zionists, because they advocated the establishment of a separate country in the Holy Land. Several highly influential Jewish sages contributed to the reaction to the political or national movements. Rabbi Yosef Rozen of Duinsk (1858-1936) was born in Rogachev, Russia, and died in Vienna, Austria. He wrote several letters opposing national Jewish aspirations. In 1904 he said: "Heaven forbid that we should test God and strive with Him concerning the length of the exile in order to be masters in the Holy Land." He added, quite forcefully: "Do you not know that Zionism and self-rule are vanity and pursuit of emptiness and imitation? Why do you despise the Torah and stretch out your hand to transgressors tainted with heresy?" He went on to denounce any Jewish aspirations for self-rule as traitors: "May the day come when we are not subjugated and oppressed by heretics originated from the Jewish people, especially seeing that they spread evil tidings about us."

This was a clever way of establishing the principle that self-rule, national identity, and its implementation in the ancient homeland are heresy, perpetrated by evildoers. Similarly, Rabbi Sholom Ber Schneerson (1860-1920) proclaimed in his writings: "In order to influence our brethren in favor of the Zionist aspiration for an independent nation and government, they have no alternative but to lead the people astray from the path of the Torah and the commandments or, at least, to weaken their attachment as much as possible, so that nationalism should prevail over the Torah, because it is known that those attached to the Torah are unlikely to change and to accept some other form of faith." Those who believed in national identity for the Jews, the Rabbi added: "entirely destroy Jewish souls." Rabbi Schneerson was the fifth Rabbi in the dynasty of leaders of the Chabad Lubavitch Hasidic movement based in Brooklyn, New York.

Rabbi Chaim Ozer Grodzensky (1863-1939) was born in Ivye, near Vilnius, Russia, and served as religious leader of the Vilnius Jewish community. In 1907 he wrote: "Zionism is the work of Satan, with all its seductions and provocations, to turn the people of Israel from the good path. A great danger arises from Zionism for the entire world Jewish community."

The virulent attacks upon the concept of national Jewish identity were not confined to the Russian rabbis. The Polish Rabbi Tzadock Hacohen (1823-1900) of the populous city of Lubbin wrote an influential missive: "The Zionists sow wheat and reap thorns, and even should the work of Satan prosper, eventually there could be a horrible end." He added: "If the Zionists gain dominion they will seek to remove from the hearts of Israel belief in God and in the truth of the Torah. All the intent of these inciters and seducers is to cast Israel into infidelity, which is destruction."

The reaction against Jewish nationalist movements for self-determination also extended to influential rabbis in Western Europe. Rabbi Nathan Marcus Adler (1800-1891), for example, considered the concept of Jewish nationalism a step backward in Jewish destiny. Rabbi Adler was the chief rabbi of London, Great Britain, and, in fact, of the Jews in the British Empire. He argued that since the Roman exile the Jews did not constitute a national entity, rather they were a *religious* entity, whose mission was to diffuse moral and spiritual ideas to the world.

In addition to attacking the concept of Jewish nationalism as religious heresy, the detractors were also concerned with the eventual consequences of embarking on a widespread national awakening of Jewish communities within their hostile environments. The greatest fear was a possible backlash of Gentile reaction, which would lead to increased persecutions. The reaction against Zionism created a union of dissimilar bedfellows. Rabbis and Jewish intellectuals who aspired to assimilate in their own countries joined forces to criticize and denigrate the Zionist idea. Thy all felt that such *duality in allegiance* would be highly detrimental to European Jews. The rabbis feared duality of allegiance to the Torah and to a national ideal, whereas the intellectuals feared the duality in allegiance to their country of residence and an idea of a Jewish national homeland. The concept of the international citizen, as a free person able to choose his own country of national devotion, had frequently been used to denigrate the Jewish existence, as people who were detached from their country of residence with allegiance to some ethereal international entity. This was prime material for theories of conspiracy and allegations of plans for Jewish world domination. The intellectuals sought to avoid any semblance of disinterest or lack of total devotion to their country of residence.

In 1897 the most influential rabbis of the largest German cities published an open letter in the German newspapers, in which they strongly declared that "the desires of those who call themselves Zionists to establish in the land of Israel a Jewish state directly contradict the Messianic destiny of Jewishness, as specified in the Jewish holy scriptures. The Jewish religion obligates its followers to faithfully serve their birth country, to which they belong, and to assist its national interests with all their souls and their best effort."[262]

The third strategy in the opposition to the Jewish national movement was the virulent attempts to vilify those who embraced the tenets of the movement. Rabbi Grodzensky of Vilnius criticized even the rabbis who showed support for national aspirations: "To our shame, some rabbis in our country have joined the Zionists, and have founded an organization called Mizrachi, and they have rejected all the rebukes of the sages. These rabbis have no faith, and do not trust in the salvation of God, and their minds have become deranged into believing that in a state founded by the hand of man there will be peace for us."

In the rabbinical teachings and counter reaction to the Jewish nationalist movement there was little concern for the suffering of the

Jewish masses. The only salvation would be by the hand of the Almighty, whenever, however, and wherever He so desired. Until then, the Jew was condemned to a life of anomaly, "a stranger in his land," and under a constant state of persecution and discrimination. The most important issue, nay, the *only* issue was the preservation of the religion. The more the suffering, the closer the era of the Messiah—such paradoxical belief made much sense to the minds and souls of a persecuted people.

Even a caring and mindful religious leader, as the "Chafetz Chaim," could not evade such a twisting of logic. Born Israel Meir Hacohen Kagan (1838-1933) in Zhetel, Poland, he chose to live in the city of Radin as an owner of a small grocery store. He was a prolific writer whose concern was mainly the decay in Jewish social practices such as slander, lying, defamation of character, and gossip. His book on the purity of language in human relations equated the desire for life ("Chafetz Chaim") with guarding one's lips from speaking deceitfully. He nonetheless believed in strict adherence to Jewish practices, without also commenting on the earthly suffering of Jews throughout Poland and Russia of his time.

"If You Will, It is No Fairytale": Theodore Herzl and the Zionist Movement

In 1897, a young Jewish writer and a journalist of Hungarian origins, proudly declared: "In Basle I founded the Jewish state." He certainly did not, but his contribution to the Zionist movement was a considerable effort at streamlining a fledgling campaign. Like a highly motivated campaign manager, Herzl provided impetus and an uncanny ability for a persuasive "spin" of the ideas embedded in the Zionist movement.

He was born in Budapest, the capital of Hungary, in 1860. In 1884 he earned a doctorate in law from the prestigious university of Vienna, and went on to serve as the Paris correspondent for the Viennese newspaper, the *Neve Freie Presse* (New Free Press). Herzl died in Vienna in 1904.

After witnessing the Dreyfus Affair, in which a Jewish captain in the French army was accused of treason simply because he was Jewish, Herzl began to ponder the Jewish question and wholeheartedly joined the Zionist movement.[263] He wrote two influential short books: *The Jewish State* (1896) and *The Old New Land* (1902). In his book about the Jewish state—as he envisioned the process of its creation—Herzl provided a succinct analysis of the "Jewish Problem" and forcefully argued that the only solution to the Jewish Diaspora is the establishment of their own country.

Herzl combined a powerful analysis and a plan with his impressive organizational abilities. He galvanized the Zionist movement by establishing the first Zionist Congress in Basel, Switzerland, in the summer of 1897. He also founded the Zionist Organization and insisted on annual congresses to evaluate the progress of the movement and to plan and execute the actions necessary to establish a Jewish Homeland, preferably and ultimately in Palestine (The Old New Land). His favorite phrase, which became the catchy slogan of the movement: "If you will it, it is not a fairytale." Thus he responded to the critics of the movement and also gave the movement a motto, a promise, and a phrase of pride and accomplishment.[264]

Herzl was both a synthesizer and an organizational genius. He brilliantly summarized the political issues and the actions necessary to achieve a political solution to the plight of European Jewry. He was a lonely force who tried to assemble the different factions of the movement and transform them into a coherent organization, capable of action.

However, besides the annual congresses-that were a forum for contentious discussions and endless posturing of the different groups and personalities in the movement—and the inspirational impacts of his books, Herzl's accomplishments were primarily ideological. His effort did not produce a massive movement of emigration to Palestine, nor any *political* structures that would and could make the dream of returning to the homeland a reality. He established a platform for action and the description of a plan that—if carried out—could result in the establishment of the Jewish state. Like so many other dreamers he disregarded the empirical barriers and the political, economic, social, religious, and organizational difficulties in creating a Jewish state in Palestine.

But Herzl gave the movement its first true leader, endowed with the traits that such a leader should possess: intellectual abilities, a gift for writing and for expressing the dreams and desires of the movement, important standing in the Gentile world, and a powerful message laced with a plan and a slogan.[265]

Herzl was a visionary who energized the Zionist movement. His detailed plan was an impressive addition to what was hitherto a society of debaters. Although various scholars and politicians attempt to link Herzl's legacy with the establishment in 1948 of the State of Israel, there was only the vision that had prevailed and the indirect impacts of his hope for a state that would be a "light unto the nations," and a true socialist country. This political perspective of socialist attributes later influenced the distorted principles upon which David Ben-Gurion and his political party based their leadership of the new state of Israel.

In the end, Herzl's political and organizational influences on the establishment of the Jewish state were merely in the form of his vision. The events that led to the formation of Israel as an independent country, fifty years after the first Zionist Congress, bore little, if any, semblance to the debates in Basel. Two world wars later and the dissolution of both the Ottoman and the British empires would create a different world into which the independent Jewish nation could finally be born.

Antisemitism: The Annals of an Implacable and Unending Global Phenomenon

In the annals of human history, the Jewish experience has been an utter failure at every step of its existence. As if addicted to suffering, Jews continued to obey their misguided leaders on a path to self-destruction. Especially religious leaders continue to this day to cling to outrageously impossible dreams and wishful ideas that have cost the Jewish people millions of precious lives.

Anger, avarice, blind ambition, greed, incompetence, pretension, stupidity, vanity, and other human frailties were, and continue to be, imbued in the leadership of the Jews. Encapsulated and bottled up in isolated communities, these horrific traits were let loose upon the inhabitants in the revered name of tradition and religious observance, like ferocious beasts in the confinement of a cage. There was no way out but to acquiesce and to play by these mortally choking rules.

By itself, tradition is not good or bad, necessary or disposable. It simply refers to repeating what others have done in the past and in the manner in which they had done so. Tradition reenacts the past with its grandeur and its faults. At its best, tradition celebrates past glory, at its worst it perpetuates a bankrupt mode of thought and action.

There is a recurrent, deeply embedded tradition in the Jewish way of life that harnesses the long-standing reality of suffering. Anchored in the irrevocable madness of a brutal manifestation of human-deity relationship, the Jewish tradition of being a perennial sufferer and condemned victim is proudly justified and insanely celebrated by the Jewish leadership and their flock.

What is Antisemitism?

To be a victim of persecution means that the Jewish people in its Diaspora were exposed to a continuous campaign by which it was singled out and specifically hounded and molested. This was the essence of the phenomenon largely described as antisemitism.

A working definition of antisemitism was recently proposed by the European Monitoring Center on Racism and Xenophobia: "Antisemitism is a certain perception of Jews, which may be expressed as hatred toward Jews. Rhetorical and physical manifestations of antisemitism are directed toward Jewish or non-Jewish individuals and/or their property, and toward Jewish community institutions and religious facilities."

But antisemitism is an ancient practice, with its own tradition and evolutionary development. It existed even in ancient times, as the Jews, upon their exile from their homeland by the Greeks and Romans, began establishing communities in Mediterranean cities, and later throughout the Roman Empire and the Islamic world. This phenomenon, a sad expression of human intolerance with global proportions, has been amply studied, researched, and dissected.[266]

It seems inconceivable that so many people, over so many centuries, from so many lands; people otherwise cultured, civilized, and humane, would turn on-a-dime and virulently express—in word and action—their passionate animosity toward fellow human beings. All people love and hate, as these are common human emotions. But to partake in a consistent pattern of hatred towards one specific group of people lasting over two millennia, this is a highly unusual phenomenon. Throughout history, tribes, cities, and nations engaged in wars and fermented mutual hatred that may have lasted for many years. But, historically, there were always acceptable and transparent reasons for such animosity and warlike conditions. Disagreements over resources, ideals, religious preferences, and even personal quarrels among royalty over women, honor, or property have been the common drivers of long-standing hate.

Why hate and persecute the Jews? What were the apparent reasons for such behavior? Many scholars, clerics, and others have devoted considerable intellectual prowess in attempts to understand the causes of antisemitism. One approach examines the various forms of this phenomenon: *religious* antisemitism, *racial* antisemitism, *economic*, *social*, and *cultural* antisemitism, and *psychological* antisemitism. The latter includes explanations such as the use of the Jews as scapegoats for all that is troubling a desperate community and for the disasters that befall upon it.

The persistence of anti-Jewish sentiments on a global basis even today is befuddling. Issues of Jewish malfeasance are routinely inserted into protests and debates that have nothing to do with the existence of the Jews. In 2004 and 2005 several protests against the war in Iraq were conducted in the United States, organized by a diverse number of groups. In several occasions speakers lambasted the Jewish and Israeli actions as "threats" to world peace and prosperity.

Imagine that one can examine this phenomenon of antisemitism from a different perspective, without overwhelming passion or prejudice. Throughout the centuries, the Jews in their Diaspora lived among their hosts as a very peculiar entity. Even a cursory observation will identify the ingredients for a recipe of distrust and ultimate hatred. All of this, of course, does not *justify* such despicable human reaction. From the perspective of the European peasant or city dweller—in the past two millennia—the Jews existed as a group shrouded in mystery. Even without the prodding of his religious leaders who singled out the Jews as traitors, lost sheep, or accomplices in the death of Jesus Christ, the average person coexisted with this group or heard stories about them.

Jewish religious practices and their core beliefs remained a mystery to outsiders.[267] Certain rituals could be, and usually were, misinterpreted. Jewish religious literature was not made available to most people outside the faith. Mystery harbors fear, begets distrust, and is open to any explanation, however wrong, that seems to make sense and to allay the fear.

To the average Gentile, the Jewish community was enclosed in its own compound, isolated, and exclusionary. Whether by choice or by law, the Jews lived in a distinct community, shrouded in mystery. They were like the nobility or the church–in glorious isolation, unreachable, and insular, except that the Jews had no power, no land, no might, and no roots in the social order of the larger community. Whatever resentment the average Gentile harbored towards his nobles and his church, he could unleash against the Jews, because they shared some fundamental attributes with the powers that ruled his life and his livelihood.

To the average Gentile, religion was a crucial and massive part of his life. In the Christian world, the events that took place in Judea, many centuries earlier, remained fresh and vivid as if they happened yesterday. But the Jews were also relating their beliefs to the same land

and to similar events of a similar time. Two different interpretations of the same slice of history! Both Jewish and Christian religious leaders had defiantly consecrated their interpretation as the only viable faith, mandated by the Almighty. The other side was a lost sheep, who strayed from the true path to salvation. Such views and related teachings had tremendous influence on how the average person perceived those of the different faiths. With both sides clinging to the past, the past becomes very real and a mighty divisive instrument of disregard and hatred.

To the average Gentile, the Jews lived in a different world with grossly different customs, garb, and culture. Where education was scarce and most people spent their entire life within a few miles from their birthplace, the Jews seemed to have connections well beyond the village, county, shire, province, or city. They were for the most part literate, and they maintained contacts with their rabbinical authorities in other places, even in other countries. As national identities became much more pronounced in Europe–following the Renaissance and the rise of Protestantism—the isolated Jewish community with its disregard for civil authority and for national borders had become a target for resentment. True, Catholics and Protestants hated each other and engaged in fierce wars, but they were French Catholics and Dutch Protestants, and Spanish Catholics versus English Protestants. Secular leaders took sides and embraced one form of Christianity or another.

The Jews remained outside these struggles, but to the average German or French, or Polish peasant or urban dweller, the Jews lacked both religious and national identities. Hence their isolation bred envy, jealousy, and hatred. The notion of internationalism was unknown and feared within the rapid spread of national pride and national ambition. Contacts with other countries and peoples were tantamount, at the very least, to an unusual and unexplainable behavior and, at worst, to utter treason.

Justification and Acceptance

These sentiments of resentment, envy, hatred, and sheer paranoia had evolved over the centuries. As persecutions mounted, so did the evolution of justification on the side of the Gentiles and the development of the notion of acceptance on the part of the Jews. This widespread popular phenomenon had to be explained and justified as a religious *and* as an intellectual movement. These explanations neatly complemented the complex justifications of nationalistic trends, even the secular uprisings against the powers and influence of the churches. Historians and sociologists began to relish the idea that within the compact of historical movements and phases, the Jews had remained an outdated constant, unable and unwilling to change and adapt. As an anachronistic existence, the Jews in their Diaspora could not and should not adhere to whatever progress was taking place in the lives of nations and peoples.

As persecutions mounted and justifications for such hateful behavior infiltrated the political and cultural elites of the Gentile world, Jewish leaders increased their belief in the notion of acceptance. They had come up with their own explanations. To them, this behavior was so abhorrent that it could not merit any intellectual justification. Instead, it was clearly the hand of the Almighty, sending an immutable message to His chosen people. Over the centuries millions of Jews perished in various forms of discrimination, exile, and persecutions. Yet, Jewish religious leaders considered these horrific events as signs of the coming of the Messiah, Son of David. In a brutally perverse way they welcomed these events and ordered their obedient flocks to accept them and to silently acquiesce to the terror.

Any solution to such treatment—other than unmitigated capitulation–was considered heresy and defiance of God's will. By the time Jewish emancipation and Jewish enlightenment had finally secured a more popular standing within the Jewish Diaspora, it was too late. Antisemitism had already matured to become an acceptable social, political, and cultural phenomenon, finely explained and diligently justified by some of the most fertile and capable minds in the world.[268]

The Jewish Question

Theodore Herzl devoted the first chapter of his book "The Jewish State" (after the Introduction) to *The Jewish Question*. In a concise manner his pamphlet defines the "question" from the Jewish perspective. He wrote: "Wherever they live in perceptible numbers, they are more or less persecuted...They are disbarred from filling even moderately high positions...The forms of persecutions varying according to countries and social circles in which they occur...In our economically upper classes it causes discomfort, in our middle classes, continual and grave anxieties, in our lower classes, absolute despair" (pp. 85-86).

But, the "Jewish Question" was also a problem for the non-Jewish leaders, governments, and countries. Perhaps initially some governments happily welcomed the popular uprising of its populace against its Jewish inhabitants–as a surrogate for rebellious ideas against the regime. These persecutions served as release valves for the sentiments of unhappiness and revolt boiling within the general population. Yet, soon enough this excuse rapidly extinguished its usefulness. Serving as scapegoats for the regime, the oppressed Jews could not absorb much, let alone all, of the pent-up popular disillusionment.

Numerous writers have expounded on the "Jewish Question," replete with opinions and counter-opinions about its origins and consequences. Yet, in the past two centuries they have not publicly raised the much needed query and the time is ripe to make it: *"Why was the "Jewish Question" a question or problem at all?* Every minority segment of a population is subjected, at some time or another, to discrimination, even oppression. Historically, in most cases, such abnormal situations are resolved by social, political, and judicial transformations. These cases are also usually confined to minorities within specific countries.

In the case of the Jews in their Diaspora, the "Jewish question" was widespread, across countries and even continents, over twenty centuries. Immune to all the social, political, and judicial transformations, to the rise and fall of empires and ideologies, the Jews in their Diaspora remained a thorn in the world's existence. Why? Why be a problem at all? Where is the promise of the Almighty to His chosen people? Why did the expectations of a bright and singularly endowed people disappear in a storm of "absolute despair"? Abandoned by its Creator, unwanted and despised by its neighbors, neglected by its leadership– the Jews in their Diaspora had become a perennial problem not only because of their tormentors, but also because they willingly contributed to the unending extension of their role as the world's and God's victims.

The Question of Victimology

Like Tuvia the milkman in the famous musical, most Jews in the Diaspora did not know they were a problem and that there existed the "Jewish Question." They lived their lives, raised their children, and worried about their daily subsistence and their children's future. They dutifully obeyed as many of the 613 rules of their religion as they could and faithfully followed their rabbinical leaders. They believed the tales of their glorious ancestry and the marvels of the salvation by the awaited Messiah. Meantime, life went on, routinely flowing within their ghetto community. Persecutions and discrimination were but a part of life, like the woes of making a living, or old age, or poor health.

Isolated from the events of the non-Jewish world, they tended to increasingly look inward, to mind their business, and to expect a future replete with bleak occurrences–as a welcome mat for the beloved Messiah. They were chosen, but also selected to be the victims of a cruel world–or so they were told, and retold, and so neatly coached by their leaders.

In elementary or pedestrian psychology, the majority of the Jews in their Diaspora could have been considered "eternal adolescents." They still lived under their parents' roof and obeyed their parents' rules because they were not mature enough to face the world on their own. They resented their parents (or religious and other leaders), and they felt the burden of the victim, bullied by other people but unable to react and to rebel. Their home-the ghetto and their community—provided them with a blanket of security and some sense of belonging and footing in some reality, albeit much distorted.

Both tormentors and their victims fueled the climate of victimization and the uniquely inadequate culture it generated. After a while, the Gentile populations and their rulers had developed a mix of sentiments towards their Jewish communities that were mostly animated by disdain and suspicion. The non-Jewish world, embroiled in transformation and revolutions, had failed to comprehend the role of the "eternal victim" played by the tormented Jewish minorities. In time, as centuries went by, this disharmonious system had become the norm in the relationship between Jews and Gentiles. Each side was *expected* to act as either tormentor or victim.

For the rabbinical leaders, this abnormal situation had the potential of strengthening their twisted hold upon their followers. Being the victims, the rabbinical authorities thus supported utter disregard for civilian laws and the secular authorities and compounded this with increased refuge within the confined ghetto-community. As victims, the Jews had developed a paranoiac distrust of all that the secular regimes represented–its laws, rules, customs, beliefs, and way of life–and continued their huddling within the relatively secure segregation of their community.

The painful consequences from this state of affairs were the alienation of the Jews and the natural course for victims: blaming themselves for their pain. Such self-hatred was further fueled by utilizing the power of the civilian regimes to settle internal Jewish disputes and to eliminate political, religious, and even economic rivals. A very different form of morality had emerged within the Jewish community, The perverted use of the odious regime of their country of residence to inflict punishment, revenge, or pain upon their fellow Jews had become an accepted mode of operation. The rationale was very simple. Since the Jew is a victim, he lacks any means of power to defend himself—even from whatever harm is inflicted upon him by other Jews. The rabbinical authorities were largely ineffective, usually deciding in favor of the more powerful members of the community. Moreover, the civilian authorities were considered the "instruments of the Almighty," for they tormented the Jews as one more step towards the waited Messiah. Therefore, how can it be unethical to appeal to such powers—by means of truth or lies—to garner some form of advantage?[269]

For the rabbinical leaders, this abnormal situation had the potential of strengthening their twisted hold upon their followers. Being the victims, the rabbinical authorities thus supported utter disregard for civilian laws and the secular authorities and compounded this with increased refuge within the confined ghetto-community. As victims, the Jews had developed a paranoiac distrust of all that the secular regimes represented–its laws, rules, customs, beliefs, and way of life– and continued their huddling within the relatively secure segregation of their community.

The sentiment of victimization also contributed to increased insulation and tribalism. Where it did not help in generating a rebellious attitude–such as with the emancipation and the emergence of Jewish political movements–victimization greatly contributed to divisions within the Jewish communities. Distrust of others, coupled with painful experiences, had made the family unit the only safe harbor, whereas all else and all others were not worthy of consideration. This behavior was constantly reinforced by the rabbinical authorities and the family-oriented religious festivals. Customs that fostered community spirit were de-emphasized, whereas the formation of groups or parties with secular purposes was utterly discouraged.

Victimization also explains how, when national identity was finally sought through the emergence of political movements, there were too many parties, almost unable to reach viable agreements. Tribalism and disunion became a dominant feature of the Jewish experience in the Diaspora.[270] Thus, ultimately, the vicious circle of victim-tormentor continued unabated for centuries, with so much suffering, lives, and dreams lost, and the wasting of a people that, in the beginning, had so much promise and an unlimited potential among the nations of the world.

The Myths of Antisemitism

By and large antisemitism was based on a set of myths. Embellished by tradition and constructed out of folklore that drank from a well of fears and ignorance, antisemitism was generally justified and encouraged by several unfounded claims.

One of the myths was the demoralization of the Jews as a powerful international concern. The misconstrued assembly of selected items of the Jewish existence in their Diaspora formed an outrageously wrong notion. The house of Rothschild and its financial power in several European capitals was a glowing observation. Most Jews, however, were engaged in petty commerce and transportable professions, *not* in international finance. The Jews were the first knowledge-workers, depending upon their individual intellectual skills for their economic survival.

The vast majority of international commerce, banking, finance, shipping, and other such global economic activities was concentrated in the hands of non-Jewish companies: Italians, Germans, British, Dutch, and French. As Karl Marx would so desperately try to explain, the means of production of the industrial revolution were not in any way in the control of the Jews nor influenced by them.

A similar myth grossly over-estimated the unity of the Jews as an international force of like objectives and modes of operation. The sobering reality was that Jews in their Diaspora were consistently divided, tribalized, and unable to form any truly unifying institutions or movements. Even the more notable attempts, such as the Zionist movement, had little appeal to the broader Jewish presence in Europe and the Americas.

The irony of the myth of Jews as an international powerhouse of like minds is that, if this was the true nature of the Jewish Diaspora, it would have much earlier formed a national identity and would have broken the vicious cycle of discrimination and persecutions.

A third myth consisted of the mysteries surrounding Jewish religion, practices, and rituals. In particular, antisemitic leaders showed considerable fascination with Jewish dietary rules ("Kashrut"). There was, and to a large extent there still is, horrific ignorance on what these rules demand, what constitutes "kosher" food, and the rituals that accompany these rules. In fact, the elementary rules about what is permitted and what is not are quite simple. These rules and the rituals that follow lack any vestige of sinister wishes nor do they harbor any inimical goals.[271]

The Who, The Why, and The Blending and Bending of Truth and Hopes

The Zionist movement finally gained some momentum in the early years of the twentieth century not because it became a roaring success or attracted millions of Diaspora Jews. Rather, it had limited success because it was the only solution to the Jewish problem that had even a minimal level of feasibility and also because at the time of Herzl and the first Zionist Congresses, there already existed a small settlement in Palestine (Zion). In 1882 the Jewish population amounted to about 24,000, and in 1914 it swelled to 85,000—due primarily to immigrations by Jews from Poland (1883), Bulgaria (1896), and a continuous influx from Russia and the Ottoman-Turkish Empire.

In 1948, upon the establishment of the State of Israel, the entire Jewish population in Palestine was less than 500,000. This amounted to less than 2 percent of the number of Jews in the world before the Nazi holocaust.

The Jewish Diaspora was the bedrock of over twenty centuries of misery, suffering, and the shattering of hopes and aspirations of an entire people. In a way, it was a conscious resolution by the chosen leaders to preserve the religion while allowing the people to wither. The fallacy of having a religion without a people to preserve it seldom seemed to disturb the rabbinical leaders. They were rather guided by the self-imposed concept of Messianic salvation, as ethereal as the invisible God. But, the crucial exception is that belief in an almighty and invisible God does not necessarily translate into inaction and the generative history of an entire people.

The belief in the Messiah and in the pains one must endure to finally "deserve" His appearance did have an enormous impact on the destiny of the Jewish people. It allowed the cabal of miserable and criminally incompetent leaders to justify their hold over their people, and thus inflict upon it centuries of evolving hatred, fear, and discrimination on a global scale.

The major disasters in the Jewish experience should not have happened. The Nazi holocaust, for example, was a result of centuries of antisemitism, not merely the deranged actions of a frustrated artist, aided by a chicken farmer and some ambitious lawyers and administrators of the likes of Eichmann and Heidrich. Many Jews would probably have perished in the Second World War as victims of the war itself, not as a result of a planned program of extermination. The main protagonist of this odious crime (Hitler, Himmler, Heidrich, and Eichmann) did not, to our knowledge, directly suffer any abuse by Jews. It was rather the *concept* of anti-Jewish sentiment that animated their horrific outbursts of hatred and mass murder. The cleansing of Europe of its Jews, as the "final solution," was simply an extension of many centuries in which the "Jewish Question" evolved as a thorn in the European psyche.

The saying that people get the leaders they deserve is wholly exaggerated in this case. The Jews in their Diaspora, nor any other people for that matter, did not "deserve" their fate of many centuries of pain and suffering. Rather, people get the leaders they *allow* to rule them. The "Jewish Question" may, perhaps should, be reframed as the acquiescence of generations of Jews in every corner of the world to a cabal of largely uncaring and terribly incompetent religious leaders. The Jewish Diaspora was originally imposed on the people exiled from its homeland. Later it became an acceptable way of life, fostered, and nurtured by the rabbinical authorities who had devised a complex, albeit tortuously disastrous, logic to justify the continuing persecutions and horrors inflicted upon their own people.

Before the modern era, by and large the Jews in their Diaspora had better elementary education than their Gentile neighbors. With the growth of cities, the industrial revolution, and the adoption of compulsory and state-supported public education, the gap was closed. Although there remained vestiges of jealousy and hatred on the part of non-Jews towards the better educated Jewish communities, this distinction largely disappeared in the wake of the dramatic rise in the levels of literacy of the general population. Such a phenomenon, coupled with Jewish emancipation, has produced encouraging results. Jews have attained high positions such as: a Prime Minister of the British Empire, a Justice of the Supreme Court of the United States, and many other elected and appointed roles in the cultural, political, economical, and social lives of their countries.

The rise and victories of democracy and human rights in the twentieth century have contributed to improvements in the fate of the Jews in their Diaspora and to the founding of the State of Israel. Nevertheless, in the final analysis, the Jewish Diaspora was an uninterrupted series of disastrous failures, betrayal, and the shattering of the hopes and dreams of a vanquished people. The religion survived and its ceremonies and rituals are still practiced by whatever is left of a promising and glorious people. But the people itself were irreparably decimated, without a trace, needlessly.

Part VII
Behind the Empty Mirror: The Epilogue

"To follow by faith alone is to follow blindly."
Benjamin Franklin (1706-1790)

The Fallacies of History's Determinism

The notion that historical events in the life of individuals, of nations, and of entire civilizations are pre-ordained and determined by fate or a superior force is utterly fallacious. Arnold Toynbee, for example, analyzed the rise and fall of human civilizations. He, and a similar school of historians, argued that the destiny is set for civilizations, with the pre-determined trajectory of growth, maturity, and fall from power. The model of biological evolution is thus transported and happily applied to the model of the life of countries and civilizations.

There is very little that is different between religious clerics who vehemently argue that history is pre-determined by the omnipotent and all-knowing deity—and those scholars who consider evolution as the model of progress, growth, and demise of individuals and their institutions. Even the randomness factor inherent in the model of evolutionary progress does not negate the ultimate result: people and institutions will perish because of the effects of natural selection and the survival of the fittest. If they happen to be unfit when unforeseen events occur, they will not survive. In this model there is very little they can do to reverse the outcome. Nature or a supreme being set the events in motion and determine the outcomes.[272]

A historical perspective of civilizations such as Toynbee's is an attractive model. It provides a macro approach that dispenses with the need or ability to measure the causes and antecedents of any conclusions one would draw. Civilizations decline and fall because of mega trends and the failure of the civilization to adapt to changes—although often adaptation may be at the root of the causes for their decline. The Roman Empire adapted itself to the presence of the barbarians in the north by incorporating them into the Roman way of life, and still the empire declined and was replaced by another civilization—albeit not as civilized. Whether it is inherent in the life of the civilization to fail or a deity so willed—the deterministic factor is the explanation for whatever happened.

Philosophers have grappled with the notion of individual choice and individual and civic responsibility versus a predetermined conception of world affairs and human destiny. The age of science and reason and the enlightenment of the past three centuries have brought to the forefront of human conscience the idea that we may not be masters of our fate, but we are certainly not enslaved to it. Even within the respect that the early scholars of the enlightenment (such as Descartes) had for their religion, these thinkers strongly believed in the human capacity to control its present and its future through knowledge and reason.

As we live in the exciting times of the new enlightenment and the age of knowledge, it doubly behooves upon us to re-examine the progression of historical events without fear or prejudice, and without resort to belief in forces of historical determinism. Marie Curie once commented that there is nothing to fear, only to understand.

If the level of analysis expands from the individual to social and political organizations and even further to nations and civilizations, the deterministic approach is no longer a satisfactory explanation of why events shaped the course of history. Different, perhaps more measurable, causes need to be identified, causes that are also more tangible and can serve as targets for blame if there have been failures and decline. In such cases there is a human tendency to look for external scapegoats who are concrete, not conceptual, and who can provide a simple yet convincing explanation to the loss experienced by the failing group, people, country, or civilization. This act of blaming outsiders offers the suffering people a rational as well as an emotional soporific to the pained souls who yearn for explanation.

The Result of Knowledge and Actions

I see historical events as the direct results from the actions of people and their leaders. There is nothing we have discovered in the genetic makeup of nations that imposes on them a limited temporal existence. Civilizations decline and some disappear because they want to, not because they must do so at the command of a superior ethereal force. Hence the difference between the longevity of countries, peoples, and entire civilizations. Some last a few centuries, others a few millennia.

Insects are less evolved than Bengal tigers or polar bears, but it is the latter who are endangered and may survive only because of extraordinary intervention of a third party—humans, not nature. The Native Americans declined in number and influence primarily because they were divided into warring tribes and unable to adequately challenge the European invaders.[273] Other societies have declined and some have perished because their leaders were unable or unwilling to lead, that is, to plan, to prepare, to understand their environment, to evaluate their friends and enemies, and to put aside greed, pettiness, ambition, vanity, and stupidity for the sake of the survival and prosperity of their societies.

In modern industrial terms, these leaders failed in their fiduciary roles. They mismanaged their organizations, thus leading them to disaster. Fate, superior force of a deity, or the malevolence of their neighbors or enemies had very little to do with their failure. Consider also that when a society fails, there are other societies that succeed and prosper (not necessarily at each other's expense). The "winning" society did not have a lock on fate or a direct line to the gods. Diamond argued that the societies who first domesticated animals and developed agriculture also had the advantage of being ahead of other societies in developing technology, writing, and management skills. However, the question that Diamond left unanswered is why did these societies take the lead in farming and animal husbandry. The answer is that at some point in their history gifted *leaders* put aside their human frailties and promoted the use of agriculture and the husbandry of animals with all the benefits to be derived from these activities, such as the accumulation of surpluses and wealth, immunity from diseases borne by animals, and the ability to feed, house, and clothe growing numbers of their people. These wise managerial actions supported the superiority of these activities, their progress, and their survival.[274]

Joseph of Egypt: How Knowledge and Actions Saved a Society

Consider the Biblical story of Joseph, son of Jacob. Some four thousand years ago a young man from a backward land was sold into slavery by his conniving brothers. He arrived in Egypt and soon his talents became known and he was made the manager of a liquor business. Joseph proved to be a very able administrator but he got into trouble by having an affair with the wife of his boss. Thrown in jail, he was nevertheless rescued by his lover who recommended him to the Pharaoh. The monarch soon employed Joseph as a consultant to help solve Egypt's problems with its cyclical economies based on the river Nile and its seven-year cycles of flooding. Joseph recommended, and the Pharaoh accepted, a series of actions. These included careful planning and making sure that surpluses of grain be stored during times of plenty, to be used in times of need. This was a program of "save for a rainy day and you shall not starve." Like so many immigrants since, Joseph was now able to bring his family to the land of opportunity.

There is a tremendous amount of knowledge necessary to plan and to implement such a program. It takes knowledge of *planning* and the understanding of the cycles of plenty and want. There is a need for knowledge of the *construction* of warehouses to store the grain collected during the years of plentiful harvests. The Egyptians needed knowledge of *logistics*, including the *transportation* of the grain and the division of the harvest between consumption and storage for future use. Even in the twentieth century the Soviet Union, for example, failed to transport, store, and distribute grain to millions of its inhabitants, thus allowing large quantities of grains to rot in the fields.

There was a need for knowledge of *distribution* of the stored grain, including the knowledge of principles of allocation to the populations and areas most in need of food. The Egyptians had to know how to defend and *protect* the grain stored in the warehouses. They needed knowledge on how to assure that the stored grain did not perish over time or be consumed by animals, insects, and human predators. Finally, they needed knowledge about the *management* and *organization* of such a program of national magnitude, including overseeing an army of farmers, transporters, project managers, inspectors, and military officers.[275] This massive effort required not only technical expertise but also knowledge of the basic principles of management at the team, project, and national levels.

Two amazing conclusions emerge from this tale. The first is that the absolute monarch of Egypt was willing to listen to a slave and to accept, even implement, his recommendations. In the story the Pharaoh entrusted the overall supervision of this effort to a former slave of foreign origin. But, even if we exclude this fine element of the rise of Joseph in Egyptian society, the act of embracing the advice of a slave confers upon the monarch the benefits of an unselfish ruler, acting in the interests of his people, rather than succumb to pettiness so prevalent among leaders.

The second amazing fact is that Joseph's extraordinary knowledge was never transferred to his kin, the Hebrews. During their exodus from Egypt many years later, the Hebrews left with many material goods, but with very little knowledge they could and should have accumulated from the Egyptians There was hardly any knowledge about architecture, construction, fluvial control, maritime knowledge, or administration. For generations afterwards, the Hebrews inhabited the land of Canaan as a conglomerate of separate tribes, composed mostly of shepherds, with little knowledge or understanding of centralized management, agriculture, or industry—a backward society made up of a blend of former nomads and former slaves.

The story of Joseph is an illuminating example of how environmental adversity does not necessarily need to be destructive to a society. Actions by a responsible leader and application of the available pool of knowledge can reverse the effects of natural forces and prevent decay and disaster.

The Thread of Jewish Destiny: From Origins To Calamity

The great German man of letters, Johann Von Goethe (1749-1832) once commented: "A comparison of the German people with other peoples arouses a painful feeling, which I try to overcome in every possible way." I very much sympathize with Goethe. Whenever I compare the Jewish people to other peoples, I also feel a painful reverberation laced with incredulity. How could a people with a promise meander through the centuries of world history guided almost permanently by a crop of wretched leaders? Since its early days, with few exceptions, the Jewish people have been led by religious and semi-religious authorities who did their best to keep their people enclosed in their ghettos, constantly awaiting the coming of their savior, and ignorant of the world around them.[276]

The Watershed Events in Jewish Experience

The three key events in Jewish history were the expulsion from their land by the Romans, the holocaust in Europe in the 1940s, and the establishment of the state of Israel. In all these events it was easy to proclaim predestination and the determinism of historical necessity. It also became convenient to blame not only the mischief of historical trends, but also—perhaps chiefly—the hatred, if not the insouciance, of the world of Gentiles. In the introspective attempts of the Jewish people over two millennia, there has been very little hard looks in the mirror. This was, and continues to be, an empty mirror.

In all these watershed events, and in so many other ancillary occurrences, the failure of the Jewish leadership has been the mortal catalyst in the unbearable suffering of so many of their people, over so many centuries.

As I conclude this narrative there is a need to reinject the issues of the essence of Judaism and the key attributes of the Jewish people—all that permitted the virtual dictatorship of the fatally unscrupulous leadership. Why did so many allow so few to lead them from disaster to disaster, without ever pausing to reflect upon the errors and the outrage of this path? Why did so many allow, and still allow today, the emergence of a few to lead the reincarnated Jewish homeland of Israel toward a calamitous end?

The Makeup of the Jewish Uniqueness

Any social, religious, or political movement whose credo relies almost entirely on the events of the past are, by definition, painfully exclusionary. Its thread to the past is its main, perhaps only, glue that holds together the society. The history of ancestors is the only link that binds current and future adherents—regardless of the content of the message of such a movement or society, however noble, enlightened or arousing.

This description aptly defines the uniqueness of Judaism and the Jewish people. For over three millennia, especially after they were driven away from their homeland, Jews have clung to the past, with almost no reference to a doable future—except that which will be provided by the mythical figure of the Messiah. Over the millennia Judaism became a mere set of dietary, ethical, and behavioral rules concocted earlier in the desert by their mythical ancestors.

Since Hammurabi, Confucius, Aristotle, and Cicero, organized humanity developed ethical and behavioral rules of existence and social behavior that have allowed and successfully maintained a rich secular life alongside religious beliefs. The uniqueness of Judaic ethics and laws had practically dissipated, to become the anachronistic manifestation of a religious society.

Other religions also grappled with similar problems. The apostle St. Paul (a Jewish scholar) understood the truisms of human nature and the essence of religious movements. His teachings emphasized the future, not the past. Although the new religion was based on the life and the crucifixion of Jesus, the *message* and the ethos it generated emphasized a present and a future. This was the key to the rupture of early Christianity with its Jewish heritage. By severing the link to Jewish historical events, the new religion could then endear itself to the Greek and Roman worlds.

How could a Roman citizen, a barbarian in Gaul, and later on a peasant in Poland or a potato farmer in Ireland relate to the covenant between God and Abraham, the exodus from Egypt, or the revolt of the Maccabeans? The entire array of Jewish religious festivals, ceremonies, and rituals are embedded in specific historical events. Any emotional value they have is anchored in the conception of the people and their link to their ancestors, all by birth rights, not by choice.

The prophet Mohammed and his successors also understood the need for a worldwide religion to abstain from unbending links to specific events and unique experiences of one people. Like Christianity, Islam is anchored in the life of an individual, not a people. Although anchored in the holy cities of Mecca and Medina (as Christianity was anchored in Bethlehem, Nazareth, and Jerusalem), the message of the new religion was universal, transcending geography and demography. The sacred localities were merely coincidental to places where the founders of the religions had spent their extraordinary lives.

By merging the religious, political, historical, and social aspects of their people into an immutable, unique, and impenetrable cocoon, Jewish leaders have created—by design—a permanent outcast in human history. With the passage of time, religious, social, and political transformations had engulfed the globe. Evolutionary and revolutionary ideas, conceptions, and ways of life have sprung and disseminated among nations and across continents. The Jewish presence remained largely unchanged.

The more isolation persisted, the more the external, non-Jewish societies became tormentors of the unique and estranged people. The more the bullying, the more Jewish religious leaders tightened their hold on their retreating and insular people and placed more emphasis on Jewish uniqueness, superiority, and their links to a glorious past. The endless cycle continued.

Whose Responsibility? Whose Culpability?

William Shirer congeniously described the tragedy of Nazism in Germany. He wrote: "No class or group or party in Germany could escape its share of responsibility for the abandonment of the democratic republic and the advent of Adolf Hitler. The cardinal error of the Germans who opposed Nazism was their failure to unite against it."

A similar distribution of blame for the forthcoming calamity can be attributed to all segments of the Jewish people. Even in present day Israel, not one segment of the society can be counted on to stop the maniacal descent of religious zealotry into nuclear perdition.

The upcoming catastrophe in the Middle East will resemble the calamity of the Bronze Age. The historian Robert Drews correctly argued that the military scenario far better explains the demise of the ancient kingdoms of the Bronze Age than, for example, the migrations hypothesis.[278]

In modern history the migrations hypothesis is not a plausible explanation to the birth of the Jewish state of Israel. The migration of over a million Jews to Palestine in the first half of the twentieth century has hardly put a dent in the over 100 million Arab population living in that neighborhood.[279] The migration of about 1.5 million Jews into Palestine and the subsequent exodus of over a million Palestinians can be numerically offset against the exodus of over a million Jews from Arab countries in the Levant and North Africa—around the same period. Jews had left or were expulsed from Tunisia to Morocco, from Egypt to Iraq. This was a massive exchange of populations based on religious grounds, in almost an eerie balance of numbers. Such exchanges have become common throughout the twentieth century, in the Balkans, in the Korean peninsula, and in the Indian subcontinent.

The only explanation befitting the upcoming nuclear catastrophe is the military solution to the conflict and the unwillingness to negotiate and to compromise. But the descent into religious dominance in the state of Israel completes the policies of the Bengurionites in the early years of the new nation, when the exchanges of populations had begun. Unlike the Indian experience, in which Hindus and Muslims were able to resolve many of their pressing differences and execute a planned exchange of populations to create India and Pakistan as independent countries, the Bengurionites never intended to do so with their Arab neighbors.

The imperative of the religious control of the state has already begun. In a manner similar to Nazism in Germany of the 1930s, the emergence of the ultra-orthodox regime is the product of the Jews in their own country. William Shirer wrote: "But the Third Reich owed nothing to the fortunes of war or to foreign influence. It was inaugurated in peace time, and peacefully, by the Germans themselves, out of both their weaknesses and their strengths. The Germans imposed the Nazi tyranny on themselves" (p. 187).

Substitute Jews for Germans and the phenomenon of ceding the country to a tyranny of zealots and it is almost identical. The religious parties are garnering economic and political power with the consent and support of the people. This time it is not the fault of the anti-Semitic actions of Gentiles. This phenomenon is entirely home grown, in peacetime, with the full acquiescence of the Jews themselves. No one to blame—look into the empty mirror.

In all of Jewish history, briefly narrated in this book, from origins to the approaching calamity, there has not been (except for very short periods) a persuasive record of civil or secular order separated from the religious controlling mechanisms. The historian Thomas Bisson described the period of the twelfth century in Western Europe as a continent without public order and government.[280] The Jewish people has experienced this lack of civilian government for generations, with the only legitimate power resting with the lordship of rabbinical authorities.

Judaism is the only major religion that has not experienced a concerted separation or division between religion and civilian order. In Christianity, Buddhism, Hinduism and, to a large extent in Islam, there has been a demarcation between the clerics and the rulers, between the religious and the secular authorities—however intertwined they might be. In Judaism, even the awaited Messiah is a descendant from a ruler, hence upon his arrival will hold both the spiritual and the earthly powers over his people.[281]

As other religions and political systems evolved since the days of the Roman Empire, most differences in goals, means, and personalities between institutions of faith and polity (some differences were significant) were resolved through combinations of conflict and compromise.

In the past two millennia, Jewish leaders have continuously resorted to shifting the blame for the isolation and suffering of their people unto others. Instead of looking in the mirror, the culpability for all misfortunes has been constantly framed as a combination of divine action and the horrors inflicted by a malevolent world. In present day Israel the redirection of blame continues with the target being the Arab world. Blaming one's neighbors is hardly the answer to one's misery.[282]

250 *Shattered Hopes Magnificent Failure*

In the final analysis, the responsibility and the culpability for the catastrophic journey of the Jews through the past and into the future rest entirely with the religious leadership. For a short period in the twentieth century, the Bengurionite leaders had wrestled control of the promised land—soon to again relinquish power to the orthodoxy—with calamitous consequences in the foreseeable future.

Behind the Empty Mirror: The Epilogue

Our most basic common link is that we all inhabit this planet. We all breathe the same air. We all cherish our children's future. And we are all mortal.

John F. Kennedy (1917-1963)

In the two millennia since the fall of Jerusalem and the expulsion of the Jews from their homeland by the Roman legions, Jewish leaders very seldom looked in the mirror. There has been a continuing descent into the disastrous path of the Jews in their Diaspora.

Modern archaeology tells us that in the beginning the Israelites may have been lower class and subjugated Canaanites who revolted against their rulers. Around the time of the story of the Exodus, about 1500 B.C., there may have been a decline in the city kingdoms in Canaan. The subjugated populations broke away from these cities (such as Hazor, Meggido, Gezer, and Ai) and established their own settlements.[283] These underprivileged people were perhaps joined by some Canaanites and similar people who escaped from Egypt. They may have arrived in Canaan via desert settlements in Midian, east of the Gulf of Aqba, where they may have assimilated the notion of a single overarching deity. Archaeological excavations in what was then Canaan have failed thus far to corroborate the destructive campaign that Joshua led into Canaan at the time of the Exodus from Egypt.[284]

The Israelite settlements in Canaan were, perhaps, attempts by displaced urban communities who overthrew their royal oppressors or left their native cities to start new lives. The story of the Exodus provided them with a specialized history that also aided in the stratification of their new identity. The story also reinforced the notion of "liberation" and "freedom" from their former lords and oppressors.

But, these settlements remained underdeveloped throughout the Israelite history in Canaan. Although they grew in size and formed regional or tribal congregations, they were unable to form centralized authority—except during the reigns of David and his son Solomon. Throughout the remainder of their history, the Israelites were an underdeveloped nation, constantly mauled by its neighbors.

The Triple Disenfranchisement

The Israelites could never form a strong and prosperous nation. They remained divided by tribal distinctions. Monotheism and the establishment of the city of Jerusalem as the political *and* religious center of the country had brought some measure of unity and a distinct identity of a separate and distinctive people. The notions of freedom and liberation echoed throughout the history of the people, whether in the Biblical story of the Exodus from Egypt or the historical and archaeological version of Canaanite revolt of the underprivileged inhabitants of the city-states in ancient Canaan.

As soon as the Romans expulsed the Israelites from Judea, the orthodox rabbinical authorities entered into the political and social void, and assumed the leadership of the scattered people. For twenty centuries these unelected, self-proclaimed, and injurious leaders have steered the Jews from one disaster to another—to culminate in the forthcoming nuclear calamity.

The religious leaders disenfranchised the concept of freedom and liberation from oppression. In their zeal for control and their orthodox interpretation of both Jewish history and the rituals of the religion, these leaders appropriated the notion of liberation to make it a myth, an unachievable myth. Instead of a unifying notion, they transformed the concept into an ethereal goal to be accomplished only with the advent of the savior, the Messiah.

In many respects, the Jewish people resemble an eternal middle school child, never to become an adult. The child constantly complains: "They are mean to me," thus continuously appealing to the parent for help without assuming personal responsibility. The Jewish people have historically been appealing to the Creator for all aspects of their existence. In the entire Jewish portfolio of traditions, festivals, rituals, and observances, there is not one in which the people are asked to commemorate a feat of their own doing, their own initiative, or their own responsibility. Even the festival of Hanukkah, the festival of light, does not commemorate the military victory of the Maccabeans over their enemies, rather it extols the miracle performed by the supreme being of letting some oil that would have lasted only one day to burn for eight days. The festivals of Passover, Tabernacles, and the receiving of the Torah at Mount Sinai are all celebrations of God's mighty actions, not the performance of the people.

The Jewish religious authorities cleverly promoted the notion of the "chosen people" to justify, both emotionally and intellectually, the constant appeal to the supreme deity. Why would the Lord listen to this Jewish people and not to its tormentors? Because, like a parent's relationship with a child, the Lord gives preference to his chosen children. Jewish prayers indeed refer to the Lord as "our father in Heaven", and this parent has the sole responsibility for the child—thus removing all sense of responsibility from the children themselves. Complaints, appeals to the Lord, and the inaction of the people have characterized the Jewish people in their Diaspora and are present in today's Israel. The uninterrupted complaints that "they are against us," "they are mean to us," and "the whole world is against us just because of who we are" perfectly reflect the corruption of the notions of liberation and freedom that were evoked by the original Israelites when they freed themselves from the shackles of the city-kingdoms in Canaan some four thousand years ago. Only when rational Jews like Theodore Benjamin Herzl took responsibility for the destiny of their people and freed them from the slavery of the Jewish orthodoxy did the concepts of a homeland and Jewish initiatives become a reality.

Instead of the concept of liberation that helped to define the ancient Israelites, the religious leaders introduced the notion of the tribulations of the Messiah ("Hevlei Mashiach"), whereupon the more the cup of suffering is filled for the Jewish people, the faster the coming of the savior. Instead of celebrating actual freedom from oppression, Jews were commanded to glorify ancient stories of liberation and put their faith in the remotely possible event of the coming of the Messiah.

A second disenfranchisement was the vicious cycle of losing the identity of a unique people to the reality of allowing other peoples to define the Jews by their own criteria and standards. With the legitimization by the religious leaders of Jewish suffering, there emerged a culture of victimization. Jews were now characterized by non-Jews as difficult, pretentious, insular, and antiquated. The more the religious leaders preached the superiority of the Jewish people, the more this approach conflicted with the abandonment of the characterization of the Israelites as a set of tribes in their land, linked by a common deity and a bunch of historical accounts. Instead, the religious leaders painted the Jews as a constantly victimized people of superior qualities that were encased in the minds of the leaders.

The third of the triple disenfranchisements was the demolition by the religious leaders of the secular element of the Jewish people. This consisted of the extinction of reason and dissent. This same approach was exercised in 70 A.D. when the religious leadership in Judea caused the demise of the state, the destruction of the temple, and the expulsion of the people from their land. By crushing internal dissent and by refusing to compromise with the Romans, the Jewish religious leaders sacrificed their people and condemned them to centuries of terror.

Behind the Empty Mirror

When Jews venture into the historical prism of looking into the mirror, they see an empty image of themselves. What they see are the Egyptians, Assyrians, Babylonians, Greeks, Persians, Romans, Christians, and Muslims—they see their tormentors, but not themselves. Their image is *beyond* the mirror, lost in the unreal space of life as it will be upon the arrival of the Messiah, not as it should be, and where the fault lies with all those reflected in the mirror.

This book was written at great mental anguish. As I see it, instead of moving toward accepting human differences as a wonderful and productive reality, today in the Middle East, Jews and Arabs see each other not as partners but as objects for destruction. Within the Jewish state, the uncompromising and ruthless religious movement is about to lead the Jewish state and half of what remains of the Jewish people in the world into the abyss of intolerance and nuclear devastation.

Where We Are Heading and What Can Still Be Done

There are today fewer Jews in the entire world than the number of inhabitants in cities like Calcutta, Sao Paulo, or Cairo. If the religious leaders in Israel have their way, the six million Jews in Israel will disappear in the nuclear devastation that these leaders will unleash. The nuclear winter in the Middle East will claim over 20 million victims and a global economic disaster.

In their pursuit of political and economic powers, the Bengurionites have over the years of their rule in Israel in effect given the "keys to the store" to the orthodoxy. By doing so, they revered the trend described in this narrative. All the sacrifices and benefits of the Jewish enlightenment and emancipation have been wasted. The trend has reversed to its original state of the Diaspora, whereby the orthodox rabbinical control has ruled unopposed. The startling difference is that in the coming years these orthodox powers will also have the keys to the nuclear arsenal.

Secular and national Jews in North America and Europe must put aside their petty quarrels and interfere in the decaying situation in the Middle East. All remaining Jews who still have their logic and who have liberated themselves from the slavery of religious mandate must look in the mirror. They may find that behind it there is emptiness, since over twenty centuries the mirror reflected a victimized and anachronistic people.

For the future of the Jewish people, religion is not the solution—it is the devastating problem. There is no substitute to peace with the Arab world and the solution to the Palestinian suffering. Secular Jews must unite to prevent the taking over of the Israeli state and its weapons of mass destruction by the religious extremists. By any means possible—including pressure on governments of the major world powers—rational Jews must act. The fate of what remains of the Jewish people depends not on the miracles of a potential savior, but on the concerted effort of Jews of good will and a reasoned approach to reality and to sanity.

This book took us on a long journey, from Canaan to the modern state of Israel. It was a journey of little pleasure and few accomplishments of which we can be proud. For the most part it was a journey of pettiness, greed, power grab, and the unmitigated desire to control a poor flock of believers who were constantly led through pain and suffering to the brink of annihilation. It is the duty of this and perhaps the next generation of Jews to make it a story not of all that went wrong, but of what went right, and that the Jewish people can live in peace and prosperity with all other peoples in this world. After all, when we put religious extremism aside, "we all cherish our children's future, and we are all mortal."

Bibliography

This is a selected list of relevant references used in this book. Additional references were books and documents in Hebrew, in the topics of Jewish and general history, philosophy, sociology, political science, and military history. Whenever feasible, a translation of these texts is included in the bibliography.

Abel, E. (2001). *Jewish Genetic Disorders: A Layman's Guide*. New York: McFarland & Company.

Adam, A. (1980). *On the Banks of the Suez*. San Francisco, CA: Presidio Publishers.

Alexander, E., & Bogdanor, P. (Eds.). (2006). J*ewish Divide Over Israel: Accusers and Defenders*. Somerset, NJ: Transaction Publishers.

Alexander, T. (2002, Second Edition). *From Paradise to the Promised Land: An Introduction to the Pentateuch*. Grand Rapids, MI: Baker Academic Press.

Applebaum, A. (2004). *Gulag: A History*. New York: Anchor Books.

Arendt, H. (1994). *Eichmann in Jerusalem: A Report on the Banality of Evil*. New York: Penguin Books.

Armstrong, K. (1994). *A History of God: The 4,000-Year Quest of Judaism, Christianity and Islam*. New York: Ballantine Books.

Armstrong, K. (1997). *In the Beginning: A New Interpretation of Genesis*. New York: Ballantine Books.

Aubert, M. (2001, Second Edition). *The Phoenicians and the West: Politics, Colonies, and Trade*. New York: Cambridge University Press.

Avishai, B. (2002). *The Tragedy of Zionism: How Its Revolutionary Past Haunts Israeli Democracy*. New York: Watson-Guptill Publications.

Avishai, B. (2008), *The Hebrew Republic: How Secular Democracy and Global Enterprise Will Bring Israel Peace at Last*, New York: Harcourt.

Bacevich, A. (2008). *The Limits of Power: The End of American Exceptionalism*. New York: Metropolitan Books.

Barber, E., & Barber, P. (2005). *When They Severed Earth From Sky: How the Human Mind Shapes Myth*. Princeton, NJ: Princeton University Press.

Bard, M. (2007). *Will Israel Survive?* New York: Palgrave-McMillan.

Barnaby, F. (1989). *The Invisible Bomb: The Nuclear Arms Race in the Middle East*. London: I. B. Tauris.

Bar-Zohar, M. (1970). *Embassies in Crisis: Diplomats and Demagogues Behind the Six-Day War*. Englewood Cliffs, NJ: Prentice-Hall.

Bar-Zohar, M. (1978). *Ben-Gurion: A Biography.* New York: Delacorte Press.

Bar-Zohar, M. (2007). *Shimon Peres: The Biography.* New York: Random House.

Bebel, A. (1971). *Society of the Future*. Moscow, USSR: Progress Publishers.

Begin, M. (1978). *The Revolt*. New York: Dell Publishing Company.

Ben-Sasson, H. (1985). *A History of the Jewish People*. Cambridge, MA: Harvard University Press.

Benvenisti, M., & Kaufman-Lacosta, M. (2000). *Sacred Landscape: The Buried History of the Holy Land Since 1948*. Sacramento, CA: The University of California Press.

Berger, D. (2001). *The Rebbe, The Messiah, and the Scandal of Orthodox Indifference*. New York: Littman Library of Jewish Civilization.

Bernstein, J. (2007). *Plutonium: A History of the World's Most Dangerous Element*. Washington, D.C.: Joseph Henry Press.

Bhagwati, J. (2007). *In Defense of Globalization*. New York: Oxford University Press; and Sen, A. (2000)

Bisson, T. (2008). *The Crisis of the Twelfth Century: Power, Lordship, and the Origins of European Government*. Princeton, NY: Princeton University Press.

Black, E. (2001). *The Transfer Agreement: The Dramatic Story of the Pact Between the Third Reich and Jewish Palestine*. New York: Caroll & Graf Publishers.

Black, I., & Morris, B. (1992). *Israel's Secret Wars: A History of Israel's Secret Services*. New York: Grove Press.

Blum, H. (2003). *The Eve of Destruction: The Untold History of the Yom Kippur War*. New York: Harper Collins Publishers.

Bobbitt, P. (2008). *Terror and Consent: The Wars for the Twenty-First Century*. New York: Alfred Knopf.

Borkenau, F. (1955). *Toynbee's Judgment of the Jews: When the Historian Misread History*. Washington, D.C.: American Jewish Committee.

Boyne, W. (2002). *The Two O'Clock War*. New York: St. Martin's Press.

Bright, J. (1972, Second Edition). *A History of Israel*. Philadelphia, PA: Westminster Press.

Bucaille, L. (2004). *Growing Up Palestinian: Israeli Occupation and the Intifada Generation*. Princeton, NJ: Princeton University Press.

Burge, G. (2003). *Whose Land? Whose Promise? What Christians Are Not Being Told About Israel and the Palestinians*. Cleveland, OH: Pilgrim Press.

Cahill, T. (1998). *The Gifts of the Jews: How a Tribe of Desert Nomads Changed the Way Everyone Thinks and Feels*. New York: Anchor Books.

Carmi, T. (Editor). *The Penguin Book of Hebrew Verse*. New York: Penguin Books.

Casson, L. (1995). *Ships and Seamanship in the Ancient World*. Baltimore, MD: Johns Hopkins University Press.

Chapman, C. (2002). *Whose Promised Land?* Grand Rapids, MI: Baker Books.

Chesler, P. (2003). *The New Anti-Semitism: The Current Crisis and What We Must Do About It*. San Francisco, CA: Jossey-Bass.

Chomsky, N. (1983). *The Fateful Triangle: The United States, Israel, and the Palestinians*. Boston, MA: South End Press.

Christman, H., Editor (1969). *The State Papers of Levi Eshkol*. New York: Funk & Wagnall.

Churchill, R. (2002). *The Six Day War*. Ripon, UK: House of Stratus.

Cohen, A. (1998). *Israel and the Bomb*. New York: Columbia University Press.

Cohen, M. (1995). *Under Crescent and Cross*. Princeton, NJ: Princeton University Press.

Collier, P. (2008). *The Bottom Billion: Why the Poorest Countries are Failing and What Can Be Done About It*. New York: Oxford University Press.

Comay, J. (1983). *The Diaspora Story: The Epic of the Jewish People Among the Nations*. New York: Random House.

Comay, J. (1988). *The Diaspora Story*. London: Weinfeld and Nicholson Publishing.

Cook, J. (2006). *Blood and Religion: The Unmasking of the Jewish and Democratic State*. London, U.K.: Pluto Press.

Cowan, T. (2004). *Creative Destruction: How Globalization is Changing the World's Cultures*. Princeton, NJ: Princeton University Press.

Cross, F. (1997). *Caananite Myth and Hebrew Epic: Essays in the History of the Religion of Israel*. Cambridge, MA: Harvard University Press.

Dalle, K. R. (2007). *Nixon and Kissinger: Partners in Power*. New York: Harper Collins.

Dawidowicz, L. (1986). *The War Against the Jews: 1933-1945*. New York: Bantam.

Dawisha, A. (2002). *Arab Nationalism in the Twentieth Century: From Triumph to Despair*. Princeton, NJ: Princeton University Press.

Dayan, M. (1976). *Moshe Dayon: The Story of My Life*. New York: William Morrow

Dayan, M. (1992). *Moshe Dayan: Story of My Life*. Cambridge, MA: DaCapo Press.

De Gaulle, C. (1998). *The Complete War Memoirs of Charles De Gaulle*. New York: Carroll & Graff Publishers.

De Gaulle, C. (2001). *The Enemy's House Divided*. Durham, N.C.: The University of North Carolina Press.

Dean P. (1981). *Les Deux Bombes*. Paris: Fayaard.

Derogy, J., & Carmel, H. (1979). *The Untold History of Israel*. New York: Grove Press

Derry, T., & Williams, T. (1961). *A Short History of Technology: From the Earliest Times to A.D. 1900*. New York: Oxford University Press.

Dershowitz, A. (2003). *The Case for Israel*. New York: John Wiley & Sons.

Deshen, S., & Zenner, W. (Eds.). (1996). *Jews Among Muslims: Communities in the Pre-Colonial Middle East.* New York: New York University Press.

Deutsch, A. (1974). Insight on the Middle East War. *The Sunday Times.*

Dever, W. (2002). *What Did the Biblical Writers Know and When Did They Know It? What Archaeology Can Tell Us About the Reality of Ancient Israel.* Grand Rapids, MI: Eerdmans Publishing Company.

Dever, W. (2003). *Who Were the Early Israelites and Where Did They Come From?* Grand Rapids, MI: William B. Eerdmans Publishing Company.

Diamond, J. (2005). *Guns, Germs, and Steel: The Fate of Human Societies.* New York: W. W. Norton.

Diamond, J. (2006). *Collapse: How Societies Choose to Fail or Succeed.* New York: Viking Press.

Draper, T. (1968). *Israel & World Politics.* New York: The Viking Press.

Dresner, S. (1974). *Levi Yitzhak of Berdichev: Portrait of a Hasidic Master.* Bridgeport, CT: Hartmore House Publishers.

Drews, R. (1993). *The End of the Bronze Age.* Princeton, NJ: Princeton University Press.

Dubnow, S. (1957). *History of the Jews.* New York: A. S. Barnes and Company.

Dunstan, S. (2007). *The Yom Kippur War: The Arab-Israeli War of 1973.* Oxford, U.K.

Easterly, W. (2006). *The White Man's Burden: Why the West's Efforts to Aid the Rest Have Done So Much Ill and So Little Good.* New York: Penguin Press.

Eban, A. (1978). *My People.* New York: Behrman House.

Eban, A. (1984). *Heritage: Civilization and the Jews.* New York: Summit Books.

Efron, J. (2001). *Medicine and the German Jews.* New Haven, CT: Yale University Press.

Efron, N. (2003). *Real Jews: Secular Versus Ultra-orthodox: The Struggle for Jewish Identity in Israel.* New York: Basic Books.

Efron, N. (2006). *Judaism and Science: A Historical Introduction.* Westport, CT: Greenwood Press.

Elon, A. (2002). *The Pity of it All.* New York: Metropolitan Books.

Eshkol, L. (1969). *The State Papers of Levi Eshkol.* New York: Funk & Wagnalls.

Eshkol, C. (1969). *Levi Eshkol, 1895-1969-Profile of a Zionist.* New York: World Zionist Organization.

Evron, Y. (1994). *Israel's Nuclear Dilemma.* Ithaca, New York: Cornell University Press.

Fellman, J. (1973). *The Revival of a Classical Tongue: Eliezer Ben-Yehuda and the Modern Hebrew Language.* The Hague, Netherlands: Mouton.

Ferraro, M. (2007). *Tough Going: Anglo-American Relations and the Yom*

Kippur War of 1973. Bloomington, IN.

Finkelstein, N. (2003, Second Edition). *Image and Reality of the Israel-Palestine Conflict.* New York: Verso.

Finkelstein, N., & Birn, R. (1998). *A Nation on Trial: The Goldhagen Thesis and Historical Truth.* New York: Henry Holt and Company.

Flavius, J. (1984, Reissue Edition). *The Wars of the Jews.* New York: Penguin Books.

Flavius, J. (2001). *The Antiquities of the Jews.* McLean, VA: Indypublish.

Frankel, G. (1996). *Beyond the Promised Land.* New York: Simon & Schuster.

Freedman, S. (2001). *Jew vs. Jew: The Struggle for the Soul of American Jewry.* New York: Simon & Schuster.

Freedman, S. (2006). *Rabbi Shlomo Goren: Torah Sage and General.* New York: Beit-Or-Vilnay.

Freudmann, L. (1994). *Antisemitism in the New Testament.* Washington, D.C.: University Press of America.

Friedman, M. (1982). *Capitalism and Freedom.* Chicago, IL: University of Chicago Press.

Ganin, Z. (2005). *An Uneasy Relationship: American Jewish Leadership and Israel, 1948-1957.*

Garaudy, R., & O'Keefe, T. (2000). *The Founding Myths of Modern Israel.* Newport Beach, CA: Institute for Historical Review.

Gartner, L. (2001). *History of the Jews in Modern Times.* New York: Oxford University Press.

Gatier, P., Gatier, E., & Gubel, E. (2000). *The Levant: History and Archaeology in the Eastern Mediterranean.* New York: Konemann Publishers.

Gibbon, J. (1978). *Canaanite Myths and Legends.* Edinburgh, UK: T&T Clark Publishers.

Gilman, S. (1990). *Jewish Self-Hatred: Anti-Semitism and the Hidden Language of the Jews.* Baltimore, MD: The Johns HopkinsUniversity Press.

Glick, L. (1999). *Abraham's Heirs: Jews and Christians in Medieval Europe.* Syracuse, NY: Syracuse University Press.

Goldhagen, D. (1997). *Hitler's Willing Executioners: Ordinary Germans and the Holocaust.* New York: Vintage.

Goldschmidt, A. (2001). *A Concise History of the Middle East.* Boulder, CO: Westview Press.

Grabbe, L. (2000). *Judaic Religion in the Second Temple Period: Belief and Practice from the Exile to Yavneh.* London, UK: Routledge.

Green, A. (2004). *A Guide to the Zohar.* Stanford, CA: Stanford University Press.

Greenfield, H. (2005). *A Promise Fulfilled: Theodor Herzl, Chaim Weizmann, David Ben-Gurion, and the Creation of the State of Israel.* New York:

Greenwillow Books.

Grodzinsky, Y. (2004). *In the Shadow of the Holocaust : The Struggle Between Jews and Zionists in the Aftermath of World War II.* Monroe, ME: Common Courage Press.

Gruen, E. (2004). *Diaspora: Jews Amidst Greeks and Romans.* Cambridge, MA: Harvard University Press.

Hahn, B. (2005). *The Jewess Pallas Athena: This Too A Theory of Modernity.* Princeton, NJ: Princeton University Press.

Halevi, Y. (1998, translated by Daniel Korobkin). *The Kuzari.* New York: Jason Aronson Inc.

George Hanus, Editor (2002). *The Compendium: A Critical Analysis of the Arab-Israeli Conflict.* Chicago, IL: Gravitas Media.

Harari, H. (2005). *A View from the Eye of the Storm: Terror and Reason in the Middle East.* New York: Regan Books.

Harper, P. (1990). *The Arab-Israeli Conflict.* Charlottsville, VA: Bookwrights Press.

Harris, S. (2004). *The End of Faith: Religion, Terror, and the Future of Reason.* New York: W. W. Norton.

Hayes, J. (1975). *Essays on Early Israelite History: From the Patriarchs to Saul.* San Antonio, TX: Trinity University Press.

Heilman, S. (1999). *Defenders of the Faith: Inside Ultra-Orthodox Jewry.* Sacramento, CA: University of California Press.

Henry, C. and R. Springborg (2001). *Globalization and the Politics of Development in the Middle East.* New York: Cambridge University Press.

Hersh, S. (1991). *The Samson Option: Israel's Nuclear Arsenal and American Foreign Policy*. New York: Random House.

Hertzberg, A. (1997). *The Zionist Idea: A Historical Analysis and Reader.* Philadelphia, PA: Jewish Publication Society of America.

Herzberg, A. (1959). *The Zionist Idea.* New York: Doubleday.

Herzl, T. (1989). *The Jewish State.* Mineola, NY: Dover Publications.

Herzl, T. (1997). *Old New Land.* New York: M. Wiener Publishers.

Herzog, H. (1984). *The Arab-Israeli Wars*. New York: Vantage Books.

Herzog, H. (2006). T*he War of Atonement: The Inside Story of the Yom Kippur War*. Greenhill Books: Newbury, U.K.

Hiro, D. (1999). *Sharing the Promised Land: A Tale of the Israelis and the Palestinians.* Northampton, MA: Interlink Publishing Group.

Hochstadt, S. (2004). *Sources of the Holocaust.* New York: Palgrove MacMillan.

Hoffman, M. (2000). *Judaism's Strange Gods.* New York: Independent History & Research Co.

Hoffman, M. (2002). *The Israeli Holocaust Against the Palestinians.* New York: Independent History & Research Company.

Hohne, H., & Zolling, H. (1972). *The General Was A Spy.* New York: Coward, McCann, and Geoghegan.

Holmio, A. (1949). *Martin Luther: Friend or Foe of the Jews.* Chicago, IL: National Lutheran Council Press.

Houghton, N. D. (Ed.). (1968). *Struggle Against History.* New York: Simon & Schuster.

Ibn Gabirol, S. (2000). *Selected Poems.* Princeton, NJ: Princeton University Press.

Isserlin, B. (1998). *The Israelites.* New York: Thames and Hudson.

Jackson, J. (2005). *De Gaulle (Life & Time).* London: Haus Publishing.

Johnson, E. (2000). *Nazi Terror: The Gestapo, Jews, and Ordinary Germans.* New York: Basic Books.

Johnson, P. (1988, Reprint edition). *A History of the Jews.* New York: Harper Perennial.

Johnson, P. (1987). *A History of the Jews.* New York: Harper-Collins.

Jones, C. (2001). *Israel: Challenge to Identity, Democracy, and the State.* New York: Routledge.

Josephus. (1981). *The Jewish War.* New York: Penguin Books.

Karp, A. (1985). *Haven and Home: A History of the Jews in America.* New York: Schocken.

Karpin, M. (2006). *The Bomb in the Basement: How Israel Went Nuclear and What That Meant for the World.* New York: Simon and Schuster.

Katz, J. (1998). *Out of the Ghetto: The Social Background of Jewish Emancipation, 1770-1870.* Syracuse, NY: Syracuse University Press.

Kenwood, A., & Lougheed, A. (1971). *Growth of the International Economy.* Albany, NY: Suny Press.

Keren, M. (1983). *Ben Gurion and the Intellectuals: Power, Knowledge and Charisma.* DeKalb, IL: Northern Illinois University.

Khoury, P., & Kostner, J. (Eds.). (1990). *Tribes and State Formation in the Middle East.* Los Angeles: Tauris Publishers.

Kimche, D., & Bawly, D. (1968), *The Sandstorm: The Arab-Israeli War of June 1967: Prelude and Aftermath.* London: Secker and Warburg.

Kimmerling, B. (2005). *The Invention and Decline of Israeliness: State, Society, and the Military.* Sacramento, CA: University of California Press.

Kissinger, H. (2000). *A World Restored: Metternich, Castlereagh, and the Problems of Peace, 1812-1822.* New York: Weidenfeld and Nicholson.

Kissinger, H. (2004). *Crisis: The Anatomy of Two Major Foreign Policy Crises.* New York: Simon & Schuster.

Klausner, J. (1943). *From Jesus to Paul.* New York: MacMillan Company.

Klausner, J. (1955). *The Messianic Idea of Israel From Its Beginning to the Completion of the Mishnah.* New York: McMillan.

Knebel, F. (1962). *Seven Days in May.* New York: Harper & Row.

Koelble, T. (1991). *The Left Unraveled: Social Democracy and the New Left Challenge in Britian and West Germany*. Durham, NC: Duke University Press.

Koestler, A. (1976). *The Thirteenth Tribe*. New York: Random House.

Kurzman, D. (1983). *Ben Gurion: Prophet of Fire*. New York: Simon and Schuster.

Laato, A. (1997). *A Star is Rising: The Historical Development of the Old Testament Royal Ideology and the Rise of the Jewish Messianic Expectations*. Atlanta, Georgia: Scholars Press.

Laguardia, A. (2003). *War Without End: Israelis, Palestinians, and the Struggle for a Promised Land*. New York: St. Martin's Griffin.

Langewiesche, W. (2007). *The Atomic Bazaar: The Rise of the Nuclear Poor*. New York: Farrar, Straus, and Giroux.

Langmuir, G. (1996). *Toward a Definition of Antisemitism*. Sacramento, CA: University of California Press.

Laqueur, W. (2003). *A History of Zionism: From The French Revolution to the Establishment of the State of Israel*. New York: Schocken.

Le Bras, H. (2008). *The Nature of Demography*. Princeton, NJ: Princeton University Press.

Lederhendler, E. (2000). *The Six-Day War and World Jewry*. College Park, MD: University of Maryland Press.

Leff, L. (2005). *Buried by the Times: The Holocaust and America's Most Important Newspaper*. New York: Cambridge University Press.

Lenczowski, G. (Ed.). (1970). *The Politics of Awakening in the Middle East*. Englewood Cliffs, NJ: Prentice Hall.

Levi-Faur, D. (1999). *Israel: The Dynamics of Change and Continuity*. London: Paul Routledge.

Levin, K. (2005). *The Oslo Syndrome: Delusions of a People Under Siege*. New York: Smith & Kraus.

Levine, A. (2003). *Scattered Among the Peoples: The Jewish Diaspora in Twelve Portraits*. New York: Overlook Press.

Lewis, B. (1996a). *Cultures in Conflict: Christians, Muslims, and Jews in the Age of Discovery*. New York: Oxford University Press.

Lewis, B. (1996b). *The Middle East: A Brief History of the Last 2000 Years*. New York: Simon & Schuster.

Lewis, B. (1999). *Semites and Anti-Semites. An Inquiry into Conflict and Prejudice*. New York: W. W. Norton & Company.

Lewis, B. (2001). *The Multiple Identities of the Middle East*. New York: Schoken.

Lewis, B. (2002). *The Assassins: A Radical Sect in Islam*. New York: Basic Books.

Lewis, B. (2003). *What Went Wrong?: The Clash Between Islam and Modernity*

in the Middle East. New York: Perennial.
Lewis, B. (2004). *From Babel to Dragomans: Interpreting the Middle East.* New York: Oxford University Press.
Liebes, Y. (1993). *Studies in the Zohar.* Albany, NY: State University of New York Press.
Lipset, S. (1971). *Jewish Academics in the United States: Their Achievements, Culture, and Politics.* Washington, DC: Carnegie Commission on Higher Education.
Losowick, Y. (2003). *Right to Exist: A Moral Defense of Israel's Wars.* New York: Doubleday Books.
Maier, P. (1988). *Josephus: The Essential Writings.* Grand Rapids, MI: Kregel Publications.
Mamdani, M. (2002). *When Victims Become Killers: Colonialism, Nativism, and the Genocide in Rwanda.* Princeton, NJ: Princeton University Press.
Mamdani, M. (2004). *Good Muslim, Bad Muslim: America, The Cold War, and The Roots of Terror.* New York: Pantheon.
Markoe, G. (2001). *Phoenicians.* Sacramento, CA: University of California Press.
Markus, J. (1960). *The Jew in the Medieval World.* New York: Meridian Books.
McCormick, J. (1999). *The European Union.* Denver, CO: Westview Press.
McNutt, P. (1990). *The Forging of Iron: Technology, Symbolism, and Tradition in Ancient Society.* Sheffield: Sheffield Academic Press.
Meir, G. (1988). *My Life.* New York: Random House.
Melman, Y. (1992). *The New Israelis.* New York: Carol Publishing Group.
Mendes-Flohr, P., & Reinharz, J. (1995). *The Jew in the Modern World: A Documentary History.* New York: Oxford University Press.
Meyer, K., and S. Brysac (2008). *Kingmakers: The Invention of the Modern Middle East.* New York: W. W. Norton.
Meyer, M. (1967). The Origins of the Modern Jew. Detroit, MI: Wayne State University Press.
Miller, S. (1984). *Studies in the History and Tradition of Sepphoris.* Leiden: Brill Academic Publishers.
Moore, B. (1966). *Social Origins of Dictatorship and Democracy: Lord and Peasant in the Making of the Modern World.* Boston, MA: Beacon Press.
Morris, B. (2001). *Righteous Victims: A History of the Zionist-Arab Conflict, 1881-2001.* New York: Vintage Press.
Morris, B. (2003). *The Birth of the Palestinian Refugee Problem Revisited.* New York: Cambridge University Press.
Morris, B. (2007). *Making Israel.* Ann Arbor: University of California Press.
Mulder, M. (2004). *Mikra: Text, Translation, Reading, and Interpretation of the Hebrew Bible in Ancient Judaism and Early Christianity.* Montville, NJ: Hendrickson Publishers.

Mullen, T. (1980). *The Assembly of the Gods: The Divine Council in Canuaite and Early Hebrew Literature.* Cambridge, MA: Scholars Press.

Nagy, R., Meyers, E., & Weiss, Z. (Eds.). (1996). *Sepphoris in Galilee: Crosscurrents of Culture.* Raleigh, NC: North Carolina Museum of Arts Publishing.

Neumann, M. (2005). *The Case Against Israel.* Oakland, CA: AK Press.

Neusner, J. (1984). *Messiah in Context: Israel's History and Destiny in Formative Judaism.* Philadelphia, PA: Fortress Press.

Nitzan, J., & Bichler, S. (2002). *The Global Political Economy of Israel.* London, U.K.: Pluto Press.

Noland, M., & Pack, H. (2007). *The Arab Economies in a Changing World.* Washington, D.C.: Institute of International Economics.

Ober, J. (2008). *Democracy and Knowledge, Innovation and Learning in Classical Athens.* Princeton, NJ: Princeton University Press.

Oberman, H. (1984). *The Roots of Antisemitism in the Age of Renaissance and Reformation.* Augsburg, Germany: Augsburg Fortress Publishers.

Oren, M. (2003). *Six Days of War: June 1967 and the Making of the Modern Middle East.* New York: Ballantine Books.

Oren, M. (2007). *Power, Faith and Fantasy: America in the Middle East, 1776 to the Present.* New York: Norton.

Patai, R. (1979). *The Messiah Texts.* Detroit, MI: Wayne State University Press.

Patal, R. (1982). *The Vanished Worlds of Jewry.* New York: MacMillan Publishing Company.

Pearcey, N. (2004). *Total Truth: Liberating Christianity from Its Cultural Captivity.* Wheaton, IL: Crossway Books.

Penslar, D. (2001). *Shylock's Children: Economics and Jewish Identity in Modern Europe.* Sacramento, CA: University of California Press.

Perman, S. (2005). *Spies, Inc: Business Innovation from Israel's Masters of Espionage.* Upper Saddle River, NJ: Prentice-Hall.

Perry, M. (1994). *A Fire in Zion: The Israeli-Palestinian Search for Peace.* New York: William Morrow and Company.

Perry, M. (2002). *Anti-Semitism: Myth and Hate from Antiquity to the Present.* New York: Palgrave MacMillan.

Perry, M., & Schweitzer, F. (2002). *Anti-Semitism: Myth and Hate from Antiquity to the Present.* New York: Pelgrave MacMillan.

Peters, J. (2002). *From Time Immemorial: The Origins of the Arab-Jewish Conflict Over Palestine.* Chicago, IL: JKAP Publications.

Pieterse, J. (2003). *Globalization and Culture: Global Melange.* Lanham, MA: Rowman & Littlefield Publishers.

Prager, D., & Telushkin, J. (2003). *Why the Jews? The Reason for Antisemitism.* New York: Touchstone Publishers.

Prager, D., & Telushkin, J. (1985). *Why the Jews? The Reason for Antisemitism.*

New York: Touchstone Publishers.

Prittie, T. (1969). *Eshkol: The Man and the Nation.* New York: Pitman.

Rabinovich, A. (2005). *The Yom Kippur War: The Epic Encounter that Transformed the Middle East.* New York: Schoken.

Rabkin, Y. (2006). *A Threat from Within: A History of Jewish Opposition to Zionism.* London, U.K.: Zed Books.

Rader, J., & Saperstein, M. (2000). *The Jew in the Medieval World: A Source Book, 315-1791.* Hebrew Union College Press.

Raviv, D., & Melman, Y. (1990). *Every Spy A Prince: The Complete History of Israelis Intelligence Community.* Boston, MA: Houghton-Mifflin Company.

Rhodes, R. (2007). *Arsenals of Folly: The Making of the Nuclear Arms Race.* New York: Alfred Knopf.

Richardson, L. (1996). *When Allies Differ: Anglo-American Relations During the Suez and Falkland Crises.* New York: St. Martin's Press.

Richelson, J. (2006). *Spying on the Bomb.* New York: W. W. Norton and Company.

Rigg, B. (2002). *Hitler's Jewish Soldiers: The Untold Story of Nazi Racial Laws and Men of Jewish Descent in the German Military.* Lawrence, KS: Kansas University Press.

Rigg, B. (2004). *Rescued from the Reich: How One of Hitler's Soldiers Saved the Lubavitcher Rebbe.* New Haven, CT: Yale University Press.

Rosenbaum, R. (2004). *Those Who Forget the Past: The Question of Anti-Semitism.* New York: Random House.

Rosenberg, J. (2006). *Epicenter: Why Current Rumblings in the Middle East Will Change Your Future.* Carol Stream, IL: Tyndale House Publishers.

Rosenthal, D. (2003). *The Israelis: Ordinary People in an Extraordinary Land.* New York: Free Press.

Roskies, D. (1999a). *Against the Apocalypse: Response to Catastrophe in Modern Jewish Culture.* Syracuse, NY: Syracuse University Press.

Roskies, D. (1999b). *The Jewish Search for a Usable Past.* Bloomington, IN: Indiana University Press.

Roskies, D. (Ed.). (1992). *The Literature of Destruction: Jewish Response to Catastrophe.* New York: Jewish Publication Society of America.

Ross, D. (2004). *The Missing Peace; The Inside Story of the Fight for Middle East Peace.* New York: Farrar, Straus and Giraux.

Rotberg, R. (Ed.). (2006). *Israeli and Palestinian Narratives of Conflict: History's Double Helix.* Bloomington, IN: Indiana University Press.

Roth, N. (2002). *Medical Jewish Civilization: An Encyclopedia.* New York: Routledge.

Rozenzweig, F. (1999). *Ninety Two Poems and Hymns of Yehuda Haalevi.* Albany, NY: State University of New York Press.

Rubinstein, D. (1991). *People of Nowhere: The Palestinian Vision of Home*. New York: Crown Publishers.

Ruderman, D. (1992). *Essential Papers on Jewish Culture in Renaissance and Baroque Italy*. New York: New York University Press.

Sachar, H. (1990). *The Course of Modern Jewish History*. New York: Vintage.

Sachar, H. (1993, Revised edition). *The Course of Modern Jewish History*. New York: Vintage.

Sachar, H. (1996, Second edition). *A History of Israel: From the Rise of Zionism to our Time*. New York: Knopf.

Sarna, J. (2004). *American Judaism: A History*. New Haven, CT: Yale University Press.

Schafer, P. (1997). *Judeophobia*. Cambridge, MA: Harvard University Press.

Scheindlin, R. (2000). *A Short History of the Jewish People: From Legendary Times to Modern Statehood*. New York: Oxford University Press.

Schoenfeld, G. (2003). *The Return of Anti-Semitism*. San Francisco, CA: Encounter Books.

Schwartz, M. (2002). *The Biblical Engineer: How The Temple In Jerusalem Was Built*. Jersey City, NJ: KTAV Publishing House.

Scott, J. (Ed.). (1997). *Exile: Old Testament, Jewish, and Christian Conceptions*. Boston, MA: Brill Academic Publishers.

Segev, T. (1993). *The Seventh Million: The Israelis and the Holocaust*. New York: Will and Wang.

Segev, T. (2000). *One Palestine Complete: Jews and Arabs Under the British Mandate*. New York: Holt and Company.

Sen, A. (2000). *Development as Freedom*. New York: Anchor Books.

Shahak, I. (1994). *Jewish History, Jewish Religion: The Weight of Three Thousand Years*. London, UK: Pluto Press.

Shahak, I. (1997). *Open Secrets: Israeli Foreign and Nuclear Policies*. London, UK: Pluto Press.

Shahak, I., & Mezvinsky, N. (2004). *Jewish Fundamentalism Israel*. London, U.K.: Pluto Press.

Shakespeare, W. (1985). *The Merchant of Venice*. New York: Barron's Educational Series.

Shanks, H. (1988). *Ancient Israel*. Englewood Cliffs, NJ: Prentice Hall.

Shapira, A., & Templer, W. (1999). *Land and Power: The Zionist Resort to Force, 1881-1948*. New York: Oxford University Press.

Shapiro, M. (2002). *Between the Yeshiva World and Modern Orthodoxy: The Life and Works of Rabbai Jehiel Jacob Weinberg, 1884-1996*. Oxford, U.K.: Littman Library of Jewish Civilization.

Sheehan, J. (2005). *The Enlightenment Bible: Translation, Scholarship, Culture*. Princeton, NJ: Princeton University Press.

Sherman, A. (1998). *Mandate Days: British Lives in Palestine*. London, U.K.:

Thames & Hudson.

Shipler, D. (2002, Revised Edition). *Arab and Jew: Wounded Spirits in a Promised Land.* New York: Penguin Books.

Shirer, W. (1960). *The Rise and Fall of the Third Reich.* New York: Simon & Schuster.

Simpson, W. (1995). *The Authentic Annals of the Early Hebrews: Also Known as the Book of Jasher.* Kearney, NE: Morris Publishing.

Slezkine, Y. (2004). *The Jewish Century.* Princeton, NJ: Princeton University Press.

Smith, M. (2003). *The Origins of Biblical Monotheism: Israel's Polytheistic Background and the Ugaritic Texts.* New York: Oxford University Press.

Smith-Christopher, D. (2002). *A Biblical Theology of Exile.* Minneapolis, MN: Augsburg Fortress Publishers.

Solingen, E. (2008). *Nuclear Logics: Contrasting Paths in East Asia and the Middle East.* Princeton, NJ: Princeton University Press.

Sorin, G. (1997). *Tradition Transformed: The Jewish Experience in America.* Baltimore, MD: Johns Hopkins University Press.

Sprinzak, E. (1999a). *Brother Against Brother.* New York: The Free Press.

Sprinzak, E. (1999b). *Brother Against Brother: Violence and Extremism in Israeli Politics.* New York: The Free Press.

Stadler, N. (2008). *Yeshiva Fundamentalism: Piety, Gender, and Resistance in the Ultra-Orthodox World.* New York: New York University Press.

Stanislawski, M. (2007). A Murder in Lemberg: Politics, Religion, and Violence in Modern Jewish History. Princeton, N.J.: Princeton University Press, 2007.

Steinsaltz, A., Hanegbi, Y., & Toueg, R. (2005). *We Jews: Who Are We and What Should We Do?* San Francisco: Jossey-Bass.

Stewart, W. (1981). *The Spymasters of Israel.* London, U.K.: Hodder & Stoughton.

Stiglitz, J. (2003). *Globalization and Its Discontents.* New York: W. W. Norton & Company.

Stiglitz, J. (2007). *Making Globalization Work.* New York: W. W. Norton & Company.

Stillman, N. (1975). *Jews of Arab Lands: A History and Source Book.* New York: Jewish Publication Society of America.

Tal, D. (2001). *The 1956 War.* New York: Frank Loss Publishers.

Telushkin, J. (1991). *Jewish Literacy: The Most Important Things to Know About the Jewish Religion, Its People and Its History.* New York: William Morrow.

Telushkin, J. (1997). *Biblical Literacy: The Most Important People, Events, and Ideas of the Hebrew Bible.* New York: William Morrow.

Tertzakian, P. (2007). *A Thousand Barrels a Second: The Coming Oil Break*

and the Challenges Facing on Energy Independent World. New York: McGraw Hill.
Teveth, S. (1987). *Ben-Gurion: The Burning Ground 1886-1948.* Boston, MA: Houghton Mifflin.
Thompson, J. (1981). *Beginnings of Christian Philosophy: The Epistle to the Hebrews.* Washington, DC: Catholic Biblical Association of American.
Thompson, T. (1992). *Early History of the Israelite People: From the Written and Archaeological Sources.* Leiden, The Netherlands: Brill Academic Publishers.
Toynbee, A. (1987). *A Study in History.* New York: Oxford University Press.
Tye, L. (2001). *Home Lands: Portraits of the New Jewish Diaspora.* New York: Henry Holt and Company.
Van Creveld, M. (1998). *The Sword and The Olive: A Critical History of the Israeli Defense Forces.* New York: Public Affairs.
Van de Mieroop, M. (2006). *A History of the Ancient Middle-East, ca. 3000-323 B.C.* London, U.K.: Blackwell Publishing.
Vermes, G. (1987, Third Edition). *Dead Sea Scrolls.* London, UK: Penguin.
Vital, D. (2001). *A People Apart: A Political History of the Jews in Europe-1789-1939.* New York: Oxford University Press.
Warschawski, M. (2004). T*oward an Open Tomb: The Crisis of Israeli Society.* New York: Monthly Review Press.
Weiss, T., Forsythe, D., Coate, R., & Pease, K. (2007). *The United Nations and Changing World Politics.* Boulder, CO: Westview Press.
Wettstein, H. (2002). *Diasporas and Exiles: Varieties of Jewish Identity.* Sacramento, CA: University of California Press.
Wheatcroft, G. (1996). *The Controversy of Zion: Jewish Nationalism, The Jewish State, and the Unresolved Jewish Dilemma.* Reading, MA: Addison-Wesley.
Wiesel, E. (1982, Reissue Edition). *Night.* New York: Bantam.
Williams, C. (1997). *The Last Great Frenchman: A Life of General De Gaulle.* New York: John Wiley & Sons.
Windschuttle, K. (2000). *The Killing of History: How Literary Critics and Social Theorists are Murdering Our Past.* San Francisco, CA: Encounter Books.
Wolin, R. (2004). *The Seduction of Unreason.* Princeton, NJ: Princeton University Press.
Wuthnow, R. (2006). *American Mythos: Why Our Best Efforts to be a Better Nation Fall Short.* Princeton, NJ: Princeton University Press.
Yergin, D., & Gustafson, T. (1995). *Russia 2010: And What It Means for the World.* New York: Vantage Books.
Yergin, D. and J. Stanislaw (2002). *The Commanding Heights: The Battle for the World Economy.* New York: Free Press.

Yiftachel, O. (2006). *Ethnocracy: Land and Identity Politics in Israel/Palestine*. Philadelphia, PA: University of Pennsylvania Press.

Yovel, Y. (1998). *Dark Riddle: Hegel, Nietzsche, and the Jews.* University Park, PA: Pennsylvania State University Press.

Zakaria, F. (2008). *The Post-American World.* New York: W. W. Norton.

Zertal, I. (1998). *From Catastrophe to Power: Holocaust Survivors and the Emergence of Israel.* Sacramento, CA: University of California Press.

Zertal, I. (2005). *Israel's Holocaust and the Politics of Nationhood.* New York: Cambridge University Press.

Notes

1. This chapter and the descriptions of places, people, and events are composed for this book from contemporary notes I made during my tenure at Dimona, and later at the headquarters of the Israeli Atomic Energy Commission. For various reasons some names and dates have been changed. All the events described in this book are described as they occurred, based on notes written at the time of the event, or very shortly afterwards.

2. Several books have been published on the Israeli nuclear program. Some emerged after Mordechi Vanunu who worked at KAMAG published photographs of the installation. He was later tried and served a prison term. Other books describe the historical progression of the program. See, for example: Jeffrey Richelson (2006), *Spying on the Bomb*, New York: W. W. Norton and Company. In particular, pages 236-262, in which Richelson described the Israeli nuclear program and the American effort to gain knowledge about its scope. Also see, for example: Michael Karpin (2006), *The Bomb in the Basement: How Israel Went Nuclear and What That Meant for the World*, New York: Simon and Schuster. Also see: Avner Cohen (1998), *Israel and the Bomb*, New York: Columbia University Press; Frank Barnaby (1989), *The Invisible Bomb: The Nuclear Arms Race in the Middle East*, London: I. B. Tauris; Yair Evron (1994), *Israel's Nuclear Dilemma,* Ithaca, New York: Cornell University Press; and, Seymour Hersch (1991), *The Samson Option: Israel's Nuclear Arsenal and American Foreign Policy*, New York: Random House.

3. Although Part V of this book is, by and large, my eyewitness account of a crucial epoch in Israel's history and a controversial and secretive weapons program, many of the details described here are already in the public domain. My personal experiences are elaborated with the hope to enhance the focus of the following parts (VI and VII) of this book. My eyewitness account is merely the historical background in support of the very painful and inescapable prognosis expounded in the latter parts of this book.

4. Plutonium also exists as isotopes Pu240, Pu241, and Pu244. Its large-scale existence today is due entirely to the production of this element in nuclear reactors. Prior to the latter part of the 20th century, plutonium was only a trace element in uranium ores, existing in miniscule quantities on this planet. Besides being used today as fuel for reactors, plutonium has no civilian applications. Its key use is as a weapons-grade core of nuclear bombs.

5. Plutonium was first isolated in 1940 at the Cyclotron at the University of California-Berkeley. One urban legend about the origins of the nuclear age tells the story that Dr. Glenn Seaborg, one of the discoverers of this element, named the element after the planet Pluto. However, instead of "plutium," Seaborg chose to name it *plutonium*, because he believed that it sounded better. See: Bernstein, J. (2007), *Plutonium: A History of the World's Most Dangerous Element*, Washington, D.C.: Joseph Henry Press.

6. The proximity of men and women in the military contingent and the pressure-filled work environment has led to several romantic relations and marriages.

7. Karpin, M. (2006), *The Bomb in the Basement: How Israel Went Nuclear and What That Means for the World,* New York: Simon & Schuster, p. 108-110.

8. There was an amusing incident during my tenure when the pipes for the cooling system at the institute were initially installed. The pipes of French origin arrived with plastic caps on each end, as protection from contamination of dirt and water. The pipes were installed and a test was ordered. When water failed to flow, it was discovered that the installers had not removed the protective caps. The French and Israeli engineers engaged in an amusing festivity of mutual recrimination.

9. Shimon Peres and Shalhevet Freier led the political and strategic group of Israelis. Both were well acquainted with French culture, politics , and languages. See, for example, Cohen, A. (1998), *Israel and the Bomb*, New York: Columbia University Press. Also, Dean P. (1981), *Les Deux Bombes*, Paris: Fayaard.

10. For a historical account of the French war hero and president (1890-1970) see: Williams, C. (1997), *The Last Great Frenchman: A Life of General De Gaulle,* New York: John Wiley & Sons. Also see: Jackson, J. (2005), *De Gaulle (Life & Time)*, London: Haus Publishing. For De Gaulle's memoirs, see: De Gaulle, C. (1998), *The Complete War Memoirs of Charles De Gaulle,* New York: Carroll & Graff Publishers. De Gaulle was president of France from 1944-1946, then again in the period 1958-1969. During his presidency, De Gaulle vetoed the addition of the United Kingdom into the European Economic Community and, in 1967, stirred political discomfort in Quebec, Canada, by supporting the French-Canadian separatist movement. For De Gaulle, the nuclear alliance with Israel represented a back-door reentry of the French into the political sphere of influence in the Middle East—at the expense of the British and the Americans.

11. In 1967, when Israel would not heed his advice to not attack Egypt, De Gaulle referred to the Jews as "an elite people, self-confident and dominating." He often later referred to the Jews as "unbending" and people of "dubious dual loyalties."

12. The Jewish population of Beer-Sheva was mostly from the North African colonies of Algeria, Morocco, and Tunisia. The bulk of this wave of immigrants had arrived in the country in the years following the creation of the State of Israel in 1948. Although many of these immigrants had been city-dwellers and professional, a large number had arrived from small villages and had little training or education. These social-economic characteristics of the local population had also contributed to the wedge between the two French-speaking groups: the locals and the visitors.

13. I recorded this conversation in my notes the day after the engineer's departure. His words have echoed in my mind for the past four decades.

14. See Karpin, M. (2006), op. cit., p. 268. Also see Cohen, A. (1998), *Israel and the Bomb*, New York: Columbia University Press, and Richelson, J. (2006), *Spying on the Bomb: American Nuclear Intelligence from Nazi Germany to Iran and North Korea*, New York: W. W. Norton.

15. Rafael was located in the basin of the city of Haifa. This was an agency of the Ministry of Defense. Its facilities had been constructed in close vicinity to the pool of technical and engineering resources of the faculty and students of the Technion, Israel's premier technological university, founded in 1924 by Jewish immigrants from

Germany. Rafael had developed the weapon itself, including the "lens," the trigger mechanism, the electronics, and the encasement. KAMAG had developed the core plutonium.

16. See, for example, Richelson (2006), and Rhodes, R. (2007), *Arsenals of Folly: The Making of the Nuclear Arms Race*, New York: Alfred Knopf. Also see the historical account of the best seller Israeli-American historian, Michael Oren (2002), *Six Days of War: June 1967 and the Making of the Modern Middle East*, New York: Oxford University Press. Also see the work by the very well connected writer and biographer of the Bengurionite elite, Michael Bar-Zohar. In particular: Bar-Zohar, M. (2007), *Shimon Peres: The Biography*, New York: Random House, and Bar-Zohar, M. (1970), *Embassies in Crisis: Diplomats and Demagogues Behind the Six-Day War*, Upper Saddle River, NJ: Prentice-Hall.

17. See Oren (2002).

18. Israeli military and political leaders would later argue that the United States had already introduced nuclear weapons into the region because it had routinely deployed nuclear-powered aircraft carriers and submarines in the regions—both types of vessels armed with nuclear weapons.

19. Although I had kept contemporary notes of my tenure with KAMAG, this narrative is not a diary. Therefore, I have dispensed with the need for exactness of dates of occurrences and names of protagonists of such events. This narrative offers the general tenor of events as accurately as possible and the atmosphere and spirit of these highly crucial events in the development of Jewish nuclear power. This narrative is not a traditional historical account. It is an *eyewitness account*.

20. By comparison, The Soreq facility had been relatively transparent and welcomed visitors and collaborators.

21. See note 19 above.

22. A "glove box" is a structure used in laboratories for the manipulation of dangerous materials. It is the size of a large crate and has two apertures in which gloves are inserted. The gloves are made of a strong material, allowing for flexibility. The gloves are the length of a human arm, so researchers can gain access to the interior of the box without being exposed to its contents. In addition, the box is connected to a ventilation system in which the external pressure is higher than that inside the box. In the event of rupture, air from *outside* the box rushes *into* the box, thus gaining a few precious moments before the pressures are equalized and the contents of the box are spilled into the environment.

23. The Hebrew term was "Mitun," characterized by rising unemployment, massive emigration, and an increasing level of economic stagnation. Some historians have chosen to elevate the economic crisis of 1966-1967 to the level of a major contributor to the military tension as the Israeli strategy to make war, thus to jump start the economy. Other historians have chosen to totally ignore the economic conditions and their possible contribution to the rise in tension in May 1967. See, for example, Oren, M. (2003) *Six Days of War*, New York: Ballantine Books. In his comprehensive book on the Six-Day War, Oren lists several catalysts for the crisis, such as increased border deployments and skirmishes, the Egypt-Syria military alliance, and a renewed

sense of power and vindication animating the Arab countries bordering Israel.

24. See, for example, Christman, H., Editor (1969), *The State Papers of Levi Eshkol*, New York: Funk & Wagnall, and Kimche, D. and D. Bawly (1968), *The Sandstorm: The Arab-Israeli War of June 1967: Prelude and Aftermath*, London: Secker and Warburg. Also Prittie, T. (1969), *Eshkol: The Man and the Nation*, New York: Pitman.

25. The facility of the department of defense was known as "Hakirya" (the town). It contained several wooden buildings, most of which were one-story offices, resembling a military compound of residence for officers. The key facility was underground, known as "The Pit."

26. The full flights and long lines of people leaving the country have spun popular reaction in the form of macabre, yet telling phrases such as "the last person leaving Israel better turn off the lights." Within a few weeks most of these people returned to resume their leading positions in Israeli politics, economy, and society.

27. "Egged" was (is) the name of the transportation cooperative in Israel. It encompassed all interurban bus lines throughout the country. A different cooperative, "Dan," served the Tel-Aviv urban area.

28. Most passwords were composed of two words, with or without specific meaning. Examples include: "green lawn," "pretty dog," "cold wind," and "burning bush." The famous password that initiated combat operations was "red sheet."

29. Personal communication.

30. For example, Oren (2003) even described how Ben-Gurion's arch political enemy, Menachem Begin, had implored Ben-Gurion to return to power (pp. 134-135). Other Bengurionites of the old regime engaged in a parade of appeals to the messianic return of the disgruntled former prime minister were Golda Meir, Shimon Peres, and Moshe Dayan.

31. Particularly those with political aspirations and loyal to the Bengurionites. Because of Itzhak Rabin's doubts about Dayan's value to the prosecution of the approaching war, the Bengurionite politicians and generals had concocted the urban myth of the time that General Rabin had suffered a nervous breakdown. While at the "pit," awaiting orders, I ran into General Rabin walking in the garden outside the building, on his way to a meeting. He appeared to me to be well in control of his self. Many years later my wife and I met him in Chicago where he appeared at a cocktail party on the city's "Gold Coast" to garner support for a memorial to his mentor Igal Alon. I approached him with the story of our encounter in the "Kyria" in late May 1967. He dismissed the story of his breakdown by saying politely "People always exaggerate." Itzhak Rabin later became Israel's fifth prime minister. He was assassinated on November 4, 1995, by a Jewish orthodox, Yigal Amir. The assassin, a religious fanatic, is currently serving a life sentence with special treatment and consideration. In 2006 and 2007 there have been numerous attempts by religious members of the Knesset (parliament) to release this venerated figure of Jewish orthodoxy in Israel.

32. Levi Eshkol and his wife Miriam have variously described the handing over of military power to Moshe Dayan as "a real putsch," "a truly undemocratic act,"

"an act of treachery," and "unforgivable." See, for example: Prittie (1969), op. cit.; Eshkol, C. (1969), *Levi Eshkol, 1895-1969-Profile of a Zionist*, New York: World Zionist Organization; and, Levi-Faur, D. (1999), *Israel: The Dynamics of Change and Continuity*, London: Paul Routledge.

33. Although the transfer of the defense ministry from the "hesitant" Eshkol to the more bellicose Dayan would be a clear signal that an Israeli attack was imminent, American intelligence did not rise to the occasion. It was the German intelligence services (BND) under General Reinhard Gehlen that provided the CIA with a detailed forecast of day and time of the planned Israeli attack. See: Hohne, H. and H. Zolling (1972), *The General Was A Spy*, New York: Coward, McCann, and Geoghegan; p. 244.

34. My free translation from Hebrew. The poem was published in the children's magazine "Haaretz Shelanu" (*our country*).

35. The rank is comparable to a full colonel in the American army.

36. Initially I believed that this was his first name. I later learned from my contact that it was his family name. The visitor was Colonel Itzhak Yaakov, who in later years became scientific advisor to the government and the acclaimed founder of the Israeli high technology industry. His nickname in military circles was "Yatsa." He was a stubborn yet worthy opponent.

37. Colonel Yaakov departed the compound soon after the arrival of the cadets. Our paths never crossed again.

38. The following assumptions are the result of personal communication.

39. Transcribed in T. Draper (1968), *Israel & World Politics*, New York: The Viking Press, pp. 255-256.

40. Knebel, F. (1962), *Seven Days in May*, New York: Harper & Row.

41. The debate continued four decades afterwards. See: Gold, D. "Occupied Territories or Disputed Territories," in George Hanus, Editor (2002). *The Compendium: A Critical Analysis of the Arab-Israeli Conflict*, Chicago, IL: Gravitas Media, pp. 75-76.

42. Karpin, M. (2006), *The Bomb in the Basement: How Israel Went Nuclear and What That Means for the World*, New York: Simon & Schuster, pp. 263-267.

43. Rafael is the Authority for Weapons Development (Reshut Pituah Emzaei Lehima). Karpin based his description of Rafael as the place where the atomic device was assembled on foreign sources.

44. Michael Karpin quotes Zvi Dinstein (with whom I worked at the Scientific Administration) that Eshkol was mentally hurt by constant criticism that his restructuring effort was detrimental to the nuclear program: "But it tormented him. I think it even may have caused his death" (p. 267).

45. This committee was the legislative body's organ in charge of the country's security.

46. See: Rabinovich, A. (2005). *The Yom Kippur War: The Epic Encounter that Transformed the Middle East*, New York: Schoken; Dunstan, S. (2007), *The Yom Kippur War: The Arab-Israeli War of 1973*, Oxford, U.K. Also see Ferraro, M. (2007). *Tough Going: Anglo-American Relations and the Yom Kippur War of 1973*,

Bloomington, IN and Blum, H. (2003), *The Eve of Destruction: The Untold Story of the Yom Kippur War*, New York: Harper Collins Publishers. Other books written by military and political figures that participated in these events include, for example: Herzog, H. (2006), *The War of Atonement: The Inside Story of the Yom Kippur War*, Greenhill Books: Newbury, U.K. The author, Haim Herzog (1918-1997) was the sixth president of Israel (1983-1993). He retired from military service in 1962 as major-general. Herzog also wrote *The Arab-Israeli Wars: War and Peace in the Middle East*, New York: Vintage Books, 2005. Also see Dayan, M. (1976), *Moshe Dayon: The Story of My Life*, New York: William Morrow and Adam, A. (1980), *On the Banks of the Suez*, San Francisco, CA: Presidio Publishers. Major General Aveaham Adam (nicknamed "Bren") was a commander of an armoured group in the Sinai battleground during the 1973 war. He also masterminded the Barlev line of fortifications on the eastern bank of the Suez Canal, captured by Israel in 1967.

47. Molded after the British model, the Chief of the General Staff of the Israeli Defense Forces (IDF) is the supreme commander of the IDF. He holds the rank of "Rav-Aluf" (the only such active rank, equivalent to a Lieutenant-General or a four-star general in the American system.)

48. General Hosni Mubarak later became President of Egypt.

49. See, for example, Boyne, W. (2002). *The Two O'Clock War*, New York: St. Martin's Press, pp. 13-14.

50. See, for example, Bar-Yoseph, U. (1998), "Israel's Intelligence Failure of 1973: New Evidence, a New Interpretation, and Theoretical Implications," *Security Studies*, 4(3): 584-609. Also Ben-Zvi, A. (1990), "Between Warning and Response: The Case of the Yom Kippur War," *International Journal of Intelligence and Counterintelligence*, 4(2): 227-242, and Bolia, R. (2004), "Overreliance on Technology in Warfare: The Yom Kippur War as a Case Study," *Parameters*, 34(2): 46-56. In this article Robert Bolia argued, as did many Israeli observers, that the key reason for the failure to ascertain the day and time of the Arab attack and to adequately react was the incompetence of Israeli military intelligence.

51. Ben-Porat retired with the rank of Brigadier General.

52. Ben Porat, Y. (1985), "The Yom Kippur War: A Mistake in May Leads to a Surprise in October," *Maarachat* (Hebrew). Also see Shahak, I. (1991), "The Israeli Myth of Omniscience Nuclear Deterrence and Intelligence,", No. 36, Spring.

53. Ben-Porat, *ibid*.

54. See some historical accounts of this crucial period in Derogy and H. Carmel (1979), *The Untold History of Israel*, New York: Grove Press. Also see Meir, G. (1975), *My Life*, New York: G. Putnam, and Ben-Zvi, A. (1995), "Perception, Misperception, and Surprise in the Yom Kippur War: A Look at the New Evidence," *Journal of Conflict Studies*, 15(2): 5-29. Ben Zvi compares the intelligence failure of the IDF in 1973 to the failure of the U.S. at Pearl Harbor in December 7, 1941, and Soviet intelligence with the German attack of June 22, 1941 (operation "Barbarossa"). In his analysis, Ben-Zvi seemed to agree with Ben-Porat that the key to the failures of these intelligence agencies was their disparaging view of their enemy's capabilities.

55. Boyne, *op cit.*, pp. 58-61.

56. These pages describe my personal recollections and my own interpretation of events as I witnessed them unfold.

57. Unlike other former chiefs of staff, such as Yitzhak Rabin and Ehud Barak.

58. See, for example, Safran, N. (1977), "Trial by Ordeal. The Yom Kippur War, October 1973," *International Security*, 2(2): 133-170. Professor Safran (1925-2003) was an expert on the Middle East. He taught at Harvard University till his retirement in 2002.

59. Dalle, K. R. (2007), *Nixon and Kissinger: Partners in Power*, New York: Harper Collins.

60. Kissinger, H. (2000), *A World Restored: Metternich, Castlereagh, and the Problems of Peace, 1812-1822*, New York: Weidenfeld and Nicholson.

61. Solingen, E. (2008), *Nuclear Logics: Contrasting Paths in East Asia and the Middle East*, Princeton, NJ: Princeton University Press.

62. See Kissinger, H. (2004), *Crisis: The Anatomy of Two Major Foreign Policy Crises*, New York: Simon & Schuster.

63. The current narrative is my interpretation of the events of October 6, 1973 to October 15, 1973. Like a puzzle, I have assembled here facts, perceptions, and conjectures from both sides of the relationship between America and Israel. It is my conclusion that in these crucial ten days in early October 1973, the nuclear option and its operationality had been the 800 lb. gorilla in the room such that everyone can see it and fear it, but not one of those present would dare talk about it.

64. Black, I. and B. Morris (1992), *Israel's Secret Wars: A History of Israel's Secret Services*, New York: Grove Press. Also see Stewart, W. (1981), *The Spymasters of Israel*, London, U.K.: Hodder & Stoughton.

65. Cohen, A. (2000), "The Bomb that Never Is," *Bulletin of the Atomic Scientists*, 56(3), 22-23.

66. Evidently, nuclear weapons on board American and Soviet vessels navigating the waters of the region were already present in the Middle East.

67. Cohen's argument that *internal* pressures of Israel's democracy are leading to a more open conversation about the nuclear program is no more than wishful thinking. Cohen published his opinion in 2000 and, as recently as 2008, such "openness" has not materialized. The "Vanunu Affair" has made it even more difficult to discuss the topic, let alone reveal the intricacies of the program. The "great deception" continues today as it has since the 1960s. Some experts on Israeli-U.S. relations believe that the Nixon-Meir "agreement" to keep the nuclear story a secret was made in 1969.

68. Frantz, D. (2003), "Israel's Arsenal is Point of Contention: The Nation Can Now Launch Nuclear Weapons from Land, Sea, and Air," *Los Angeles Times*, 12 October, 2003, p. A1.

69. After the "Vanunu Affair," there has been a flurry of activities to force Israel to publicly acknowledge its nuclear capability. On 15 September 2003, the International Atomic Energy Agency in Vienna, Austria held meetings to discuss Israel's "capabilities and threats." On Friday, 7 January, 2005, Israel's television channel 10 broadcasted a program on the reactor at Dimona (KAMAG). In August 2004 there was

a public relations fiasco in the southern region of Israel. The government had begun distributing *Lugol* tablets, designed to protect the thyroid gland from the damaging effect of Iodine 131, a radioactive isotope. The government explained this action as an attempt to protect the population residing within 30 kilometers from KAMAG. The Israeli public and some members of the Knesset reacted with anger and dismay at the lack of an adequate explanation to the urgency of this sudden action by the government.

70. Iran is a Muslim country but its inhabitants are not Arabs.

71. This fact also applies to Teheran in Iran.

72. Pakistan is the exception to this rule. As the only Muslim country with a nuclear arsenal, the Pakistani leaders have largely remained on the ideological and political margin of the Arab-Israeli conflict. The strong ties of Pakistan with the United States have also mitigated their involvement in the Middle East. This scenario may change if and when Islamic fundamentalists assume control of Pakistan, as they have done in Iran.

73. A similar collapse appeared to take place in early October 1973.

74. The original plan did *not* consider a pre-emptive nuclear strike.

75. This is further elaborated in part VI of this book.

76. There is a possibility that the principle of the nuclear deterrence has been a motivator for some of the Gulf states to show some positive initiatives towards Israel. Although it is doubtful that they knew the specifics of the plan and their role as secondary targets, this thought and suspicion may have animated their political reasoning.

77. In the original plan of four decades ago. There is no reason to believe that this principle has changed since then.

78. Douglas Frantz (2003), note 69 above.

79. George Perkovich review of Michael Karpin "The Bomb in the Basement," *The Washington Post*, February 19, 2006, p. BW03.

80. Kober, A. (2008), "The Israeli Defense Forces in the Second Lebanon War," *Journal of Strategic Studies*, 31(1): pp. 3-40.

81. Appeared in www, smallwarsjournal.com, August 17, 2008. Retrieved from the internet on September 12, 2008.

82. General Mattis listed several elements of the EBO concept which seem to contribute to its shortcomings: "Assumes level of unachievable predictability; cannot correctly anticipate reactions of complex systems; calls for unattainable level of knowledge of the enemy; too prescriptive and over-engineered; discounts human dimensions of war; promotes centralization and micromanagement; fails to deliver clear and timely direction to subordinates."

83. Mattis, op. cit., p. 2.

84. Compared with losses of American lives in Iraq and Afghanistan, because the United States has 50 times the population, Israel's 120 dead are equivalent to 6,000 Americans. The Second Lebanon War also exerted a very high economic price, with thousands of reservists called from jobs and much of the north of the country almost

paralyzed for several weeks.

85. This was the initial philosophical rift between my father and the regime. Seven years later it led to the harsh treatment he received from the Ben-Gurion government when the possibility arose—that he would run for the post of Mayor of Tel-Aviv, opposite Mrs. Golda Meirson.

86. Jewish Virtual Library, except of minutes of the 1947 conference by S. Har.

87. Dor Borochov: "Our Platform," written in 1906.

88. See Avishai, B. (2002), *The Tragedy of Zionism: How Its Revolutionary Past Haunts Israeli Democracy,* New York: Allworth Press.

89. See Avishai, B. (2008), *The Hebrew Republic: How Secular Democracy and Global Enterprise Will Bring Israel Peace at Last,* New York: Harcourt.

90. See, for example: Efron, N. (2003), *Real Jews: Secular Versus Ultra-Orthodox: The Struggle for Jewish Identity in Israel,* New York: Basic Books. Noah Efron is a writer living in Israel. He laments the vitriolic rhetoric used by the secular and ultra-orthodox Jews against each other. Dr. Efron explores the interface between science and religion (see: Efron, N. (2006), *Judaism and Science: A Historical Introduction,* Westport, CT: Greenwood Press. Dr. Efron reached a conclusion similar to mine: the issue of the ultra-orthodox Jews is a threat to the future of the Israeli state. This conclusion, however, is anchored in the peril of the intense conflict between secular and religious Jews, whereas my contention is based on the Israeli movement toward a theocratic state, armed with weapons of mass destruction.

91. Grossbongardt, A. (2007), "Religion and Secularism in Israel: Unhold Conflict in the Holy Land," *Der Spiegel,* March 7, 2007 (downloaded from the magazine's website www.spiegel.de on 20 October 2008).

92. See Stadler, N. (2008), *Yeshiva Fundamentalism: Piety, Gender, and Resistance in the Ultra-Orthodox World,* New York: New York University Press. Nurit Stadler studied in this book the life and beliefs of ultra-orthodox men in Israeli Yeshivas. She argued that the new generation is rejecting the tendency of their community to insulate themselves from Israeli life. Rather, these men are increasingly participating in civic activities and institutions. Stadler's findings lend support to my proposition that the new generation of ultra-orthodox Jews in Israel are rapidly accomplishing their political ambitions and moving toward a substantial controlling role in Israeli government.

93. A favorable biography of Rabbi Goren: Freedman, S. (2006), New York: Beit-Or-Vilnay.

94. See, for example, Shapiro, M. (2002), *Between the Yeshiva World and Modern Orthodoxy: The Life and Works of Rabbai Jehiel Jacob Weinberg, 1884-1996,* Oxford, U.K.: Littman Library of Jewish Civilization.

95. Shahak, I. (1994), *Jewish History, Jewish Religion: The Weight of Three Thousand Years,* London, U.K.: Pluto Press. Also see: Shahak, I. and N. Mezvinsky (2004), *Jewish Fundamentalism Israel,* London, U.K.: Pluto Press.

96. See: Shahak, I. (1997), *Open Secrets: Israeli Foreign and Nuclear Policies,* London, U.K.: Pluto Press. For issues of demographic growth patterns see: Le Bras, H.

(2008), *The Nature of Demography,* Princeton, NJ: Princeton University Press.

97. Begin, M. (1978), *The Revolt,* New York: Dell Publishing Company.

98. Pieterse, J. (2003), *Globalization and Culture: Global Melange,* Lanham, MA: Rowman & Littlefield Publishers. Also: Cowan, T. (2004), *Creative Destruction: How Globalization is Changing the World's Cultures,* Princeton, NJ: Princeton University Press.

99. Zakaria, F. (2008), *The Post-American World,* New York: W. W. Norton.

100. Weiss, T., D. Forsythe, R. Coate, and K. Pease (2007), *The United Nations and Changing World Politics,* Boulder, CO: Westview Press.

101. Stiglitz, J. (2003), *Globalization and Its Discontents,* New York: W. W. Norton & Company.

102. See note 101 above

103. Stiglitz, J. (2007), *Making Globalization Work,* New York: W. W. Norton & Company.

104. Imagine your bank changing the administration of the credit you use for a project in your company by suggesting that these changes will improve the successful completion of your project. This evidently ignores critical attributes of your project that are factors in its success, such as your managerial abilities and skills, honesty, integrity, and a host of market factors.

105. Easterly, W. (2006), *The White Man's Burden: Why the West's Efforts to Aid the Rest Have Done So Much Ill and So Little Good,* New York: Penguin Press.

106. Collier, P. (2008), *The Bottom Billion: Why the Poorest Countries are Failing and What Can Be Done About It,* New York: Oxford University Press.

107. Paul Collier, a professor of economics at Oxford University in the United Kingdom, has even suggested that the richer countries should engage in selective military interventions in the developing countries to remove corrupt government, to restore peace to civil wars, and to save millions from starvation.

108. See, for example, Bhagwati, J. (2007), *In Defense of Globalization,* New York: Oxford University Press; and Sen, A. (2000), *Development as Freedom,* New York: Anchor Books. Both Bwagwati and Sen are highly respected economists.

109. Yergin, D., and J. Stanislaw (2002), *The Commanding Heights: The Battle for the World Economy,* New York: The Free Press.

110. See, for example, a wonderful book: Ober, J. (2008), *Democracy and Knowledge, Innovation and Learning in Classical Athens,* Princeton, NJ: Princeton University Press. Josiah Ober brilliantly proposed the thesis that the ancient Athenians implemented knowledge and technological innovations through their democratic form of government to achieve unprecedented measures of power and prosperity. This was a first such age of enlightenment in the ancient world.

111. The European enlightenment had also experienced counterforces from the established centers of political, economic, and religious powers. Nonetheless it has survived and has prospered. The key difference between then and now is that the new enlightenment is global, rather than regional. Thus, it has even more power and reasons to survive and prosper. Why? Because there are many more bearers of

its flags, much more to lose, and much more to gain by so many around the world. Whatever happens in Africa or Asia today is flashed around the world in seconds. In the eighteenth century the lessons from the American revolution took several years to reach France and to influence its own thinking and ideas which contributed to the revolution of 1789.

112. See, for example, Meyer, K., and S. Brysac (2008), *Kingmakers: The Invention of the Modern Middle East*, New York: W. W. Norton.

113. Henry, C. and R. Springborg (2001), *Globalization and the Politics of Development in the Middle East*, New York: Cambridge University Press.

114. See, for example, Noland, M., and H. Pack (2007), *The Arab Economies in a Changing World*, Washington, D.C.: Institute of International Economics.

115. See: Tertzakian, P. (2007), *A Thousand Barrels a Second: The Coming Oil Break and the Challenges Facing on Energy Independent World*, New York: McGraw Hill. Also see: Bobbitt, P. (2008), *Terror and Consent: The Wars for the Twenty-First Century*, New York: Alfred Knopf. Bobbitt contends that because more countries are moving toward a "market state," terrorism remains a form of resistance to these changes. He calls for a more drastic application of force in the "war on terror." My proposition challenges Bobbitt's. I believe that globalization and market economies will strongly deter rather than encourage global terrorism. An increasing number of countries converted to the notions of globalization will view terrorism as an intolerable impediment to peace, prosperity, and political stability in their own countries. The unprecedented global interdependence makes it impossible for one country to remain untouched when another country across the globe is the target of a terrorist act.

116. See, for example, the case of Russia and its transformation in: Yergin, D. and T. Gustafson (1995), *Russia 2010: And What It Means for the World*, New York: Vantage Books.

117. Gatier, P., E. Gatier, and E. Gubel (2000), *The Levant: History and Archaeology in the Eastern Mediterranean*, New York: Konemann Publishers.

118. Quoted in the electronic version of the Israeli daily newspaper *Haaretz* at: www.haaretz.com on November 5, 2004. Mr. Sharansky is proposing that former Israelis who reside abroad travel to Israel to vote. Israel does not allow absentee ballots and Israelis have traditionally regarded such emigrants with scorn, as traitors to the Zionist ideas of settling in the Holy Land.

119. Cyprus itself gained its independence from Britain in August 1960.

120. For an exploration of this dark side of the Jewish settlement of Palestine and the holocaust, see for example: E. Black (1999) *The Transfer Agreement*, New York, Carroll and Graf Publishers.

121. The numbers are revealing. Almost ten thousand survivors lack adequate medical assistance. Mr. Zeev Factor, a holocaust survivor, said in 2006: "These people are barely surviving, but the crisis begins when a real sickness befalls them. The Government of Israel has received money from the German government...but I think the government didn't use enough for the survivors."

122. The uprising of the Warsaw ghetto in the spring of 1943 is a glaring exception. About 300 thousand Jews, under the command of the 23-year old Mordecai

Anielewicz, resisted thousands of elite troops of Nazi Germany. On May 16, 1943, the uprising ended. Israelis honored the fallen hero of the ghetto by establishing a kibbutz: "Yad Mordecai" (a memorial to Mordecai Anillewicz).

123. This image is reflected in speeches by key Israeli politicians and generals. In June, 2006, the dean of Israeli political figures, Shimon Peres, declared in a policy statement: "we are not "freiers" (the Hebrew popular term for "gullible" or a "dupe"). In July 2006, the Israeli government retaliated against Lebanon with all its force, following the abduction of two Israeli soldiers by Hezbollah, the terror organization operating from Southern Lebanon. Many commentators deplored the "disproportionate" response of the Israelis. The key driver for such military response was the image of "never again," and "any injury, however minor, inflicted upon us will be retaliated with all our punitive and preventative power."

124. A revealing account of the forging of the new Jewish mentality is given in: Melman, Y. (1992) *The New Israelis*, Birch Lane Press.

125. An exception is the ultra-religious orthodox Jews whose internal rate of natural growth equals that of Arabs. The secular population of Israel is continually losing ground. The demographic future of the country favors a much more theocratic population in both the Jewish and Arab sectors.

126. The following example is revealing of the global perception of the Jewish state. In October 2003, a poll conducted by the European Commission of the European Union with a sample of 500 respondents in each E.U. country concluded that Israel poses the most threat to world peace–more than Iran, Iraq, Libya, and North Korea. Israeli officials expressed their unmitigated outrage. Minister Natan Sharansky argued that the poll represents "nothing other than pure anti-Semitism."

127. Some examples: M. Keren (1983) *Ben-Gurion and the Intellectuals*, Dekalb, IL, Northern University Press; D. Kurzman (1983) *Ben-Gurion: Prophet of Fire*. Israeli writers who chronicled Ben-Gurion's life include: S. Teveth (1987) *Ben-Gurion: The Burning Ground 1886-1918,* Boston, Houghton-Mifflin Company; and, M. Bar-Zohar (1978) *Ben-Gurion: A Biography*, New York, Delacorte Press.

128. For instance: Bar-Zohar (1978) wrote: "Seeing Ben-Gurion at work, studying his way of thinking and speaking, observing his behavior, feeling almost physically the crushing weight of his personality in private meetings as well as in public rallies, allowed me, I believe, to grasp the magnetism he exuded and to witness the exertions of those indefinable qualities of authority, inspiration, and leadership that turned men into his devout followers..." (p. xvii).

129. The description of David Ben-Gurion and "Bengurionism" in this narrative is the result of the author's interpretation of the literature, historical and current events, and personal experiences of the author and others.

130. Although many changes have taken place in Israeli society and its economy, particularly in the 1990s and into the first years of the twenty-first century, much of Bengurionism remains well entrenched in Israeli polity, its institutions and its way of life.

131. The Socialist movement led by Ben-Gurion had started with the "Poalei Zion" (workers of Zion) socialist group in Warsaw, Poland, under Ben-Gurion's leadership.

This movement later evolved in the 1920s into the "Histadrut" (organization or federation), a federation of trade unions in Palestine. This federation still exists and is a thriving concern and a major force in contemporary Israel. The "party" which ruled Israel in its first twenty years of existence, established in 1930, and led by Ben-Gurion was the "Mifleget Poalei Eretz Israel–MAPAI" (Part of the Workers of the Land of Israel). In 1968 the MAPAI party joined another socialist party to form the Israel Labor Party, later known in Israeli politics as the "Maarach" (The Front). In this narrative "party" functionaries are the leaders and operatives of the various configurations of political parties that populate the Israeli economic and political landscapes.

132. This narrative is not a historical account of the events associated with the establishment of the State of Israel or its aftermath. It is rather this author's interpretation of such events in the life of the Jewish state under the prism of the attributes and the legacy of David Ben-Gurion.

133. The city of Jerusalem was declared a separate entity (corpus separatum) under a special regime, to be administered by the United Nations. The U.S.A. and the U.S.S.R. voted in favor of Resolution 181. The Arab countries voted against it, and the United Kingdom had abstained. See, for example, Sterman (1998) and Segen (2000).

134. From the text of the Declaration of Independence. It should be noted here that a constitution has never been formulated nor established in the State of Israel.

135. At the time of the declaration, the Jewish population in the country is estimated at about 650 thousand. In the 1920s and 1930s about 300,000 Jews immigrated to Israel from Europe. To some extent the "histadnut", dominated by Ben-Gurion, influenced this immigration by steering immigrants with labor political affiliation to established settlements and to the existing trade unions.

136. It should be pointed out that one of the signers of the declaration, Rabbi Yehuda Leib Hakohen Fishman (Maimon) was a cousin of my maternal grandmother and my "sandak" (godfather).

137. Dr. Haim Weitzman later became the first president of Israel, a largely ceremonial position.

138. See a warm description of Berl Katznelson's legacy in Golda Meir's autobiography: "My Life."

139. This interpretation of Berl Katznelson's ideology is based on this author's analysis of Katznelson's writings.

140. Lacking a well-defined political agenda, and animated by rulings of their rabbinical authorities, the orthodox parties had traditionally cooperated with any secular partners who could provide them with the best *economic* incentives to join a coalition in the government. Following the victories of the Begin party in the late 1970s, the "Likud" (union) combination of centrist and right-wing nationalist parties continued the tradition of very close cooperation with the orthodox and the ultra-orthodox parties.

141. On August 13, 2006, the *New York Times* reported that Olmert and Peretz "have been wounded by the perception that they mishandled the war." In the same article, Tom Segers, author and historian, argued that "again the government looks to be bad managers."

142. Many of the reserve soldiers who participated in the Lebanon Campaign (including officers of elite units) have openly challenged their commanders and civil leaders. Upon their return from the battle fields, these reservists had bitterly complained that their units lacked basic equipment and supplies–including food and water–and that while the top commanders of the IDF (Israel Defense Forces) spent their lunch time in fancy restaurants in Tel-Aviv, the combat troops lacked basic necessities and had to invade Lebanese homes in order to acquire food and water (Report by Einau Ben-Yehuda, *Haaretz* daily, 18 August 2006). In comments made to an Israeli Internet site, another reserve officer had suggested that the failures in Lebanon in the summer of 2006 point to a lack of a cohesive ideological framework of the governing elite. This is also a reflection of the lack of a *national* framework of goals and an understanding of what the country is about, what its mission is, and its founding principles (www.news.walla.co.il of 24 August 2006). In this author's view, the said lack of ideological framework at both the national and institutional levels is the product of the Bengurionite tradition and its legacy. By focusing on petty political, tribal, and trade unions' interests at the expense of a national constitution and a set of guiding principles, Bengurionism has engendered a culture of ineptness and petty tribalism.

143. The five most feared words in Israeli Hebrew are not: "He is a suicide bomber" but "You know who I am?" For example, the former commander of the Israeli Air Force, General Ezer Wietzman (1924-2005) who later became the seventh president of Israel) drove his car in the Tel-Aviv suburb of Ramat-Aviv at high speed and caused the death of an elderly man who was crossing the street. When brought to trial, the Judge apologized to the General for the inconvenience. Weitzman (the nephew of the first president, Haim Weitzman and brother-in-law of General Moshe Dayan) later joined the Begin government and his career was crowned with his service as Minister of Transport (!) and he was awarded the country's Presidency in 1993 and again in 1998. Due to allegations that he received substantial unreported income and gifts, Weitzman resigned in disgrace from the presidency in July of 2000. He was replaced in the presidency (which is primarily a ceremonial post) by Moshe Katzav, who in 2006 was accused by several women on his staff that he had illicit and unwelcomed sexual relations with them.

144. Eshkol became Prime Minister in June 1963 and served in this post during the Six Days War of June 1967. His most memorable achievement (often neglected by historians) was his fateful meeting with President Lyndon Johnson in 1965, and the establishment of the Israel-America link that continues today.

145. This writer's childhood experience best illustrates the persecution of private commercial enterprises in the early years of Israel's existence. The family business consisted of a small company trading in fabrics, in downtown Tel Aviv. The business received in the 1950s monthly visits from the "economic police" of the Bengurionite government. Often this meant a detail of 4-6 young men who would ransack the warehouse, at their leisure and amusement, and concoct some outrageous reason for the periodic harassment. They had no need for a court order or a plausible cause to enter the premises. The legal concepts of individual rights do not exist in the Bengurionite legal system.

146. The economic situation inside Israel has been less than stellar, even after the "liberalization" of the 1980s-1990s. The Office of Social Insurance of the Israeli government published its *2005 poverty report* in August of 2006. An astounding one quarter of Israelis are considered to be living *below* the poverty line. Over 1.5 million Israelis live in poverty. The picture is even more serious for Israeli children. Almost *half* of those in poverty are children. In 2005 almost 35 percent of Israeli children lived in poverty–one in three children!

147. The story of the shipping company Maritime Fruit Carrier is a good example of the Bengurionite tactics of using economic incentives to gain political inaction from its opposition. Two members of Begin's opposition party, Mila Brenner and Yaakov Meridor founded the shipping company in the 1950s. They purchased reefers from Norway in a deal that was *guaranteed by the government of Israel*. In the Bengurionite era of the early days of statehood, not a pin dropped in Israel with the carefully vetted licensing of the government. The official support given by the Bengurionites to the political adversaries was highly uncharacteristic of the regime. These and similar incentives had worked their magic to dramatically attenuate the opposition's stance against the government–thus allowing the Bengurionites three decades of an almost monopolistic control of the state. It should be noted that several years earlier, in the 20th of June 1998, there occurred the *Altalena Affair*. The ship *Altalena*, with a cache of weapons purchased by Begin's Irgun organization of resistance to the British Mandate arrived in Tel-Aviv. Ben-Gurion had issued an ultimatum to Begin and his comrades to deliver the weapons to his government forces. Yaakov Meridor was Begin's deputy and he held negotiations with the government to transfer the weapons peacefully. In the afternoon of that day, with Begin on board Altalena, Ben-Gurion ordered the shelling of the ship. Menachem Begin was able to leave before the ship had caught fire. The toll in human life was 22 of Begin's comrades and three soldiers of the newly established army killed. See, for example. Ehud Sprinzak (1999).

148. For example, Daniel Kahneman, born in Tel-Aviv, Israel and a Professor at Princeton University, USA, received the 2002 Nobel Prize in Economics (based on his cooperative work with Professor Amos Tversky of Stanford University, born in Haifa, Israel, 1937-1996).

149. Kenwood and Lougheed (1971); also McCormick (1999).

150. See Koelble (1991).

151. Ben-Gurion's famous uttering was: "Um-Shmum" (Never mind the United Nations–is a rough translation). He consistently ignored the international body in his calculations and his adventures and overtures in global affairs.

152. Ben-Gurion's tragic miscalculation and his perverted sentiments toward the United States are similar to those of Germany's Adolph Hitler who said in January 1942: "I don't see much future for America. . . . It's a decayed country, and they have their racial problems and the problems of racial inequalities" (Shirer, 1960).

153. Although in the beginning such cooperation–primarily Israeli assistance to the African countries in medicine, agriculture, technology, and military expertise–has benefitted the Israelis in commercial terms and in political assistance by favorable votes of African countries in the United Nations–the relationship has substantially cooled off in later years (Robert Greenberger, *Israel's Technical Assistance Program*

to the Developing Countries in Asian and Africa as an Implementation of her Foreign Policy, Masters Thesis, Kent State University, 1963).

154. Richardson (1996) and Tal (2001). An unexpected outcome of this war was the rise to power in France of Charles de Gaulle (1890-1971), and the establishment of the 5th republic, in which he was president from 1958 until 1969 (see C. DeGaulle, 2001). This development led to the warming trend in the relations between France and Israel, and ultimately to the cooperation between the two countries in nuclear science, and the transfer of nuclear technology from France to Israel.

155. Seymour Hersh (1991).

156. Eshkol and Johnson had much in common, thus striking an immediate friendly understanding. Both had stepped into the position previously held by a charismatic leader. Both had much to prove to their countrymen, and both were largely considered by the elites in their country to be unsophisticated party politicians with little experience in foreign affairs. Such affinities between these two leaders had paved the way to what remains today a very special relationship between Israel and the United States. For example, in the period 1982-2005 the United States has applied its veto power in the United Nations Security Council to derail resolutions against Israel.

157. There is a myth deeply ingrained in Israel's popular culture that Golda Meir paid two surreptitious visits to King Abdalla of Jordan, in order to discuss a peace arrangement. The first meeting supposedly took place in November 1947. In May 1948 Golda Meir presumably traveled again to Amman, Jordan, and disclosed to the king that Ben-Gurion was about to declare the statehood of the Jewish homeland. According to the story, the king asked why the rush to declare statehood, to which Golda Meir supposedly replied: "We have been waiting for two thousand years. Is this a rush?" There is not a body of irrefutable historical corroboration of these events. It is highly unlikely that the Hashemite king, a proud chief of a long-standing dynasty which traced its origins to the Prophet himself, would have agreed to so malleably meet and confide in a common woman, who at that point in time lacked any official capacity and was technically a colonial subject of the British Crown and an avowed socialist! The myth itself is an attempt by the Bengurionites to stress the overarching attempts by Ben-Gurion and his cronies to "talk peace" with the Arabs, and to indirectly justify the usurpation of power in the new state by the sudden declaration of statehood.

158. As in the previous pages of this narrative, this analysis is based on the author's consideration of historical events and the subsequent personal interpretation of the historical trends.

159. Most universities in the United States, Canada, and the European Union, which are equivalent in size to Israeli universities, have degree programs and research centers on Islam and Arab Studies. This is a reasonable policy by institutions of higher learning, considering that Islam is practiced by over one billion people worldwide and is the religion of scores of countries in at least three continents.

160. The congruence of commercial needs by private organizations and the military requirements for intelligence finally inflicted so much pressure in the 1980s and 1990s that more resources had been assigned to better understand the Arab world and the Arab countries. Yet, even this pressure has not resulted in a better focus within the government-run educational system on Arab studies and rabic as a compulsory

second language.

161. And for that matter the entire country of Israel.

162. The founder of the chain, this author's father, and the Russian born Hebrew poet Shaul Tchernichowski would meet regularly at the bookstore before the birth of the Jewish state to discuss topics in culture and politics. The proliferation of bookstores throughout the country occurred only after the death of Ben-Gurion and because of the influx of Jews from the English-speaking world in the 1980s and 1990s. During Ben-Gurion's years in power, Mr. Steinmatzky used to complain to this author's father of the difficulties imposed by the government of any plans he had to expand his business and to open additional stores.

163. Even with the so-called liberalization of the Bengurionite economy, the government still maintains inordinate control over the means of mass communication, including radio and television. The advent of the age of the Internet is a thorn in this stronghold, because the population can freely communicate with the rest of the world.

164. Including the Army's own radio station, *Galei Zahal* ("The IDF's Waves").

165. For example, one of the families, the Brothers Ofer, who own a shipping concern, received in 2000 and 2001 3.2 million Shekels from the government, as subsidies to employ Israeli sea personnel (from the Report by the country's Inspector General Judge Eliezer Goldberg, 30 July 2003). In the same report, as published in the daily "Haaretz," Judge Goldberg declared that "favoritism" is endemic in the distribution of economic goods and services in the Israeli economy.

166. Ran Rimon in: The Marker.com, 21 August, 2005.

167. There have been continuous attempts since the 1990s to privatize the Israeli economy. Many government entities became privately owned. However, Bengurionism remained as an economic, social, cultural, and, above all, political system that permeates the Israeli existence. Moreover, in a perverse exercise in outrageous irony, Israeli politicians named the country's main airport and a major university after Ben-Gurion. He was fervently opposed to travel outside the country. He viewed air travel as both an act of treason and tourism as a capitalistic sin. Except for the former Soviet Union, Israel had the most restrictive rules for travel abroad. In the area of higher education, although Ben-Gurion offered much lip service for the need of a university in the southern part of the country, in practice he opposed the establishment of such an institution. The university came into being only after Ben-Gurion had left the government. This was a calculated political perspective–vintage Bengurionism: restrict higher education and restrict travel to avoid the diffusion of ideas other than the socialist and trade unionist agenda.

168. In a meeting with business leaders in 18 February 2007, Netanyahu said: "This body we call the Authority of the Land of Israel ... is intolerable and clearly leads to corruption. This absurdity which does not exist in any other country must be eliminated."

169. From contemporaneous notes taken by the author and from reports by family members present in these meetings.

170. The key protagonists in this sad event, this author's mother and her cousin, are deceased.

171. The Bengurionite government structure in Israel has established the High Court of Justice. This is the manner in which justices of the Supreme Court of Israel are supposed to rule on the legality of government decisions. Although the title of this court includes the lofty term "justice," the incestuous relations between the judiciary, legislative, and executive branches of government severely restrict the court's efficacy to help the common citizens.

172. The impacts and legacy of the Ottoman Empire's rule over the Middle Eastern region are aptly described and analyzed in the books by Professor Bernard Lewis.

173. Another incident which happened in the mid-1950s better illustrates the Bengurionite excesses. This author's father, a wholesale merchant of textiles, had endured countless visits from the economic police to his store on Lilienbloom Street in Tel Aviv. The "inspectors" would take with them rolls of fabrics, without a warrant, and without cause, in what amounted to theft. When he finally complained to the authorities, this author's father was taken from his store and arrested—again, without a warrant or a cause. For several days his wife and family were not notified of his arrest. His wife hired a friend of the family, a lawyer named Tussia-Cohen, who was able to locate him. While in prison, this author's father was brutally beaten by his jailers. He was denied food and water for several days, and when located by the lawyer, the prison authorities refused to "pay for his food" and proposed that his wife provide his meals. When finally the case appeared before a court, the judge said that he would release him if no mention was to made of the treatment he received while incarcerated. Mr. Tussia-Cohen agreed. Shortly after his release this author's father and his family emigrated. The barbaric torture he endured broke his body but never his spirit. He died a few years later at the age of 50. In the vast tapestry of human misery in which millions are starving, injured, or dying of diseases, cruelty, and neglect, the attempted expulsion of an elderly widow from her ancestral home and the torture of a businessman may hardly be worth mentioning. These unfortunate incidents, bolstered by the subsequent expulsion of thousands of settlers, are indicative of the power of the regime and the frailty of the Jewish existence in its reinvented homeland. A small elite effectively controls the rights of Israeli citizens to own property and even to reside in any given area of the country.

174. Several Jewish and Israeli readers of an earlier draft of this chapter criticized its harshness, its direction, and its uncompromising negative portrayal of life in Israel and the Bengurionite legacy. They argued that although emigration trends were troublesome, many Israelis are satisfied with their government despite its shortcomings. Clearly, there are always segments of any population who see benefits in any regime, no matter how ineffective or unsavory it and its leaders may be—as was the case in the previous century with Fascism, Nazism, and Communism.

175. See, for example, Warshawski (2004), Grodzinsky (2004), and Zertal (2005). The analysis in this chapter is the author's.

176. The Anholt Nation Brands Index of late 2006.

177. Such despair may *not* be largely attributed to the security and military pressures of the Israeli populace. Rather, it is more likely to be the result of the social and economic difficulties and the indifference of the regime. The policies aimed at the privatization of large government concerns have been another factor in the

deteriorating climate in the Israeli society. During 2004-2006 there has been a rise in the number and severity of strikes in several key sectors of the economy, such as university students, teachers, and employees of government agencies and concerns, including the electric company and airport personnel.

178. The use of the political instrument of trading "land for peace" that was practiced by Israeli governments on several occasions tends to reinforce, in my view, this exercise in power. Only when the government has control over the land through unimpeded ownership, does it also have the ability to trade it for political gains, without constantly resorting to approval by owners-citizens, other institutional organs, legal barriers, or public opinion. Instead of a national patrimony belonging to the people, large tracts of land are viewed as commodity, ripe for the trading.

179. Generally known as "Haredim" (those fearful who tremble in awe of God), the orthodox movement in Judaism is highly conservative and dogmatic. These religious "fanatics" believe in the divine nature of their laws and practices—as directly given to them from God through Moses on Mount Sinai. The compilation of both the written laws and rules in the books of the "Torah" and the interpretations by rabbinical scholars (the oral form of the law) is the "Halacha" (The Way). This is the sacred, indisputable, and overarching code of behavior for the Jew, covering virtually *every* aspect of the way of life: dietary, moral, physical, legal, religious, economic, political, and any other aspect of life. When in doubt, rabbinical authorities interpret the query and their ruling has the power of ultimate determination and judgment. Because the entire way of life is derived from the written code, there is a pressing and altogether practical need to learn the code and to ponder its various implications. Hence the Jewish custom of compulsory learning of religious scriptures which will guide men and women in the ways of their entire life.

180. Also see Biale (2010), Brenner (2012), Sternhell (1999), and Halbertal (2007).

181. See, for example, Wheatcroft, G. (1996), *The Controversy of Zion,* Reading, MA: Addison-Wesley; Bard, M. (2007), *Will Israel Survive?,* New York: Palgrave-McMillan.

182. Jones, C. (2001), Israel: Challenge to Identity, Democracy, and the State, New York: Routledge.

183. See Christa Case Bryant, "Israel's Jewish State Hangup: Why Netanyahu and Abbas Can't Agree," *Christian Science Monitor*, March 17, 2014, Internet Edition.

184. This scenario is similar to the restrictions imposed by the Spanish Inquisition following the Reconquista on the Jews who would not convert to Christianity. Another similar example is the Nuremberg Laws imposed in 1935 by the Nazi regime on German Jews. In the Spanish example the discriminatory criterion was religious. In the German example, it was racial. The Nazi regime also applied a complex test to determine "Who is a Jew?". This test examined the *racial* background of the person, inquiring several generations into the person's past. The criterion called for a measure of "Aryan purity". The measure itself and its rationale are not far removed from the measures of purity applied in the Israeli criterion of "Who is a Jew?"

185. The source of the content of these conversations is contemporaneous notes

taken by the teacher.

186. Dever, William (2003).

187. The term "Habiru" in ancient Akkadian and "Apiru" in ancient Egyptian probably had a connotation of a disruptive bunch or a bellicose mob. It is possible that these early mentions of these people of Amorite descent are similar to the way the Vikings were described by their neighbors in the Middle Ages.

188. See, for example, Isserlin (1998). The use of language to trace the origins of the Israelites is also problematic. For example, language can be a friend or a foe in the explanation of the distant past. The Hebrew word *haver* means friend or companion, and the word *havura* means a band. The words *ivri* (Hebrew) and *avar* (passing, to pass, or passerby) may equal: a band of people passing through, or nomads. So, the origin of the word *Hebrew* from *Habiru* may have remained in the Hebrew language as a band of companions who is passing through. This is clearly a speculation and linguistic scholars may attribute other ancient meanings to these terms. There is agreement today that the Hebrew language originated as a mixture of the Aramaic and Canaanite languages.

189. These accounts were perhaps composed during the Hebrew monarchy, in the period 1000-800 B.C.E.

190. The rewriting of history for the fulfillment of current aims was a common practice in antiquity–and still is in our time. The power of a cohesive history of a people is indisputably a useful instrument in cementing the unity of the people–particularly when divided into both tribal and regional factions, as were the Hebrews during the monarchy. Even today, historical facts and traditions are used as instruments of public opinion in the Israeli-Palestinian conflict. In 2004 an Egyptian law professor, Nabil Hilmi, argued that the Jewish state should pay reparations to Egypt for the "spoils of the Israelites". On the other side, Israeli archaeologists had been actively pursuing Biblical accounts in their search for evidence of the veracity of the Biblical stories of the Exodus, the wandering in the desert, and the conquest of Canaan and the Transjordanian territories.

191. See the fascinating study by Barber and Barber (2005). They argued that "before writing, myths had to serve as transmission systems for information deemed important; but because we–now that we have writing–have forgotten how illiterate people stored and transmitted information and why it was done that way, we have lost track of how to decode the information often densely compressed into these stories, and they appear to us mostly gibberish" (p. 2).

192. Some historians of religion compare terms used to describe deities in antiquity, and they find similarities across cultures. The term *el* used in Semitic cultures can be compared to *Helios*, the Greek term for the sun, perhaps reminiscent of Akhenaten's short-lived attempt to worship the God-Sun. See, Armstrong (1994).

193. Some historians of religion tend to refer to such a god as the "Sky God," because it inhabits the heavens.

194. Although the Ten Commandments were similar to the legal code of the Sumerian King Hammurabi, they are a very concise summary. The Hammurabi code contained 282 rules or provisions of conduct and punishments, usually extremely

severe. The commandments do not specify the type or level of punishment associated with breaking each commandment. In fact, only the fourth commandment: "Honor thy father and thy mother" contains an incentive: "so that you may live a long life on this earth." Many scholars have examined this anomaly and some Jewish scholars have argued that since the fourth commandment is the first of the commandments that deals with relations with other people (parents) rather than with God, there was a need for such an incentive. The previous three commandments deal with the person's relations with God. By offering an incentive for the first "human relations" commandment, the believers would feel more enticed to honor such a commandment. The issue of "enforcement" is discussed in the text.

195. Moses was not allowed to cross over to the Promised Land because he doubted the power of God. David was punished for his lust after Bat-Sheba with the death of his favorite son; and Solomon was punished for his lavish lifestyle and foreign wives by the partition of his kingdom. The Romans had adopted a similar mode of enforcing discipline in their military cohorts and legions. Acts of cowardice in the face of the enemy carried a brutal form of punishment for the *entire* unit. This was collective punishment for the transgressions of the few. Each tenth soldier would be executed (hence the term "decimation"). Such enforcement of discipline also supported the Roman's policy of inculcating in its armies a sense of camaraderie among the soldiers and a strong bond, fealty, and pride in their military cohort and their legion. In modern armies such bond and pride are encouraged in the military units of a regiment, squadron, battalion, and division.

196. Although this analysis also belongs to the story of the collapse of the Israelite state in their promised land, the seeds of destruction are embedded in the essence of the religion created by Moses and his followers. The innovativeness of the monotheistic and omnipresent deity was also a harbinger of chaos and destruction. Some recent books on a similar topic are: Harris (2004) and Windschuttle (2000).

197. The promise of God to his people was not a promise of grandeur or of conquests or imperial expansion. In return for obeying God's rules, the Israelites were promised a peaceful as well as prosperous existence *in their land*. To a modern observer this constituted a sensible arrangement of stability and prosperity in exchange for civilized conduct and devotion to the one God. But, the "promise" also carried the principle of the special treatment given to a single people, chosen without a sensible set of selection criteria–at least in the eyes of a modern observer.

198. Even after the Roman conquest, the destruction of Jerusalem, and the banishment of the people by the emperor Titus, the Jews continued a deliberate but uncoordinated movement to return and rebuild some parts of the country. Not all the inhabitants had been expelled by the Romans, and those who remained had managed to maintain their lives, albeit without a political entity of an independent state. A thousand years later, during the early Crusades, there was a sizeable Jewish presence in Jerusalem and other parts of Judea.

199. See, Toynbee, A., *A Study of History*, New York, Oxford University Press, 1987.

200. Diamond's book is a continuation of his Pulitzer-Prize book: Diamond, J., *Guns, Germs, and Steel: The Fates of Human Societies* (New York, W. W. Norton,

1999). In this book Diamond explained the success of Western culture in its domination of the world with the lens of a combination of biology and technological superiority. The joint impacts of geography, environment, and the drive to colonize had shaped the modern world and may account for the stunning success of Western expansion. His follow-up book (2004) is the flip side, where he explores how those civilizations that were conquered had succumbed to the factors that made their conquerors' history's winners.

201. The Jews are not the only such society. Another example are the Armenians who, like the Jews, are dispersed throughout the world, and who maintain ties to their ancestral homeland– although for centuries they lacked political existence as a nation and a state. In the 1870s the Armenians who inhabited the land on the border between the Russian and Turkish empires found themselves squeezed between the two powers. It was at that time that the "Armenian Question" surfaced in discussions about them, very similar to the "Jewish Question." Beginning in 1915 there were Turkish actions against the Armenians. Although Turkish scholars dispute these events, many historians describe them as the "massacre of the Armenians."

202. In ancient Peru, for example, several societies and cultures existed and became merged with newer societies. The Chavin were prominent in the period before 400 B.C.E. and the Paracas culture existed between 600-175 B.C.E., followed by the Nazca culture and the Inca.

203. This argument is an example of an effort to explain the failure of the Israelite tenure in their land with variables that were beyond their control. Such inclement conditions of the land itself are similar to a less than favorable "hand of cards," dealt by destiny to an otherwise promising people, thus contributing to the inevitability of its ultimate tragedy. It is evident in the text that I wholly reject this approach.

204. See Flavius, J., *The Antiquities of the Jews* (McLean, VA: Indypublish, 2001).

205. Henry the Navigator (1394-1460) was the king of Portugal who founded a school for navigation and maritime science at the coastal city of Sagres. He assembled there an extraordinary group of technologists: shipbuilders, engineers, cartographers, sail makers, and astronomers. His effort helped to launch the Portuguese maritime adventure of the late fifteenth to the eighteenth centuries, and may be credited with the making of the Portuguese colonial empire.

206. See Samuel II, 23-26. These passages describe the distribution of national offices or ministries under the king. Yoav, son of Zruya, was in command of all the armed forces; Bnaya, son of Yehoyadah, in command of the foreign mercenaries who joined David's military; Adoram in charge of taxation, and Jehoshaphat, son of Ahilud, the secretary of the realm.

207. See Samuel II, 17-18.

208. I must mention at this point that my great-grandparents, my greatparents, my mother, and I are native to Jerusalem.

209. The "Dead Sea Scrolls" are the writings of a sect of religious hermits that describe related narratives of the biblical account of the history and traditions of the Israelites during the first century A.D. They do not contain any *secular* knowledge.

210. Isserlin (1998), Chapter Ten, describes the development of the Hebrew

language. He argued that the more popular form of Hebrew, as spoken by the non-elite population, is "not well documented" (p. 207).

211. The reader may wish to consult Schwartz (2002); McNutt (1990); Khoury and Kostner (1990), and Sheehan (2005).

212. The term "Jew" originated with the Hebrew word "Yehudi", meaning a person from Judah. The first mention of the term in ancient documents dates to the second century B.C.E. The term perhaps was initially used by the Hebrews of the era (in Judea and the Diaspora) to define themselves and to ascribe their link to Judea and to Jerusalem.

213. See the book of Ezra, 7, verses 1-6.

214. The word *Torah* means a book of learning in Hebrew.

215. In a separate development this framework was both an incentive and a deterrent to the Apostle Paul when he preached the new religious concepts to Jewish communities in the ancient near Eastern nations. See Klausner, J., *From Jesus to Paul* (New York: McMillan, 1943).

216. From here on I shall refer to the country in the term used by the Romans.

217. Klausner, J. (1955).

218. See, for example, Laato (1997).

219. See, for example, Dubnow (1957). He described the events of the era in terms of the injustice and unbearable actions of the foreign forces. In the essay on the revolt against the Romans, Dubnow wrote, "Albinus was succeeded by Gessius Florus (64-66), the last procurator of Judea. His cruelty kindled revolt....He came to Judea like a hangman for the execution of the condemned" (p. 767). His analysis rests on historical facts and the inevitability of the reaction of the Jews to the actions by the Roman envoys. Social, political, and economic variables are conspicuously absent from Dubnow's analysis.

220. The Maccabeean kings even entered into an agreement with the emerging power of the Roman Empire in its eastern expansion. They served, however, in the dual roles as monarch and high priest. This led to an untenable position where they were unable to adequately perform either role, to internal strife, and to civil war. The Jewish political entity had begun to deteriorate from within, prompting Pompeii to mediate and, in order to restore the peace, to declare the country a province of Rome (in 63 B.C.E.) and to nominate his choice of rulers over the province.

221. It should be emphasized that this form of Jewish theocracy is indeed unique in world history. Even theocratic frameworks, such as those that emerged in Christianity and Islam, had some separation and workable distinction between religion and state.

222. As a historical note, the Palestinian Talmud was completed around 375 C.E. and the Babylonian Talmud around 500 C.E.–well into the period in which Christianity had been adopted as the state religion in Rome and its philosophical and religious foundations had become well defined and codified.

223. The events in Alexandria coincided with the timing of the Jewish revolt against the Romans in Palestine. The remaining Jews in Alexandria revolted again in 115 C.E. and were brutally massacred. Their house of worship, the synagogue of Alexandria,

was destroyed. The community ceased to exist in the ancient world of the Roman Empire until its rebirth in the eighth century C.E., following the establishment of the Muslim Caliphate in Cairo. Again, in modern time, in 1948, after the establishment of Israel, the community was displaced and most of Alexandria's Jews went into exile.

224. Critics of this view have long argued that this is tantamount to "blaming the victim" for the injuries inflicted upon the victims (see, for example, Schoenfeld, 2003). The concept of being the victim of historical malfeasance and unhappy turns of events which continually punished the Jewish people became enshrined in the religious notions of "sin and punishment" and as the precursors to salvation by the Messiah." These topics are further elaborated in Part IV: The Diaspora: Recreating a Religion, But Losing A People.

225. Military leaders did emerge to lead short-lived rebellions. They were dedicated patriots but were largely animated by religious fervor rather than national and civic interests.

226. See, for example, Miller (1984) and Nagy, Meyers, and Weiss (1996).

227. Klausner, *From Jesus to Paul* (1943), p. 275.

228. There are very few topics that received equal or more attention than the rise of Christianity, its characteristics as a religion, and its distinct features compared with Judaism. The reader may wish to consult such literature. Here I simply suggest that the promoters of early Christianity had encountered the Jews in the Diaspora, as well as in Palestine, without a national identity and a social-political structure. The initial clash of the two sets of beliefs was purely religious–contrary to Klausner's thesis. This phenomenon of the growth of Christianity among the Jewish population of the Roman Empire was a natural extension of the failure of Jewish life and existence in the land of their ancestors.

229. This phrase has been sometimes used to describe the passing of important people.

230. Josephus Flavius (Joseph Ben-Matityahu), the soldier and scholar who chronicled the Jewish revolt against Rome, offered several underlying causes for the war. These may be clustered under two main categories: (1) the corruption and excesses of the Roman governors, and (2) the internal Jewish conflicts on the basis of class, religious direction, and ethnicity. He wrote: "Great disputes and differences have arisen between them; but the Sadducees are able to persuade none but the rich, and have not the populace obsequious, while the Pharisees have the multitude on their side" (*Antiquities of the Jews*, 13.10.7). He also added: "Each of the factions got for itself a company of the boldest revolutionaries and became leaders to them.... There was nobody to rebuke them; they acted with full license, as if there were no government over the city" (*Antiquities*, 20.9.2).

231. Shirer, W., *The Rise and Fall of the Third Reich* (New York: Simon & Schuster, 1960, p. 93).

232. The Romans destroyed Carthage only because it was a threat to their hegemony in the Mediterranean Sea.

233. The siege of Masada is described by Josephus Flavius in "The Wars of the Jews" (Penguin Books, Reissue Edition, 1984). The events at Masada left an indelible

mark upon Jewish culture and mythology. There has been a revival of the event in modern Israel. Elite units of the Israel Defense Forces are sworn with weapon and the Bible at Masada in a nocturnal ceremony with torches and a sentimental link to the brave ancestors who sacrificed their lives. The phrase "Masada shall not perish again" is a battle cry for the Israeli state and its armed forces.

234. This paragraph may be a comprehensive definition of the failure of the Jewish antiquity. What constituted the outcomes or consequences from the people's inability to continue its existence may be used as indicators of the failure I described in this narrative.

235. I am taking the liberty of omitting the religious aspects of the interest in Jewish history and in the Jewish destiny. In the United States there is a growing interest in the fundamental Christian denominations–in the fate of the Jewish people, their link to the Christian fate, and to prophecies.

236. See the list of myths in the Preface.

237. In the twentieth century the term "ghetto" was extended to the urban concentrations of other groups in America, such as African-Americans, Porto-Ricans, Italian, and Irish. As new waves of immigrants arrived in the New World, they tended to congregate in segregated communities. The difference was that, by and large, this was by choice. Clearly, in many instances, some groups were not allowed to reside in certain areas, but they were not *ordered* to reside only in a given enclave.

238. In the early travels of the disciples and the apostles of Christianity they usually targeted the well-established Jewish settlements in Rome's dominions.

239. Simon Dubnow (1957), for example, offers a robust sociological study of the Jewish colonies in Egypt, Asia Minor, Syria, and Mesopotamia during the first and second centuries of the Common Era.

240. During the Babylonian exile there was a serious attempt to rebuild the promised land, and after Ezra and Nehemiah, there existed a considerable Jewish population in Palestine, even to the point of achieving a thriving political, cultural, and social existence. After the Roman exile, all attempts in twenty centuries of the Diaspora have been sporadic and unsuccessful.

241. There are several spellings of his name, such as Zevi, Tsvi, etc. In Hebrew it means "deer."

242. Palestine was at that time under the control of the Turkish Sultan, as a province of the Ottoman Empire.

243. My free translation (M. Hertz). Other translations may differ. See: T. Carmi (Editor), *The Penguin Book of Hebrew Verse*, New York: Penguin Books, 1981.

244. My translation (M. Hertz).

245. This is "Tisha Be'av." The ninth day of the month of "Av," which is a day of mourning.

246. Rabbi Samuel Drisner wrote an excellent account of Rabbi Levi Itzhak of Berdichev (1974). Rabbi Drisner visited with me several years before his death in 2000. He kindly gave me a signed book about the life and accomplishments of the Rabbi from Berdichev. We amiably disagreed on my point that the Rabbi routinely

ignored established rituals in order to better communicate with his God and to appeal to God by means of good deeds rather than structured prayers and rituals.

247. Some inbreeding did produce, however, genetic diseases that are more prevalent in certain Jewish communities. The most notable example is Tay-Sachs disease, which is a fatal, untreatable lipid storage disorder affecting children. The disease is highly prevalent in Eastern European Jews. For other disorders common among Jews, see: Ernest Abel (2001), *Jewish Genetic Disorders: A Layman's Guide*, New York: McFarland & Company.

248. Unfortunately, this became a minority view. See the case of the teacher and the rabbi.

249. The "Talmad" ("Study") is a collection of rabbinical discussions, rulings, and interpretations of Jewish laws, customs, case histories, and ethical and moral issues. The Talmud is composed of: (1) the "Mishnah" ("Repetition") which is a written record of the oral laws of Judaism, and (2) the "Gemara" ("completed study"), which is the rabbinical discussions of the "Mishnah."

250. In Jewish folklore the name of Maimonides is sometimes compared to the prophet Moses. A popular saying is: "From Moses to Moses (Maimonides), there has never been another Moses."

251. The Hebrew phrase is: "Yehareg ubal yaavor." It contained three key sins of transgression against the Almighty that Jews *must* obey, even with the sacrifice of their life. According to the "Gemara," the three are: idolatry, murder, and forbidden sexual relations such as incest. There are several divergent opinions in the Talmud that argue for resistance to transgressing even the slightest of the rules of Jewish life.

252. In some schools of ethics, such as Immanuel Kant, if all living Jews would choose death to save their religion, and if all thus died–the religion would perish with them and the outcome would be disastrously unethical.

253. The horrific significance of the notion of "kidush hashem" is a preference for the preservation of the faith over the survival of the people.

254. Hence the Judaic custom of insisting upon burial of *all* the parts of the deceased body.

255. Mark Cohen (1995) has written a compelling historical narrative of Jews under Islamic rule. He concludes that although regarded with more respect, Jews under Islam had been subjected to violence and persecution because they were viewed as "infidels." The difference between Christendom and Islam was a matter of the degree to which Jews suffered persecution.

256. The "Black Death" which killed over 25 million people in Europe between 1346 and 1351 was regarded by rabbinical authorities as a sign of the turbulent times. Clerics from other religions also interpreted the plague as divine wrath and a punishment for sinful lives.

257. In the early part of the twentieth century, before the Nazi Holocaust, over 12 million European and world Jews spoke Yiddish as their main language. Today, worldwide there are about 4 million Jews who speak, read, and write in Yiddish. The word means "Jewish."

258. My great-grandparents in Palestine of the mid-nineteenth century had adopted Hebrew as their home language. They were also pioneers in the establishment of a Hebrew printing shop and later a Hebrew newspaper in Jerusalem.

259. In time there emerged a saying in Jewish parlance: "To live on the account of the Baron," as a great many Jews in Europe and Palestine had benefitted from the Baron's charitable endowment.

260. Some members of my grandmother's family (the Frankels) emigrated to Argentina as part of Baron Hirsch's colonization program. To my knowledge their descendants are today integrated within Argentine society.

261. A "Pogrom" is a Russian term, later also used in Yiddish, describing the massacre of innocent people, particularly the Jews in nineteenth century Russia.

262. Free translation by the author of this book.

263. The French novelist Emile Zola immortalized Captain Alfred Dreyfus and the injustice of his trial in his book *J'Accuse* (I Accuse).

264. The term "Zionism" was originally proposed by Nathan Birnbaum (1864-1937). Like Herzl, he also studied at the University of Vienna. In 1884 Birnbaum published a book about Jewish assimilation and in 1890 he suggested the term *Zionism* to describe the movement designed to reestablish the Jewish people in its ancient homeland. In 1892 he coined the term *political Zionism*. Birnbaum worked with Herzl during the first congress in 1897, but later had severe disagreements with the leaders of the movement and he resigned from the Zionist organization. Birnbaum died in the Netherlands in 1937.

265. In his book "The Jewish State," Herzl discussed the establishment of the Jewish company to fund the new state. He also examines the topics of the purchase of land, construction of homes and buildings, and even the format of the army, the legal system, and even the flag. (He proposed "a white flag with seven golden stars. The white field symbolizes our pure new life; the stars are the seven golden hours of our working day. For we shall march into the promised land carrying the badge of honor" (p. 147).

266. Several illustrative references are given in the bibliography.

267. Often even to the Jews themselves–as the interpretations and re-interpretations of the 613 rules of Judaism grew in sometimes-conflicting abundance.

268. In his book *The Jewish State*, Herzl listed the causes of modern anti-Semitism as a result of the emancipation of the Jews. He argued that by entering the non-Jewish world of commerce and the professions, the emancipated Jews had now initiated "fierce competition" with their fellow Christians (p. 90). He ignored other root causes of anti-Semitism but suggested a vicious circle in which "oppression naturally creates hostility against oppressors, and our hostility aggravates the pressure" (p. 91).

269. Historical examples span the millennia. In the Roman era, rabbinical authorities in Jerusalem used the Roman secular power to eliminate opponents. Jesus of Nazareth offended the rabbinical elite particularly when–according to tradition–he spoke against the moneychangers at the Temple, thus challenging economic stability. Recently, during Nazi Germany's occupation of Europe, some Jews utilized the powers of the regime in their relations with their fellow Jews.

270. This trait also spilled over to the Jewish community in Israel.

271. In October 2003, the European Union conducted a poll of European citizens from the 15 nation members. The poll's surprising finding was that Israel was considered "the biggest threat to world peace" (59 percent of respondents), followed by Iran, North Korea, and the United States (53 percent). This perception is but a continuation of the paranoiac fear harbored by so many Europeans over so many centuries of the Jews and even their new-founded country.

272. Toynbee, A. (1987), *A Study of History*, New York: Oxford University Press (originally published in 1947, the second volume in 1957).

273. See a different explanation in: Diamond, J. (2005), *Guns, Germs, and Steel: The Fate of Human Societies,* New York: W. W. Norton. Jared Diamond takes the position of an evolutionary biologist. He argued that the differences in the habitats of societies have determined their progress. In a later book he explored the demise of selected societies: Diamond, J. (2006), *Collapse: How Societies Choose to Fail or Succeed*, New York: Viking Books. In this book he argued that harmful environmental practices and disregard for ecological disasters have greatly contributed to the demise of societies such as the Anasazi and the Maya civilizations. In effect, these were failures of leadership, not pre-ordained events.

274. I recognize the fact that evangelical Christians, for example, support the notion of historical determinism and are also convinced, as I am, that the Middle East is heading toward a catastrophic war. See, for example: Rosenberg, J. (2006), *Epicenter: Why Current Rumblings in the Middle East Will Change Your Future*, Carol Stream, IL: Tyndale House Publishers. The evangelical path differs from mine, as theirs is based on scriptures and prophecy. The outcome, however, is the same. I offer here a more mundane explanation of why such an Armageddon is inevitable. Whether such a cataclysmic event will result in the coming of the savior is a matter of individual faith.

275. The account of Joseph of Egypt when viewed through the prism of the principles of modern management is an excellent example of how the wise and unselfish actions of a knowledgeable leader could counteract the powerful tricks and dangers of the natural environment and could ensure the long-term prosperity of his people.

276. A similar viewpoint is also expressed by other authors. See, for example: Elukin (2013), Dollinger (1998), Biale (2010), and Reiter (2012).

277. Shirer, W. (1960), *The Rise and Fall of the Third Reich*, New York: Simon & Schuster.

278. Drews, R. (1995), *The End of the Bronze Age*, Princeton, NJ: Princeton University Press.

279. I must offer some form of an apology since we in America often pay excessive homage to numbers and we tend to look at the world in quantitative terms.

280. Bisson, T. (2008), *The Crisis of the Twelfth Century: Power, Lordship, and the Origins of European Government*, Princeton, NJ: Princeton University Press.

281. Within Israel there are well-developed trends of intersector hatred and mistrust. In 2006, a survey of the Israeli population found that over half of the secular Israelis believe that the religious sector consistently rob the country's treasury.

Similarly, over 60 percent of religious Jews will not live in a building inhabited by secular Israelis.

282. Despite my grievous and grave concerns about the future of the Jewish people and the Middle East, I will most probably be criticized in many quarters. Like Sir Winston Churchill during his lean years in the 1930s, I shall be characterized as "disgruntled," or "out of touch," or "ignorant of historical imperatives," or "insensitive to the suffering of my people," and "blind to the evil perpetrated by the enemies of the Jews."

283. Dever, W. (2003), *Who Were the Early Israelites and Where Did They Come From?*, Grand Rapids, MI: William Eerdmans Publishing Company.

284. Plus 40 years of wandering in the desert, as the Bible's story proposes.

Index

A

Adan 36
Adan, General Avraham 36
Afghanistan 64, 88
age of knowledge 72–73
Akhenaten 136
Akiva, Rabbi 196
Alexander the Great 173
alpha radiation 3, 5–6
Altalena Affair 106
Amorites 131, 133, 143, 149
Antiochus 165
antisemitism 229–234
  myth of, 236–238
Arab-Israeli conflict 38, 45, 47, 56, 58, 64–68
Arab Spring 73
Arc of the Covenant 150, 157
Arik (also: General Ariel Sharon) 122
Asher, tribe of 154
Asher, Tribe of 148

B

Babylonian Diaspora (also: Galut Bavel) 160
background radiation 13
Balfour Declaration 80, 123
Balfour, Lord Arthur 80
Bank Hapoalim 96
BBC 19
Beer-Sheva 10, 18–19
Begin, Menachem 59, 66–67, 92, 118
Ben-Gurion, David 20–22, 89–123
Bengurionism
  and America 104–108
  and foreign policy 101–104
  and life in the "Promised Land" 113–114
  and the Arabs 107–110
  and the control over information 110–113
  and the culture of favoritism 114–120
  and the economy 99–102
  illegitimacy of 93
  the nature of 90
Ben-Gurion, Paula 104
Benjamin, tribe of 156–157, 159
Ben Matityahu, Joseph (also: Josephus Flavius) xii
Ben-Porat, Yoel 33–34
ben-Yair, Eleazar 181
Ben-Yehuda, Eliezer 216–217
Bible 131, 133–134, 148, 173
Bohr, Niels 24
Bolsheviks 57
border guard, Israel 22, 25
Borochov, Dov Ber 57–59
British Mandate of Palestine 2, 56, 80, 92–94, 116–117
Bronze Age 132–133, 248

C

Canaan, land of 131–138, 139–141, 143, 147–152, 169, 194, 245, 250–260
Carthage 154–155
Central Intelligence Agency (CIA) 12
Chafetz Chaim 226
chosen people 141, 151, 163, 174, 182–183, 210, 252
Christianity 139, 169, 171, 174, 177–179, 183, 203–204, 210–211, 221, 231, 247–248, 249
Churchill, Winston 34, 37, 55, 99, 110
Cohen, Avner 41
Collier, Paul 70
Cunningham, Sir Alan 92
Cyprus, Island of 81
Cyrus, King of Persia 163

D

Dado (also: Elazar, General David) 32, 35
Davar (also: The Word) 96
David, King (also: Son of Jesse) 113, 150, 156–157, 202
Dayan, Moshe 21–22, 25, 28–36

De Gaulle, Charles 9–10
Der Spiegel 61
Dever, Wlliam 131, 133, 153
Diamond, Jarred 146–147, 243
Diaspora (also: Jewish Diaspora) 79–80, 87, 124, 147, 149, 152, 155, 160, 164, 165, 168, 170, 174, 176, 178, 180, 182–185
Dimona, city of 2, 3, 7–8, 11, 12
Disraeli, Benjamin 37, 218
Doomsday Plan, The 42–54
Dostrovsky, Israel 30–31
Duality Paradox 168–169
Dulles, John Foster 105

E

Eban, Abba 103
Effects Based Operation (EBO) 51–52
Egypt 17, 19, 28–30, 32–35, 37, 43–45, 59, 87, 112, 131–134, 140–141, 149–151, 152, 159, 161–166, 169, 173, 192, 210, 243–244, 250
Einstein, Albert 24, 94
Eisenhower, Dwight 105–106
Eitan, General Rafael 36
Elazar, General David (also: "Dado") 32–34, 35–36
Ellsberg, Daniel 38
emancipation, concept of 211–213
Eshkol, Levi 12, 16, 17–22, 28–32, 74, 99, 107
European Union (EU), (also: Treaty of Rome) 69, 74, 76, 102, 103
Exodus 131–134, 215, 245, 247–248, 250–251
Ezra 160, 166–170, 172

F

false Messiah (also: Meshiach Sheker) 191, 192
Fein, Monroe 106
Fermi, Enrico 24
Flavius, Josephus (also: Joseph Ben Matityahu) 152, 171, 177, 182
France 9, 10, 18, 34, 69, 72, 85, 105–106, 112, 123, 173, 204, 213, 216, 217

Freier, Shalhevet 31, 34
French Invasion 9–10
Frost, Robert 24

G

Galut Bavel (also: Babylonian Diaspora) 189
gamma radiation 3, 5–6, 24
Gandhi, Mahatma 94
Geiger counter 6
globalization 68–71, 72, 76
glove box 17
Goethe, Johan Wolfgang von 47, 245
Golan Heights 29, 34
Gordon, Yehudah Leib 221–223
Goren, Rabbi Shlomo 63–64
Gottlober, Abram Ber 221
Greece 146, 155, 175, 217

H

Haifa, City of 49, 94, 109, 148, 154
Haig, Alexander 36–37, 39–40
Halevi, Yehuda 194
Halutz, General Dan 49
Hammurabi, King 131, 135, 246
Haolam Hazeh 111
Haredi 121
Harel, Isser 111
Haskalah movement 212–216
Hebrews 131–132, 141–143, 145, 148, 159, 245
Hebrew University 1, 64, 109
Hegel, George Friedrich 84
Heine, Heinrich 217
Helms, Richard 12–13, 15–16
Herod, King 119, 167, 181
Herut party 66, 101
Herzl, Benjamin (also: Theodore Herzl) 59, 61, 80, 89, 226–228, 232, 237, 252
Herzl, Theodore (also: Benjamin Herzl) 80, 226–228, 232
Hezbollah 49–52
Hirsch, General Gal 50
Histadrut 95
Hitler, Adolf 66, 83, 90, 106, 238, 248
Holocaust 80–87, 237, 245

homeland, Jewish 43, 57–59, 82, 88–89, 92, 97, 100–105, 118, 140, 171, 185, 186, 188, 188–190, 189, 192, 194, 198, 204, 208, 213, 221, 227, 237–239, 246
Hussein, King 19, 59
Hussein, Saddam 43
Hyksos 131, 133
hypothesis of failure 163–186

I

Institute Number One 4, 14
Institute Number Two 10–15
International Atomic Energy Agency (IAEA) 14
Iraq 14, 44, 88, 230
Irgun organization xi
Islam 43, 191, 192, 204, 209–212, 247, 249
Israel Defense Force (IDF) 18, 20–21, 28, 32–34, 51, 112
Israelites 131–134, 139–143, 145–152
Israel Security Services (also: Shin Bet) 111
Israel, State of 34, 56, 60, 75, 79–138, 227, 237, 245, 248

J

Jacoby, Johann 217
Jerusalem, City of 29, 56, 77, 150, 151, 152, 155, 157–159, 164–169, 192
Jewish Diaspora (alsoL Diaspora) xii, 85, 165, 186–195, 198, 204, 208, 213, 227, 237–239
Jews and Germans 83–85
Jinnah, Mohammed Ali 94
Johnson, Lyndon 12–13, 15–16, 20, 107
Jordan, Kingdom of 81
Jordan River 92
Joseph, son of Jacob 243–245

K

Kadima party 66
Kagan, Israel Meir Hacohen 226
KAMAG 4–6, 7–8, 10–12, 14–16, 22
Karpin, Michael 8, 10, 12, 30, 48
Kashmir 56
Kashrut (also: kosher) 236

Katzenelson, Berl 57
Kennedy, John Fitzgerald 12, 105, 106, 119, 250
Kidush Hashem 209
Kingdom of Judah 145, 157, 164
King James Bible 203
King Solomon 132, 151–152, 156, 158–159, 202
Kissinger, Henry 36–41
Klausner, Joseph 169, 177
Knebel, Fletcher 28
Knesset (Israel's parliament) 28, 32, 101
kosher (also: Kashrut) 127, 236
Kupat Holim 96
Kurzman, Dan 89

L

land of Zion 221
Langley Air Force Base 36
Lawrence, Ernest 24
League of Nations 92
Lebanon 43, 44, 48–53, 98–99, 154
Lenin, Vladimir 105
Levant, the 75–78
Levy Itzhak from Berdichev, Rabbi 197–198
Lieberman, Senator Joseph xiv
Likud party 66
Lincoln, Abraham 91
Luther, Martin 203

M

Maccabeans (also: Judah Maccabee) 171, 251
Maccabee, Judah (also: Maccabeans) 165, 175
Maimonides (also: Moses Ben Maimon) 126, 205
Maimon, Moses Ben (also: Maimonides) 205
Maimon, Yehuda Leib xi
MAMAG (also: Yavne Reactor) 4
Marcoule Center 8
Masada Plan, the 43
Masada Syndrome, the 39
Mashiach Sheker (also: false Messiah) 191

Mattis, General J. N. 51
Mediterranean Sea 4, 17, 19, 34, 40, 92, 150, 153–154, 191
Meir, Golda (also: Meirson) 32–34, 35, 41, 104–105, 118
Meirson (also: Golda Meir) 104
Menachem Begin 101
Mesopotamia 131–132, 139–140, 149–150, 152, 159, 162, 164–167, 172, 210
Messianic Idea 167, 168–170
Metternich, Prince Von 37
Middle East 37–38, 40–41, 47, 48, 51, 58, 59, 64, 68–70, 72–75, 81, 83, 87, 108, 177, 248, 253, 253–254
migrations hypothesis 248
Ministry of Defense 21, 31, 34
Montefiori, Sir Moses 218
Mosaic law 62
Moses 75, 132, 134–135, 138–140, 149
Mutually Assured Destruction (MAD) 44

N

Nahal 15
Nahal Soreq 4
Nasser, Gammal Abdel 11, 17, 18, 19, 28, 102, 105
Nations Security Council) 92, 103
Nehemiah 166, 170, 177, 178
Nehru, Jawaharlal 94, 102
Nero, Emperor 178
Netanyahu, Benjamin 115
new enlightenment 71–74
Nixon, Richard 36–43
nuclear power 9, 44
nuclear reactor 2, 4, 10
nuclear weapons 10–12, 15, 16, 34, 39, 41, 42–44, 46, 48, 52–53, 63, 67, 76, 122, 128

O

Old Testament 151, 166, 167
Olmert 52
Olmert, Ehud 49–50, 98
Oppenheimer, Robert 24
Oren, Michael 21, 28
Ottoman Empire of Turkey, 72

P

Pakistan 42, 55, 81, 248
Palestine 57–58, 80, 83, 92–97, 101, 108, 167–173, 177, 179–182, 183, 189, 217, 221–222, 227–228, 237, 248
Paradox of Jewish Isolation 85
Peres, Shimon 105
Peretz, Amir 98
Peretz, I. L. 209
Petek, culture of 115
Philistines 143, 147, 148, 150, 161
Phoenicia 153–155, 158, 161, 162
Plutonium (also: PU 239; PU 240) 5, 8–9, 8–10, 24, 28–29
Poalei Zion (also: Zionist Workers Party) 57
promised land 113–114, 151, 169, 196, 202
Pu 239 5

Q

question, Jewish 226, 232–237

R

Rabin, General Yitzhak 21
radiation safety 36–37
Rafael 11, 30–31
Ramon, Haim 118
Rashi (also: Rabbi Shlomo Yitzhaki) 204–205
Rehavam, King (also: son of Solomon) 158, 202
Roman Empire (also: Rome) 177, 182, 193, 210, 229, 241
Rome (also: Roman Empire) 102, 154, 171, 179
Ron-Tal, General Yiftah 51
Rothschild, Lionel Nathan 80, 218
Rozen, Rabbi Yosef 223

S

Sadat, Anwar 32–33, 59–60
Samuel, prophet 169
Sapir, Pinhas 99
Sarajevo 35

Saul, King 147
Schlesinger, Arthur 106–107
Schneerson, Sholom Ber 224–225
science, Jewish 24, 84
Scientific Administration 30–32
Sea of Galilee 34, 205
Second Lebanon War 48–50, 52
Second Temple 145, 151, 160, 163–186
Settlement (also: Yishuv) 81, 93, 96, 125, 165
Shabbetai, Zvi 191–192
Shahak, Israel 64
Sharansky, Natan 79
Sharon, General Ariel, (also: Arik) 36, 118, 122
Shin Bet (also: Israel Security Services) 111
Sinai Peninsula 19, 29, 133
Sinai War xi
Six-Day War 16–31
socialism 57, 60, 90, 96–97
socialist-Marxist ideology 57
son of Jesse (also: King David) 147, 169
son of Solomon (also: King Rehavam) 158
Soustelle, Jacques 9–10
Soviet Union 18, 37–38, 44, 71, 79–80, 88, 90–91, 94, 104, 113, 244
Spinoza, Baruch xiv, 208
Stiglitz, Joseph 70–71
Suez Canal 36, 105
Syria 18, 32, 33, 34, 43, 45
Szilard, Leo 24

T

Talmud xiv, 172, 173, 204
Tel-Aviv, city of 4, 31, 45, 89
Tel-Aviv-Jaffa (also: city of Tel-Aviv) 154
Tel-Aviv University 1
theocracy, Jewish 74–75
Third Temple 34
Tiran, Straits of 18, 19, 28
Toynbee, Arnold 145, 146, 241
treaty of Rome (also: European Union) 102
Triple Disenfranchisement 251–254
Truman, Harry 76

U

ultra-orthodox Jews 61–62, 125, 129
unholy alliance 60, 97, 122
United Kingdom 72, 105, 213, 218
United Nations (also: United Nations Security Council) 50
United Nations Resolution 92
United Nations Security Council (also: United Nations) 50, 286
United States 11–13, 14, 16, 18, 28, 36–38, 42, 45, 60, 61, 69, 71–73, 87–88, 103, 105–108

V

victory 35, 38, 52, 251
Von Clausewitz 45

W

Wailing Wall (also: Western Wall) 29
Watergate scandal 38
Western Wall (also: Wailing Wall) 29
Who is a Jew 123–126, 168, 289
Winograd, Eliyahu 50
Word, The (also: Davar) 96
World Bank 70–71

Y

Yaakov, Colonel 26–27
Yavne reactor (also: MAMAG) 4
Yiddish 200, 216, 222
Yishuv (also: Settlement) 81
Yitzhaki, Rabbi Shlomo (also: Rashi) 204
Yom Kippur War xi, 29–44, 52
Yugoslavia 35

Z

Zakaria, Fareed 68
Zeira, General Eli 33
Zionism 57, 90, 101, 119, 223, 224, 225
Zionist Congress 79, 227, 228, 237
Zionist movement 80, 221, 226–228, 236–237
Zionist Workers Party (also: Poalei Zion) 57